D0762443

THE
HIPPOPOTAMUS MARSH

Lords of the Two Lands
Volume One

Pauline Gedge

VIKING

VIKING

Published by the Penguin Group

Penguin Books Canada Ltd, 10 Alcorn Avenue, Toronto, Ontario,
Canada M4V 3B2
Penguin Books Ltd, 27 Wrights Lane, London w8 5TZ, England
Penguin Putnam Inc., 375 Hudson Street, New York, New York 10014, U.S.A.
Penguin Books Australia Ltd, Ringwood, Victoria, Australia
Penguin Books (NZ) Ltd, cnr Rosedale and Airborne Roads, Albany,
Auckland 1310, New Zealand

Penguin Books Ltd, Registered Offices: Harmondsworth, Middlesex,
England

First published 1998
1 3 5 7 9 10 8 6 4 2

Printed and bound in Canada on acid-free paper ∞

CANADIAN CATALOGUING IN PUBLICATION DATA

Gedge, Pauline, 1945–
    The Hippopotamus marsh

ISBN 0-670-88376-x

1. Title.

PS8563.E33H56 1999   c813'.54   c98-932257-2
PR9199.3.G42H56 1999

Visit Penguin Canada's website at www.penguin.ca

This trilogy is dedicated to Prince Kamose, one of the most obscure and misunderstood characters in Egyptian history. I hope that in some small way I have contributed to his rehabilitation.

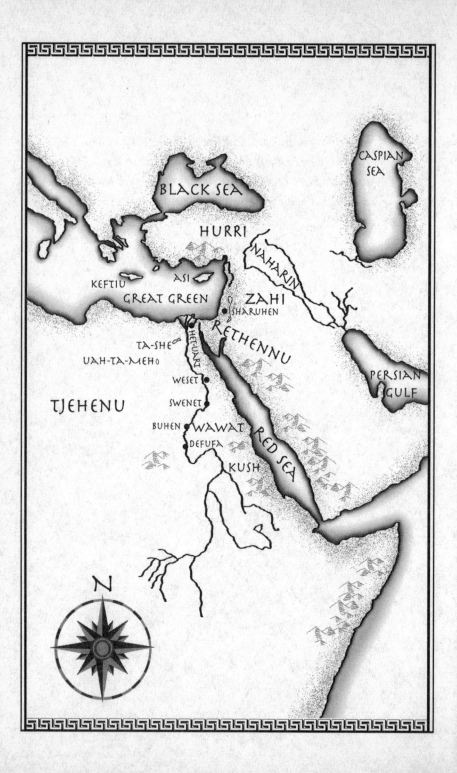

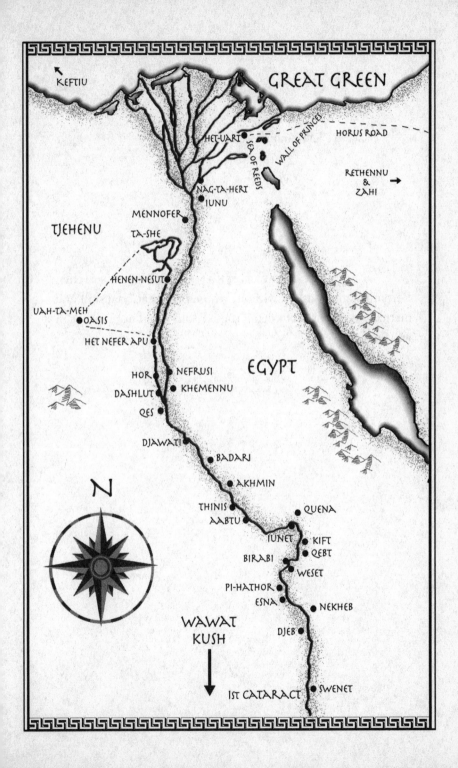

Acknowledgement

HEARTFELT THANKS TO my researcher, Bernard Ramanauskas, without whose organizational skill and meticulous attention to detail these books could not have been written.

Character  List

THE FAMILY

Seqenenra Tao—Prince of Weset

Aahotep—his wife

Tetisheri—his mother

Si-Amun—his eldest son

Kamose—his second son

Ahmose—his third son

Aahmes-nefertari—his elder daughter

Tani—his younger daughter

Ahmose-onkh—a son of Si-Amun and his sister/wife Aahmes-nefertari

MALE SERVANTS

Akhtoy—the Chief Steward

Kares—Steward to Aahotep

Mersu—Steward to Tetisheri

Uni—a Steward

Ipi—the Chief Scribe

FEMALE SERVANTS

Isis—Tetisheri's body servant

Hetepet—Aahotep's body servant

Heket—Tani's body servant

Raa—Ahmose-onkh's nurse

RELATIVES AND FRIENDS

Teti—Governor of Khemennu, Inspector and Administrator of Dikes
and Canals, and husband of Aahotep's cousin

Nefer-Sakharu—Teti's wife and Aahotep's cousin

Ramose—their son and Tani's betrothed

Amunmose—High Priest of Amun

Turi—Ahmose's wrestling partner

THE PRINCES

Hor-Aha—a native of Wawat and leader of the Medjay

Intef of Qebt

Iasen of Badari

Makhu of Akhmin

Mesehti of Djawati

Ankhmahor of Aabtu

Harkhuf, his son

Sebek-nakht of Mennofer

OTHER EGYPTIANS

Paheri—Mayor of Nekheb

Het-uy—Mayor of Pi-Hathor

Baba Abana—Guardian of Vessels

Kay Abana, his son

THE SETIU

Awoserra Aqenenra Apepa—the King

Nehmen—his Chief Steward

Yku-didi—his Chief Herald

Khian—a Herald

Itju—his Chief Scribe

Pezedkhu—a General

Dudu—a General

Foreword

AT THE END OF the Twelfth Dynasty the
Egyptians found themselves in the hands of a foreign power
they knew as the Setiu, the Rulers of Uplands. We know them
as the Hyksos. They had initially wandered into Egypt from the
less fertile eastern country of Rethennu in order to pasture their
flocks and herds in the lush Delta region. Once settled, their
traders followed them, eager to profit from Egypt's wealth.
Skilled in matters of administration, they gradually removed all
authority from a weak Egyptian government until control was
entirely in their hands. It was a mostly bloodless invasion
achieved through the subtle means of political and economic
coercion. Their kings cared little for the country as a whole,
plundering it for their own ends and aping the customs of their
Egyptian predecessors in a largely successful effort to lull the
people into submission. By the middle of the Seventeenth
Dynasty they had been securely entrenched in Egypt for just
over two hundred years, ruling from their northern capital, the
House of the Leg, Het-Uart.

Chapter ONE

SEQENENRA CAME OUT onto the roof at last, panting a little from his exertion, and lowered himself so that his back was resting against the sagging remains of the windcatcher. He drew up his knees with an inward sigh of satisfaction. This was his sanctuary, this rubble-littered corner above what had once been the women's quarters of the old palace. He could sit here and think or brood or simply rest his eyes on river and fields, his estate or the straggling town of Weset that hugged the bank and encircled the two temples. Often, in the somnolent afternoons when his wife slept or gossiped with her women and the children had taken their bodyguards and gone to swim in the river, he would slip away, walk through the vast, silent courtyard of this derelict god's home, and enter the shrouded, empty rooms. Few physical reminders of his ancestors remained. Here the swift glint of yellow paint on a pillar, there the black-and-white shock of a wadjet-eye and an indecipherable cartouche still cast a lingering spell over the untenanted shadows, but the halls and passages, the intimate bedchambers and mighty reception areas with their gloomy pillars, were scoured by wind and echoed when he walked through.

The structure was swiftly becoming dangerous. The mud

bricks from which it had been built were decaying. Whole walls were nothing but piles of dust. Ceilings had collapsed, letting in shafts of light whose very brilliance often seemed to him sacrilegious. Sometimes he went and stood in the principal audience chamber where the Horus Throne used to rest on its dais, listening to the silence, watching the squares of light that came through the high windows move imperceptibly across the sand-sullied floor, but he could not long endure the atmosphere of solemn sadness.

Today he had not retreated here to gnaw at some administrative problem or even to pursue a line of uninterrupted thought in peace. As Prince of Weset and Governor of the Five Nomes he was a busy man, his duties predictable but regular, and he had come to cherish the few hours he was able to spend alone, high up where the irritations and responsibilities of his position and his family shrank to their proper proportions under the spell of the panorama laid out below him. It was spring. The Nile was flowing with a ponderous, powerful slowness, its banks a tangle of hectic green reeds and feathery papyrus fronds nodding in the sweet breeze. Beyond it the western cliffs shivered, dun and arid, against a pure blue sky. A few small craft bobbed aimlessly, masts bare, disturbing the ducks and an occasional heron that rose white and languid from the marshes.

Seqenenra's gaze wandered north. The river swept around a bend and was lost to view, but on the east side, his side, the black fields criss-crossed with palm-lined irrigation canals lay wet and fallow, still too soft to be trodden by the peasants who would soon scatter them with grain.

Closer in, just beyond the broken wall that had once completely surrounded the palace, his servants squatted planting vegetables, their naked brown backs gleaming. He could hear their voices, a spasmodic but pleasant murmur, as they worked. The roof of his house could be clearly seen, lower than he was.

Cushions and scattered linen made a bright, intermittent splash between the branches of the sheltering sycamores and acacia that gave shade to his garden. Farther out he watched the flags fronting the pylons on Amun's temple ripple, and past the holy precinct, a corner of Montu's shrine thrust like a brown knife edge into the near horizon.

Seqenenra felt himself begin to relax. The Inundation had been generous, flooding the land with both its necessities, water and silt, and if the crops sprang up healthy and strong the harvest would be equally bountiful. It was too early yet to have received word from the overseer of his vineyard in the western Delta, but he presumed that his grapes would hang heavy and bursting on their vines this year. The fruit from the trellis that shaded a portion of the path running from his watersteps to the house were always used for juice, not wine. My cattle have no disease and my people's bellies will be full, he thought gratefully. Of course, a great deal of my wealth will go north in taxes but I will not complain. Not as long as I am left to my own devices.

He stirred, all at once aware of a piece of chipped brick lodged between the sole of one foot and his sandal, and as he reached down to pick it free, his mood became tinged with a brief anxiety. I delude myself if I believe that I am forgotten here in the south, that the only time I occupy Apepa's mind is when he sends out his overseers to collect the taxes, his thoughts ran on. The miles between us are no guarantee of my safety. I wish it were so, but to him I am like this little shard, pricking him uncomfortably in the moments when there is nothing else to distract him from the knowledge that I exist. I cannot change my lineage, melt into the anonymity of minor nobility. I am a reminder to him of his own foreign roots, and what are they compared to the mighty gods who sired me? Well, I will not consider these things today. I did not clamber up here to ponder either Apepa's past or my own. How glorious is my corner of this beautiful Egypt! Leaning back he half-closed his eyes.

For perhaps an hour he drifted on a tide of somnolence, enjoying a gentle but steady breeze that mitigated the after-noon heat of the sun, and he had just decided that he had lingered long enough and ought to be leaving the roof when a shout brought him reluctantly to his feet. He walked to the edge and peered down. Si-Amun was standing in a gap of the decaying enclosure wall, his twin, Kamose, behind him. Both young men were naked but for their loincloths.

"I thought you might be up there, Father!" Si-Amun called, pointing north. "We've been swimming and we saw a royal boat beat round the bend. By the way the sail is coming down, I believe it will head for our watersteps. What do you think?"

Seqenenra glanced in the direction of his son's arm. A slim craft was labouring towards him, triangular sail even now being furled. Blue-and-white pennants fluttered fore and aft. Several men stood on the deck, liveried in the same colours. It was indeed a royal craft. It will go by, Seqenenra thought. Most of them go by on their way to Kush, eager for gold from the mines, for slaves, for ostrich feathers and other exotic trinkets. Si-Amun is probably hoping that it will indeed put in here. He would like nothing better than a visit from one of the King's representatives and would wring from him every last detail of life in Het-Uart, though his loyalty to me would forbid him to express too much joy in such an opportunity. But I will breathe more freely when I see it glide past and dwindle out of sight. "I think that they are merely negotiating a change in the wind's direction," he called back. Si-Amun gave a resigned shrug.

"You are probably right," he said loudly, "and I am bored today." He waved and turned towards the house. Seqenenra watched him for a moment, but then his attention returned to

the river. He had expected to see the bow of the vessel with its
sail being hoisted again, but to his dismay the oars had been
run out and the craft was already veering towards his watersteps. Alarmed, he hurried down the stairs.

He emerged into the courtyard, and when he reached the
gap in the wall he found Kamose waiting for him. "Si-Amun
was right. They are not going on," he said tersely. "They are
coming here." Kamose stood back as he pushed his way through
and both of them looked towards the river.

"What can they possibly want?" Kamose asked worriedly.
"New Year's Day was five months ago. The tribute was paid, the
gifts sent and acknowledged, and it is too early for our tax
assessment."

Seqenenra shook his head, glancing at his son's handsome
face as they started for the house together. "I cannot guess," he
replied heavily, "but it will be nothing to our advantage, you
may be sure."

"Let us pray that they only want a flagon of wine, a good
meal and a night under your roof before sailing on into Kush,"
Kamose observed. "I think they see us as the last bastion of civ-
ilized comfort before they brave the rigours of the south. How
they fear and despise the desert! Ahmose! Where are you
going?" Seqenenra's youngest son ran past barefooted, his kilt
rumpled and dusty.

"I am meeting Turi on the practice ground for a wrestling
match!" Ahmose yelled over his shoulder. "We have a small
wager between us!"

"Be present at dinner, Ahmose!" Seqenenra shouted after
him. "We have guests!" The boy waved his acknowledgement.

"Guests," Kamose repeated bitterly. "They were not invited
and we have no choice but to receive them." Seqenenra
answered the salute of the soldier on duty at the main entrance.
As he and Kamose entered the house, Uni left the shadows and

came swiftly towards him. Kamose disappeared in the direction of his own apartments in the men's quarters.

"A royal craft is about to dock at the watersteps," Seqenenra told the steward. "Send an escort to meet whoever is on board. Tell Isis to warn the Lady Tetisheri and my wife, and have fruit and wine ready in the garden. I want to pray and change my kilt." Without waiting for Uni's nod he strode towards his rooms. "Water, quickly!" he ordered the body servant who had appeared in answer to his call and was bowing. "And I will need fresh linen. We have company from the Delta." Do not look for trouble where there is none, he told himself sternly as he unloosed his sandals and reached for the water jug. Stay calm. Do not antagonize Apepa's messenger. Do not upset the balance of today's Ma'at, O Prince of Weset!

Opening his shrine, he took up the incense holder lying beside it, lit the charcoal from the candle kept burning for that purpose, and sprinkled a few grains of incense on it. Bowing to the image of Amun the Great Cackler, lord and protector of Weset, he made his obeisance and then prostrated himself on the cool floor. Help me to keep my temper, he prayed. Give me the gift of wisdom to hear whatever it is that has brought the King's herald this far, without betraying either impatience or contempt. Guard my tongue, that I may not offend him to my detriment and the peril of my family. Veil my thoughts from him so that he sees only politeness behind my eyes. There was nothing more to say. Rising, he took a moment to inhale the sweet smoke from the burner before snuffing it out, closing the shrine, and submitting to the ministrations of his servant who had returned with a basin of warm water and linen cloths.

An hour later, freshly clad, he walked into the sunlit fragrance of his garden. His eyes were kohled. On his brow he wore a plain silver circlet and around his neck went ankhs and silver wadjet-eyes. Rings glittered against the almost black skin of his hands. Beside his pool, under the shade of the trees, mats had been spread and the royal visitor and his two companions sat cross-legged, listening to his wife Aahotep's soft, measured tones. Kamose sat a little apart, also formally painted, his hands folded on the clean white pleats of his kilt.

At Seqenenra's approach all rose and bowed. A servant moved to offer him a bowl of fruit but he shook his head, accepting the wine Uni held out. He motioned, sinking to the grass, and all went down with him. "Greetings," he said amiably. "We are honoured to give hospitality to the servants of the One. To whom am I speaking?"

"I am Khian, Herald of the King," one of the men replied. He was slender and fair-skinned, his eyes thickly kohled against the southern sun. His kilt was gossamer-fine, his leather belt studded with carnelian, and the two gold chains lying on his chest sparkled with his breath. "These are my guards. I thank you for your greeting, Prince. It is my pleasure to bring the good wishes of the Lord of the Two Lands to your whole household and particularly to the Lady Tetisheri, your mother, to whom he fervently conveys life, health and prosperity."

Seqenenra nodded. "We are grateful. Are you on your way to Kush, Khian?"

The herald took a delicate sip of his wine. "No, Prince," he explained. "I came especially to extend to you the salutations of the One and to bring you a letter." Seqenenra's glance met Kamose's and passed on to his wife. Aahotep was studiously watching the antics of the sparrows among the newly opened leaves of the trees.

A small, awkward silence fell. The herald drank again. Kamose brushed an invisible speck of dust from the date in his hand and bit into it cautiously. Seqenenra was about to make an innocuous comment that good manners demanded, when a shadow fell across him and he turned to see Si-Amun and

Aahmes-nefertari standing hand in hand at his back. He breathed a quiet sigh of relief. The pair bent smiling, kissed Aahotep, greeted Khian gracefully, and settled onto a mat beside Kamose.

A general conversation began, full of the prospects for this year's sowing, the new life stirring in the precious vines and the number of calves born in the Delta. Khian was an enthusiastic husbandman who took a personal interest in the running of his own small estate outside Het-Uart and the slight hiatus that had followed the mention of a letter was forgotten. The sun westered slowly, filling the garden with an orange light, and the fish in Seqenenra's pool rose to the surface as the mosquitoes began to gather in clouds. Uni distributed fly whisks and the talk was punctuated with their gentle swishing.

Tani came at last, running over the lawn with the dogs panting and grinning behind her. One of them, Behek, loped to Seqenenra and laid his sleek head in his master's lap. Seqenenra stroked it gently. "I am sorry to be so late," Tani remarked as she reached for some fruit and settled next to her mother. "But the dogs needed a good run. I took them out to the edge of the desert and then through the town to the river so that they could cool off. What a beautiful day it has been!"

Seqenenra motioned to Tani's bodyguard and the man whistled and shook the leashes he held. Reluctantly the dogs obeyed, Behek licking Seqenenra's hand before trotting away. Aahotep rose. "It is time to refresh yourself before the meal," she said to Khian "Uni will show you to the guest rooms and then escort you to the reception hall. Your men can go with our servants. Tani, come with me. You need a good wash." She smiled around at them all and Seqenenra marvelled at her composure. No strain showed on her face or was betrayed in any hesitancy of her gestures. At once Khian and his soldiers stood, bowed, and followed the steward. Si-Amun flung an arm around Aahmes-nefertari's neck.

"He is more like a farmer than a herald," he remarked. "Although he would find hoeing weeds a chore without any muscles. Why does the King send us such an inferior creature? Surely we are worthy of a Chief Herald's attention at least! What does he want of us?"

Seqenenra knew that his son was half-joking but beneath the bantering tone was a hint of affront. You have too much of the wrong kind of pride, Si-Amun, he thought to himself. I wish that you did not take offence so easily over the petty insults that cannot threaten either your manhood or your noble blood unless you let them. "He has brought another letter from Apepa," he said. "I have not read it yet. I want to do so on a full stomach." Kamose came close to his father.

"Always letters, always stupid, niggling demands," he said in a low voice. "Last time it was an order to grow more barley than flax when the barley crop already promised to be abundant, and then there was a request for the numbers of pairs of sandals in our household. What stupid game is the King playing?"

Seqenenra gazed at the placid surface of the pool. The fish were making peaceful circles that spread and broke against the stone surround. Long shadows were growing across the sunset-tinged grass. The servants were rolling up the reed mats and gathering the debris of the greeting-meal. "I don't know and it doesn't matter," he answered at length. "We do as we are told and in exchange for our obedience we may order our nomes and our lives as Amun desires. Many are not so fortunate." Kamose grimaced, and scrambling up he walked away.

"I could go and talk to the herald, Father," Si-Amun offered. "I might be able to glean some useful information from him."

"I forbid you to do so," Seqenenra said sharply. "A herald is a messenger, nothing more. He is not required to advise his master or give any opinions and it should be beneath your dignity, Si-Amun, to accord this Khian any more respect than the laws of hospitality require. Moreover, he is the servant of a King who wishes us ill. Remember that and take care how you address him." Si-Amun flushed.

"Forgive me," he said. "You are right. But it is very hard to know myself the child of Kings and yet be forced to curb my tongue in the presence of a mere herald." He rocked forward onto his knees and then stood, pulling his wife with him. "There will be no feast for a while yet," he finished. "Walk with me by the river, Aahmes-nefertari."

Seqenenra watched them disappear into the growing dusk. Si-Amun was nineteen, a few moments older than Kamose and therefore Seqenenra's heir. Physically he was his brother's double and they could hardly be told apart from each other except for the small mole at the corner of Si-Amun's mouth, but their personalities were dissimilar. Si-Amun's self-confidence bordered on arrogance. He was a clever scholar, a good marksman with the bow, but chafed at his existence in this provincial backwater. He wanted to go north, to wait upon the King, to be where the power in Egypt resided, and Seqenenra could only hope that as he grew his arrogance would become a Princely competence and his restlessness would be channelled into the exercise of a proper authority.

But Kamose seemed to have inherited an aura of serenity from his mother. He had all the quiet self-confidence of a man twice his age, and was secure enough in his own maturity to mind his own business. At sixteen, Ahmose, the youngest son, was a flame, a darting, vigorous, happy man proficient with his weapons, a fine wrestler who asked little more of life than that it should continue unchanged under the blessings of the gods.

I have everything a man could desire, Seqenenra reflected. I am a Prince of Egypt. I have a close and loving family. I suffer no want. My duties are taxing but straightforward, unlike the responsibilities of a King. He looked up, and almost against his will his eyes were drawn to the massive, straggling hulk of the ancient palace, now cloaked in the coming night. For as long as he could remember it had dominated the estate he had inherited from his father, Senakhtenra, and his father before him. Most regarded it as an anachronism. Familiarity had bred an indifference to its slowly crumbling presence. But from the time of his childhood his mother had put him to sleep with the stories of his ancestors who had inhabited it, one god following another, Kings of Upper and Lower Egypt, the Red Land and the Black Land, fighting monarchs whose blood was fiery with the seed of desert forebears and numinous with the legacy of Ra himself. They lay beautified in their tombs. They rode in the Holy Barque with the gods, while he . . .

Suddenly he shivered in the evening breeze, and rising he began to walk towards the house. He was no more than a loyal Prince to the god who sat on the Horus Throne in Het-Uart. The power of the Kings of old had waned. Egypt had split in two. Prince had squabbled with noble. Private armies had ravaged the land and the last true god, weak and useless, had surrendered his authority to foreigners who had for many years been seeping into Egypt from the east and gradually taking upon themselves the responsibilities of a country in chaos. The Setiu now ruled Egypt. That was the reality of the age into which Seqenenra had been born and in which he would die.

So deep were his musings that he almost collided with his steward, waiting in the gathering dimness of the passage. With an effort he wrenched his thoughts into the present. "Does Khian have everything he needs?" he asked. Uni nodded. "Good. See that the torches are lit, Uni. Darkness seems to have come early tonight." He moved slowly towards his own quarters, knowing he had no appetite either for the food whose aroma was even now stealing over the precincts or the game of words he would be forced to play yet again with his King.

The feast was eaten in an atmosphere of forced cheerfulness. Family and guests were anointed with scented oils and garlanded with delicate early wild flowers. Seqenenra's harpist played, and later Tani left her place by her grandmother, Tetisheri, and danced, weaving among the crowd with all the sinuous grace of her thirteen years.

Apart from Khian, there was a Weset merchant, Seqenenra's Overseer of Cattle, who had arrived earlier from the acres in the Delta where the Prince was allowed to graze his herds, and several priests from the temple of Amun, whose shaven skulls gleamed in the torchlight. Tetisheri, regal yet elfin in a tightly fitting white sheath, her grey hair hidden under a chin-length black wig topped by a circlet of gold leaves, had exchanged brief, cool greetings with Apepa's representative, answered the message from the King politely, and retired to her meal and conversation with her steward, Mersu.

As the evening grew cooler, braziers were lit. The merchant, drunk and appreciative, bowed and went home. The priests retired. Seqenenra, looking about the emptying hall from his position on the low dais, knew that he could no longer postpone the moment of reckoning. The servants had cleared away the remains of the meal and vanished. Khian was fidgeting surreptitiously with the bracelet on his thin wrist, and the expectant faces of the family were turned towards Seqenenra. He nodded to his scribe, Ipi, and at once the man went to Khian and took the proffered scroll. At Seqenenra's invitation he broke the seal and began to read aloud.

"A message from Awoserra Aqenenra Apepa, Lord of the Two Lands, Beloved of Set, Beloved of Ra, he who causes hearts to live, to Seqenenra Tao, Prince of Weset. Greetings! It distresses me to make this command to my friend Seqenenra, but the pool of the hippopotamuses which is in Weset must be done away with. For the noise of their bawling is in my august ears day and night and they permit me no sleep. Life, health and prosperity to you and your family. May Sutekh the Magnificent smile on you and Horon bring you good fortune. I anticipate your favourable reply."

The scroll rolled up with a dry rustle. Wordlessly Seqenenra held out a hand and Ipi relinquished the papyrus quickly, as though it had sullied his fingers. "You are doubtless tired, Khian," Seqenenra said evenly. "You may go to your couch." The herald bowed with obvious relief.

"Thank you, Prince," he replied. "I must leave very early in the morning, for I wish to make a speedy return to Het-Uart and the river current will be against me. I am grateful for your indulgence." He sketched a reverence to the rest of the family and was gone.

For a long time no one stirred. The lamps were burning low and shadows encroached into the airy room and insinuated themselves across the floor. The braziers spat and settled. Then Tani spoke. Her voice shook. "You won't kill the hippopotamuses will you, Father?" she pleaded. "Surely the King does not mean what he says! The marshes would be like deserts without them!"

"There is no need to discuss this at length," Tetisheri said determinedly. "Apepa is insane. He has probably already forgotten that he even dictated such a nonsensical piece of rubbish. Toss it into the nearest brazier and let us go to bed." Seqenenra placed the scroll very carefully among the bruised flower petals that now littered his small table and stared at it pensively.

"He is not insane," he said. "If he had come under the special protection of the gods, the whole country would know about it, and that is not the case. No." He felt all at once weighted down, as though he had eaten stones instead of goose meat. "This is yet another attempt to puzzle and frighten us, to push us towards something, away from something, I don't know what."

"Perhaps he simply wishes to emphasize his authority over us and humiliate Weset at the same time," Kamose interjected. "He knows our lineage. We are a long way from Het-Uart, more than six hundred miles. Does he lie sleepless in the night because he wonders what plots we might be hatching here so far from his control? It is not the coughing of the hippopotamuses that he fears."

"But we have a legal treaty with him," Aahotep put in. "We pay tribute. For generations we have been loyal subjects. His father did not torment your father this way, Seqenenra . We do not hatch plots, Kamose. We see to our five nomes and mind our own affairs."

"I think he wishes us to violate our ancient agreement with him," Seqenenra answered quietly. "He wants us to give him an excuse to bring his army here, to exile us, or worse, to install a governor without a drop of royal blood in his veins. Then he will be able to sleep."

"But why now?" Tetisheri urged. "I can just remember the terrible plague that struck Het-Uart forty years ago when Apepa's grandfather Sekerher sat on the Horus Throne. The citizens were dying in their hundreds. Their bodies were thrown into open pits within the city. The Setiu were vulnerable then, but we in the south did not take the opportunity to rebel. Why this suspicion now?" Seqenenra shrugged.

"But it was after the plague had burned itself out that Sekerher threw up the mighty earthen defences that now encircle the mounds on which the city was built," he pointed out. "Hindsight told him that his security had been hanging by the slender thread of the south's goodwill. He woke to a danger that had not materialized but had become a possibility to be considered in the future. Apepa may not rule actively here, but neither are we absent from his calculations. He does not trust us."

"Het-Uart is not worth defending," Aahotep said. "It is a treeless jumble of filthy alleys where rats forage among the offal. I cannot imagine why the Setiu should have chosen to live in such squalor with the whole of the verdant Delta at their disposal."

"Yes you can," Tetisheri retorted. "They are not Egyptian, that is why. They are foreigners who live without Ra. Het-Uart!" she snorted. "The House of the Leg! It used to be a rather delightful little town before the Setiu discovered it. What a pretty picture such a name conjures now!"

"We are not planning a rebellion," Kamose objected calmly. "Mother is right. We do not hatch plots. Let us not discuss this at length. 'Power is in the tongue, and speech is mightier than fighting,' as one of the Osiris Kings once said. Send yet another clever letter, Father, and then we can return to the more important matters of sowing and calving."

"This talk is ridiculous!" Si-Amun interrupted. He frowned at Kamose. "Rebellion, trust, these words should be meaningless to us. Who do we think we are! What business do we have in trying to circumvent a directive of the One? If he wants the hippopotamuses dead, then kill them! Anything else is sacrilege!"

Kamose struggled to his feet. "This has nothing to do with the wretched hippopotamuses and you know it," he began, but Aahmes-nefertari tugged at Si-Amun's arm.

"Father will decide what to do," she said. "Won't you, Father? Why is there always such a fuss when the One makes requests of us? I am tired and I want to go to bed." Seqenenra smiled at her faintly. Aahmes-nefertari, the peacemaker, he thought.

Aloud he said, "Yes, I will decide what to do. You can go,

both of you, unless you have something else to say, Si-Amun? I know your feelings on this matter and I do not take your opinion lightly. You are my heir. But Kamose is right. We will not appease the King by slaying a few animals. If I can save them, I will." Si-Amun turned his smooth, dark face to his father.

"I am not stupid," he retorted harshly. "I understand. But Apepa is King and god. Apepa is all-knowing and all-powerful. We owe him our allegiance and our obedience." He hesitated, pushing Aahmes-nefertari's hand away. "Otherwise," he finished flatly, "he will destroy us." He got up, bowed shortly to his grandmother and Seqenenra, and putting his arm around his wife left the hall.

There was a moment of silence. Seqenenra broke it. Walking to the nearest brazier, he thrust the scroll into the orange coals. "Tani shall have no cause to cry," he said tonelessly. "Tomorrow I will dictate yet another proof of my skill as a scribe and there the matter will end."

"Good." Tetisheri gathered herself up and glided to the doorway. "Do not disturb me before noon tomorrow, any of you. Come, Kamose. You can read to me as I fall asleep." Kamose rose, bade his parents good night, and the pair of them melted into the shadows.

"Stay with me tonight, my sister," Seqenenra spoke softly. "I am unsettled." Aahotep left her place and went to him, putting her arms around him and laying her head against his bare chest.

"You did not need to ask," she murmured. "How exhausting it is to entertain the representatives of the One when we know that they only bring us trouble! You have the wisdom of Thoth in that heart of yours, my husband. You will compose a good letter."

He lifted her chin, cupping her brown, warm face in one large hand, thinking how typically Egyptian her features were with their full mouth, straight nose and dark eyes. A year younger than he, she had kept her youthful looks and vitality in spite of the fan of tiny lines radiating across her temples. She came of sturdy stock. Her family were members of the old minor nobility who ruled in Khemennu, the city of Thoth, their roots in good Egyptian soil, their ancestors making old bones. Aahotep, too, would live long, he reflected. There was the strength of bronze, the new metal the Setiu had brought into Egypt, under her sensuous flesh. No luxury would ever taint her. The wealth of a Kingdom could be hers and she would remain inviolate.

And how splendid she would look, he thought as his mouth sought her own, with a wig of golden plaits, the vulture feathers of Mut in gold and lapis lazuli crowning her, her breasts covered in pectorals of jasper and gold! These are not wise thoughts, not sensible, he told himself. Apepa's Chief Wife wears the Queen's crown. Desolation swept over him and he groaned and buried his face in his wife's tumbled hair.

He slept badly and rose a little before dawn, performing his ablutions carefully before ordering a litter to take him to the temple for the morning's rites. He was carried along the path by the river and he left the curtains open, enjoying the smell of the morning air, briefly moist and laden with the scent of earth and the greenness of spring. The river was calm and grey, flowing noiselessly. Birds and small unseen animals made the rushes tremble. The light was pale and limpid, but as his bearers turned away from the river, passing the temple watersteps, the sun lifted above the eastern horizon, shimmering gold, and by the time he alighted and began to walk towards the pylon he could feel its warmth on his face.

The outer court was quiet. A pair of dancers wrapped in linen and talking together in low tones paused and turned to bow to him and he smiled at them, passing into the half-light of the inner court. The High Priest and an acolyte came to greet him through the shafts of new light pouring down from the clerestory windows. Seqenenra sat. The acolyte removed his sandals and washed his feet, then Prince and priest approached the door to the sanctuary beyond. Behind them there came a scuffling and whispering interspersed with the tinkle of the systra as the singers prepared to welcome the god to another day. Seqenenra knelt before the door, prostrated himself, then rose and broke the clay seal. The High Priest pulled away the cord and swung open the door. Immediately the singers burst into song. The systra in their hands beat time to the words of praise.

Seqenenra and the priest entered the sanctuary. It was dark and stuffy. The lamps left burning beside the great golden figure of Amun had almost gone out. Averting his eyes the priest replenished them, charged the tall copper censers to each side of the figure, and began to remove the wilted flowers and stale food from the night before. Out by the doors, priests were placing fresh food, wine and flowers together with new linen reverentially on the floor. The singing ceased. The music of finger cymbals and drums began and Seqenenra could hear the glide and shuffle of the dancers' feet as they took the place of the singers, swaying and bending for Amun's entertainment while his morning ablutions were performed.

Seqenenra began his duties, taking the gossamer-fine, starched linen from the hands of the High Priest, the food, the scented water for the washing, his own hands moving gently over the massive golden limbs of the god, his voice carrying beyond the small sanctuary as he said the accompanying prayers. This was his god, the totem of his family, his town, the one who had once raised his ancestors to supreme power in Egypt. He deserved the utmost respect.

When Amun had been washed, clad in fresh linen, and

offered the food and wine, the dancers retired. The door was shut. Seqenenra stood looking up into the benignly smiling face and tall golden plumes while the High Priest began the prayers for the day. "O power that quickened the waters of chaos, breathe life into thy son Seqenenra. O power whose eyes brought light to the earth, bring understanding to thy son Seqenenra. O Divine Goose from whose mighty Egg all things were created, spring forth in abundance over thy city of Weset . . ."

Seqenenra listened, anguish in his heart. What will I dictate to Apepa, Amun, my Lord? he thought dismally. To what dark end are we being herded? Do you no longer care that your divinity is shrouded, that it does not shine forth triumphant over the whole of Egypt?

The High Priest finished the official prayers and there was a pause. Seqenenra closed his eyes and inhaled the sweet, pungent smoke hanging thickly in the motionless air. It was time for the Admonitions, when the priest reminded the god of his duties to his city and nome, of the promises not yet kept and perhaps forgotten, and often the words were for the Prince himself, couched in warnings to the god. This morning Amunmose spoke of fertility for the soil, protection from diseases, and the need for better offerings to maintain the temple and its staff. Seqenenra smiled. He would have to remind his friend that need must wait upon circumstance.

Then the High Priest chanted, "Take up your cause, Mighty Amun, against the false gods of the Setiu in Egypt. Muzzle the dogs of Sutekh, blind the dancers of Anath, strike dumb the singers of Baal . . ."

Seqenenra started. His heart began to pound. On impulse he knelt, and laying his cheek against Amun's gleaming shins he began to laugh. The High Priest paused. Seqenenra stood, still laughing, and motioned for the man to continue. Of course! he thought, trying to stifle his mirth. My thanks, Great Cackler. Muzzle the dogs of Sutekh. That will do. That will do very well...

Later when the doors had closed behind them, and the acolyte had tied Seqenenra's sandals back onto his feet, and he and Amunmose were strolling across the outer court, Amunmose said, "The offerings are no laughing matter, Lord. Certainly the temple is small and my staff not overly large and I do understand that gold is doled out to us in return for levies of labourers and other favours not specified in our agreement with the One, but to laugh at the needs of the god is almost blasphemy."

Seqenenra took his shoulder and swung him to a halt. They stood squinting at each other in the blinding sunlight. The court was busier now. We'eb priests came and went through the tall pylons, receiving the offerings of the common people together with their requests. A few nobles were performing the purifying ritual before being allowed into the inner court, ignored by the temple women who talked or prayed or sat in the shade of the wall and gossiped. Seqenenra's escort could be glimpsed squatting by the litter, their spears beside them in the sand, playing knucklebones.

"Do not reprove me, my friend," he begged. "Do I not maintain the house of my father? Do I not see that the shrine of Montu is pleasing in his eyes? Is the habitation of Mut not lovingly repaired out of my own treasury? What other governor in this sick and miserable land cares for the sacred places as I do?" He had not meant to say all those things. He had wanted to remind the High Priest that he, Seqenenra, had appointed him and therefore expected a degree of indulgence, but a cold pain had gripped him with his first words and anger had surged from his chest onto his tongue with an appalling familiarity. Amunmose had gone white. He dropped his eyes and began to murmur an apology. Seqenenra cursed himself inwardly. "Forgive me," he begged. "I am not angry with you. I laughed in the sanctuary because my father had answered a prayer, that is all." Amunmose touched his left hand to the leopard skin draped over his right shoulder. It was the obeisance of a subject to a King.

"Nevertheless you are right, Prince," he said. "I was presumptuous."

"You have worries also, I know," Seqenenra sighed. "I have received another senseless directive from the One. I cannot divine what direction these odd missives are taking. Perhaps I should consult Amun's oracle."

"Perhaps." Amunmose hesitated. "Prince, may I give you some advice?" Seqenenra looked at him blankly.

"Of course."

"Then, be careful whose ears are open around you when you speak of the One and his divine commands. You mentioned blasphemy to me. Sometimes your opinions might be construed by loyal Egyptians as blasphemy against the Lord of the Two Lands. You are changing, Seqenenra Tao." He smiled faintly. "The old contentment is gone. You are no longer governor of Weset and Prince of Egypt." Seqenenra's throat went dry.

"What do you know that I do not?" he whispered. "My servants are the children of my father's servants, loyal to my name and my authority." Amunmose held up a hand and shook his head.

"I know nothing. On the august plumes of the Cackler I swear it. I simply beseech you to be cautious. Your father was an honest governor under the One and he gave his servants no cause to examine their deepest loyalties. It would be unwise to cause any of yours to panic." Seqenenra stared at him.

"Am I so innocent, then?" he muttered half to himself. "Am I so stupid? I will ponder your counsel." Amunmose bowed and turned away.

Seqenenra went to his litter, and, drawing the curtains, sat hunched against the cushions. You are changing, Seqenenra Tao . . . no longer governor of Weset and Prince of Egypt . . . Not so, not so, he thought vehemently. I am content with peace. The restlessness I sometimes feel is simply the blood of my fighting ancestors demanding release. It passes in time.

After breaking his fast he received his Overseer of Lands and his Treasurer in his office, dealing quickly with their questions before sending for Ipi. The man came and bowed, taking up his position at Seqenenra's feet and settling his scribe's palette across his knees. Trimming his brushes and shaking his pot of paint, he waited. Silently Seqenenra weighed the words that must be couched in phrases of correct worship.

Outside, beyond the pillared loggia, he saw Ahmose run past unpainted and unshod as usual, followed more slowly by Si-Amun and Kamose who were obviously on their way to the training ground with their weapons. A servant staggered into view, laden with cushions which he spread by the pool under the thick shade of a fig tree, and presently Tetisheri appeared, picking her way delicately, Isis holding a large sunshade over her head. She folded onto the ground, clapped, and Mersu knelt beside her, dropping several scrolls. Seqenenra smiled to himself. His mother knew perfectly well what he was doing and she would wait to hear what he had dictated. "Uni," he called into the passage. "Bring beer." His steward went away to comply. Seqenenra nodded. "I am ready."

"Thoth guide my hand and your thoughts," Ipi replied dutifully.

"Good. Begin with the usual salutation, 'to Awoserra Aqenenra Apepa Beloved of Set, Beloved of Ra, Lord of the Two Lands, from his governor and servant Seqenenra, greetings.' Then—'My distress was great upon hearing the words of your letter. Let it not be, I said, that my Divine Lord's rest should be disturbed by the voices of the hippopotamuses in the marshes of his loyal city.'" He paused, for Uni had returned, setting a cup and a small flagon on the table beside him. The steward poured, tasted, then passed the cup. Seqenenra drank deeply. Uni returned to his post behind his master. "Read it back to me," Seqenenra ordered. The scribe did so. Seqenenra continued, a tremor of laughter in his voice. "'I have accordingly commanded my leatherworkers to design and construct muzzles for these noisy beasts. Thus will my lord's sleep be deep and uninterrupted. May my lord's name live forever. Life, Health, Prosperity! Given this day, the twentieth of the month of Tybi in the season Peret, by the hand of my scribe Ipi.'" He watched the rapid, black script dry into the papyrus. "Seal it and give it to Men. He is due to leave for the Delta. Make a copy for the archives." Ipi slid the lid closed on his brush box, tucked the scroll into his kilt, and backed away respectfully.

Seqenenra stretched, poured more beer, and turned to Uni. He felt as though the weight of foreboding that had settled on his shoulders the night before had just rolled away. "What do you think of my solution?" he asked.

"The One will see it as a joke at his expense," Uni warned. "He will be angry."

"Oh, I do not think so," Seqenenra disagreed. "The Setiu only laugh when donkeys fall down or old women trip in the street. Our King will close his eyes at night on visions of every one of my hippopotamuses' noses swathed in leather thongs."

Uni cleared his throat. "I do not think so, Prince. He will know you have been disrespectful."

"But I mean him no disrespect," Seqenenra replied emphatically. "I have tried to answer his letter in the same tone as it was addressed to me."

"And what tone was that, Prince?" Seqenenra sighed.

"Uni, you are an efficient and valuable steward. Sometimes you are even the sharer of my secrets. Do not be impertinent." Uni bowed stiffly.

Seqenenra took his beer and went out into the garden. Seeing him come, Tetisheri gestured and Mersu stopped reading. Tetisheri waved Mersu away. He gathered up his armful of scrolls and withdrew. Seqenenra sank onto his haunches before his mother. She drew one hennaed finger down his cheek. "Well, Prince?" she urged softly. "What did you tell the servant of Sutekh?" His gaze met her lined, kohled eyes. The bones of her face were as fine and dainty as a fawn's. At sixty, her skin had the hue of parchment. Her hair was white, the veins of her hands blue and knotted, but her voice, her movements still held an echo of the lightly graceful girl she had been.

"I told him I would muzzle the hippopotamuses," he said. "I think Uni was horrified at my presumption." Tetisheri laughed.

"Uni is an old woman," she commented. "Well, thank the gods, that is that. A brilliant solution, as always. Aahotep and I are going to visit a friend today. What will you do?" He glanced over her head, above the trees and the sheltering wall, to the mute invitation of the old palace baking in the sun. No, he thought determinedly. Not today.

"Tani and I will take a skiff to the marshes," he said, "and we will tell the children of Set how fortunate they are!"

He and his daughter, with several bodyguards striding beside the litters and Behek and the other dogs lolloping behind, rode the short distance to the edge of the marshes. There they got into a skiff, Tani hauling Behek down beside her and leaving the others in the care of the soldiers, and were poled between the whispering papyrus swamps and beds of lotus that floated, waxy and fragrant, in their small wake. Fish flicked away just out of Tani's reach. Frogs leaped with sudden abandon from the reed pads into the pale, cool water. A cloud of blue dragonflies settled briefly on Tani's linen and she cried out in delight. Egrets rose beside them with a flutter of white wings and beat their way up towards the sun. Tani was soon drenched.

Seqenenra watched her contentedly. At length she became

quiet and from the shelter of the river growth they peered out at the hippopotamuses. Today only three of them were standing shoulder deep in the river, ears flicking lazily, bright eyes narrowed. One yawned, exposing a cavernous throat, water running from its nostrils, its teeth festooned with limp weeds. "I do love them so," Tani whispered. "Even though they belong to Set. If the One could only see them thus, he would not want to kill them, I know."

"He has seen them," Seqenenra reminded her. "But perhaps you were too young to remember." He kept a careful eye on the beasts as he spoke. They were slow, their movements cumbersome, but they could also be dangerous. "You were only six. The One had just ascended the Horus Throne in Het-Uart and he wanted to visit all his governors. He came and stayed with us, or rather he stayed on the royal barge tethered at the watersteps. We had some grand feasts while he was here." One of the hippopotamuses lowered itself until only its nostrils and tiny eyes could be seen, then it started for the bank. Seqenenra signalled to the servant and the skiff turned and began to glide back through the papyrus.

"I think I remember," Tani said doubtfully. "Did he have a beard?"

"Yes. A small one. I believe he did not keep it long."

"Oh. Father, look up! A falcon!" Seqenenra followed her pointing finger. He shaved off the beard, he thought, but there was nothing he could do about his eyes, set too close together, or the clumsiness of his hands as he held the Crook and the Flail. "Go on, Behek!" Tani was urging the dog. "Jump in and swim! Call him, Hor-Aha!" Seqenenra dismissed his own pettiness and gave himself up to the pleasures of the afternoon.

Kamose stared at the scuffed, baking dirt of the practice ground now inches from his nose. He flexed his shoulders slightly, testing Si-Amun's lock on his throat, and felt his brother's elbow tighten against his neck. Si-Amun's spare hand gripped Kamose's wrists like a vise behind his back. Both young men were pouring sweat and breathing hard. Si-Amun's harsh breath rasped in Kamose's ear. "You still must put me on the ground," Kamose croaked with difficulty. "My feet are firm." If I can make him shift his centre of balance, he thought, I can throw him. Si-Amun was bent over Kamose's slick back. Kamose let himself go slightly limp, felt his brother move imperceptibly to automatically adjust his hold, and in the second when Si-Amun's balance was disturbed Kamose spread his legs and leaned forward. With a shout Si-Amun dove into the dust. In a flash Kamose was on him, kneeling well back on his chest so as not to be toppled forward. "Last throw," he panted, grinning and rising, holding down a grimy hand to his brother. "I can't believe I actually won this time." Si-Amun pulled himself to his feet and they embraced.

"Make the most of your victory," Si-Amun teased him. "It will not be repeated. You won because I am not in top form today. I drank too much wine last night."

"Excuses." Kamose walked to where their kilts lay in a white pile on the hot earth. "I think I am going to be the better wrestler in the end, Si-Amun. I spend a lot more time training with Hor-Aha than you do. You're getting lazy." He flung Si-Amun's kilt at him and wound his own around his waist.

"You're right," Si-Amun agreed good-naturedly. "I like to keep fit but I don't want to attain the physical perfection of the soldier. I can't see why you bother either." He waved an arm towards the far end of the training ground where a large number of men were being drilled. The sunlight glinted on the tips of their spears and their sun-blackened, muscular bodies gleamed with oil. The sharp commands of the officer in charge came echoing to the two brothers as they watched the formation wheel smartly. "They are an expensive toy for Father,"

Si-Amun went on, wiping his forehead vigorously with his kilt before fastening it in place. "Of course, the bodyguards are necessary, and a few retainers when we travel, and perhaps a spare contingent or two for the nomes when there's trouble, but with the King's whole army available for any serious defence, Father could send half his five hundred troops back to their homes. Supporting them drives Uni crazy."

"They may be needed one day," Kamose replied, picking up his sandals and shaking them free of sand, and Si-Amun jumped on his words with an immediacy that betrayed his secret preoccupation.

"To do what?" he snapped. "The only need Father might have for a true private army would be against the One himself and I know such thoughts are in his mind because of the way he reacted to the King's scroll. No one is more aware than I that royal blood flows in our veins, which is why I do not understand our self-imposed exile in this lamentable burning backwater when we might be sitting beside Apepa in Het-Uart and enjoying his favour. Father has too much pride."

"It is the pride of a Prince who would rather govern his ancestral seat with authority than lick the King's leather boots every day in a region of Egypt where he has no friends and no roots," Kamose shot back irritably. "I wish I had been born before you, Si-Amun, for then you would be free to go north and fawn upon our King while I prepared to take upon myself the responsibilities of a Prince of Weset."

"How humourless you are!" Si-Amun mocked him gently. "How sober! Don't you ever just have fun, Kamose, make love to a few serving girls, get drunk in your skiff at midnight on the river? You are so solemn most of the time!" Kamose bit back a stinging answer.

"I take life a little more seriously than you, Si-Amun, that is all," he said, beginning to walk towards the gate in the wall that gave onto the rear of the courtyard. Si-Amun hurried to keep pace with him.

"I apologize," he said. "If we were similar in more than our looks, our lives would be simpler. Yet I love you." Kamose smiled across at him.

"I love you also."

"All the same," Si-Amun emphasized, always needing the last word, "if Father ever took it into his head to commit treason against Ma'at and march against the King I would not join him. I worry about that."

"So do I," Kamose admitted, "but not out of loyalty to the King. I worry at the dissolution of the family and the destruction of the life we lead here at Weset. But we are foolish to make ourselves even more sweaty than we are already by arguing over a puff of cloud. Let's bathe. I want to be oiled before my muscles stiffen into soreness. In any case," and here he graced Si-Amun with one of his rare, dazzling full smiles, "Apepa is not Ma'at in Egypt. Father is."

To that, Si-Amun had no reply. They pushed through the gate, crossed the courtyard beyond in the sudden shade of the granaries, and headed for the bath house together.

No reply to Seqenenra's letter came from the King. Men returned from the Delta several weeks later and reported that he had not personally been received by Apepa. He had handed the scroll to Itju, the King's Chief Scribe, and had been told the next day that he could go. He had toured his master's cattle, which were growing fat and sleek on the lush pastures watered by an abundant Nile that branched out and meandered slowly through the Delta to the Great Green, and could tell Amunmose that Amun's cattle likewise fared excellently. He had watched the King's charioteers practising manoeuvres outside Het-Uart. On his way home he had spent a day admiring the marvels of Saqqara, the ancient city of the dead, and had climbed one of the lesser pyramids close by, as so many other travellers did.

Seqenenra had few questions for him. In the days that followed, his anxiety lessened and finally disappeared as he watched royal craft ply the river on their way to Kush or from Kush to the Delta, passing Weset with oars flashing and flags afloat. Apepa's quixotic demand and Seqenenra's equally irrational reply were relegated to the back of Seqenenra's mind and often forgotten altogether.

Chapter TWO

As SPRING MOVED INTO summer and the season of Shemu began, Seqenenra left Kamose to govern in his absence and took Aahotep and the rest of the family north to Khemennu where Teti, Aahotep's relative by marriage, was governor. Tetisheri declined to go, preferring to order her time as she wished. Kamose was more than content to see to the affairs of the nomes, do a little hunting in the desert hills, and enjoy the peace of his own solitary routine. Seqenenra did not insist that Si-Amun fulfil the duties of an heir. He would get much more pleasure from the bustle of Teti's estate than Kamose. Ahmose was content to make no choices. He was happy wherever he found himself. The crops had sprung up thick and promising in the little fields. The canals bordering them were full of the water imprisoned by mud dykes as the Nile sank after the last Inundation. In the gardens the leeks and onions, radishes, lettuce and melons were forming and flowers trembled, pink, blue and white, beside the pool. Monkeys perched in the palm trees that lined river and canal, gibbering at passersby, and in the thick papyrus beds young crocodiles lurked, watching with lazy greed the antics of the newly hatched fledglings.

The Inundation had been generous. Isis had cried copiously,

flooding Egypt with fecundity, and Seqenenra knew that the resultant crops would pay his taxes to the One and leave his personal treasury amply filled for another year. Si-Amun and his older daughter had come to him just before they were all due to leave, both solemn and full of importance, with the news that Aahmes-nefertari was pregnant with their first child. Delighted, Seqenenra congratulated them. Aahotep gave Aahmes-nefertari a menat-amulet for special protection and the whole family burned incense before Taurt, who stood fat and smiling, her great hippopotamus's body swollen with her own promise at the entrance to the women's quarters. Tani had always treated the statue of the goddess with happy affection, rubbing the vast stomach as she ran to and from her room beside her mother's, but now Aahmes-nefertari brought a flower or two daily to lay on the goddess's feet and assiduously said her prayers there morning and evening.

It was a cheerful group that waved farewell to Kamose and Tetisheri. Aahotep watched until the last glimpse of the tree-shrouded house and the glint of sun on the white watersteps had sunk from view. Behind her barge came the one carrying Si-Amun and Aahmes-nefertari. Ahmose and Tani shared the third craft. The servants who would set up quarters for the family on the bank each evening had gone on ahead. Aahotep signalled, going to the mats laid under the canopy against the small cabin where Seqenenra already sat, and as she went down beside him, Isis handed her a cup of water.

Already Weset, with its clusters of whitewashed mud houses, narrow donkey-crowded streets and women squatting to slap their linen against the river's surface, had receded and the Nile wound peacefully through reed marshes that opened on the east to fields in which peasants bent and on the west to unculti-vated tangles of papyrus and then blinding sand that covered the feet of the western cliffs.

"I wish Tetisheri had decided to come with us," Aahotep remarked, sipping the water. "It would have done her good to get away from Weset for a while."

"Khemennu is under the One's direct control," Seqenenra reminded her. "My mother likes to foster the illusion that we are all free, or at least she does not like to have to swallow her words or bite her tongue. She and Kamose understand one another very well. They will enjoy the opportunity to tussle over minor matters of administration."

"I suppose you are right. And I know she will spend much time taking offerings to your father's shrine and praying there. She speaks of him so little, yet I know she misses him a great deal. I shall go to my parents' tomb in Khemennu also while we are there, and eat a memorial meal. Seqenenra, could you talk to their priest and make sure the endowment is being used correctly? Kares exchanges correspondence with him, but in these times one never knows . . . Seqenenra?" He came to himself with a start.

"I am sorry, Aahotep. I was wondering whether I should visit my mayors and assistant governors on the way north or as we come home. It is good for them to talk with me and not an overseer sometimes."

"No, you were not." She took his hand and her fingers closed around it. "You were thinking of Si-Amun's unborn child."

Seqenenra stared up at the roof of the canopy, its yellow tassels bobbing in the wind, and then beyond it. The sky was densely blue and as he squinted against the sun he saw a hawk wheel into sight, wings outstretched and motionless, a black speck in the vastness. He heard the helmsman give a sharp order, answered by one of the sailors. His gaze dropped slowly to Isis and Kares, leaning over the side and talking quietly together with that air of permanent alertness that all good servants developed. Bending, he kissed Aahotep's full, hennaed lips, brushing her tousled black hair away from her cheek as he did so.

"You are right," he admitted. "I am happy for them both and yet..."

"And yet you wish that Kamose could be persuaded to wed Tani and give you grandchildren also, in order that your inheritance might be doubly secure." He drew away grim-faced, sitting with one leg extended, his arms clasping the other bent knee as a guest in his own garden might sit. Aahotep waited, and when he did not speak she continued in a low voice, "You are the rightful King of this land by blood and birth. You would have married your sister if she had not died so young. That is why you feel so naked. I was given to you because my family is also ancient though it carries no royal blood. True Ma'at in Egypt hangs by a thread. Kamose resists all your efforts to push him towards a union with Tani when she comes of age next year so that you wonder whether you will be forced to command him. Yet life that seems so bright and strong may at any time flicker and vanish, dear brother. Si-Amun's child will be fully royal. Kamose might be dead tomorrow, next month, next year." She fingered the silver ankh at her neck and the amulet of Sekhmet on her arm to negate the doom of her words. "We know nothing. Rejoice for your son. If Kamose decides to see reason and he and Tani have children, that is fine. If not, there is still Ahmose."

"You are right," he broke in harshly. "I grieve for myself, for my father, for a wounded Ma'at. I mourn because I will go to my tomb and Si-Amun to his, yes and Kamose too, as lowly governors. I will never touch the Crook and the Flail, Aahotep."

"Yet you have always done right in the sight of the gods," she reminded him. "When your heart is weighed, nothing else will matter. Isis!" The woman left the view and came bowing.

"Bring the sennet. Look, Seqenenra." She pointed to the bank. "This village seems to be inhabited solely by little boys and oxen. I suppose they have driven them into the river to cool them. Do you want to play the cones or shall I?"

They played several games, ate and drank, and played again, Aahotep being careful not to force Seqenenra's piece into the square that denoted the cold, black water of the underworld where the dead wailed for the light of Ra, and Seqenenra's mood soon lifted. He was not a man given often to self-pity and like everyone he knew he was addicted to the magical tussle between the cones and the spools. As the afternoon heat intensified, Aahotep took Isis to fan her and went away to rest.

Seqenenra rose, stretched, and made his way to the side of the barge, first hypnotized by the steady running of the wake the craft was making and then fixing his eyes on the bank gliding past. Villages, stiff palms, canals mirroring a bronze sky, sometimes a nearly-naked peasant leading a donkey, all appeared, imprinted themselves briefly on his consciousness tinged with a haze of heat, and slid away like waking dreams. He knew them all. Since the time of his youth he had travelled up and down the Nile, from Weset south to Swenet and north to Qes, the boundaries of the portion of Egypt he and his fathers before him were allowed to administer. Year by year he had seen the apparent changelessness of his domain. Changelessness was a part of the rightness of Ma'at, the eternal order that had been laid down by the gods when Egypt rose from Nun, the primeval waters, and Osiris had still been a god of the living.

When he was younger, travelling with Senakhtenra, such familiarity had been reassuring. Yet now he knew that the changelessness of the villages was the only part of Ma'at that remained. The barge was passing a shrine, crumbling and overgrown, and even as he had to turn his head to keep it in view he saw a pack of dogs come running from its gaping entrance and head towards the water. The Setiu who ruled Egypt now had brought their own gods with them, uncivilized deities with hard names, and the homes of the gods of Egypt were turning to dust. How is it that I never noticed before? he asked himself, deeply disturbed. Khentiamentiu, jackal of Aabtu, your temple and a hundred others, not changeless, no. Falling down, falling apart as I sailed by year after year, while Set and Sutekh slowly became one and Hathor and Ishtar blended. Horus and Horon . . . He shivered. My body lives in the shadow of the old palace. My ka inhabits the past so that I keep the present comfortably at bay. And why not? Wearily he left the barge's side and cast himself down on the cushions. Uni padded to him immediately, but with one arm over his eyes Seqenenra waved him away. Let Kamose marry whom and when he will. Let Ahmose continue to run wild and laughing through his life. In five hentis or ten there might be change but not in my lifetime or the lives of my children. That is the Ma'at of today. That is the law of the One, Apepa, Beloved of Set, foreign usurper in Het-Uart. He felt no anger, only surprise that today the full force of his country's situation was brought home to him, today during a small voyage of no great import. He considered, but the heat brought him a welcome lassitude and he slept.

At Khemennu they were guests of Aahotep's cousin Teti, a wealthy man who had secured from the King the position of Inspector and Administrator of Dykes and Canals. In addition to travelling through the nomes of his jurisdiction after the Inundation had receded in order to see to the reconstituting of the dykes and the repair of the major irrigation canals in Upper Egypt, he held much property. His wife was a priestess in the temple of Thoth, a deity revered not only as the god of wisdom and writing and therefore every scribe's patron but also as the essence of the moon. Khemennu was his city and Aahotep, a lover of Thoth all her life, spent much of her time in the temple there when she was not visiting relatives. Khemennu was a pretty place surrounded by dense fig trees, its mud streets lined with date palms and its docks busy. Teti's estate lay on the northern limit beside the temple of Set that had been built fifty years before. He had many minor officials under him and his watersteps were often crowded. Seqenenra, walking with him through the town, taking a skiff with him as he was poled to some dispute or other over a field boundary that the winter flood had washed away, and sitting beside him at the evening meal when his reception hall was full of the dignitaries of Khemennu and noisy with musicians and acrobats, felt out of place. It was not so much the faster pace of the life of his relative by marriage. It was Teti's quite unselfconscious air of cheerful fulfilment. He worshipped Thoth as his nome's totem and Set as the lord of the King. He organized his family and his staff, received the frequent heralds from the Delta with assurance and warmth, even talked to Seqenenra with just the correct balance of comradeship and deference that Seqenenra's superior blood but inferior relationship with the One demanded. Teti, Seqenenra decided, was a man without dark dreams or stabs of remorse. He envied him.

With Seqenenra's permission, Teti had placed Tani in the care of his son Ramose, a sixteen-year-old who loved fowling and who promised to care for his second cousin as though she were Hathor herself. Tani, to her father's surprise and secret amusement, blushed at the young man's earnest words and the pair of them had gathered up servants and throwing sticks and disappeared into the swamps.

"They get along very well together, those two," Teti commented one evening. He and Seqenenra were sitting by Teti's artificial lake, small but grandly ornamented with blue tiling, drinking pomegranate wine while Ra lowered himself towards the mouth of Nut beyond the western hills. "Ramose is a responsible son and Tani must surely be nearing the age of betrothal?" Seqenenra shot him a surprised glance and Teti chuckled. "Have you not considered it, Prince? We may be members of the minor nobility but I am a rich man, enjoying the favour of the One, and a further cementing of our families would be a blessed thing."

"Perhaps," Seqenenra responded slowly. "Yet Tani is still very young and I would not force her if she and Ramose felt nothing more for each other than friendship." Besides, he thought, there is Kamose. He may change his mind. Tani may find her brother a safer and more familiar haven in the end than the prospect of Khemennu's noise and bustle.

"Neither would I want to force her," Teti retorted. "After all, it would not be a royal match of necessity." He signalled for more wine to be poured for them, casting Seqenenra a shrewd look. "Si-Amun and Aahmes-nefertari's children will keep your blood line pure. Tani could do a lot worse than my son." Seqenenra leaned forward apologetically.

"Teti, I did not hesitate out of arrogance. I am sorry. The idea had not crossed my mind, that is all."

"I don't suppose it had," Teti replied, eyes narrowed. "But give it some thought, Prince. The One would be more than pleased." Seqenenra stiffened and looked him full in the face. He was lifting his gold cup and drinking, but his eyes were coolly fixed on Seqenenra.

"Is this match his idea?"

Teti lowered his cup and tossed the dregs into the water of the pool, now rippling red with the sun's last lingering rays. Already servants were moving about the garden with lamps.

"Not directly. But lately on several occasions when I have been granted an audience with him at Het-Uart regarding new acres to be flooded, he has expressed an interest in my son and your daughter, separately in the conversation but with, I think, a hint of his new desire."

"But why?" Seqenenra did not want to say the words himself. It was safer here, in a city where a Setiu governor's estate lay barely a stone's throw away, to hear them from Teti's lips.

"You know why," Teti said shortly. "The One has your oaths of obedience and the scroll your grandfather signed, but Weset is a very long way from Het-Uart and the holy sleep is sometimes disturbed, I think, by the fear that Seqenenra Tao's sons may both end up married to Seqenenra Tao's daughters. A potential for treachery would have been created."

Seqenenra laughed abruptly, though he felt cold. "But you know me, Teti. You know my sons. We live quietly, we serve Amun in peace, we administer our nomes with honesty. The One's suspicions are unjust."

"They are not yet suspicions," Teti assured him. "Only moments of unease, I am sure. But quite apart from that, Seqenenra, wouldn't Ramose and Tani make a good pair? Look at you and my cousin!"

Full dark had fallen. The hot night air was suddenly laden with the odours of lotus, pomegranate blossom and a waft of roast goose from the kitchens across the sandy courtyard. Lamps cast pools of yellow light on discarded cushions and the remains of the small greeting meal of fruit and wine the men had been picking at, but did not illumine their faces to each other. "You are right," Seqenenra managed, fighting down the wave of reluctance the idea had stirred. "But let us wait and see what Tani and Ramose themselves have to say about it by the time we must go home."

"That is fair." Teti rose with a gesture and Seqenenra rose with him. "Now we will go inside and see what the women have been doing today. My wife ordered out the litters early this morning, so it is likely that they have been visiting merchants! In any event, I am glad Aahotep and your daughters are here. I wish they would come more often. My wife loves them dearly. You know, I must adjudicate a terrible wrangle in the Delta between a group of peasants and the Overseer of Set's Acres. It seems that one of the dykes between their adjoining fields was completely washed away in the Inundation this year and the Overseer is claiming more land than was originally the god's, or so the peasants say. I must consult the land titles and the original survey and I hope I can find some wisdom there. The One says..."

Seqenenra listened to him politely but absently as they moved from the garden, between the pillars of the entrance hall, along the brightly painted passage. Danger snarled at him suddenly, and he felt anxious and alone. "Teti!" he blurted. The other man stopped talking and turned to him.

"Yes?"

"Your grandfather was once an erpa-ha Prince and governor of the Khemennu nomes, was he not?" Teti stepped closer and when he spoke his voice was scarcely above a whisper. "Yes, he was. What of it?"

Oh gods, Seqenenra thought in despair. What is the matter with me? Teti's wounds, my wounds, scars now, dry and healed. Amun, prevent me from ripping at them any more! The lamp on the wall behind Seqenenra's head was flickering and the tongues of light jerked spasmodically across Teti's face, making his eyes glitter.

"Why are you not governor of Khemennu? An erpa-ha is an hereditary title." He had overstepped the bounds of hospitality and family affection by a mile, yet he could not help himself. Teti bit his lip.

"I thought you knew, Prince," he murmured huskily. "My grandfather led an insurrection against Osiris Sekerher, Apepa's grandfather. It got no further than Henen-Nesut, south of

Ta-she. My grandfather was pardoned but he had his tongue removed for treason and his title was taken away. Yet our King and his father were merciful. My father, Pepi, redeemed himself in the first Apepa's army and I am grateful for what I have." He drew away into deeper shadow but Seqenenra could still see his eyes, veiled and cautious. "I sway with the wind so as not to be broken," he said with more confidence. "I suggest that you do the same, Seqenenra Tao. Indeed I had always thought you a mild and biddable man. There is no other way."

They looked at each other in silence. At the end of the passage where the reception hall opened out and guests and other diners were already chattering and laughing, light blazed out but did not reach them. At length Seqenenra wet his lips. "Is there not?" he croaked. "You know about the letters, Teti?" Teti took one step forward, and grasping his friend's arms shook him once, violently.

"Yes, I know! All Egypt knows! Treat them with patience and respect and they will cease! I don't know what demon has found a way into you, Prince, but run to the magicians and be exorcised!"

"No other way?" The words were so softly spoken that Seqenenra could not be sure Teti had heard them. Teti let him go. For a long moment he regarded Seqenenra, and slowly his face fell into lines of sadness and regret.

"No." he replied. Turning on his heel he walked into the welcoming cacophony of the hall. Dazed, heart pounding, Seqenenra followed. That is the end of it, he thought, as Aahotep saw him and came hurrying through the crowd. He bent as a serving girl reached to tie a cone of perfumed wax on his head and another with a word of submission set a wreath of blue lotuses around his neck. Aahotep kissed him.

"You look ill," she said. "Come and sit down. Too much rich wine, Prince?" He managed to smile into her painted face and allowed himself to be led to the low table strewn with flowers that awaited him. The other guests were settling themselves before their own tables throughout the hall and the musicians, harps and drums under their arms, were threading their way towards the dais. The end of it, end of it! Seqenenra thought fervently. Tomorrow I will apologize to Teti. I do not even have the excuse of being drunk. I will invite him and his family to Weset. I will make amends. But as he lowered himself beside Aahotep and turned to politely greet the woman on his other side, rebellion rose in him like a sick red tide. I am a King, he thought fiercely. I am Horus. Horus does not make amends.

He drank too much that night, singing with the singers, dancing with the naked women who twirled and dipped between the tables. He was not alone. By the time dawn inched coldly into the room the floor was littered with guests too drunk to get onto their litters and go home. Aahotep, Uni and Isis half-dragged, half-carried Seqenenra to his couch in the guest quarters where he muttered, groaned, and fell into a sodden sleep.

He woke towards noon with a raging thirst and a headache that threatened to split him in two. Rolling off the couch he sat waiting for the room to swim into focus. Outside, he heard voices in the garden, and farther away, splashes and shrieks. Dogs were barking. A knock came on the door and Uni entered carrying a tray. Seqenenra smiled at him weakly. "I suppose most of the servants are ministering to guests as sorry for themselves this morning as I am," he said. "Is there water, Uni?" The man set the tray on the table beside the couch.

"Yes. I drew it myself from the urn in the passage. It is fresh. There is also bread and some figs, though they are very early ones and I fear they are too green. If you don't want them, I can bring leek shoots." Seqenenra lifted the cup and drained it.

"The figs will do. Go to the bath house and make sure there is hot water for me in a moment. Where are the others?"

"The Princesses Aahotep and Aahmes-nefertari are in the garden with the other women, watching the weaving. Tani and Ramose are swimming. Ahmose has gone fishing. Teti and his steward have taken litters into Khemennu and I believe Si-Amun is with them."

"Thank you. You can go." Uni bowed himself out.

Seqenenra picked through the figs without appetite. With his thirst quenched, the headache was receding. Carefully he reviewed the curious and frightening exchange he and Teti had had, all his own fault of course, and he discovered that the wine he had swilled so copiously had somehow acted as a purge. He felt cleansed in his mind. Despair and anxiety had gone. He could go home in peace.

Padding into the passage, he drew more water from the waist-high stone jar, drank, then wrapping a sheet around himself, he made his way to the bath house. Standing on the slab while the bath servant deluged and scrubbed him, he told himself that life was good. Damp and cooled, he made his way back to his room, opened the house-shrine to Thoth, and thanked the god for giving him the new wisdom to accept gladly that which could not be changed. Uni did not reappear. Annoyed, Seqenenra dressed himself in a plain kilt, a silver chain and his sandals, then he ventured out into the sparkling early afternoon.

Slipping by the garden where his wife and his daughter, cross-legged on mats under a canopy, were talking animatedly with Teti's wife who was sitting on a stool before a loom, he strolled past the trellises of grapevines, across the paved court, and came to the watersteps. Several dogs lay panting and indolent in the shade of the acacias that clustered close to the water and Teti's pet baboon shuffled up to him, inspected him curiously, and put out a furry hand. Amused, Seqenenra took it, stroked it, and the beast, seemingly satisfied, bared its teeth in a parody of a smile and shambled into the shrubs.

Seqenenra lowered himself onto the steps. Tani and Ramose were out in deep water, beating each other with rushes amid shouts of laughter. Seqenenra watched contentedly. Presently Tani saw him, waved, and she and Ramose swam towards the steps and clambered dripping and puffing out of the river. "Greetings, Prince," Ramose said, bowing. "I thank you, if I have not done so before, for the company of your daughter."

"Oh, I believe you have done so before," Seqenenra assured him, grinning. Ramose looked discomfited, then grinned in return.

"I must put in some practice at the butts now," he said. "Please excuse me. Tani, I will ask Father about the chariot ride later today." He strode away, his bare feet supple and sure on the sandy paving, the sun glittering on the beads of water spraying from his body. Tani wrung out her hair and rubbed the water from her face.

"Such a polite young man," Seqenenra observed. "You like it here, don't you, Tani?" She pulled the sopping linen sheath away from her brown skin. Seqenenra noted how transparent it was when wet, how it moulded to the budding curves and long lines of her. She was lithely beautiful, this precious daughter of his, and in a very few years she would have the added assurance of maturity and an awareness of her own magnetism. All at once he was very proud of her, proud and hungrily possessive.

Yes," she answered. "I do. There is always something going on. Oh, Father," she hastened to correct herself, "it is not that I'm bored at home. Home is my preferred place. I do not mean to be disrespectful. But being here is fun."

"I seem to recall that on your last visit you sulked and couldn't wait to weigh anchor and be off back to Weset."

"Yes, well that was four years ago. Ramose threw spiders at me then, and teased me, and so I refused to come with you the next few times. But now it is different. He is a man now."

"He doesn't tease you any more?"

"Well, yes, he does, but not spitefully. And he looks after me too." For the second time he saw her blush, a russet stain under her dark cheeks. She began to scrub at her scalp with vigour. "I want him to come and stay with us. Will you invite him, Father?" You have flashes of true adulthood, my Tani, he thought before he answered. I, too, would like to see Ramose in a setting other than this opulent estate.

"Yes, I will," he agreed. "His father is talking of a betrothal between the two of you." She did not seem surprised. Folding her hands between her knees she gazed out over the sun-dimpled Nile.

"No one has said anything to me," she responded, "but it may be. I think he is very fine and I think he likes me too." Suddenly she turned an astute stare on her father. "But what about Kamose?" Inwardly Seqenenra relinquished that foolish dream and found he was not sorry to see it dissolve into noth-ingness.

"If you and Kamose had shown the slightest sexual interest in each other, I would be pushing for a marriage between you," he confessed. "But Tani, I will never force you into something abhorrent to you. If you and Ramose continue to learn to care for one another, you will make many people happy." She kissed him swiftly on the cheek.

"Thank you, Father. You are really quite wonderful. Kamose is not going to get married for a very long time, you know. He is too serious about everything. I think I will go and get oiled."

He did not watch her go. He sat with chin in hand, his eyes on the far bank now shimmering in the heat haze. She is only partly right, he thought. Kamose is indeed a serious man, but his character is full of deep feeling and intensity. If he ever meets a woman who stirs him, he will commit himself to her for the rest of his life.

Si-Amun delighted in his time in Khemennu. He was at home with the elegant, smoothly polite representatives of the King who came and went in Teti's busy reception hall. He blossomed with curiosity when talking to the merchants and traders from Rethennu, Keftiu and Zahi, and his confident questions betrayed an avid excitement. He also enjoyed the twittering attentions of Teti's many female servants. He was tall, sinewy, handsome and a prince. He received all deference as his right.

He and Teti had always been fond of each other. Teti was as affable and open as Seqenenra was lordly and aloof, and though Si-Amun loved his father and was fully conscious of the tincture of royalty in his blood, there were times when he would have preferred to be a son of Teti. Such thoughts made him feel ashamed but did not detract from his pleasure. He had gone with Teti and Seqenenra to pay the obligatory call on the governor of Khemennu and its nomes. Seqenenra had been effusively good-mannered, sampling every sweetmeat at the welcome meal, enquiring after the health of the governor's family and raising his goblet with words of praise to the King on his lips, but Si-Amun knew that under the exquisite conventions his father was hating himself for his dishonesty.

On this day he and Teti had returned to the governor's estate and spent a delightful morning inspecting the man's hunting dogs, sampling a rare vintage of palm wine, and listening to the latest gossip that came out of Het-Uart. He had taken his leave with regret. He and Teti had then got onto their litters and had been carried to a rocky outcrop in the desert where there were some ancient tombs, now open and pillaged. Si-Amun had his countrymen's avid interest in the monuments of the past. He exclaimed over the wall paintings and felt the sadness of the desecrated place. After a prayer for the kas of those who had once lain there and a petition to Anubis to remember them, he and Teti had returned to the cultivated fringe of greenness where Teti's servants laid down mats, put up canopies, and spread bread, beer and fruit for their lunch.

"You are a very generous man, Teti," Si-Amun complimented him as they sat cross-legged under the shade of a fig tree and gratefully drank their beer. "You do not come to Weset often enough for us to repay you for your hospitality." Teti smiled across at him.

"The gods and the King have been good to me," he replied, "and besides, I love to have company, Si-Amun. My other relatives are not congenial people."

"Father was congenial enough last night!" Si-Amun laughed. "He does not often get drunk and have such a good time. I think it relaxes him to be here. He takes his responsibilities at home too seriously." As soon as the words had left his mouth, he wondered if he had been disloyal. He glanced anxiously at Teti, but Teti had drained his cup and was smiling warmly across at him, eyes narrowed.

"As a Prince of this realm your father has a certain dignity to maintain," he answered. "Yet I do not think he drank out of relaxation and pleasure, Si-Amun. He has been troubled and withdrawn since he arrived. It is the scrolls from the One, isn't it? I wish he would confide in me as an old friend, and let me help him." Si-Amun hesitated, wishing he had not blurted out his observation so freely, but Teti continued to smile. He leaned forward and placed a soft, hot hand on Si-Amun's. "You need not speak of it, if you do not wish to," Teti said. "But know, Si-Amun, that I love you and your father and the rest of your family. There is blood shared between us, however distant the connection. Relatives should aid each other." Si-Amun now felt disloyal to Teti. To dismiss the moment would seem rude, and it was true that he had a sudden urge to confide in this man. His father would listen to his doubts, indeed he knew them already, but his sympathetic ear did not bring agreement. Teti would be different. Teti would understand.

"Yes, they should," Si-Amun returned. Teti relinquished his hand. "It is nothing truly important, Teti," Si-Amun went on. "But the scrolls seem so arbitrary in their demands, so senseless. Each time one arrives, Father becomes more tense and angry." He looked up. Teti's eyes were commiseratory and understanding. The man nodded.

"And you are afraid that one day your father will grow tired of an unrewarded loyalty to the King and will take some reckless action that will bring disgrace on you all." Si-Amun nodded miserably.

"I think there is already rebellion in his heart. It is so unfair!" he burst out. "Our house has been loyal to Het-Uart for hentis! Why is the One pushing so?"

"Calm yourself," Teti said soothingly. "Have you eaten well? Good. A little more beer and then we will make our way home." Si-Amun watched as the dark liquid spilled into his cup. "You are not a child, Si-Amun," Teti reproved him gently. "You know the King's fear. It will be laid to rest as long as your father strives to obey." He drank, sighed, and wiped his mouth on a piece of linen a servant discreetly passed to him. "You and I must do our best to make sure that Seqenenra rides out this storm in peace. I say again, it will pass. I am your friend, young man, and your father's too." He bent a solemn gaze upon Si-Amun. "I would be desolate if anything happened to either of you. Let me help." Si-Amun looked gratefully into the plump, painted face.

"You are very kind, Teti," he said huskily, "but I don't know what you can do."

"I can speak for your father in Het-Uart. The One knows

that my own loyalty is without question. I can be an intermediary, tactful, pouring oil on these troubled waters. I can also come and visit your father, talk to him of sense and preservation if his anxieties become too much to bear."

Suddenly Si-Amun knew what was coming. He cringed inside, wishing fervently that the whole subject had never arisen, and then wondering if it would have surfaced in any case. He was caught. He could not back away after having expressed his concern for his father. It would seem callous. He could not refuse Teti's offer of assistance, for that in turn would appear to render the problem frivolous and his own words an exaggeration. But they were not my words even though they were present in my heart, he thought while Teti regarded him fondly. Teti spoke them aloud, not me.

"But if I am to be of any help I must know how things stand with Seqenenra," Teti went on. "Someone who cares must keep me informed so that I can come to Weset at a moment's notice." Seeing Si-Amun's expression, he shook his head violently. "No no no, my loyal young man! Gods! Do you think I am asking you to spy on your father?" His thick black eyebrows rose. "Well, I suppose that in a sense I am, but my request comes from love, Si-Amun. Do not let Seqenenra go down under Apepa's heel! Help me to help him!"

It is a reasonable request, Si-Amun thought, indeed, it is a risky one. Teti himself might be seen by the One to be conspiring with my father if too much correspondence begins to flow from Khemennu to Weset and back again. How can such an expression of familial concern be wrong? Yet he hesitated. "Very well," he said reluctantly, "but my father would be furious if he believed that I did not trust his judgement in this matter and was deferring to yours. You are right that he must be watched for his own sake, but . . ."

Teti drew a ring from his finger and showed it to Si-Amun.

"This is my family's seal," he said. "I shall imprint my letters to you with it. You in turn shall write under the seal of—what? What shall it be?"

"A hippopotamus," Si-Amun said slowly.

"Very well." Teti pushed the ring back onto his thick finger. "You know that Mersu, your grandmother's steward, grew up in the same village as my steward? You may give any messages for me to Mersu to be sent north. You and Ramose have known each other since your youth. You can say they are for him. Or you can say nothing at all and let Mersu draw his own conclusions. But given his loyalty to your family, I'm sure he would understand."

He heaved himself to his feet, gestured, and the waiting servants sprang to roll up the mats. The litter bearers readied themselves. Si-Amun scrambled up. "But you will speak to the King?" he croaked. "You will assure Apepa of my father's good faith?"

"Of course I will." Teti stepped forward and embraced the young man. "It will be all right, Si-Amun, I swear. Perhaps we are being foolish, you and I." He let Si-Amun go and they started for the litters. As they stepped from the shade, the sun smote them. "Perhaps all this will resolve itself and we will laugh at our own solemnity." Si-Amun did not reply. I can always go home and do nothing, he thought, settling himself on his litter and twitching the curtains closed. I can ignore it all. But he knew he would not. His father's secret rage at Apepa must somehow be diverted, rendered harmless, or it would destroy them all.

They stayed in Khemennu for a month, eating, drinking and sleeping, talking with Teti's visitors and going regularly to the temple of Thoth. Seqenenra went once into Set's temple, carrying offerings of rare wine and three gold bands, knowing that the King would hear of it and be pleased and reassured. But he was not allowed into the sanctuary. Only the King himself and the senior priests of Set could greet the god face to face, though at home where Amun was totem of city and family and he himself was lord over all, he had the right to commune directly with his god. He was not sorry to be denied access to Set. He did not want to see the renegade brother of Osiris, the red-haired, red-eyed ruler of the desert, wild and unpredictable though he might be, represented as the Setiu saw him, melded with their own barbaric god Sutekh.

He and Teti regained the easy familiarity of their relationship. Seqenenra, having decided not to apologize, pretended that the conversation in the passage had never taken place and Teti did not refer to it. Amid embraces and renewed invitations to visit more often, Seqenenra, the family and their retinue set off for Weset. The journey was slow. Seqenenra stopped at every town over which he was lord, talking to priests and mayors, overseers and his minor officials, and the family did not dock at the watersteps until the end of Phamenoth.

All was well. Kamose had performed his duties quietly and efficiently. Tetisheri questioned Aahotep briefly about the health and well-being of her relatives but did not seem particularly interested in Aahotep's replies.

Chapter THREE

Spring ended and Weset sank into its summer somnolence. In the arbour the grapes formed and began to swell, green and hard. The crops began to lose their willowy brightness and stiffen to yellow. The crocodiles could often be seen basking immobile, with eyes closed on the sandbanks of the rapidly shrinking Nile, and over all that self-contained, placid domain the sultry timelessness of Shemu exhaled its burning breath.

Seqenenra, lying on his couch in the stultifying afternoons with sweat pouring from his body or prowling the relative coolness of the old palace while family and servants alike waited languorously for the benison of sunset, knew that he would not wish to exchange this tranquil, satisfying life for the sophisticated bustle of Teti's estate. There was contentment in the predictability of the coming harvest, and reassurance in the annual Beautiful Feast of the Valley when Amun was carried over the river to visit the mortuary temples and tombs of the ancestors and the citizens of Weset followed him with food to eat beside their dead. Aahmes-nefertari would add to the family. Tani would be betrothed to Ramose, and once a settlement was decided upon by himself and Teti, she would go to live at Khemennu. His mother would go to join his father before too many years were out, and he himself would grow old and fat, Aahotep beside him, and give the reins of governorship to Si-Amun. I ask for nothing more, he said to himself fervently, standing in the dusty shade of a palm tree to watch the peasants work the shadufs, tipping the sun-caught pure water into the now stagnant and empty canals. My land, my family, my life.

Tani dictated many letters to Ramose and spent much time hanging about the watersteps, shading her eyes and waiting for a messenger's skiff to appear round the northern bend, a bored Behek lying at her feet. Sometimes Teti's skiffs did bring scrolls from Ramose. Sometimes the young man gave his messages for Tani into the hands of a Royal Herald who delivered them at Weset on his way to Kush. Seqenenra had ceased to fear the sight of such a vessel tacking towards his watersteps, indeed, he welcomed them, for they made Tani bubble with joy.

Payni and Epophi came and went in a remorseless heat that shrivelled the leaves on the trees and sapped energy from beast and human alike. Mesore began, and all at once the lazy, halcyon days were over. The gardeners loaded vegetables into baskets. Servants began to strip the vines, and in the white dazzle of the big courtyard to the south of the house the men trod the grapes, singing and dancing.

Si-Amun, Kamose and Seqenenra were seldom home. Day after day they strode the fields, watching the overseers direct the reapers. The sickles rose and fell. Of particular concern was the flax harvest, for much of the crop would go north to form fine linen for the King's household, traded for the family's needs, and the rest Isis and the other servants would weave for Aahotep and the girls. Barley was set aside for the season's new beer. The harvest was plentiful, and master and peasant alike worked cheerfully.

Towards the end of Mesore when Si-Amun, Kamose, Seqenenra and Uni were closeted together tallying the yield and trying to apportion the taxes and tribute that must go to Het-Uart, Aahmes-nefertari knocked and came towards the littered desk. Her pregnancy was now in its eighth month but being her first, her slim body was not much distorted. She was suffering more than usual from the heat and no longer spent so much time roving the grounds. Today she was barefoot but wore an ankle-length white sheath caught under her breasts by two thick linen straps that covered her nipples. The menat-amulet given to her by her mother was hanging from a leather cord around her neck. Her arms were bare of ornament but yellow ribbons trailed from her hair, sticking to the sweat on her shoulders, and as she approached she pushed back her wet tresses. Behind her, Raa, her childhood nurse and favoured companion, came padding, bearing a large starched fan.

The men looked up from their work. Aahmes-nefertari sank gratefully onto the stool Seqenenra pushed forward. "Thank you, Father," she said. "I am sorry to disturb you, but a royal skiff has just pushed off again from the watersteps. The herald could not stay to speak with you. He said he had urgent business with the Prince of Kush. He gave me a scroll for you. Tani is very disappointed!" Seqenenra laughed.

"Tani is becoming spoiled. She imagines now that every craft plying the Nile is doing so for her benefit. I suppose the scroll is our tax assessment from Het-Uart. It will be heavy with the harvest so bountiful, and Men tells me that the cattle in the Delta have calved as never before. Well I suppose I must look at it." Aahmes-nefertari produced the scroll and Seqenenra took it.

"The Overseer of Lands has also come, with reports on the harvest from our nomes," the girl went on. "Grandmother is giving him wine by the pool. She asks that you join them. The Tchaus Nome is complaining of a lessened yield due to rust on the grain." Kamose smiled faintly.

"The Tchaus Nome always complains about something," he said.

"Better a complaint than the silence that hides one," his father answered, breaking the seal. "Aahmes-nefertari, please tell your grandmother we will join her shortly." The girl rose and left, Raa behind her.

Seqenenra unrolled the scroll. Si-Amun and Kamose waited expectantly. Then Seqenenra exclaimed softly, "No. No! This is not to be believed." The hand holding the message dropped to the table. Kamose stepped up and touched his father's shoulder. It was trembling.

"May I read?" he asked tersely. Seqenenra nodded.

"Read it aloud. I may have misinterpreted a portion of the script." Kamose and Si-Amun exchanged a swift glance, then Kamose picked up the scroll. His eyes ran rapidly over it and he cleared his throat.

"'To my...'"

"Not the salutation!" Seqenenra cut in harshly. "That hypocrite!" Uni started, then regained his composure beside the desk. Kamose continued.

"Very well, Father. 'For a time I slept peacefully in my palace, disturbed by no more than the night cries of birds, but soon once more the coughing of your hippopotamuses intruded on my dreams so that my voice is weak and my eyes are dim from lack of rest. The muzzles of your leatherworkers have not prevented the beasts from tormenting their King. Therefore I have consulted with the priests of Set the Mighty, whose children the hippopotamuses are, to enquire of them why the god's charges are still calling to me.'" Kamose paused, even his customary control almost deserting him. Seqenenra sat rigid, his mouth grim, looking down at his tightly clasped hands. Si-Amun's patience was a motionless, tense thing. Taking a deep breath, Kamose went on. "'The children of the god are angry because their lord's homes are far from Weset. They are sad because there are no priests to do them homage. Therefore I, Awoserra Apepa, Beloved of Set, recommend to you, Seqenenra, that a southern home be built for my lord the god Sutekh so that he may be worshipped in Weset and his children may be appeased. When word of this intention becomes known in the nomes of the governor of Weset, the people will rejoice, and will flock to the site of the god's home to build it, and will make tribute to the god's servants who will tend it. If the governor of the south does not answer my message, let him no longer serve any other god besides Sutekh, but if he makes answer and he does what I tell him to do, I will take nothing whatsoever from him and I will bow myself down never again before any other god in the whole earth besides Amun, the King of the gods.'" Kamose put the scroll on the desk with exaggerated care and folded his arms.

"I am surprised that he had the intelligence to string so many coherent words together all at once," Seqenenra grated. "Filthy aati!" The anger that had sprung upon him with such familiarity and had so shocked him during the intense and now almost forgotten exchange with Teti burst into immediate life. Its sudden force balled in his stomach and he winced. Si-Amun started forward.

"Father, you are speaking blasphemy," he said, his face pale. "Think whom you are calling a fever and a pestilence! It is true that Set has no temple south of Khemennu. It is possible that the god is displeased. That he spoke to the King through his children and his priests." Si-Amun's sweat was soaking the band of his short black wig and trickling down his neck, and the stifling heat in the room seemed to intensify. "If he wants a home here in Weset, you must comply." Seqenenra looked up at him slowly.

"A son who says 'must' to his father is in danger of discipline," he snapped, but he was calmer. "Of course, it is possible that the god spoke to his priests, but I do not think so. Kamose?" The young man began to pace.

"I do not think so either, Father. Apepa is tightening the vise. A temple for Set here will mean royal representatives in Weset at all times. Our every move will be watched. For us and for the nomes it means large numbers of conscripted farmers for construction and an even heavier tribute to pay architects, stonemasons, engineers." He reached the step that led down between the small lotus pillars to the garden beyond, turned, began a measured walk back. "If we agree to the King's veiled command, our lives will change forever. We will lose whatever freedom we may have. If we refuse, we give him an excuse to charge us with disobedience both to a divine directive and disrespect to Set." He smiled coldly. "I do not think that you can dictate an ingenious letter to deflect the King's intention this time."

"I think you are right," Seqenenra agreed woodenly. "I would need the complexity of Thoth's mind to do so." He swivelled on the chair. "Uni, you are my right hand in this house. You order my staff. What is your opinion?" Uni bowed.

"Set is not only the god of foreigners," he replied. "He is also the sovereign of deserts. Are we not children of the desert as much as of the fertile land, O Prince? A temple to Set here in Weset would be most appropriate." He was obviously very uneasy, swallowing often between his words, his glance moving rapidly between Seqenenra's attentive face and Kamose's damp back.

"Could the nomes support the labour and expense?" Kamose asked, reaching the door and turning. "Apepa wants you to refuse, you know that, Father. He wants to ruin you." The words fell flat and sinister in the thick afternoon air.

"His insecurity is a dangerous thing," Seqenenra said in a

low voice. "I have served him faithfully and honestly but my devotion has counted for nothing beside his secret fear." He got up clumsily, and leaning both hands on the desk, tried to smile reassuringly at Uni. "Do not be ashamed that you are troubled," he said kindly. "You are loyal to this family but also to our King, and any word spoken against him goes to your heart. I could not do without you, Uni. I know that if you were in the King's presence when something was said against us, you would be equally distressed. Forgive me." Uni's features cleared.

"I obey the One and you," he answered. "And now Lord, will you join your Overseer who is surely overstuffed with fruit and sloshing with your wine by now?" Seqenenra managed a laugh.

"I had forgotten about him. I will be there directly. You can go." When Uni had bowed himself out, father and sons looked at each other. Si-Amun came and stood close to Seqenenra.

"You will have to do it," he said uneasily. "As you said, you have served him faithfully and honestly. The alternative is unthinkable."

Seqenenra's mind filled with visions of Tani and Ramose flinging reeds at one another and shrieking with laughter, of Si-Amun and his other daughter, arms around each other, oblivious to the rest of the world, of Aahotep and his imperious, adored mother sipping wine and gossiping together under the summer shade of his trees. Yes, the alternative Si-Amun had grasped with such quick intuition was unthinkable, yet his whole being revolted at the injustice of the King's tortuous manipulations. "I must ponder the matter," he said, "but not now. I need wine." Morosely they walked out of the office and into the white furnace of the afternoon.

For seven days Seqenenra kept the contents of the message from the women. He had no intention of burdening Tani with it at all, but knew that eventually the others must be told. He shrank from the inevitable discussion that would follow. He knew that his mother's sharp eye noted his preoccupation, but she tactfully, if impatiently, waited to share his confidence. Aahotep, too, was disturbed by his silence, but she attributed it to a second scroll arriving hard on the heels of the first, which listed the taxes and expected tribute for the year. As Kamose had predicted, it was heavy. But the load was a familiar one, carried by them for years, and Seqenenra tossed it to Uni with an abstracted word and forgot it.

He did not seek comfort and counsel from Amun. Though he went every morning to perform the rites of washing, clothing and feeding the god, and stood with Amunmose while the High Priest chanted the Admonitions, Seqenenra could not bring himself to ask the god's advice. He was afraid of what Amun's oracle would say. The presence of Set in Weset would diminish Amun's power. There would be rivalry between the two gods and their servants. Set was unpredictable. At one moment he could protect a desert caravan from lions or marauding Shasu, and the next bare his teeth like the ravening wolf he was, and tear the same caravan to pieces. Seqenenra respected him but could never have trusted him. He demanded a devotion that turned his priests into fierce-eyed cubs. He had never forgiven Horus, his nephew and Osiris's son, for taking half of Egypt away from him, and even if Seqenenra had chosen to do him homage, Set would do no favours for the living Horus-in-the-Nest. How infinitely more insulting, also, to stand before the creature, half-Set and half-Sutekh, that Apepa would install in the new temple. Seqenenra made his prostrations before Amun's gentle smile and feathery golden plumes with a sick heart.

He did not often cross the river to visit the mortuary temple of his ancestor Mentuhotep-neb-hapet-Ra, for it lay well back from the tombs of others of his forebears and his more recent family in a valley which curved in a great bay and was bounded by the rugged, pocked cliff of Gurn. He had often wondered why the Divine One had chosen such a site, far from fertility and habitation, a lonely, windless place where the sun beat in with remorseless intensity unimpeded by any shade. But in the week before he spoke to Tetisheri about Apepa's demand he had himself poled across the Nile and made the journey to the secret valley, and in his agony of mind, believed he had found a reason.

Walking alone up the ramp in the middle of the terrace, shading eyes that watered in the blinding sun in spite of heavy kohl, so that he could contemplate the small pyramid jutting against the unbearable blueness of the summer sky, he felt the uniqueness and courage of the man. Like Seqenenra himself, Mentuhotep had been a governor of Weset paying tribute to a King in the north, until his blood cried out for justification and he had taken up arms against the usurper.

Why? Seqenenra wondered, blinded and beaten by the sun as he stood exposed high upon his ancestor's monument. The King you served was an Egyptian. He had stemmed the flow of foreigners from the east into the Delta. He had fortified the eastern border. He had raised Mennofer to the power that venerable city had once had, he brought new trade, new peace, he was a good King. But he was not divine. He did not rule by the power of Amun.

Seqenenra sank onto the hot stone, despair flooding him. And when you could bear the humiliation no longer, you made a war of desperation, and you won, and you set the Double Crown on your head at last. Egypt again became a united country, the Red Land and the Black Land, and Ma'at was restored. That is why you chose this forbidding place for your last home. Your destiny set you apart in life. It changed and drove you. It set you apart even in death. Oh, do not let such a destiny overtake me!

With a groan he straightened, passed down the ramp, and walked between the dead remains of the grove of tamarisks. Mentuhotep's likenesses watched him go from their shade under the sycamore figs, and it seemed to Seqenenra as he passed that the statues spoke to him dumbly of both his duty and his pain.

In the valley, scorched by the sun, he could not think. He could only feel. He sought refuge in Mentuhotep's derelict palace where there was coolness of a sort. He paced, he brooded. Unfolding his canopy on the roof of the women's quarters, he sat cross-legged in the thin shade and looked out over the summer barrenness of his domain. The Nile was a sullen brown dribble. The fields were turning to desert, riven with cracks so deep that a man might stand in one almost knee-deep. The trees were shrivelled, the palms drooped. Nothing living was in sight. As he spared a glance behind him to where the desert danced in the breathless haze, golden sand rolling away to meet an infinity of azure sky, he realized that he was looking at his own soul.

When he knew that he could face neither solution, could turn neither to right nor left even though the choice was now as clear as his own reflection in the copper mirror his body servant held for him every morning, he took the scroll to his mother. Tetisheri was on her couch. It was the middle of the afternoon. Isis was fanning the stale air over her sheeted body and Mersu had just replenished the water jug on her table. The room was dim but the thick mud brick walls could not keep out the full force of Ra as he prepared to burn his way into the west.

Seqenenra requested admittance and was waved forward. Isis laid down the fan and retired. Tetisheri struggled up and patted the couch and Seqenenra sat, handing her the scroll. She read it through, raised her eyebrows, and read it again. Seqenenra helped himself to water. Tetisheri dropped the message on the floor and sighed.

"The dagger has been coming closer for years," she said. "Now it pricks our skin, waiting for a final command to be driven into our heart. I have prayed that this moment might be averted but somehow my ka knew that it could not. What are you going to do?"

He barked a laugh. "I stand on the square of the Beautiful House," he said, "and my opponent has thrown the number that will send me plummeting into the water of the Under-world. I cannot jump." She wiped her face with a corner of the sheet and tapped him on his arm.

"The sennet is not won until the last piece is carried off. We must discuss the alternatives. We both know what they are. Do you sacrifice your pride for the sake of the family and leave Si-Amun nothing, not even the title of governor, to inherit? At least our dear ones would be safe. Or do you contemplate . . ."

"No!" Seqenenra slapped the bedclothes. "It is what he wants. What hope of winning would I have? What do I have? A few chariots for the purposes of pleasure. A few weapons for my bodyguard. I would be defeated before I had even left Weset."

"You have the Medjay," his mother objected. "The men of Wawat are the best fighters in the world. They have no love for the Prince of Kush. They are desert creatures who fear, above all, that Kush will one day try to take over their villages. The few in your service are loyal and happy. Recruit more. Talk to Hor-Aha. You have not called him the Fighting Hawk for nothing."

His thoughts finding life in her mouth terrified him. It was as though, in hearing them spoken aloud, a decision had already been made and he was committed.

"Are you so ruthless, Mother?" he said quietly. "Would you

wish to sacrifice all of us to satisfy your own pride?" He had hurt her, he saw it. For a moment her eyes filled with tears.

"No," she ordered, holding up a hand as she saw him begin to apologize. "Do not say it, Seqenenra. There is a grain of truth in your accusation. I have great pride. It is the pride of a woman who was married to a King. Without a Kingdom, I know, yet still a god. But that pride is not an evil thing. It would never demand the lives of those I love."

"I am sorry, Mother. I know. You speak only of an alternative." She nodded once.

"And the other is this. Build Set's temple. Impoverish your people to do it. You know what would happen afterwards?" He smiled without warmth.

"Oh yes. Another letter, demanding what? That I take over the governorship of another city perhaps? Somewhere farther north, nearer to Apepa?"

"Or perhaps a call to active duty in a border fort. There is no escape, Seqenenra. I don't think there ever was."

Silence fell between them. The house was utterly still. Tetisheri lay against her cushions with eyes closed. Seqenenra watched the steady rise and fall of her breast. At length he said, "If I fight and am defeated, I condemn all of us to death."

Without opening her eyes she replied coldly, "We have already been fighting one long rearguard action and are being slowly defeated. We have nowhere left to run. Do we stand and fight, or kneel and receive the longer death?" Her eyes flew open. "Damn Apepa! We have been so willing. So willing!" Her hand found his knee and at her touch he leaned forward, taking her in his arms. She was tiny and fragile, this mother of his who stood as straight as an arrow and whose spirit had always dominated her dainty body.

"Tetisheri," he said, striving to keep his voice even, "I am very much afraid."

"So am I." She disengaged herself. "You do not need to make this decision immediately. Think about it a little more."

"I will." He stood up. "But I know that no amount of thinking will present a fresh alternative. If I hesitate too long, I will run away. I will become impotent. Perhaps Si-Amun and Kamose..."

"Perhaps." She moved her head wearily on the pillows. "Ask them for their opinion. The most difficult task will be winnowing out those you can trust." Seqenenra was finding it hard to breathe in the hot, stuffy room. He nodded and turned away.

He spent the afternoon in a restless perambulation of the house. At first he tried to sleep away his anguish but the heat and his feverish thoughts sent him wandering the passages, the reception hall, the men's quarters where Kamose lay oblivious and Ahmose squatted on the floor of his room, tossing dice. He circled the grain silos ranged neatly against the southern outer wall of the estate, startled the servants in the kitchen that was set in the shade beside the granaries, and knelt in the kennels to feel the comfort of Behek's great head thrust against his neck.

In the scentless dusk when the sky had gone from red to the palest blue and the stars were beginning to prick clear and white, he sat by the river in a thicket of brown reeds that rubbed together with the dry whisper of death, his feet covered in warm dust. Time and again he began a conciliatory letter in his mind to the King but got no farther than the salutation. There were no clever words to say. Apepa demanded a yes or a no. The matter was that simple. 'Treat them with patience and respect and they will cease,' Teti had said of the scrolls from Het-Uart, but Teti was wrong. Seqenenra had submitted all the patience and respect for his King that he could, but he had emptied himself to no avail.

He forced himself to appear cheerful at the evening meal,

listening to Tani's prattle, enquiring after Aahmes-nefertari's health, advising his wife to isolate the children of the servants who were ill with a fever, and when he could bear the idle conversation no longer he excused himself and went to his couch. At his word Uni extinguished all but the night lamp beside him and went away.

Exhausted, Seqenenra fell into a heavy sleep, but he dreamed of Apepa with the massive wet body of a hippopotamus standing shoulder high in a foetid Nile, his eyes glaring furiously above a leather muzzle that threaded over and around his quivering snout. He was trying to snap the bonds, his lips straining, but they were too strong. In his dream Seqenenra began to speak a spell of malediction. "He shall hunger! He shall thirst! He shall faint! He shall sicken!" and Apepa's eyes went on blazing at him so that in the end Seqenenra's voice faltered and died away.

He woke suddenly, drenched in sweat and struggling for breath, and sitting up gasping he looked around the room. The shadows were immobile and tenantless. The house was deep in slumber. He lay down again and this time fell into a healing unconsciousness.

The following day when he returned from his duties in the temple he sent one of his bodyguard to find Hor-Aha. He met with the commander of his Medjay soldiers once a week as a matter of course to make sure that the men's needs were being met, his sons' military training was progressing well and to discuss any changes in routine. Hor-Aha was not a voluble man. He discharged his responsibilities efficiently, was deferent but not obsequious to his master, and like all the desert fighters was not at all forthcoming about any life he had outside the confines of the practice ground. Seqenenra liked and respected him but did not feel he knew him well. He received him in his office, alone.

Hor-Aha came smoothly across the floor, enveloped in the thick woollen garment he wore in winter and summer alike. Beads of sweat stood out on his black forehead. He kept his hair long as most soldiers did, braided in two plaits that hung stiffly on his naked chest. Under the voluminous folds of the cloak he wore a kilt and a stained leather belt in which a short dagger was stuck. Silver bracelets tinkled on his wrists. Seqenenra greeted him politely. Hor-Aha returned the greeting, then stood expectantly, his ebony eyes questioning. Seqenenra's heart began to race. Today I commit myself, he thought tensely. If Hor-Aha cannot be trusted, then today I also fail.

"Hor-Aha, how many Medjay do I order?" Hor-Aha's eyebrows rose.

"You have five hundred, Prince. I rotate their duties a hundred at a time and divide the rest between exercise, training and leave."

"Chariots?"

"Ten only, and twenty-two horses."

Seqenenra swallowed a laugh. What a mighty army indeed, he thought. "How many of the men are armed with the new bows the Setiu use?"

Hor-Aha considered a moment before replying. "Very few of them. The bows are expensive, commanding much barter, and as you know, Highness, they require a different technique of use to our Egyptian weapons. They are taller and more unwieldy to handle, and men must be retrained to use them, for they require much strength to draw. But they are very powerful and more accurate than our bows."

"Do you have one?"

Hor-Aha smiled. His white teeth flashed at Seqenenra. "I do."

"Would they be difficult to make?" He watched his commander's eyes narrow in swift speculation. The man shifted his weight from one wide, bare foot to the other, and folded his brawny arms.

"It could be done, but the principal material is birch wood from Rethennu and if you wish to make bows in any great number, you will need permission from the One to trade with the country from which his ancestors came into Egypt and where the chieftains call him brother."

"There must be a substitute for birch," Seqenenra pressed. "What else is needed?"

"Sinews and tendons from bulls, preferably wild ones. Horns from goats. Again, wild goats have more durable and stronger horns than domestic ones. But it is the splicing and fashioning that require a military craftsman's hand."

"Could you do it?"

"Perhaps. If you obtain the wood." Seqenenra waved him down. Hor-Aha sank to the floor, tucking his legs under his robe. Seqenenra poured beer for them both, handed a cup to the commander, and collapsed onto a chair. The moment had come.

"I want to greatly increase the number of troops at my command," he said, "and I want to arm them with the new bows. I need chariots, too, many more of them. I wish to strengthen the security of my nomes." He drank, glancing at Hor-Aha over the rim of the cup. Hor-Aha's gaze became expressionless and fell to the brown liquid still moving between his hands.

"As you wish, Prince," he said at last. "I think that another hundred infantry, with twenty stationed in the head town of each nome, would be sufficient. We are, after all, at peace in Egypt." His head was down but Seqenenra had the distinct impression that the man was smiling. When Hor-Aha looked up, however, the thick, even features were bland.

Seqenenra cast a quick glance towards the portico where sunlight flooded between the pillars and blazed in the deserted garden. The door at the other end of the room was firmly shut. He swallowed convulsively twice and then leaped over the wall of safety.

"You are my Fighting Hawk," he said huskily. "You came to me from the desert when I was in my twenties, and you took over my military training. You gave me a steady eye and a strong arm. I am about to place myself in your hands yet again." Hor-Aha regarded him steadily. "I am going to assemble an army," he went on unevenly. "I am going to march it north and do battle with the One. I intend to commit sacrilege, Hor-Aha, because I can no longer bear the insults done to me, and if I do not take this desperate course now, the One will take away everything I have. I do not think that I can win. Perhaps I can do no more than sacrifice myself to Ma'at. But I would rather die for Ma'at than live in the agony I now endure. Will you help me?"

Hor-Aha drank reflectively, pursed his lips, and put down the beer. His hands suddenly disappeared into the sleeves of his garment. "A Prince in defeat may be punished but is not often killed," he observed, "but his officers are put to the knife. If I side with you, Highness, I will probably lose my life." Seqenenra waited. Then the dark head came up. "I know nothing of the King," Hor-Aha said. "I have never been farther north than Aabtu. You are my King. Your commands are well judged. I will continue to serve you." Seqenenra felt his bowels loosen.

"I can promise you nothing at present but an empty title, General. I cannot even give you more bread and beer." Hor-Aha shrugged.

"I have sufficient for my needs, and General is a title that will do very well. For now. Later, if Amun smiles on your Highness, you may care to make me Commander of the Braves of the King." Seqenenra grinned at him weakly and he smiled back.

"I would like nothing better," Seqenenra agreed. "Now may we discuss practical things? I want as many new Medjay recruited as possible. Can you trust your men?"

"They are content to follow my orders."

"Good. Send them to their tribes in the desert. I need many young men. But they cannot be quartered here. I must build a barracks out on the desert or perhaps on the western bank behind the dead where people seldom go, so that they may be trained without attracting too much notice." Hor-Aha's hands reappeared, lifted the beer, and the cup was drained. He licked his lips carefully.

"Perhaps you might ask Prince Si-Amun to visit the nomes and conscript peasants," he suggested. "They will do what they are told." He forestalled Seqenenra's next question. "I will approach your craftsmen. We will unlock the secrets of the bow. But, Highness, although you can order more chariots, you cannot obtain horses. We must just steal them as we move north."

They talked for a while of fundamental things, including the possibility of obtaining axes and knives made of the new metal, bronze, that the Setiu used with such success, but neither voiced Seqenenra's greatest worry. How was he to pay for this explosion of activity? By the time Uni requested admittance to tell him that the noon meal was ready, he felt completely separated from himself, unreal, as though his ka had discussed treason and rebellion with Hor-Aha while in the real world he himself was swimming or checking the accounts with his scribe or sitting with Aahotep by the pool. He dismissed his Commander and followed Uni on unsteady feet.

Before the end of the week Hor-Aha and the majority of the soldiers had vanished unobtrusively from Weset, leaving a token bodyguard for the family. Summer was a time of lethargy and only Kamose noticed the same faces day after day by the main gate to the estate and in the passages. Puzzled, he found Si-Amun. Together they went to their father with an idle query, and Seqenenra, his dice thrown, told his sons everything.

"Si-Amun, as my heir I want you to travel the nomes and conscript men," he ordered. "Hor-Aha is even now deep in the south, trying to persuade the Wawat wildmen that joining my army will secure them freedom from Teti-the-Handsome, Prince of Kush, and much booty. You and he will command together under me." Si-Amun had lost colour as his father was speaking. Now he was grey, his nostrils pinched, his eyes huge with shock. He put out a hand, then let it drop.

"Father," he said urgently. "You cannot do this thing. Please! As you love me, as you love us, do not do this! It is blasphemy. It is death for us, surely you see that?" His voice had risen and then cracked. He was trembling. Abruptly he sank into a chair.

"We have been over this ground enough," Seqenenra put in harshly. "I know how you feel, but the time has come to put your personal opinions aside and stand with me. You are my son. Your loyalty must go first to Amun and to me."

"I can't!" Si-Amun bit his lip. His hands were clenched into fists in his lap. "As an Egyptian my first loyalty is to the King. So is yours. It's treason, Father! Forgive me, but I can't!" Seqenenra went and stood over him.

"Are you saying that you will not fight for me?" Si-Amun's long-lashed black eyes rose and met his. He was on the verge of tears.

"If you give me a direct order, I will of course fight for you, Prince," he choked, "but I will not go to the nomes and help you to hasten the moment of our destruction. I abase myself before you. I humble myself. But I will not go." Seqenenra struggled with his anger, sympathy and an overwhelming sense of betrayal. Sympathy won. He pulled Si-Amun to his feet.

"Very well," he said curtly. "I honour your decision because I know that my son does not speak from cowardice. Leave this room." Unhappily Si-Amun drew himself up, and stalking past a silent Kamose, went out. For a moment Seqenenra and Kamose could not look at each other. Then Kamose straightened his shoulders.

"He has great courage," he reminded his father. "He is a good warrior. You must not blame him." Seqenenra, hurt and aching, did not respond.

"I will go to the nomes and conscript men," Kamose went on grimly, "but I think your reason is impaired, Father. How long will it be before your rashness reaches the ears of the One? He has spies in the house, that is certain. I wish with all my heart that you could build the temple instead of an army. I do not want to die."

"I am terrified for all of us," Seqenenra replied, "but you have an inner strength that will never betray you. It is for Ahmose and Aahmes-nefertari and Tani that I grieve." Kamose's lips had thinned. He was livid under his deep tan.

"How will you pay for it all?"

"I must take Uni into my confidence. And Amunmose. He must beg Amun for the greatest favour he has ever shown this family."

"Why not climb onto the roof of the sanctuary with a horn and announce your intentions to the whole of Weset?" Kamose shot back caustically. "It will come to that anyway, Father, and you know it. You must move very fast if you want to strike even the feeblest blow before Apepa sends a fraction of his horde south and demolishes us all."

"Will you help me?"

Kamose clenched his fists. "Of course. The blood of the god is in my veins, too."

Seqenenra looked at him curiously. It was the first time

Kamose had ever referred so directly to his lineage. I hardly know you, Seqenenra thought. I hardly know you at all.

With an effort of self-control Si-Amun forced himself to walk to his quarters, answering the greetings of servants affably as he went. His head was whirling. Why are you so surprised? he asked himself sternly. You knew it would come to this, or you would never have made the agreement you did with Teti. Then why this feeling of stunned disbelief? Did you think that Father would wake from his fantasy?

Si-Amun had not communicated with Teti since his return home. Life had seemed to settle into normality and his father had been his usual taciturn self. Si-Amun, with a curious sense of relief, had allowed himself to smooth away the memory of the lunch with Teti under the fig tree, but now as he reached his own door and entered his bedchamber with weak legs and a pounding heart, it came back to him in horrifying detail. Why horrifying? he thought as his steward came forward and bowed. "Bring me a piece of papyrus parchment and a palette," he ordered, and the man went away.

Si-Amun pulled off his kilt, then tore the sheet from his couch and began to rub down his sweat-streaked body. Horrifying, because you doubt Teti's good intentions, he said to himself. There. I have formed the words. I am not a wide-eyed innocent. Teti may wish me to spy on my father for his own ends. Yet he may be sincere. We share blood through Mother. He has always been a good friend to this family and I cannot rely on my own misgivings, caused surely by nothing but guilt at going behind Father's back. Father must be stopped and Teti is the only one to whom I can turn. Grandmother would tear out Apepa's eyes if she could. Mother does whatever Father wants. Kamose also. Ahmose cares for nothing but his freedom. It is up to me to save us all.

The steward returned with the scribe's palette and parchment. "Find Mersu and ask him to come," Si-Amun said, taking the things. "And then tell my wife that I would like to walk with her for a little by the river. You can go."

He sank cross-legged onto the floor, settled the palette across his bare knees, and selecting a thin brush he began to write carefully on the papyrus, willing his hand not to tremble. 'Father has received another letter,' he printed. 'He is raising an army. Please come before he goes too far. I do not know what to do.' He did not sign it. Rolling it, he tied it with a piece of string, sealed the knot with hot wax, and painstakingly drew a crude hippopotamus in the wax.

By the time he had finished, Mersu was bowing himself into the room. Si-Amun, still naked, held out the scroll. Mersu looked at him enquiringly but took it. "I believe you are a friend of Teti's Chief Steward," Si-Amun said. Mersu nodded.

"He and I were raised in the same village, next door to one another, Prince," he replied guardedly. "We attended the local scribes' school at the same time."

"I see." Si-Amun folded his arms. "I want you to make sure that this scroll reaches him. It is for Teti. A private matter." He had been going to lie, but if he had said that the scroll was for Ramose, Mersu would have wondered why it had not been given to a regular messenger plying the river. Try as he might, Si-Amun could come up with no good excuse for his request. The older man was gazing at him steadily, a question in his eyes. Impatiently Si-Amun dismissed him. He did not bother to wash. Rummaging in his chest he pulled out a clean kilt, wrapped it on, and hurried out to find Aahmes-nefertari. He needed to feel her arms around him, reassuring him that he had done the right thing although she herself was ignorant. Teti would come. Father would listen to his relative's appeasing words. All would be well.

Chapter FOUR

BEFORE THE MONTH was out, gangs of peasants from Weset were raising barracks on the desert behind the western cliffs. Hor-Aha and his soldiers returned, and soon dark, quick men began to trickle across the Nile and disappear into the hills. Seqenenra made his fifty seasoned retainers officers to form the core of his army, and set them over the new recruits. There was no time to train them properly. They would have to sink or swim on their own. Those with the new bows must teach those receiving the ones Hor-Aha was feverishly trying to construct. All must be marched and drilled, issued spears, axes and clubs, fed and watered. Seqenenra made no attempt to answer the King's letter. It would be at least two months, he knew, before Apepa began to wonder why no word had come from the south.

When matters could no longer be hidden from the family, he had told them what he had decided to do. "I do not have time to organize this thing properly," he said to the bewildered little group. "I have few career officers, no seasoned Scribes of Assemblage and Recruits, no skilled charioteers. Forgive me for doing what has to be done." Tetisheri had said nothing. Neither had Aahotep. Kamose was away touring the nomes, but Ahmose had exclaimed immediately, "Kamose and I will fight, of course. Ma'at is on your side, Father. We will see the Horus Throne returned to us before next New Year's Day!" Looking into the sixteen-year-old's bright eyes Seqenenra wondered whether Ahmose indeed believed that the Setiu would be driven out of Egypt by then or whether he was offering cheer to the despondency he sensed in his father.

Aahmes-nefertari tried to control her tears and could not. Sobbing, she struggled to her feet, flung her arms around Seqenenra's neck, then fled the room. At his father's nod Si-Amun went after her. Tani clung to her mother, her eyes huge and frightened.

"Father, this is treason," she whispered. "The gods will punish you. What will I do without you? Why are you doing this to me?" There was nothing he could say. To Tani this suicide must seem the height of selfishness.

"What can I do?" Tetisheri asked quietly.

"Keep the estate running as normally as possible, you and Aahotep. Make excuses for my absences. Deflect questions." His shoulders slumped. He had been about to say that it did not matter in the end, but the sight of Tani's disfigured, uncomprehending face had stilled his tongue.

Uni had spluttered and expostulated when Seqenenra had told him why he needed a full accounting and a revision of the budget of his governorship.

"This is madness, Prince. Madness!" he had shouted. "I shall have to purify myself of this stain every day so that the gods will not punish me!" Wearily Seqenenra heard him out without rebuking him for his insolence.

"Uni, I know that like Mersu your ancestors were Setiu," he said. "You are free to leave my service and do what you wish with the information I have given you, but please know that I need you." Uni had bowed shortly and turned away sullenly.

"I will make a report on the state of your holdings, Prince," he had muttered. "I will also glean a list of new sources of revenue. If there are any." He had stalked away stiff with anger and Seqenenra had let him go. In spite of his outrage he had indirectly given Seqenenra the answer he craved.

He did not have much time to reflect on his undertaking. His days were spent with Ahmose in the burning heat of the desert behind the western cliffs watching Hor-Aha and his new officers try to beat and cajole the new men into soldiers. New bows were coming out of the craftsmen's shops. A substitute for the unobtainable birch wood had been found. Hor-Aha had experimented unsuccessfully with various possibilities until out of desperation he had applied his glue to the stripped ribs of palm branches. The results were surprisingly good, and once full production was underway, he had left the task to the military craftsmen and had turned his attention to the recruits.

Seqenenra and his younger son sweated with the rest, enduring Hor-Aha's taunts and insults as they struggled to draw the bows. Both had experience with the weapons but had only used them for an occasional friendly competition. Now they worked in earnest, Ahmose glorying in his swift progress, Seqenenra grimly drawing and loosing, cursing under his breath, feeling time flow by him like the river in flood while Ra tried to boil his blood and blister his skin.

Sometimes Si-Amun came to the practice ground and stood beside his father and brother, handling the bow with silent preoccupation or racing in his chariot during the mock charges Hor-Aha had decreed, but he did not appear often. Seqenenra tried to force aside his disappointment in his son and behave as though all was well, but Si-Amun had withdrawn into an icy arrogance. At meals, in the temple, during the informal moments of each day when the family gathered by the pool, Si-Amun's eyes slipped past the gaze of his relatives. He talked readily enough when the conversation remained general, but at any mention of the activity beyond the western cliffs he quietly closed his mouth.

Seqenenra ached for him. His refusal to do any more than fight beside his father had not seemed to influence Aahmes-nefertari's attitude towards him and for that Seqenenra was grateful, but Tetisheri was openly cool to him.

"That boy is hiding something," she said emphatically to Seqenenra one evening as they sat over the remains of the last meal of the day, too indolent to stroll outside before going to bed. "It is understandable that he should be defiant around us, prepared to defend his position, but the Si-Amun of the shifty eyes and long silences I do not know." She leaned back and put both hands on her knees. "His behaviour conceals some sort of guilt."

"He is hardly a boy, Mother," Seqenenra answered. "And surely a little guilt is not surprising. What conflicting loyalties lie behind the respectful faces of our servants, let alone a member of the family? The situation is terrible for everyone. Si-Amun feels it keenly."

She slapped her knees. "Guilt! He should be angry, hotly defending his position, arguing whenever plans are discussed. I know my grandson, Seqenenra. This dumb brooding creature is unnatural. It is not the Si-Amun I know." Her voice dropped. "Have him watched, Prince."

Seqenenra was horrified. "You cannot possibly believe that my own son, my heir, would betray me? Sometimes I think that you are a disciple of Set, Tetisheri. I will not spy on my own flesh."

Tetisheri was unmoved. "Something is eating away at him," she insisted. "I love him and so do you, but don't trust him."

Seqenenra pushed his table away and rose. "It is a long step from familial disagreement to treason," he said. "The web of your mind is too complex, Mother, too dark. Your thoughts are dishonourable."

"And yours are dangerously innocent!" she called after him as he walked away. "Love him, Seqenenra, but don't trust him!"

Later, when Isis had slipped her sleeping gown over her head and pulled back the sheets on her couch, Tetisheri sent the woman for Mersu. When Isis returned, the steward bowing behind her, Tetisheri spoke to both of them.

"I am a suspicious old lady," she said, "but I will sleep better if you will both perform a small task for me. You know that Prince Si-Amun is against the coming war. I do not know whether or not he is so against it that he would betray us all. Therefore I want you to take note of his doings, where he goes, who he sees, and particularly to whom his correspondence is addressed. Oh don't look so shocked, Isis," she said irritably as the servant gaped at her. "I love the young idiot, as you well know. Mersu, you seem unmoved by this command." Mersu bowed slightly.

"I am not unmoved, Highness, and I will, of course, fulfil your request, but it does seem a trifle dramatic." Tetisheri dismissed them with a curt wave.

"It is not important what you think. Simply do as you are told."

Yet when they had gone and she was alone under the sheets, her eyes fixed on the shadows hanging in the ceiling, she was almost inclined to agree with him. Si-Amun has always been drawn to power, influence, all that is fashionable, she thought. It has not made him weak, only restless and occasionally envious. His heart is sound. Perhaps I am indeed an evil old woman. She turned on her side and closed her eyes but sleep eluded her. She felt ashamed of spying on her grandson, but uneasy also, and the unease had no roots. Stoically she prepared for a long night.

Seqenenra dismissed his mother's warning and thought no more about it. He was feverishly preoccupied with the slow drawing together of his rebellion, and with its coming to gradual fruition it brought a darkness of mind and a continual apprehension that seldom lifted. One incident served to lighten his heart, however. He was lying on his couch one afternoon while his body servant massaged oil into his aching muscles when Uni announced that the mayor of Weset wished audience.

"He and his deputies have been escorted to the reception hall," Uni told him. Seqenenra signalled for the man still kneading his protesting flesh to take the dish of oil and go.

"What do they want?" he asked testily.

"They did not say," Uni responded. "I put wine by their hands and left them."

"Very well. Send Ipi with his palette to the reception hall." Uni acknowledged the order and Seqenenra rose, went quickly into the passage beyond, answered the salute of the guard at the far end, and made his way to where the mayor and three other men stood awkwardly waiting, goblets full of untouched wine in their hands. As he approached, they bowed low. Seqenenra settled himself on the seat of audience and bade them relax. "Now," he said, keeping his uneasiness hidden. "What may your Prince do for you?" The mayor straightened, put down his wine, and clasped his hands behind his back.

"Highness, we know that our lord Kamose is journeying through the nomes gathering men. We know that you, Highness, have no building projects underway at the present time." Here Seqenenra hid a smile of approval at the mayor's tact. I have no architects, let alone plans for monuments, and you know it, he thought. I made a wise choice when I appointed you as chief representative of my town. "Therefore," the mayor went on, "these men are not needed to haul stone. We respectfully wish to know if our Prince is raising an army, and if he is, whether or not he intends to move against Het-Uart?" There was a small disturbance as Ipi glided in, sank to the floor by Seqenenra's feet, and slid open his brush box, and in the few seconds of grace Seqenenra considered and decided.

"The answer is yes to both questions," he said tersely, "although I doubt if I will be able to fight my way as far as Het-Uart." The mayor smiled. His companions murmured to each other.

"Then, Prince, we wish you to know that we will not wait for his Highness Kamose to command us to deliver conscripts. We have brought a list of all men able to carry arms for your Scribe of Recruits."

"Why, Your Excellency?" Seqenenra was genuinely taken aback. "If I choose to conscript your citizens, you have no choice in the matter in any case." The mayor drew himself up.

"Because many hentis ago Weset was a city sacred to all Egypt. The Incarnation of the God ruled the land from here. The people of Weset love you. Whether or not the Double Crown sits on your head, you are the Beautiful of Risings, the One Who Causes Hearts to Live, the Son of the Sun. We are your cattle, Majesty, but we share the long grief of your royal family." He raised his shoulders. "Can I say more? We also offer whatever goods each household can afford to give."

Seqenenra was overcome. Tears burned behind his eyelids. I seem to spend most of my time these days snivelling like a lovelorn girl, he berated himself, yet today I am surely forgiven. I have never heard myself called Majesty before, nor could the word be any sweeter if it came from the lips of a Vizier himself rather than from this portly, dignified son of Egypt.

"I accept this great gesture with a thankful heart," he managed huskily. "You have honoured Amun also today, and if by his will I am able to return the Horus Throne to its rightful place in Weset, both I and my father the god will be eternally grateful. Ipi, take the list." The scribe reached out and took the scroll offered by one of the men. "Drink your wine now," Seqenenra told them. "Return this evening with your wives and be my guests at dinner. I can offer little in the way of hospitality, but perhaps there will be good entertainment." After a while he dismissed them and went to the office where Uni waited impatiently, the day's problems cluttering the desk, and he was humming as he opened the door and greeted the steward.

Kamose returned shortly, weary and taciturn, and leaving his brother to organize the men he had brought and get them across the river and into their billets, he sought out his father. Seqenenra had been talking with Tani, a pleasure he had had little time for lately. The girl did not fully understand the events that had overtaken the family and was watching, terrified, for the retribution she was sure would fall on her father from the gods for disturbing the balance of Ma'at, but she was trying to keep her anxiety to herself. There was still Ramose, expected for a visit soon, and his messages that she reread many times to comfort herself in the long, hot afternoons. Still, her efforts at cheerfulness did not deceive her father. She had recently turned fourteen and her youth lock had been removed and burned. Seqenenra fervently wished that not only a betrothal but a marriage might take place soon between her and Ramose and she might be removed from any danger at Weset.

He was casting about for some way to accomplish this when he came to the end of the passage to the women's quarters and was met by Kamose. They embraced. Kamose was still covered in the dust and grime of his journey. Seqenenra sent a servant running for beer and he and his son went into the garden, settling themselves under the faint shade by the pool. Kamose tore off his crumpled linen helmet and used it to wipe his face and neck. After a few words of unimportant conversation he said, "Ahmose tells me that the soldiers' new quarters are very cramped and rations are short. Also there are not enough donkeys to carry water into the desert. Apart from these things the river will begin to rise in less than a month and in two months marching will be impossible." He began to rub the grit and sand from his legs. "It is not too late to change your mind, Prince." Seqenenra watched the nimble fingers slap at the stained calves.

"Hor-Aha tells me the same thing," he replied. "But I cannot wait another year, Kamose. You know that. I intend to march ahead of the Inundation. How many men have you brought me?" Kamose lay back on one elbow.

"A thousand and three hundred. I could have brought more if we had not been forced to send so many north to the King's labours. There were no questions asked, of course. How many Medjay did Hor-Aha manage to persuade?" Only thirteen hundred. Seqenenra pushed away the wave of panic that constricted his chest.

"Two thousand, but every one is worth two of Apepa's men and, of course, we have our own five hundred troops. I am hoping to gather support from the cities and nomes we pass."

"Not even a division," Kamose said drily. "We need another seventeen hundred men for that. Rumour has it that Apepa commands more than one hundred thousand Setiu troops in Het-Uart alone." Seqenenra heard the rebuke in his son's voice but did not respond to it.

"We will call our soldiers a division in spite of the numbers," he decided. "The Division of Amun. The original fifty Medjay bodyguards will be the Braves of the King and Hor-Aha is training five hundred tribesmen as Shock Troops. It will be a miniature army, Kamose, but still an army."

"You will command in the field?"

"Of course. But I do not want Ahmose to fight." Kamose sat up but said nothing. His gaze was fixed intently on his father. Seqenenra went on, "Our line must not die out, Kamose. If I fall in battle, there must be an heir to the governorship here. If he is clever, he can persuade Apepa that I alone was stricken with this madness and he tried to prevent it."

"I can see that Ahmose must not fight," Kamose agreed. "The promise of the future should be preserved if possible. If we die, Ahmose is still here."

"I know you do not really want to fight," Seqenenra said gently. "If the choice was yours, you would do everything in your power to keep all as it is, to preserve our blood for a time in the future when the Setiu will be gone from Egypt. But I tell you that the time is here, now. Besides, Apepa will make sure that war or no war this family disappears into oblivion."

Kamose sighed. "You are right. I just want with everything in me to believe it is not so. I hate him!" The black eyes, heavily kohled and red-rimmed, suddenly blazed at Seqenenra. "I hate what his stupid suspicions are doing to Aahmes-nefertari and her unborn baby and to you most of all! I need to bathe." His burst of fury vanished as swiftly as it had come. Getting up, he brushed off his kilt and strode away. Seqenenra himself left the garden a moment later, walking to the shallow, oily river to be poled to the west bank to inspect the conscripts. There was as yet no sign of the flood and for that he was grateful. An early Inundation would have made an already foolhardy gesture into an adventure in futility.

Seqenenra was leaving the temple precincts late one morning after several hours spent with Amunmose, both of them trying to wring every last uten's weight the god could spare for the coming conflict. The High Priest had not demurred when Seqenenra had asked for his help. It would be, after all, Amun's war as well as the Prince's, and Amunmose with his scribe had emptied the temple treasury. The priests would have to tighten their belts and apart from the god's food, clothing and the vital incense, the chests were gutted. "It is a pity that your Highness cannot trade off some of your cattle in the Delta, and Amun's also," Amunmose had observed. "Cattle always fetch much grain and perhaps even a little gold. But the One would ask why."

"The One will soon ask why in any case," Seqenenra had replied. He was becoming concerned that Apepa would begin to look for a reply to the letter. Two months had passed since the King's outrageous demand and Seqenenra's heart missed a beat every time a barge bearing the royal colours hove into sight. So far they had sailed on or stopped only to deliver scrolls for Tani. But one day soon a final ultimatum would arrive. By then, Seqenenra thought to himself, stepping from the temple pylon's deep shade into the full glare of the morning sun and walking to his patient litter bearers, I will be on my way north fighting anyone who gets in my way. Will Apepa have been alerted? Will there be an army standing waiting, at Aabtu, at Akhmin or Djawati?

He was about to lower himself onto the litter and the bearers were taking their places when he heard Tani call "Father!" Squinting into the light he watched her run towards him, the gossamer sheath tight against her tanned body, her sandals kicking up puffs of sand. She came up to him, panting and laughing, dark eyes alight under their dusting of green eyepaint. It had been a long time since he had seen her so excited.

"Calm yourself!" he said, smiling. "No one should run in this heat. What is it, Tani?"

"Ramose and his father are here!" she almost shouted. "Teti is on his way to inspect Tynt-to-amu before the Inundation begins and they decided to pay us a visit!"

"Here, sit beside me," Seqenenra gestured, getting onto the

litter. "I think the men can carry both of us. Close the curtains, it's too hot to look out." Tani let the curtains fall and turned to him, eyes shining. The bearers lifted them and they began to sway the short distance to the house. "And is the great and mighty Ramose as wonderful as the last time you saw him?" Seqenenra teased her, his own lightness of heart due to the relief he felt. I could have been coming back from the training ground across the river with Hor-Aha and my weapons, he thought. Thank the gods I was in the temple today!

"Oh, twice as wonderful!" Tani vowed. "He has brought me the most beautiful pectoral you ever saw and the balance-pendant at the back is in gold and turquoise, the crown of Mut to ward off the attacks of the evil ones from behind! Mother made me put it away for now." She leaned towards him anxiously, all huge eyes and moving hair, and her breath smelled of the honeycomb she had been sucking when she saw the barge approaching. "I think Teti also brings a betrothal contract," she whispered. "He will want to discuss a dowry. What shall we do?" He smoothed back her tresses and kissed her on the cheek.

"That is not your concern," he reproved her. "Do not worry. Are you not a Princess, my Tani?" You shall have your dowry even if I have to sell all my cattle to pay for it, he promised her mutely. One of us at least shall have his greatest desire.

The litter slowed and he heard the bearers exchange a polite greeting with someone. Parting the curtains he saw that they were now moving along the dusty street dividing his domain from the trees that lined the river. Two men were standing back to let them pass. One was Mersu, Tetisheri's steward, who saluted Seqenenra with grave respect. The other, even now bowing as he saw the curtain part, was unknown to Seqenenra.

"I think that is Teti's Chief Scribe," Tani told him as he let the hangings drop and the litter turned towards the house. "Or perhaps it is his steward. Anyway, I believe I saw him on the estate at Khemennu. Greetings, Ramose!" The litter had been lowered. Tani swung her feet to the ground and the young man's hand came out to help her. At the same time, he managed to bow to Seqenenra.

"My greetings, Prince," he said. "I hope my frequent written salutations to Tani did not annoy you. I had to make sure that no handsome count's son caught her eye while I was not near her!" Seqenenra placed a hand on his shoulder.

"I was not annoyed," he replied with a smile. "I am almost persuaded that you are worthy of my daughter. We shall see." He turned to Tani. "You may go with him now, but be in the garden soon to share the greeting meal. Both of you!" They did not scurry away as they might have done a few months before. Holding hands they strolled back along the street, dappled in shade, heads together, their bodyguard behind. It did Seqenenra good to see them so. He set off across the tired grass towards the house.

Teti rose from his stool beside Aahotep and came smiling to greet Seqenenra. He had put on weight since Seqenenra had seen him last, but not enough to make him corpulent. It only served to emphasize the impression of authority Teti carried with him. Gold sparked from his bracelets as he held out his hands. He was resplendent in a yellow-and-white-striped linen helmet, a dazzling white, stiffly starched kilt and a soft white shirt. Several rows of solid silver chains studded with jasper encircled his neck. The fingers that Seqenenra clasped were heavy with rings. "Teti!" Seqenenra exclaimed, waving him down and lowering himself into the grass beside him. "This is an unexpected pleasure! Tani tells me you are on your way to inspect the first cataract before the Inundation comes thundering through it!" He caught Tetisheri's eye and read his own relief mirrored there. Uni bent and offered him wine and a dish of dried plums. He took the wine and sipped. Teti pulled his jewelled fly whisk from his belt and began to apply it to the folds of flesh at his waist where the flies were gathering in search of salt.

"That is in response to my command from the One," he answered. "My own purpose, happily combined with his, is to offer you a betrothal contract between Ramose and Tani." He made a playful face over the rim of his cup. "I think it is written on the last piece of papyrus in my office. Ramose has stolen all the rest for his letters to her." They all laughed.

"I am very pleased, Teti," Seqenenra said. "And yes, it is time to join the two of them. There is no doubt in Tani's mind that it is Ramose she wants."

"So we will celebrate?" Teti signalled for more wine. "A wedding in the spring when Egypt will be green again?"

"Agreed." They raised their cups together. "But let us not discuss the details now. We will do it tomorrow morning in the office. I will give her a good dowry, as befits a Princess."

"Of course you will!" They drank again. Seqenenra felt waves of wine-induced contentment flow over him and for just a moment he forgot that outside this garden, this house, Weset seethed with military activity.

But Teti's next remark brought him back to earth with a jolt. "What is going on over the river?" the man asked. "We saw loaded donkeys following a track into the hills and a contingent of soldiers behind them. Surely only the dead inhabit West-of-Weset?" Seqenenra stared at him and it was Tetisheri who answered.

"Some of the tombs have been pillaged," she said coolly, "and when Si-Amun went in person to inspect the damage, he found a number of burials not only disturbed but the tombs themselves in a bad state of repair. A small village for workmen and soldiers has been built out on the desert so that the tombs can be attended to and then guarded."

"Have you found the thieves?" Teti asked with interest. Seqenenra shrugged.

"Not yet, but we will. Questioning the peasants yields little information, but they are simple men and sooner or later the culprits will try to trade what they managed to steal. Then we will punish." He put his cup carefully in the grass and braced himself for further discussion, but the moment was saved by the arrival of Tani and Ramose and in the general chatter the subject of the tombs was dropped. Teti did, however, ask where Si-Amun, Kamose and Ahmose were. Aahotep told him they were overseeing the work on the west bank. Teti seemed mollified. Shortly afterwards, Tetisheri called for Mersu and went to her apartments with Aahotep to consult over the feast that had to be prepared.

Teti, the perfect guest, presented Aahotep with three brace of ducks he and Ramose had killed in the reeds the evening before when they made camp, and several delicacies he had stored for the long trip to Tynt-to-amu. Seqenenra's harpist played and sang. Tani danced, wearing the pectoral Ramose had given her, a white, gilt-threaded ribbon wound through her short, curling hair. There was plenty of beer and wine. Si-Amun, Kamose and Ahmose, warned discreetly by the ever-vigilant Uni, had arrived at sunset freshly washed to support Seqenenra's story. Aahmes-nefertari, heavily pregnant but full of fun, told a bawdy story Hetepet, her body servant, had heard in the market that day. Yet Seqenenra did not think that his relative by marriage was deceived. Teti laughed, ate and drank, kept up a constant stream of conversation, but his kohled eyes were watchful. Ramose had eyes only for Tani. He teased her about her hair, still growing after the youth lock had been shaved off, and fed her by hand like a beloved pet.

On the following morning Teti and Seqenenra met in the office to haggle over Tani's dowry. The final agreement would not be made until the marriage contract was drawn up, but the initial offer would have to be made and considered. Teti, hearing Seqenenra talk, was clearly uneasy. For a while he nodded, grunted, nodded, then he held up a hand and Seqenenra was silent.

"Pardon me, Prince," he interrupted. "I do not wish to appear rude but you seem absent, preoccupied. Are the fortunes of your family a little strained? Has the One raised your taxes too high this year?"

"I am not offended," Seqenenra replied reassuringly. "This is one occasion when you have a right to enquire into my financial health. It is true that the taxes were high but then so were my revenues. It was a bountiful harvest." Fierce pride swelled in him and he wanted to deny that he was living on the edge of ruin and tell Teti to mind his own business. But as he had said, Teti had a right to the assurance of the dowry, and, in any case, word of his army must surely be leaking steadily north. "My nomes have been complaining of raids on their villages by the Shasu," he explained. "I decided to conscript a small army to deal with them. When the men are trained, they will be stationed in the various villages, but until then I must bear the cost of feeding and arming them." He spread his hands. "It is an expensive undertaking."

"I have heard rumours of this army of yours," Teti said slowly, and at his expression Seqenenra was very glad he had kept his explanation as close to the truth as possible. "But Seqenenra, why did you not simply ask the One for a few detachments from Het-Uart? He would not want the security of his people threatened." His people? Seqenenra swallowed his hot reply.

"I do not want to excite the King's attention," he said frankly. "I know that I make him anxious and it would be foolish to take the chance of being relieved of my governorship on any pretext. The One could say that I was incompetent, that I did not control the nomes properly. Or he could say that the situation was more grave than it is and put a Commander in charge of Weset." He felt suddenly hotter. His kilt scratched his thighs and he was all at once aware of the taste of grit in his mouth. Teti's black eyebrows rose.

"The One will hear of it in any case," he said.

"But by then I will have the situation in hand," Seqenenra cut in swiftly. "The conscripts might even be disbanded." I sound like a haggler in the market running after a steward already walking away from my stall, he thought in despair. Rising, he rubbed both hands over his face and smiled wanly at Teti. "You do not believe me, do you?" Teti chuckled abruptly in surprise.

"Why would I not?" he asked. "The Shasu often pick away at outlying villages. But Prince, if your resources are so stretched to supply this army, I advise you to swallow your pride and ask the One for help. It is exceedingly dangerous not to explain your true situation to him." They looked into each other's eyes for a long second. "You have not answered his last letter, have you?" Teti continued softly. "That is why you do not wish to approach him. You are very foolish, Seqenenra." Seqenenra felt himself loosen. Teti had grasped the wrong conclusion.

"Do not worry about Tani's dowry," he said, trying to keep the quiver of relief out of his voice. "I may be impoverishing myself temporarily to victual my soldiers, but I still have great wealth in my cattle in the Delta. Tani is precious to me and if she wants Ramose she shall have him." Teti knew that his implied criticism had stalked the boundary of good manners. He bowed his head once.

"So be it," he acquiesced. "In that case we ask two hundred head." Seqenenra resumed his seat and objected. Ipi, on the floor by the desk, silent and unobtrusive, picked up his brush, and the haggling began again.

Si-Amun was about to climb onto his couch that night when Mersu bowed his way into the bedchamber. The young man had sat uncomfortably through the feast, tense and polite, and had escaped to his rooms as soon as possible. Kamose had sought him out there and they had cast the dice for a while. He had gone to Aahmes-nefertari's apartment afterwards, lying beside her on the couch with her head against his shoulder while Raa massaged her swollen legs, but after she had begun to doze he had gently extricated himself, said good night to Raa, and gone back to his own rooms. He felt cold and restless, and knew that he would not be able to sleep.

"Your pardon, Prince, for disturbing you so late," Mersu said, "but your kinsman wishes to see you privately in the guest rooms."

"Well, let him come here," Si-Amun responded sharply. "A Prince does not answer a summons from a mere nobleman." Mersu continued to stand by the door just outside the lamp's steady glow.

"That is true," he replied softly, "and Teti asks forgiveness for his request, but he thinks that it will excite less comment, if you are seen, for you to go to him. I agree."

"Oh, do you?" Si-Amun said sarcastically. He had conceived a dislike for his grandmother's steward since handing him the scroll for Teti some weeks ago. It seemed to him that an oily complicity had been growing behind Mersu's impeccable manners, but he was careful to admit to himself that his own guilty imagination might be at work.

It is I who have changed, he thought, as he came reluctantly to his feet and reached for his sandals. I certainly do not like him, but truthfully I cannot fault his service or his attitude. "It is not a steward's place to proffer agreement," he snapped pettishly. "But I suppose I must see what Teti wants. Go."

Mersu bowed and slipped away. Si-Amun could not hear his bare feet on the floor of the passage. Going to the door he peered out. The torch on the wall showed him nothing but the sleepy guard at the far end.

The men's guest quarters were in the same wing of the house as his and his brother's rooms and it did not take Si-Amun long to arrive at Teti's door. He knocked and not waiting for an answer, walked in. Teti rose from beside the couch and inclined his head. He was wearing a thin, yellow linen coat with full sleeves that brushed the floor and showed every well-fed line of him with the night light behind it. "I was rude to beg you to come to me, Prince," he said before Si-Amun had a chance to speak. "Please forgive me. But I needed to be careful. Ramose and Tani are out looking at the stars," he explained in answer to Si-Amun's glance around the room. "I will not keep you long, Si-Amun." Si-Amun swallowed his irrational anger, and closing the door, came forward.

"I expected some answer to my message, Teti," he said. "I was beginning to think that it had gone astray." Teti indicated the dried figs and wine by the couch. Si-Amun shook his head. Teti folded his arms.

"You asked me to come, not write to you," he pointed out. "I am sorry if I caused you any distress. I knew that the One would require an inspection of the cataract this year as it was not done before the last Inundation, so I decided to wait. Your father seems set on this course." Si-Amun began to wander the room, touching walls, fingering the alabaster lamps.

"You have spoken to him about it?"

"Yes. I mentioned it briefly. I told him that rumours of the army are filtering north and will reach Het-Uart soon. He said that the soldiers are for the defence of your nomes against the Shasu."

"That is a lie." Si-Amun forced himself to stand still and face Teti. "Father's Medjay bodyguard have been recruiting Shasu. Teti, you must stop this!" He spread his arms. "Why should I have compromised my conscience if you can do nothing?"

"Is that what you feel you have done?" Teti enquired in a low voice. "What of your conscience towards our King, young Prince?"

"I know, I know." Si-Amun spoke more impatiently than he had intended. "I am relying on you, Teti, to contain this thing and keep it from the ears of the One."

"And how am I supposed to do that if your father brings his army north? I tell you, Si-Amun, he will not be persuaded. All we can do is to have his effort aborted before it can flower."

Si-Amun was stiff with the need to move, to fidget. Resolutely he put his hands behind his back. "Is that possible?"

Teti frowned, pulling his coat more tightly around him. His bald head shone in the pale light. "I can write to the One and request that Seqenenra be ordered north on some pretext, to organize the nomes around Ta-she perhaps, to regulate the taxes, anything. The King will comply." He met Si-Amun's troubled gaze. "The flood is almost upon us and a man cannot march through water."

"There is no time for that."

"Then your father must be stopped on the way. Apepa must be told, warned. Seqenenra must take the consequences."

"No!" Si-Amun started forward. "I trusted you to help us, Teti! What use have you been? What have I done?" Teti strode to him and took his shoulders in a firm grip.

"You have done your duty as a loyal Egyptian," he insisted. "Do not weaken now, Si-Amun. Apepa's justice will fall more kindly on your father for your loyalty. I know him. But you must not falter now. Keep me informed. Send me the time of the march and its direction and first destination. If you do not,

Apepa will think that you have changed allegiance and will punish you severely. There is no time to do more!" Si-Amun wrenched himself from Teti's grasp.

"Talk to Father again!"

"If I do, he will know that someone has been telling me what has been going on. He will suspect you."

It was true. I should have seen it from the beginning, Si-Amun thought bitterly. Well, let Father suspect me. Let him be cold towards me, let him hate me. I will go to him myself and tell him what I have done. But he knew he could not. He did not believe in the rightness of Seqenenra's rebellion. It has all gone too far, he thought again with despair. I am committed. "The King knows what is going on already, doesn't he?" he whispered. "You sent him my scroll. You betrayed me."

"Yes, he knows." Teti poured wine and thrust it between Si-Amun's trembling fingers. "Yet he waits to see what Seqenenra will really do. He does not wish to be unjust if your father changes his mind."

"Gods!" Si-Amun stood staring stupidly into the red depths of the cup. "I have sold my father!"

"No. You have saved your inheritance. Think, Si-Amun! With Apepa waiting to surround him, your father will suffer little bloodshed. Otherwise the damage he inflicts before he is defeated could be enormous. The revolt will be a small thing, quickly forgotten. Seqenenra will be disciplined and his officers executed, but is that not better than the loss and destruction of all you have here?" He watched Si-Amun suddenly empty the cup, draining it in long, gasping swallows. "Keep me informed, I tell you."

With exaggerated care Si-Amun placed the cup on the table. He nodded at Teti, turned, and walked unsteadily to the door, but before he could leave, it opened and Ramose came in. Si-Amun was too dazed to step aside and Ramose barely avoided hitting him. "Good evening, Prince!" Ramose said. Si-Amun pushed by him and the door slammed. Ramose looked at his father. "What is the matter with Si-Amun?" he asked. Teti sank onto the couch and passed a weary hand over his shaven skull.

"I made him angry," he said. "It is nothing, Ramose. I shall be glad to be on our way tomorrow."

"That sounds ominous." Ramose smiled. "Is it something to do with Tani's dowry?" Teti looked startled.

"No! Seqenenra and I have arrived at a satisfactory agreement and you can marry at sowing time."

"Wonderful." Ramose yawned. "Where is the body servant? I want to go to bed. I love Seqenenra's estate, it's so easygoing and everyone is unconcerned with the rigidity we live with, but it does make for lax staff. Shall I call him?"

"If you like."

Ramose waited, but as his father continued to sit on the edge of the couch gazing into space and frowning, the young man shrugged to himself, bellowed for a servant, and fell to humming the tune Seqenenra's harpist had played that evening. He was supremely happy.

Chapter FIVE

IN THE END TETI and Ramose sailed with a promise of a hundred head of cattle, twenty offering rams and thirty uten's weight of silver as Tani's bride price. Seqenenra, embracing them and watching them walk up the ramp into their barge in the brief moment of transitory coolness before Ra rose in shimmering heat over the horizon, wondered where he would obtain the silver, but as he had asked that that portion of the agreement be deferred for one year after the marriage, he resolved not to worry about it. Tani was ecstatic, saying goodbye to Ramose in floods of happy tears, his necklace proudly at her throat.

Shortly after the last ripple of wash from the barge had vanished, she took her bodyguard and went to visit the hippopotamuses. Aahotep, eyes still swollen with sleep, gathered her loose cloak around her and went back into the house for food. Kamose and Ahmose sat on the watersteps, their bows beside them, waiting for the skiff that would pole them once more over the river where Hor-Aha was already drilling the soldiers. Uni and Mersu stood a few paces away, immobile and freshly washed, while Tetisheri took Seqenenra's arm and gently pulled him to face her. Without kohl, her lips free of henna, her wiry grey hair streaked with black tumbling about her shoulders, she looked old and tired but her grip was firm. "Does he suspect?" she asked abruptly. Seqenenra shook his head.

"I don't know. Perhaps. In any case there is nothing we can do about it if he does. It is too late. I told him I was conscripting to protect the nomes. He knows I have not answered Apepa's letter."

"How does he know that?" Her black eyes nested in a myriad of wrinkles were suddenly alert. "Is he in closer contact with the One than we suspected or does he only surmise?" Seqenenra was suddenly angry at the greedy complicity in her face. He plucked her fingers from his arm.

"How in the name of Amun would I know?" he snapped. "Am I a Seer?" He felt trapped by her will, by the King, by his poverty, by his fate. Kamose and Ahmose had stopped conversing together at his loud tone and were both staring across at him. He wanted to apologize but instead swung away and started for the house.

"Where are you going?" she called after him, unperturbed.

"I want to march in three days' time," he shot back without slackening his pace. "There is much to do. Uni!" His steward fell in behind him. At Tetisheri's impatient jerk of the hand Mersu went to her, but after that one gesture she stood still, frowning. The skiff nudged the watersteps and Kamose and Ahmose gathered their weapons and clambered aboard. Tetisheri came to herself at the shouts of the helmsman and Ahmose's lighthearted reply. The sun's new rays were already dimpling the sluggish water.

"I am going back to bed," she said. "Mersu, bring me beer at noon."

Seqenenra spent the next two days conferring with Hor-Aha and checking every detail of his pitifully small army. Of the three thousand three hundred soldiers, only three hundred could be said to be fit to function as Shock Troops, those who entered the field first and took the brunt of a chariot charge, and of those a mere hundred had the advantage of the Setiu's composite bows. Their construction was time-consuming and although the craftsmen had been working feverishly, no more were ready.

Fifty men, the members of Seqenenra's original bodyguard, were named Braves of the King, but Seqenenra insisted that the precious bows be used by the Shock Troops and not his personal defenders in the field. They would carry the smaller ancient weapons. The ten chariots had been refurbished, but again there had been no time to produce more and certainly no time to teach men to drive them. Horses were in short supply. So was food. Grain, water, onions and dried vegetables were piled in sacks and skins, waiting to be loaded onto donkeys. None of the men would shoulder bronze-tipped spears, bronze axes or bronze clubs. Neither Men nor Hor-Aha could obtain the new metal. But at least Men bartered well and they will all have new shields and tight sandals, Seqenenra thought as he moved from Uni's disapproving face in the office to the baking hard-packed sand of the hidden training ground to a few stolen moments with Aahotep on his couch. And our ancient weapons may serve them better than the unfamiliar heft and weight of bronze. May Amun grant it may be so!

Kamose kept to himself during this time, apparently savouring the precarious security and last peace of the untidy estate. Ahmose wandered the riverbank with his throwing stick, and Si-Amun did not leave Aahmes-nefertari's side. The whole family had prayed that her baby might be born before the men marched away, but the evening of the second day came and she was still moving awkwardly about her apartments, hot and uncomfortable, Si-Amun watching her disconsolately.

Seqenenra knew that his son had diligently prepared to march with Kamose. His steward had packed his clothes. His chief bodyguard had sharpened his spear, restrung and broken in his bow, cleaned his shield, and the chariot he would drive stood ready in its stall.

His travelling Amun shrine lay closed, a box of incense beside it. There was something pitiful in Si-Amun's careful, dumb arrangements in the face of his heartfelt opposition that made Seqenenra's heart ache. He would have liked to tell Si-Amun to stay home, to rule the nomes and run the estate in his absence, but he knew that would only increase the young man's weight of misery. It is one thing to die for something one believes in, Seqenenra thought, but quite another to go to one's death against every dictate of one's ka.

He had tried to talk to Si-Amun, but his son had only confronted him, dark eyes large with rage and unhappiness, and begged him to send the soldiers home. Seqenenra had the impression that Si-Amun wanted to say more, but Si-Amun, on Seqenenra's refusal, had pursed his lips, swung on his heel, and stalked away. If I had known in the beginning that he cared so violently I would have sent him away, Seqenenra thought. He could have gone to Teti perhaps, or even to Apepa's court. His lack of pride in his blood cuts me deeply, but his anguish wounds me even more. I have not been a good father to him, my handsome young heir.

On that last night Seqenenra could not rest. He and Aahotep had made love, exchanging words that were reassuring from long usage as they caressed each other in the dim, stifling room, but an hour after Aahotep had drifted into a deep sleep, Seqenenra lay beside her, eyes pricking with weariness, irritated by the damp sheet that stuck to his limbs and tormented by his racing thoughts. In a few hours the army would muster on the west bank. The chariots would flash in the sun. The blue-crested horses would stamp and chafe at their bits, eager to be gone. Amunmose and his acolytes would come with incense and a white ram to make the sacrifice for good fortune.

Tomorrow I will cease to be Prince Seqenenra Tao, governor of Weset, he said to himself, moving restlessly against Aahotep's soft, relaxed body. I will greet the dawn as King Seqenenra Tao, Son of the Sun, the Mighty Bull of Ma'at, Lord of the Two Lands, the Horus of Gold. A Fledgling no longer. How long will I keep the titles, I wonder? How far will we march before Apepa crooks his little finger and we are scattered like chaff under the winnowing fork? Best not to think of that. Think of the nobles and governors along the Nile who will see us pass and flock to join us. Think of arriving outside Het-Uart in the morning mists of the Delta, ringing the city, taking the Double Crown from Apepa's barbaric head, the Crook and Flail from his filthy hands . . .

It was no use. Behind the images of success with which he tried to lull himself to sleep was the fear, a black pulse beating like a muffled oar on the lightless waters of the Underworld. He sat up, felt for his sandals, and wrapped his discarded kilt around his waist. On impulse he crept to Aahotep's side of the couch, and bending, he kissed her temple then her cheek. She groaned a little and opened her eyes. "Seqenenra," she murmured. "Can't you sleep? Shall I go to my own quarters so you can have the couch to yourself?"

"No," he whispered back. "I think I will walk a little, and pray. I love you, Aahotep." Wide awake now, she heard the loneliness in his voice. Reaching up, she drew him close and kissed him on the mouth.

"If I could fight beside you I would," she said. "Come home safely, my lord." Gently he pushed her back onto the pillows.

"Go back to sleep," he replied.

The passage was dark. Two of the torches had gone out and

only one sputtered beside Uni's door, open in case his master called him in the night. Seqenenra heard him mutter as he passed. No soldier stood on guard where the corridor branched. All men were sleeping across the river. Seqenenra hesitated, looking along each untenanted, drowsy arm, then turned towards the garden and the crumbled cleft in the wall through which he could clamber and so come to the old palace. He slipped past the door to Mersu's room. His mother's steward had lodgings close to the way to the women's quarters so that Isis could rouse him if Tetisheri needed him. The door was ajar. Glancing in, Seqenenra saw a hump on the couch. It was hard to imagine the stately and silent Mersu with limbs disordered in sleep. Seqenenra smiled and went on.

The night was hushed, hot and still. As he padded across the garden, skirting the black square that was the pool and ducking in under the dry trees, he spared a glance for the sky. The moon was already setting, a stark white sliver in a spangle of stars whose sharp brilliance held his breath for a moment. He paused, whispering a prayer to Thoth, god of the moon and its soul, before stepping carefully over the almost invisible rubble that had tumbled from the wall of the palace and squeezing through the hole.

The palace loomed above him, a jumble of sharp angles high against the velvet sky. He was not intimidated. Many feared the night because of the dead, but here Seqenenra felt only the welcome of ages gone, time peopled by his own flesh and blood. He had a right to be walking across the churned courtyard and plunging into the shadowed great reception hall. He crossed it swiftly, moving more by instinct than by the faint grey light filtering down from the clerestory windows. In the audience room he did not look towards the throne dais. I will rebuild this place, he thought as he passed on. I will bring the Holy Throne from Het-Uart and place it here.

At the foot of the stairs leading to the roof of the women's quarters he suddenly stopped, listening. It seemed to him that he had heard a sound behind him. "'Is anyone there?" he called quietly, but the darkness was undisturbed. "Osiris Mentuhotep neb-hapet-Ra, if it is the flutter of your ba-wings I hear, please bless me and protect me, I beg," he called again, but if the bird with Mentuhotep's head had left his tomb and was exploring the ancient King's derelict home, it did not show itself. Still, Seqenenra was comforted. He mounted the stairs quickly and came out on the roof.

As he folded onto the still-warm brick, he felt his tension flow away. He had imagined that to come here would be to order his thoughts, but in the end there were no thoughts to order. Only a dreaming reverie that calmed and raised his spirits. His house was in darkness but for one pale light in the women's quarters that he knew was Aahmes-nefertari, unable to rest. A night bird sang briefly and harshly. Down by the river he caught the whicker and shuffle of the tethered horses, and the water itself drifted on towards the north, in the direction he himself would soon go, faint moonlight greying its surface. As usual, he turned for a moment towards the desert, but the horizon was indistinct. I talked to Tani today but not Aahmes-nefertari, he thought. I meant to go to her, my quiet one, but I was afraid that my farewells would only upset her further. Better a brief embrace in tomorrow's chaos. His eyes were drawn back to the faint glow of her lamp and he began his prayers to Amun.

He prayed for bravery in battle, for a public vindication of his claim as Amun's Incarnation, for the safety of his sons. He was just beginning the thanksgiving when again he fancied that he heard a noise behind him, this time the rattle of a piece of dislodged brick on the stairs. The words died on his lips. A sudden foreboding swept over him, prickling his scalp and running down his spine, and the dread of a terrible certainty seized him even as he swung round and began to scramble clumsily to his feet. He did not complete the movement. There was a rushing shadow between himself and the black stairwell, the dull glint of waning moonlight on the blade of an axe, and a blow so swift and stunning that he did not have the time to raise his arms in defence or to cry out.

The sun had already risen above the eastern horizon, dispelling the strange grey shadows of dawn, when Seqenenra's body servant knocked on Uni's door. It was customary for the Prince to be woken, bathed and dressed before the steward was summoned to accompany his master to Amun's ablutions, and Seqenenra had left instructions that he was to be roused a little earlier than usual on this morning. The body servant, bowing his way into the Prince's bedchamber before dawn, had found only Aahotep breathing quietly, lost in unconsciousness. Waking her timorously he had enquired whether the Prince had already gone to the bath house. Aahotep muttered that she did not know, and went back to sleep.

The servant accordingly searched the bath house, and thinking that the Prince might even now be enjoying an early breakfast, he hurried to the reception hall. Kamose and Si-Amun were eating fresh black bread and dried grapes, standing silently while they were served. Tetisheri was there also, the remains of her meal before her, already painted and wigged in order to face the army's farewell. The servant questioned them nervously. His duties never extended beyond the chores of the bedchamber. But they answered him absently. Having wandered throughout the house, he went to Seqenenra's steward.

Uni was already up, kilted, fed, and waiting for the Prince's summons. Seqenenra had given him instructions for the running of the house in his absence and they had discussed what Uni, together with Mersu, might do if the King's armies came, but there were always last-minute matters to be aired even when the family made short trips, and Uni had a scribe squatting in the passage outside to accompany him and the Prince to the temple and take notes if necessary on the way.

"Have you looked in the women's quarters?" Uni asked after hearing the servant's complaint. "The Prince was intending to visit the Princess Aahmes-nefertari for a moment." The man nodded. "Well, what about the kennels? You know how the Prince loves his animals." The servant spread his hands.

"I have looked everywhere, Master." Uni considered. Perhaps the Prince had gone to the temple early and alone on this fateful day. Perhaps Hor-Aha had called for him with some military problem. Uni dismissed the servant.

"Send Isis to the Princess if she is not yet up," he ordered, "and then you can take the linen to the wash house and begin the cleaning. Do not bother to put fresh linen on the Prince's couch." The man hurried out and Uni followed him more slowly.

As soon as he reached the end of the passage, he saw how high the sun already was. A din of men shouting, horses neighing and donkeys screaming reached him from the opposite river bank where the army was beginning to rank for the coming march. As Uni stepped from the portico down into the garden, Kamose and his brother hurried by, bows slung over their shoulders and quivers bouncing against their backs.

In the garden Aahmes-nefertari turned at the steward's approach. She was swathed in wafting linen to modestly hide her pregnancy but she had tied a white ribbon around her sleekly brushed hair and her eyes had been kohled. "Uni, have you seen my father?" she asked. "He promised to meet me here before we all went to the river to say goodbye. Has something detained him?" Uni bowed.

"I do not know, Princess," he replied, "but I will find him. You should not stand here in the sun. Send Raa for a mat and a canopy." Aahmes-nefertari spoke to her companion and as she did so Uni's eyes found the cleft in the wall and the palace beyond, its walls now warm beige in the morning light. He smiled sourly and walked towards it. Of course. Where else would the Prince go to snatch a few minutes of peace before the day's events claimed him? But he should have kept watch on the sun, Uni thought, annoyed, as he strode across the empty courtyard, now full of blinding light that made him squint. By now he should have completed his duties in the temple, said goodbye to his family, and be gone. It is not like him to keep the soldiers waiting under this sun.

Uni did not like the old palace. As he walked into the cooler dimness he wished that he had a charm hanging between his shoulder blades. He touched his amulet, crossed the audience chamber as Seqenenra had done, and turned towards the stairs he knew his master favoured. A sudden flurry above him and a thin piping made him shrink against the wall, his face distorted with disgust. Bats. It would be necessary to speak to the peasant detailed to drive the beasts into the open each morning in case the Prince needed to mount these steps.

Uni pressed on and up, coming at last to the chipped and broken doorway. Heat beat at him as he emerged blinking, and he stood for a moment until his eyes had adjusted. "Prince, are you here?" he called politely. There was no answer, but answer was not needed. Uni saw his master almost immediately.

Seqenenra was lying face down in the dust and blown sand, his cheek against a chunk of brick, his arms invisible beneath him. His splayed legs were in full sunlight and the edge of his kilt stirred in the erratic puffs of breeze. Uni felt his heart stop, then lurch in his chest. Scrambling forward he touched Seqenenra hesitantly, and it was then that he saw the smashed skull, the brown, dried stain of blood pasted across the grey face. "Ah, gods, gods," he whispered.

Straightening, he looked around desperately for help. Soldiers from the eastern barracks were milling under the trees by the river, a confused mass of brown limbs, white kilts and sun-fired spears waiting to embark for the west bank. He could not call that far. No one would hear him. Then he caught a flicker of movement passing the cleft in the wall surrounding the garden. "Here!" he shouted, but his voice was a croak. He took a deep breath. "Here! Up here!" He continued to shout. Presently a figure appeared, leaning through the gap and looking up, shading his eyes with one hand. It was one of the gardeners. "Run as fast as you can and bring servants and a litter!" he ordered. "When they are on their way, find the Princes Si-Amun and Kamose. I saw them going towards the river. Send the physician to the Prince's bedchamber immediately. Immediately! Run!" The man looked bewildered, but at Uni's hysterical tone he disappeared.

Uni crouched by the body. There was nothing more he could do until the litter arrived. Hesitantly he ran his fingers across Seqenenra's shoulder. The skin was harshly dry and cold. *Is he dead?* Uni thought, sudden nausea making him pant. He could see no more than part of the Prince's face, but one eye was glazed under a lid that was only half-closed. The sun was rapidly dispersing the shade the Prince lay under. Uni removed his kilt and laid it over the exposed flesh. As he did so, he realized for the first time that one does not tear open one's skull by tripping and falling, nor can one fall up steps. Someone had crept up behind the Prince and done this terrible thing.

"Uni!" a voice shouted. He looked down. Aahmes-nefertari was leaning through the gap. "What is happening up there? What are you doing?" He knew that he must persuade her to go into the house, that she must not see the thing lying behind him, but something about his stance must have alerted her.

Before he could remonstrate, she was forcing her distended body through into the courtyard.

"Princess, no!" he shouted. "I will talk to you in a moment! Please return to the house!" But she ignored him. After her, Uni saw the litter bearers come hurrying. He went down to meet them.

He could not stay at the foot of the stairs with a pale and anxious Aahmes-nefertari. He left her and returned to the roof to supervise the Prince's transference to the litter as gently as possible, sensing from the glances of the men that they considered such care pointless. Seqenenra was dead. They were probably right. He ushered them back down the stairs, acutely conscious of the Princess's upturned face at the foot, and he was powerless to prevent her from drawing close as the litter reached the ground. She bent over her father, puzzlement evident in her gestures, then the full significance of what she saw struck her. She screamed once, swayed with one hand pushed into her cheek, and Uni took her shoulders and forced her gently onto a step. "Stay here, Princess," he said. "I will send you Raa." She wrapped her arms around her protruding abdomen, looking up at him with huge, frightened eyes.

"Is he . . . is he dead?" she managed.

"I do not know. Stay here." He bowed without being aware of the obeisance, an unconscious act of long habit, and ran after the bearers.

For fear of jolting him, they carried Seqenenra out through the huge, gateless aperture at the end of the courtyard that had once been hung with copper and had seen the resplendent passing of kings and nobles. Uni, watching the limp form anxiously, saw not the slightest evidence of life. The eyes were partly open but dull. Dried blood had oozed from between the slack jaws and dribbled down the chin to dry in the hollow of the neck. The scalp was a mess of crinkled skin. Uni was beginning to suffer from the effects of the shock he had sustained. His legs were shaking and his head swam. He was very glad to see Kamose and Tetisheri hurrying along the passage towards the bedchamber at the moment the litter turned from the hallway. The physician was already waiting within. While the servants lifted Seqenenra onto the couch, Kamose gripped the steward's arm. "Speak to me!" he grated.

"No one could find the Prince," Uni explained, beginning to shiver, "but I thought that he might be in his favourite spot so I sought him there. He was lying on the roof of the women's quarters," he pointed into the room, "like that."

Kamose indicated the stool by the door. "Sit," he ordered. "You look ill. When you feel recovered, send a servant to Si-Amun and Hor-Aha. Si-Amun is on the west bank hitching horses to the chariots. He must come at once. Hor-Aha is to ferry the troops back across the river. They may rest today, and have him give them plenty of wine. Then command Mersu to wait upon me. You are excused for the day, Uni. You have done well."

Uni looked curiously into the hard, set face. Kamose's lips were a thin line, his nostrils pinched, his eyes completely black. The steward had known the Prince since the time of his birth. He had been a quiet baby, a brooding youth and a self-contained, self-controlled young man. He could talk lightly and easily of many things, and his slow smile had warmed the heart of many a guest. Uni suspected that he was deep, that Kamose's true life was lived far beneath the tranquil, graceful gait and tolerant conversation. Now he knew instinctively that Kamose was in the grip of a vast rage. The young Prince's words had the sharp edge of complete authority. Uni did as he was told.

In the bedchamber there was a tense, unbelieving silence broken only by the physician's soft movements. Kamose and Tetisheri stood rigidly side by side. Aahotep had pushed past

Kamose while he spoke to Uni and was kneeling by the head of
the couch, tears running down her freshly painted cheeks, but
she was obviously in command of herself. For a long time they
all watched the physician make his examination, their eyes
moving with his hands as though mesmerized, then Aahotep
stirred. "Is he alive?" she asked. The man checked his motions
and regarded her with surprise.

"Of course he is alive, Princess, or I would not be doing this.
I would have called in a sem-priest. See for yourself." He drew
a small copper mirror from its wooden case and held it close
to Seqenenra's mouth. It misted with a thin film of conden-
sation.

"Ah, Seqenenra," Aahotep breathed. "Who has done this to
you?" At the question the others loosened. Tetisheri stalked to
the couch.

"What is the extent of my son's injury?" she barked. The
physician put his mirror away.

"When he is washed, Princess, you will see that, apart from a
graze on his cheek where he fell against something sharp, his
only wound is this dreadful blow to the skull. The axe penetrated so far that the contents of the pan are exposed."

"Axe?" Kamose exclaimed tersely. "He was attacked with an
axe? How do you know?"

"I can tell by the shape of the wound," the physician
answered. "I can also tell you that the axe was made of bronze.
One of our own axes would not have been able to penetrate so
cleanly. It would have been too soft, and the force of the blow
would have resulted in many splinters of bone embedded in the
brain. There are splinters which I shall have to remove, but not
many." He would have gone on, but there was a commotion at
the door and Tani's voice rose above the remonstrations of
Mersu.

"Father! What is it, what is going on? Let me pass please,

Mersu!" Aahotep rose quickly. Her hands, as she pressed them against the sheet, were trembling.

"Amun forgive me, I had forgotten about Tani," she said, and before the harassed Mersu yielded she was across the room and out the door. Kamose turned back to the physician.

"Will he die? What hope is there?" The physician raised his eyebrows and his shoulders.

"I can shave his head, wash him, and remove the splinters, but I cannot return him to consciousness. I suggest that a priest be present to sing spells of healing."

"You believe that he will die."

"Yes," the physician said simply.

They were interrupted by Si-Amun who came running into the room, his blue linen helmet still framing his face, a whip coiled in one hand. "What is happening?" he demanded. "Hor-Aha has been told to take the troops back over the river and the servants are falling over each other in the house like beheaded geese!" For answer Kamose stepped aside. Seqenenra lay on his stomach and his hideous wound was exposed to Si-Amun's view as the young man moved closer. For a moment there was silence, then Si-Amun swayed. Kamose put out a hand to steady him. "What is it?" Si-Amun croaked. Kamose let him go.

"Someone tried to murder him with an axe," he said grimly. "And not just any axe. It was a Setiu weapon."

"No! "

Kamose looked curiously at his brother. Si-Amun's face had lost all its colour and Kamose was afraid he would faint. Something in Si-Amun's tone as he had shouted had made Kamose's hackles rise.

"Calm yourself, brother," he said quickly. "Father lives. For how long we cannot say, but . . ." He got no further. Si-Amun had left the room.

But Seqenenra did not die. All that day the physician worked on his flaccid body, washing him, shaving away his thick black curls, removing the flaps of scalp that had been torn so grievously and picking out the tiny pieces of bone embedded in the thick membrane that protected Seqenenra's brain. Seqenenra did not so much as sigh. His breathing remained shallow and spasmodic. Kamose stayed with him for many hours, unmoved by the physician's grisly ministrations, but eventually he was forced to go with Hor-Aha, who was trying to appease the disgruntled soldiers. The chariots were returned to the stalls. The horses were turned out onto the sparse, brittle grass beside the barracks of the family's bodyguard. "What do you want me to do with the men?" Hor-Aha, asked Kamose when they were at last on their way, tired, filthy and disheartened, to Seqenenra's office. "Shall I send them home?"

"No," Kamose replied adamantly. "Not yet. We have victualled them at great inconvenience to ourselves for many weeks and we will go on doing so. I have much to consider, Hor-Aha, and until I have reached a proper decision you can go on drilling them with mock battles and the like. We have the time to make more bows at least." Hor-Aha ventured a small grin, but quickly sobered.

"The Prince is dying, is he not?" he said, turning his dark face to Kamose. "If he dies, what will you do?" Kamose knew what the General was asking. He answered vehemently.

"My father will not die. Our physician is a fine one. The High Priest himself is saying the spells. The couch is surrounded by powerful amulets."

"But if he does?" Hor-Aha pressed. Kamose walked on, not looking at the tall Medjay. "Then someone will pay," he promised grimly.

Si-Amun had left Seqenenra, his thoughts in turmoil, and was running panting through the house, when Raa met him.

"Your pardon, Prince," the woman said, "but your wife has gone into labour, and she is most distressed. Can you come?" Si-Amun, stunned and confused as he was, had not hesitated. Without bothering to reply to Raa, he had swerved towards the women's quarters. One of the midwives from Weset had been summoned but had not yet arrived.

Aahmes-nefertari was pacing beside the couch, both hands across her abdomen, weeping. One of the family's priests was lighting incense in a long holder. Kares, Aahmes-nefertari's steward, waited just inside the door for any orders. When Si-Amun's breath had slowed, he went to his wife and kissed her. "Is the pain bad?" he asked, and she turned her tear-stained face to him.

"No, not yet," she sobbed. "It is Father, the way he looked when the litter bearers brought him down, so grey, and that terrible hole in his head. Hold me, Si-Amun!" He put his arms around her and she buried her face in his neck. "He will die," she choked, her voice muffled. "My baby will be born under dreadful omens! I am so afraid!" He comforted her as best he could, while behind them the priest began to chant and the sweet odour of the holy smoke began to envelop them. Its scented haze calmed Aahmes-nefertari. "I have prayed and brought offerings to Taurt every day," she said, her voice stronger. "Surely she will not betray me now. Si-Amun, thank you for coming. Please leave, and send Mother. Is the midwife not here yet?" Her tone had risen, become strident. He took her face between his brown hands, and kissing her wet eyes and her tremulous mouth, bade her have courage. His own voice was none too steady.

"Kares, send after that stupid midwife," he ordered. "The rest of you, stop gaping and make yourselves useful. Music would be soothing and perhaps a board game or two." He spoke sharply, knowing that the uneasiness in the room stemmed from the drama being played out in another part of the house and not wanting its effects to panic his wife. The servants sprang to obey him and he left them.

He could not stay in the house. Shock and anger at the attack on his father was mixed with anxiety over his wife, and in the end he took a skiff and one bodyguard and had himself poled into the reed swamps. There he let out a fishing line and lay back in the boat, eyes on the gently swaying papyrus fronds above his head. He was twenty now and Aahmes-nefertari four years younger. From the time of their childhood, they had been betrothed to each other according to the ancient custom whereby the heir to the throne must marry a fully royal princess, usually his sister, and so keep the blood line pure. He and Aahmes-nefertari had always known that they would marry, in spite of the fact that the males of their line no longer sat on the Horus Throne, and the knowledge had made him protective of her as they grew up together. He loved her, though he had secretly scoffed at his father's insistence on a tradition that no longer had validity. If I am proud with a prince's arrogance, he thought, eyes squinting against a dazzling sky, then Father is doubly so with his dreams of this family's return to godhead in Egypt. Is. Was. Aahmes-nefertari will be all right, but Father...

Groaning, he sat up. There was a tug on his fishing line but he ignored it. He knew he must consider the terrible consequences of his moment of weakness with Teti. Am I responsible? he wondered, no longer able to hold worry about his wife as a shield against his first sight of Seqenenra lying like a sacrificial bull, impotent and near death. If I had not sent that message to Teti, if Teti had not betrayed me to Apepa, would Father even now be marching along the river road towards the north? Surely word of the army would have reached the King in any case! Did Apepa order a murder? Or was Father struck by some frightened servant or soldier?

He knew he was simply pushing words around in his mind while all the time he was filling with guilt and self-hatred. It is as though I myself wielded that cursed axe, he thought miserably. I, Si-Amun, Prince of Weset. But who struck the actual blow? Mersu? Mersu with his Setiu ancestors, his kinship with Teti's Chief Steward? Now that I consider it, he was not very curious about the scroll I asked him to send, almost as though he were expecting me to approach him. I send to Teti. Teti sends on to Apepa. And the King reads, considers, and decides to punish his proud southern subject once and for all? His ka responded with a bleak assent. Dismally Si-Amun drew in his line and gave a strangled command. The skiff began to glide back through the rushes to the bank.

The kitchen staff prepared a scanty evening meal but no one wandered into the hall to eat it. There was no change in Seqenenra's condition. A pall of grimness settled over the house. Aahotep, desperate to be with her husband, encouraged and comforted her daughter. Tani, forgotten by all in the confusion and tragedy of the day, went to her couch early and lay rigid and utterly miserable while Heket told her stories to try and take her mind off her father's state. A desolate silence came with the night, the only area of bustle and noise being the women's quarters.

Si-Amun returned to his rooms and took a dagger from his box. It had been cleaned and honed, ready to lie at his belt on the long chariot ride north. Placing it inside his shirt where it rested cold against his skin he made his way to Mersu's small cell. He did not want to summon the man. Someone in the future might remember that he had done so and wonder why. Reaching the passage and acknowledging the guard's salute, he walked to Mersu's door and pushed it open.

The room was empty. It was furnished sparsely but adequately. Mersu's pallet lay against one wall, a very low table and a stool beside it. Two chests holding the steward's possessions lay side by side against another wall. A lamp stood on the table. Smiling grimly, his heart pounding, Si-Amun closed the door behind him and lowered himself onto the stool. He could have searched the chests, lifted the pallet, but he did not. Folding his arms so that he could feel the lethal comfort of the knife, he leaned back against the wall and waited.

The time for the evening meal came and went but Si-Amun was not hungry for food. His appetite was for absolution, cleansing. He thought of Seqenenra, fighting for his life as Ra's thin light faded from the tiny window high in the wall and the room sank into darkness. Rousing himself, Si-Amun took a spill from the table, went out into the passage, lit it from the torch blazing above the patient soldier, and went back into the room to light the lamp. He considered dismissing the guard but did not do so. Soldiers were expected to ignore the actions of their superiors. The room filled with a warm, steady glow. Si-Amun was about to resume his seat when the door was flung open and Mersu's angry face appeared. Si-Amun stared, bemused. He had never seen the steward with other than a bland expression.

"I saw the light under the door," Mersu began. "How dare you enter my . . ." but then he recognized Si-Amun. Immediately a mask fell across his features and he was once again the well-trained servant. He bowed. "Forgive me, Prince," he murmured. "I thought one of the underlings had been prowling and the guard had somehow failed to challenge him. I am sorry." Si-Amun had swung round to face him, hands at his sides.

"Close the door," he ordered. For a fleeting second he thought he saw fear flicker over the steward's face but it could have been a waver of the lamplight. Mersu silently obeyed. "Now, Mersu," Si-Amun went on calmly though his stomach knotted with tension. "Tell me where you were last night." Mersu inclined his head.

"I suppose the family is questioning everyone," he observed. "Such a terrible thing has not happened in all the time I have been serving the Lady." He sighed. "To answer you, Prince, I waited upon the Princess until she closed her doors. I then went to the kitchens and ate with Uni. I spent about an hour with him. As the night was so hot, I persuaded him to swim with me, and I came back to my cell at about midnight, just before the temple horns blew. The swimming had tired me. I fell asleep immediately. But I left my door open," he added. "If anyone passed along the passage they would have seen me on my pallet."

His expression had not changed. It registered nothing more than deference as he spoke, and his eyes were clear. Yet the words are too smooth, Si-Amun thought as he listened. I am quite sure that Mersu did indeed eat and swim with Uni and go to bed shortly thereafter, but I am equally sure that he did not stay there. Oh gods, if I am wrong and I have insulted Grandmother's favourite she will never forgive me. "Mersu, do you remember the scroll I gave you to deliver to Teti's steward?" he asked. Mersu nodded. "You were not at all surprised at my strange request. Why?" Mersu looked startled. He spread his hands.

"I barely considered the command," he answered. "What business was it of mine anyway, Prince? You wished to communicate with your mother's cousin. That was all." I want to believe you, Si-Amun thought in the tiny silence that fell between them.

"I do not think so," he said slowly, and Mersu's hand dropped and found the sleeves of his cloak. "I think that Teti or his steward told you to expect such a request from me. I think you are a spy for Apepa in this household." Mersu's eyes grew round with shock.

"Prince, I am deeply affronted," he said harshly. "I have served the Princess Tetisheri for thirty years and she has never once complained of my care. My loyalty to the House of Tao has never been questioned before!" Si-Amun took a step towards him.

"Perhaps that is because there has never been a need to question your loyalty until now, when Father decided to place a final breach between himself and the King," he spat back. "Your soul is Setiu, Mersu." Mersu did not reply. His whole stance conveyed his disappointment and mortification. Si-Amun knew that he had already done irreparable harm to the relationship between Mersu and the family. He swallowed. "Turn out your chests," he ordered.

Anyone other than a servant would have demanded to know why, but Mersu, the consummate steward, went immediately to his chests, lifted the lids, and began to pull out the contents, piling them on the floor. Si-Amun went and stood behind him. There were six or seven long pleated steward's gowns, a razor, a spare pair of sandals, a plain wooden cosmetic box which, when Si-Amun gestured, revealed a pot of scented oil and a pot of kohl, and several wigs. The other chest contained a pretty carved box in which Mersu kept the gold he had saved, several amulets, a small statue of Amun, another of Sutekh, and assorted bracelets and necklaces, all of copper but finely decorated with carnelian and turquoise. Tetisheri had been generous to her servant.

Si-Amun felt his heart sink. Bending, he scoured the chests, fingered the belongings, and at last nodded curtly. Mersu began to put the things away. There was no scroll here, no message for Mersu. But then, if I were Mersu, Si-Amun thought, and I had received an order to murder my lord, I would certainly not leave the papyrus lying about. I would burn it immediately. Despair seized him. I know Mersu is guilty but I cannot prove it, and now the wretched man will hold a grudge against me forever.

Mersu had risen and was waiting politely, but behind the downcast eyes Si-Amun sensed relief. Perhaps even triumph? Then another thought struck Si-Amun. What if the message was not written on papyrus? Apepa is no fool. He would not send an expensive scroll to an underling for fear of detection. Surely he would send words scratched on a piece of broken pottery, like the bits used by students or scribes who were learning their craft. Pots were broken in large households all the time. A steward holding a bit of such a pot would be remarked by no one.

He began to pace the floor, scuffing the dirt with his feet. The floors of the servants' cells were not tiled but made of smooth mud bricks whose surfaces became gritty and deposited a fine film of dry soil underfoot. He sensed Mersu become alert as he moved, but his sandals did not catch on anything. Baffled, he stared at the lamp, pondering. Mersu said nothing.

Then all at once, Si-Amun knew. With a grunt he strode to the lamp, pushed the burning wick aside as it floated in the warm oil, and retrieved a small piece of red pottery. He heard Mersu exhale, a long sigh of defeat. Si-Amun wiped the piece clean on his kilt, tensing for Mersu's escape, but the steward merely stood with hands still buried in his sleeves. The lamp spat and the shadows flickered as the wick settled once more. Si-Amun held the message to the light. "Kill the traitor," it said. It was signed "Itju," above a crude depiction of Sutekh. Itju was the King's Chief Scribe. Si-Amun stared at Mersu, and Mersu stared back. "You should have smashed this as soon as you received it," Si-Amun whispered at last. "Then nothing could have been proved against you." Mersu smiled faintly.

"I did not have the time," he said. "I tried. If you had not been here tonight, I would have done so. I received it yesterday from a herald passing on his way to the second cataract. Your grandmother kept me busy all day, and if I had refused to eat and swim with Uni as I do every evening, he would have been suspicious. I hid it in the kitchen, in a pile of refuse. I should have left it there. I could not go back for it until after I had struck the Prince, and then it was too late. There was consternation, errands of panic to run . . ." He shrugged. "Amun has punished me for my perfidy." He swallowed. "Believe me, Prince Si-Amun, I love your father and this family. Weset is my home. But my duty lay with the King and his orders must be obeyed."

Si-Amun listened in horror. The last words might have been his own.

"The King used me," he said, still whispering. Mersu inclined his head.

"Yet is the King not entitled to use any of us, his subjects?" he replied. To that Si-Amun could find no answer. Seeing him hesitate Mersu came forward eagerly. "I know that you share my loyalty to the Horus Throne in Het-Uart," he said urgently. "What I did was dreadful, Prince, but necessary. I should not be blamed for it. Say nothing, I beg!"

"Say nothing?" Si-Amun laughed harshly. "Amun! You try to murder my father and then ask me to say nothing? I will take you at once to Kamose and your mistress and you will be tried and executed!"

"I think not," Mersu said softly, "for if you try, I will tell your brother how you betrayed your father's plans to Apepa. You will be forced to kill yourself as a matter of family honour." Si-Amun's face flushed red. He clenched his teeth.

"You filthy worm!" he ground out. Mersu was unmoved.

"I am sorry, Prince, but it is the truth. I will keep your secret, if you will keep mine."

"It is not the same!"

"Yes," Mersu said firmly. "It is."

I should kill him now, Si-Amun thought, feeling the dagger

move against his waist. I can tell Kamose that I discovered the truth and struck in grief and rage. But Kamose will ask me how I knew to search Mersu's cell. A sweat of fear and claustrophobia drenched him suddenly. I am encircled, he thought desperately. I have no choice any more. Amun forgive me! I deserve to die too. He wanted to wrench out the dagger and push it through the steward's lightly breathing chest, but he did not have the courage to kill the man who had bent over his basket when he was a baby, who had fed him by hand and been there to catch him when he took his first unsteady steps. Nor could he face the sure aftermath of such an act.

"But I swear by Amun, by Mut and Montu," he said aloud, "that if you attempt to complete your terrible deed, I will reveal all both you and I have done. I hate you, Mersu. Hate you!" He stumbled into the passage, and as he ran blindly in the direction of his apartments, it came to him that it was not Mersu he hated. It was Apepa, and himself.

Chapter SIX

TETISHERI ADVANCED into Seqenenra's office where Kamose sat sprawled in a chair, his head propped on one elbow, gazing into the room. He was alone. One lamp on the desk shed a pool of light over the litter of scrolls and the still-full wine jug and empty cup Kamose had ordered and then forgotten. He looked up wearily as his grandmother greeted him, and rose to pull a stool forward. He lowered himself onto it, and Tetisheri slumped onto the chair. She looked drawn, with dark pouches under her eyes, and the lines around her pale mouth were accented by the slowly shifting shadows. "Is there any change?" Kamose asked. Tetisheri shook her head. One tendril of grey hair had fallen on her breast and she pulled at it absently.

"None at all, but the physician said that if he survives another day, he has a good chance of living. I did not dare ask what permanent damage such a wound could cause. I sent Amunmose back to his cell in the temple. He needed rest. The physician has a pallet on the floor in Seqenenra's room and, of course, Uni is hovering. There is nothing more I can do." Kamose knew how frustrating it was for her to admit that no word or action of hers could alter what was to be.

"And what of my sister?"

Tetisheri made an effort to smile.

"She is strong. She will give birth with no more trouble than a cow dropping a calf. I pray that the birth will not suck life from Seqenenra." Her freckled arm fell on the desk. "You must begin to question the servants and the members of the bodyguard, Kamose," she said harshly. "What were they all doing last night? Early this morning? What of the soldiers? Did any of them have bronze axes? Is this the work of a stranger, an assassin from the Delta sent by the One to deal quickly and quietly with a rebellious subject?" She smiled coldly. "An assassination would be much cheaper and cause less turmoil in Egypt than the need to dispatch a division from Het-Uart to defeat us."

"I have been thinking about it," Kamose answered. "If an assassin smote him, then the man will be long gone. Was he watching Father? Is that how he knew where Father was? And if not, then we have a spy in our midst who is full of hatred for us. Did an order come from the King to someone we know, someone under our very noses?" He moved restlessly on the stool and sighed. "I will have the staff questioned and I will tell Hor-Aha to suborn one of his trusted men to move among the soldiers, picking up any gossip there may be. Soldiers love gossip and often know things we could never surmise. Otherwise . . ." He ran limp fingers through his dusty hair. "We have very little hope of running a suspect to ground. Just as well for him. I would love to dash out his brains, and I would sleep the sleep of the justified afterwards."

"It is the helplessness I cannot bear," Tetisheri said. "That, and the humiliation of our failure to protect one of our own or to find his attacker. Our pride as well as the one we love has suffered a crippling blow." She stopped speaking as soon as her voice began to betray her, paused, poured a little wine that she did not even sip, then she resumed. "Will you take the army north in your father's stead, Prince?" Kamose turned a level gaze upon her.

"No," he replied firmly. "It would be stupid to do so until we know whether or not the King ordered Father's death. If not, our chances remain as they were." He grinned sardonically. "Almost nothing. If so, then this is a warning not to proceed any further. I will continue to support the soldiers and I will wait. I will also question most closely all members of our staff with Setiu ancestors, Uni and Mersu among them."

"Mersu has been with us for many years, as has Uni. You will insult them both very deeply."

"What do I care for their feelings? Someone dared to lay violent hands on a god, and someone will pay." His words, spoken with a firm steadiness, were striking.

"If he dies," Tetisheri said smoothly, "Si-Amun will be a god." He did not answer. He merely rose and trimmed the wick of the lamp as it began to flicker. "We must buy time," she went on after a while. "I suggest that you dictate a letter to Apepa. Tell him that your father was struck by falling rocks as he hunted near the cliffs in the desert. Tell him that Seqenenra was engaged in carrying out the directives of Apepa's scroll and was thus too busy to answer. Perhaps add that he wanted to surprise and please the King by not answering until the work was well underway." Kamose was staring into the lamp's flame.

"Very good, Grandmother," he said. "I will add that Father found it necessary to increase the numbers of the bodyguard because of desert marauders temporarily harassing the villages of the nomes. It happens every few years, as Apepa knows. I will also tell him that many men have been conscripted to begin work on the temple to Set and the One should be pleased at his faithful governor's eagerness to honour the god."

Tetisheri nodded. "That will throw him into doubt if we do have a spy here in the house. He will wonder at the accuracy of the man's reports and thus we may breathe freely for a little while."

"Or a woman's reports," Kamose cut in. "The spy may be a woman. Gods! It could be anyone. I will dictate the letter tomorrow." Neither commented on the growing certainty they shared, based on nothing but their instincts, that Seqenenra's attacker had been a spy in the household.

As they remained in silence together, Tetisheri slumped in the chair and Kamose moodily staring into the lamp, they were aware that the amicability they had always shared was growing into a warm complicity. Kamose was musing on the knowledge, accepted until now without question, that under her imperious-ness and his retiring, sometimes cool, aloofness, they were very alike. He had always enjoyed her company. She made no demands on him. If he did not choose to see her for days, she was not offended. Her frankness refreshed him, mirroring the uncompromising authority of mind he seldom showed out-wardly, and she was not in the least discomfited by his long silences. With a jolt he realized that although Si-Amun was the head of the household now, and temporarily the governor of Weset, he, Kamose, would have to shoulder the practicalities of the job. At least, he thought fervently, I hope the task will be only temporary. Si-Amun seems to be sunk in some dark world of his own these days. Ahmose will be of no help to me. He will cheerfully agree with everything I propose and then go back to his archery, his chariot and his dogs. Mother is popular and a careful thinker, but concern for Father will render her useless and colour all her advice. Tani is, well, Tani. But you . . . He went to Tetisheri and helped her to her feet. "You are definitely not beautiful Little-Teti tonight," he said gently. "Go to bed, Grandmother." He kissed the soft, loose parchment of her face and ushered her out the door.

He was about to follow her, his vision blurred and his limbs leaden with weariness, when a servant appeared out of the darkness of the passage, flushed and excited. He bowed. "Your pardon, Prince, I know it is late," he said when Kamose had demanded his business. "But I thought you would want to know. The Nile markers have registered a small rise in the level of the river. Isis is crying. The Inundation has begun."

The following evening at sunset Aahmes-nefertari gave birth to a boy, squatting flushed and exhausted by the couch. Murmurs of congratulations and approval ran through the equally tired women, and a servant was dispatched to summon her husband and spread the good news. Raa helped the girl onto the couch where she relaxed, drank thirstily, and submitted meekly to a washing. The baby, now clean and wrapped in new linen, was placed carefully beside her, and she propped herself on one elbow and gazed down on it with foreboding. It had not cried much when the midwife had slapped it gently. It had uttered a weak, mewling sound like a kitten and then fallen silent. Aahmes-nefertari noted the greyness of its skin and the way its tiny limbs remained limp. When Si-Amun shouldered his way to her side, she began to cry tears of fatigue. "I am sorry, dearest brother," she choked. "I can take no joy in this son, for Father cannot see him or hold him. Forgive me." Si-Amun soothed her, his eyes on his child, his heart sinking. The boy did not look as a newborn should look, red and angry. His wife had been right. The omens for this birth were all bad.

"Sleep now," he advised, stroking the damp hair from her forehead and kissing her. "I am proud of you and my son. Tomorrow I will consult the astrologers about a suitable name for him, but for now you must rest and grow strong again."

"Father?" she asked drowsily. He took her hands and put them under the sheet, drawing it to her chin.

"There is no change," he told her. "The river is rising,

Aahmes-nefertari. Soon the heat will abate. Do not worry." By
the time he had reached the door she was asleep.

News of the birth stirred Weset into traditional rejoicing,
but it was hollow and soon over. Under ordinary circumstances
their response would have been genuine, but now anxiety over
their Prince and fears for themselves because of their commitment to his revolt pushed away any happiness for Si-Amun and
his sister-wife. The mayor came with small gifts and prepared
speeches and that was all. Si-Amun could not blame them.

The astrologers had advised that the boy be called Si-Amun.
He had been born on a day with unlucky auspices, therefore
their choice was conservative and reflected caution. Aahmes-
nefertari, already bouncing back to vigour, approved. But little
Si-Amun did not seem much interested in life. He lay in whatever position he was placed, cried with great effort, and could
not keep down his milk. Si-Amun knew his son was going to
die. Somehow the evil that he had helped to conjure infected
the house and had penetrated Aahmes-nefertari's womb to
destroy his firstborn. It had destroyed something within himself
also, something too fragile to survive the blows. If his wife had
given birth before the attack on Seqenenra, he would have
treated the matter with cheerful pride and gone back to his military exercises, wrestling and boating. But now he spent many
hours sitting with Aahmes-nefertari as she healed, holding the
baby in silence.

On the day that Seqenenra opened his eyes for the first time
since the attack, little Si-Amun died. It was shortly after noon.
Si-Amun, bending over the reed cot, saw that the baby lay on
his back with one loosely clenched fist above the sheet as the
wet nurse had put him down. His eyes were open but dull, his
lips slack. Si-Amun did not cry out. He put one hesitant finger
against his son's temple. There was no pulse and the skin was
cold. "Why are you taking so long?" Aahmes-nefertari called

from the other room. "Is there something wrong?" Si-Amun came to her and at the sight of his face she knew. Dropping the red linen belt she had been sewing tassels onto, she rose, both hands going to her mouth. Then she gripped the neck of her sheath and tore it to the waist, her first gesture of mourning. "One sem-priest will be able to carry him in one hand," she said tonelessly. "In one hand. Send for him at once."

One hour later Aahotep sat beside her husband, watching the physician and his assistant bathe the inert body. Two weeks had gone by since he had been laid on his couch. His heart still beat. His breathing had settled to an even rise and fall of the chest. He had lost much weight. His stomach was sunken, his legs were losing their definition, and his cheekbones protruded as though they would break through the skin of his face. Uni had fed him milk and bull's blood mixed with honey, forcing open the jaws every day and placing the liquid at the back of the throat as though he were tending a motherless calf. Seqenenra had swallowed. Once or twice he had groaned. He took water. He had even moved his head sometimes and Aahotep, heart in mouth, had believed several times that he would wake.

But on this day, as the wet cloth moved over his body, he opened his eyes. Aahotep sprang to her feet with a cry. Immediately the physician bent. He straightened again, watching intently. At first Seqenenra's gaze was fixed vacantly on the ceiling but presently it began to wander dazedly. Aahotep saw that his left eyelid had not opened properly, and drooped as though he were squinting. She leaned forward. The eyes slowly focused on her. "Aah . . . Aah . . ." he rasped, deep in his throat. She lifted his hand from the sheet and kissed it, tears welling.

"Yes!" she said. "Oh, Seqenenra, Amun has answered my prayers! Please do not close your eyes again, do not go to sleep!" His mouth worked. Puzzled, then grief-stricken, she noted that the left corner of his mouth dragged downwards while his lips moved, and she shot a glance of terror at the physician.

"Wa ... Wa wa wa," Seqenenra said.

"Water? Water!" Clicking her fingers she summoned the assistant. The physician took the cup, placed a reed in it, and Seqenenra swallowed a little water with difficulty. The small effort had exhausted him. His eyes closed and he said no more. Aahotep looked at the physician.

"In a few hours we must try to wake him again," the man said. "He will live, I think. But, Princess, he is grievously damaged."

Aahotep nodded, ashen. "His eye, his mouth . . . But he knew me, I'm sure."

The physician did not commit himself. He bowed and did not answer.

"I must tell the others," Aahotep said, almost running to the door. Wrenching it open, she sent Uni hurrying to find Kamose and Tetisheri, but he had scarcely gone when Raa ran down the passage towards her. Aahotep noticed for the first time the shrieks and cries coming from the women's quarters, the sounds of ritual mourning. Raa was crying.

"The baby is dead!" she said. "The sem-priest has just taken him away. The Prince Si-Amun held him for a moment. Tani is screaming . . ." Aahotep raised a hand and the woman fell silent. Poor Aahmes-nefertari, Aahotep thought. Oh my poor daughter. And you, Seqenenra, your grandson was born and has died while you wandered in the places of darkness. Was there a link? She shuddered.

"I will go to Tani and we will both come to Aahmes-nefertari," she said. "Keep the women away from here, Raa. I don't want the Prince disturbed." She will have more children, Aahotep thought as she walked to Tani's apartments, but none will have the place in her heart that little Si-Amun had. It will not be the same.

The full seventy days of mourning were held for the baby, and by the time he was carried to the west bank and laid in the tomb Si-Amun was preparing for himself there, Seqenenra was sitting up, taking nourishment, and trying to communicate with those around him. The wound in his head still gaped and Aahotep had ordered that a white linen scarf be tied to hide it. To her dismay the Prince could not use his left arm or move his left leg, but she concealed her horror as best she could from him. If he had a need he would grunt and try to describe it with his right hand, and Aahotep, relying more on the expressions in his dark eyes than on the wavering fingers, became his interpreter. He was not yet strong enough to hold a scribe's brush. It was often agony for her to look into those eyes, to see helplessness, pleading, anger and the constant frustration of not being understood.

Once she had sent for a spray of persea blossom, pleased with herself for believing he had asked for flowers, but he had grabbed the branch and flung it across the room, showering her and the floor and the couch with pink petals. She had risen and begun to brush them away from him but he had slapped her arm, then gripped it. His right eye and the half-closed left one blazed sheer rage at her, but at her shocked glance the rage had faded and he had begun to weep without sound. His hand had crept to her shoulder, pulling her against his chest, and at last she too had broken down and cried, her face buried in persea blooms.

His children had finally been allowed to see him. Kamose, after kissing him, had said nothing, only stood and stared at him expressionlessly. Ahmose had been all jokes and smiles. Aahotep knew that Seqenenra had noted Aahmes-nefertari's new slimness and the fact that she was wearing blue, the colour of mourning. She cursed herself for her carelessness but Seqenenra managed a slow, laborious nod at his daughter and

Aahotep knew that he had absorbed this news calmly. He beckoned Aahmes-nefertari, placed a hand on her stomach, tugged at her blue sheath, then indicated his own wound decorously hidden under the white scarf. They were both suffering, he was saying. They grieved together for all of it.

Tani surprised her mother. She began to come to her father every morning when he was strongest, taking a stool beside him and prattling on about the small incidents that made up her life. Teti and Ramose had sent good wishes for his recovery. Ramose had assured her of his love and support and would come to visit as soon as the river regained its banks and his sailors could struggle upstream. The hippopotamuses were enjoying the deeper water, and one of them had actually given birth. Tani described the new baby with such enthusiasm and vividness that she drew a twisted smile from her father. She also read to him from scrolls she had borrowed from the small library, retelling the stories he had known and loved as a child and had read to her when she was small. Aahotep saw a maturing taking place in the girl. Tani was becoming a strong and selfless young woman.

Through the months of Paophi and Athyr the river continued to rise and then spill over onto the parched land, softening it, flowing with cool fingers into the cracks, loosening and revivifying the dead earth. Small pools in the fields joined, became lakes reflecting blue sky and the march of palms whose drowned roots sucked once more at life. The air became limpid, the breezes did not cut with the fiery knife of Ra, and Khoiak was a month to sit on a roof for hours and contemplate the still, peaceful expanse of submerged fields.

With the slow sinking of the river during Tybi, Seqenenra's strength grew. The physician allowed him to be carried out into the garden and placed on a camp cot under the trees where he could lie and watch the branches, heavy with leaf buds, move against the sky. The garden was full of heady delights at that time of the year. The smell of wet soil mingled with the odours of freshly opened lotus flowers on the pool and the shoots in the vegetable plots. Behek was brought, an inspiration of Ahmose's, and when Seqenenra was lying by the pool, the dog would lie beside him, muzzle resting on his paws or against the Prince's hand, his nose twitching.

Soon Seqenenra was sitting upright against many pillows. Tani piled flowers on his lap and danced for him the steps she was learning in order to take her turn as a priestess of Amun in a few months. But Seqenenra grew restless. At last he was able to take a scribe's brush in his hand, and while Aahotep held the piece of potsherd, scrawled "Kamose. Hor-Aha."

Aahotep exclaimed, "Oh not yet, Seqenenra! I do not think you are strong enough yet. Wait a few days more." He growled, his signal that he was impatient.

"Now," he said. Aahotep rolled her eyes. "Oh, very well. Uni! Fetch Kamose and General Hor-Aha. You need not wave at me like that, Seqenenra. I am going into the house." She kissed him swiftly and swayed towards the shady portico.

Seqenenra kept his eyes on her until the shadow claimed her. He heard her speak sharply to someone, heard her sandals slapping in the hall beyond. The garden was riotous with bird-song, and close by a bee was hovering over a white, waxy bloom. Behek was snorting and running in his sleep and Seqenenra longed to wake him up, imagining that he bent down, rubbed the rough stomach, said "Come on Behek! They are only the devils of nightmare!" but he could not move.

His head ached today. It ached most days with a constant, dull throb. Sometimes it itched, but the physician had warned him not to touch the wound, even through the linen that was changed every day. He did not remember the blow, did not remember going into the old palace, did not even remember the things he had said and done the day before he was attacked. Perhaps it was a merciful forgetting. His life before the blow and his life now were entirely separate. He did not know why he had not been allowed to die there on the roof of the women's quarters. He did not think it was Amun who had spared him. It was Set, cruel wolfish Set who had intervened in a mood of cunning and revenge so that he, Seqenenra, might be punished for his sacrilege.

No. Seqenenra leaned forward to where his left leg was slipping from the cot, and struggled to lift it. Set would never commit an act of such horror on an Egyptian unless someone had deliberately insulted him deeply. Surely his pride revolted against the slow coupling of himself with the Setiu Sutekh. No, Seqenenra thought. Amun has spared me so that I might finish what I began. They tell me that they cannot find my attacker. I am not surprised. The arm of Apepa is longer than I imagined, and it struck, and was withdrawn. I have been warned, and if I lie quiet now, lick my wounds and behave myself, nothing more will happen. Must I admit to myself that I have failed, and not only failed but been defeated?

At the image of the King gloating self-righteously in Het-Uart he groaned, and his body servant, standing patiently beside him, began to flick him with the whisk. It is not the flies! Seqenenra wanted to snap at him, but could not face the effort of making himself understood. My body has become a living tomb, he cried out silently, pushing away the panic that always waited to engulf him in such moments. My thoughts can no longer reach my tongue or my limbs. The way has been sealed against them. I look at Aahotep, at her anxious eyes, at the loneliness behind her forced cheerfulness, and I want to fold her in my arms and protect her, but those days are gone. Do not dwell on them. Do not see yourself balanced in the chariot, arrow to bow, with a lion bounding ahead of you across the desert. Try not to feel the glorious tensing of muscles and the rippling caress of water against your chin and shoulders as you strike out farther into the river.

And do not think, oh, never again think of Aahotep lifting the sleeping robe, letting it slide down her arms, her thighs, stepping towards you with eyelids swollen and a lazy smile. Sweat was trickling down his temples. He shook his head vigorously at the servant, then cried out in pain. The man laid aside the whisk, and taking up a cloth, wiped his face. Gods, Seqenenra thought, must I suffer these indignities for the rest of my life?

Voices reached him. Kamose, Hor-Aha and Si-Amun came round the corner of the house, Kamose and Hor-Aha keeping stride with each other, Si-Amun a little behind. His oldest son had been often at his bedside, particularly at night. Seqenenra would wake to see him sitting, an indistinct shape in the faint glow of the night light, chin sunk in his hands and elbows on his knees, his face turned towards the bed. If Seqenenra stirred, Si-Amun would rise and bend over him, lift him gently to shake the pillow, call Uni if he was able to make it clear that he wished to relieve himself, yet he seldom addressed his father directly, though his hands betrayed his concern. His presence there in the night sometimes made Seqenenra uneasy, he did not know why. Perhaps, he reflected, watching them come, it was just the nightmares. My dreams were terrible.

They skirted the pool, came in under the shade, and bowed to him. He waved them down into the grass. Kamose and Hor-Aha sat close together, but Si-Amun took a place on the other side of the cot where, Seqenenra thought with a flash of irritation, I will have to turn my head to see him. He put away the spurt of an invalid's querulousness. "I am well enough now to hear the state of the army," he said slowly and carefully, forcing his distorted lips into exaggerated movements. At the sound of his voice Behek woke, sat up, and licked his arm before sinking into the grass once more. "Tell me how it fares." Kamose and Hor-Aha were watching his mouth intently. There was a puzzled silence. Then Kamose put a hand on Seqenenra's ankle.

"I am sorry, Father, but we cannot understand you. Shall I send for Mother?" Rage flowed over Seqenenra, followed by a feeling of helplessness that he abruptly refused. Struggling into a sitting position he signalled to Ipi, squatting motionless just out of earshot. The scribe came, laying his palette across Seqenenra's legs and holding it steady. Seqenenra took a brush with his right hand, dipping it in the ink and writing "how is army" before tossing the piece of pottery to Kamose.

"You wish to know about the army," Kamose said. "We are still feeding it at great expense, Father, and Hor-Aha is still training it. Si-Amun and Uni have already begun to assess this year's planting with regard to its continued support."

"Things do not look good," Si-Amun broke in, and Seqenenra rolled his head in order to see him. "The flood was bountiful and the planting has begun, but as you know we had to open the family's personal treasury to help support the soldiers last year in spite of the wonderful harvest. Must we continue to impoverish ourselves in this way?" Seqenenra took up the brush again and Ipi set another piece of potsherd before him. "Their health, readiness, prowess," he wrote, all at once tired and wanting to sleep. He lay back, pulled his left arm onto his stomach, and cradled it. Ipi handed the piece to Kamose who glanced at it and passed it to Hor-Aha.

"The health of the soldiers is good, providing the officers keep them working hard," Hor-Aha responded, his dark face upturned thoughtfully, his long black braids stirring on his naked chest. "But, Prince, it seems wasteful to have them on battle alert continually. They are drilled every day and more and more of them are becoming proficient with the bows the craftsmen are turning out, but they grumble and often fight among themselves. They want to go home if there is to be no war." Seqenenra considered, watching a scarlet butterfly hover over Behek's oblivious head before fluttering erratically in the direction of the blue lotus blooms resting on the limpid surface of the pool.

"Disband them, Father." The voice was Si-Amun's. He had risen and was standing over Seqenenra, his shadow deepening the shade in which Seqenenra lay. "Your dream of rebellion has come to nothing. The gods considered, and moved against you. They are content with Apepa, and if you take your plans to the limit, their retribution will be final. I am afraid of a curse falling on us all, I am afraid of Apepa's loss of patience. Besides," he cast a glance at his brother and Hor-Aha, "we cannot afford a standing army. We never really could. Every day that goes by drains our emergency stores. I, for one, would be relieved to see Weset return to its state of peaceful somnolence." Kamose laughed with amusement.

"I never thought to hear you of all people plead for a peaceful life!" he joked. "Yet there is truth in what you say. Amunmose should be consulted as to the will of the gods for us."

"He only knows the will of Amun," Seqenenra put in, "and I believe his will to be clearly against a letting-go." At their polite, expectant expressions he cursed inwardly, grabbed another piece of potsherd from Ipi's dwindling supply, and applied the brush furiously, feeling his face redden with exertion and frustration. "Send them home for own sowing," he wrote. "Bring back end of Pharmuti." He flung the message at Si-Amun.

"No," the young man said, passing it to Kamose. "No, Father, please." He sank beside the cot, kneeling in the warm grass, his hands rising to grip Seqenenra's arm. Seqenenra turned to him with difficulty. He was frowning, his lips pursed, his eyes troubled. "We have braved loss of wealth, the King's anger, the disapproval of the gods," Si-Amun went on passionately. "You have been grievously wounded, perhaps for ever. I have lost a son. All this to pursue the righting of what you see as a wrong." He glanced at his twin and away again. Kamose was staring at him without expression. Hor-Aha's gaze had gone to his smooth, folded knees. "Fate has answered your dream with the sternest suffering. Turn back and do not fight it any more. Please!"

Kamose broke in. "It was more than that, Si-Amun," he said. "The letters, the knowing that we were, we are, being driven. That has not changed."

They all turned to Seqenenra. Suddenly he was too tired to pick up the scribe's brush. Gathering his energy, he said, "No. We ... go ... on." This time they understood. Kamose came to his feet, Hor-Aha after him.

"I am sorry, but I will of course obey," Kamose said. "I will send the conscripts and the men of Wawat home, and the officers can round them up again at the end of the planting season. It may be that the King, seeing us send the soldiers home, will be mollified and cease to suspect us." He smiled across at his brother, and Seqenenra, lying under them, watched Si-Amun try to answer Kamose's gesture of optimism. For a moment they were still, their identical profiles etched against the softly moving leaves of the sycamore and the densely brilliant sky beyond like two figures from a painting on some palace wall. Then Si-Amun said curtly, "Father's assassin was not caught. We do not know who did this terrible thing, but if we have been warned and do not heed the warning he may try again. I for one do not want Father's blood on my conscience!" He spoke with such fervour that Seqenenra was surprised, and the uneasiness of the nights returned.

"But Father has made the decision, not us," Kamose objected.

"We are not responsible for his death in any case, because he will stay here and you or I will command in the field, Si-Amun. Supposing we have been warned by Apepa. How does that change anything? He is determined to destroy us whether or not we choose war."

Si-Amun answered hotly and the two of them began to argue over Seqenenra's head, chins almost touching, necks taut and fists clenched. Kamose's voice stayed controlled, but Si-Amun's rapidly became shrill. Hor-Aha stood with his eyebrows raised and his brawny arms folded, his woollen cloak loose about him. Seqenenra waited, and then, reaching up, he slapped each cheek smartly in turn. Kamose stepped back.

"I am sorry, Father," he said. "We forgot where we were. May we be dismissed?"

For a moment Seqenenra bitterly resented Kamose's formality. He waved them away.

Now he had the garden to himself. He knew that before long someone would come, Tani perhaps, to wriggle onto the narrow cot at his feet and talk to him as though she were chattering to a friend, or Aahotep with Isis or Mersu in attendance, or perhaps Tetisheri. Ahmose would be on the river in the late afternoon with rod and throwing stick and would bring his catch to display before his father with beaming pride. I am becoming like a household god, Seqenenra thought wryly. They come to me bringing the gift of their words and thoughts. But we no longer revolve around each other. Soon I will be able to stand, yet still my progress through the house will be occasions of fuss and proclamation like a divine journey. I should have told them that I intend to ride with the army in the summer. I cannot send them out to fight and perhaps to die while I hobble about the estate like a lame horse. I can no longer dream of the Horus Throne, power and might for myself, the unifying of Egypt under my strong hands, but I can end this agony with honour and pray that Si-Amun wears the Double Crown.

He was tired and uncomfortable. Signalling to the servant that he wished to be laid down, he began to turn onto his side, but he saw Aahmes-nefertari leave the dimness of the portico and come quickly towards him. "Oh, I see you are tired," the girl said, lowering herself beside him and taking his useless hand. Her pale linen floated into the grass around her and her thick copper bracelets clinked. Seqenenra, receiving her kiss, thought that she looked drawn under the blue eyepaint and hennaed mouth. "Don't try to speak to me," she went on. "I could hear Si-Amun and Kamose shouting all the way to the reception hall where Mother and I were making lotus wreaths. It was inconsiderate of them to tire you." Seqenenra felt his left eyelid begin to twitch as it usually did when he had attempted too much. He put a finger to it and the impulse stopped. He turned his right hand palm upwards and Aahmes-nefertari nodded. "I just came to tell you that I am pregnant again, Father. You are the first to know. I haven't even told Si-Amun yet." She paused. "I hope he will be pleased. So little pleases him these days."

Seqenenra felt a surge of joy coupled with anxiety. He knew that she was still grieving for the little corpse whose beautified body lay alone in Si-Amun's tomb. Doubtless Aahotep had urged her to have another child to help erase the old memories. He thought of himself being carried down from the roof of the old palace, of her standing there at the bottom, of how terrible the sight must have been. Kamose had told him. She herself had not mentioned it.

He reached over with his right hand and squeezed her fingers, smiling his lopsided smile. She responded. "You must not worry about me," she went on. "We are a tough family. All of us are strong. I must go now. Shall I dismiss Ipi and tell the servants to take you back to bed?" He nodded gratefully. He had forgotten his scribe who still sat cross-legged somewhere behind him. Aahmes-nefertari spoke briefly, smiled at him again, and walked away.

I am guilty, Seqenenra thought, as Ipi bowed and left him and other servants came hurrying with a litter. She thinks it is all over but it is not. It has only just begun. His head was throbbing, and though the servants were reverently careful he could not help crying out as he was lifted from the cot to the litter. Before he was rolled onto the couch in his bedchamber, he had fallen into a light doze.

He insisted on being carried out into the fields to see the peasants complete the sowing, lying under a canopy with Uni beside him and his servants ranged around him, watchful in case his litter should sway and tip him into the warm mud. Sometimes Ahmose accompanied him, running along the dykes, weaving in and out of the date palms with Behek at his heels, and Seqenenra found comfort in his youngest son's vigour and unquestioning lust for life.

As his strength improved, he tried to return to his former routine: being woken early so that he might be carried into the temple for the morning rites where Amunmose as his delegate performed the ceremonies he could no longer attempt, receiving Men who came from the Delta with the twice-yearly report on his and Amun's cattle, and feasting with the heralds and other ministers of the King who plied the river between Het-Uart and the vast holdings of Teti-the-Handsome, Prince of Kush and Apepa's friend.

He did not try to hide his condition from these men. It was good that they should see him maimed and disfigured, should go back north to Apepa with tales of the proud Seqenenra's twisted mouth and drooping eye, his leg and arm like a doll's limbs stuffed with straw. Let them gloat, he thought in the evenings when he sat in the reception hall, propped in his chair with pillows, his left arm supine in his lap. Let Apepa hear of me chastened and cowed, my lesson learned. The laughter and chatter flowed around him on these occasions. The harpist sent rippling music over the throng, the dishes steamed in the hands of the servants, his women arrayed themselves in their best linen and jewels. Seqenenra presided mutely, Aahotep close by, Uni at his right hand to anticipate his every need.

The soldiers had gone back to their villages, Hor-Aha's Medjay to see to their tribal affairs in Wawat and the Egyptians to till and plant their tiny fields. Seqenenra knew that this word also had gone north.

But the bows of palm ribs continued to come from the hands of the military craftsmen and pile up in the armoury, and in the granaries, grain from the last harvest was laid aside for next year's assault. Hor-Aha had sent a scout to buy horses, a few here, a few there, and chariots were being made. This time, Seqenenra reflected grimly, we will be prepared. The men will be better trained, the stores more plentiful. Kamose and Si-Amun will be older and hardier. Yet by the time he allowed Aahotep to usher him to his couch at night, he was always feverish and consumed with a despair that he hid from them all.

The hole in his head that he came to regard with a mounting disgust and horror was closing slowly. New bone was growing on the old, jagged teeth of the wound. Yet to him it was a symbol of everything he now was, an object of concern and pity to his family and an affront to himself. He would not allow Aahotep to kiss him on his lips, or anyone but his body servant to touch his face. At night, with throbbing head and anguished heart, he wished that Apepa's crafty tool, whomever he might be, had struck a little deeper.

The months of Mekhir and Phamenoth passed. The crops began to spring up lush and thick in the fields. The canals, still full of calm, stagnant water, became playgrounds for the brown peasant children who leaped and splashed in them with innocent abandonment. The nights were soft, the stars gentle in a black sky.

Aahmes-nefertari had announced her pregnancy to the family and once more Taurt was honoured, but Seqenenra, watching her come and go, sometimes with her arm linked through Si-Amun's but more often followed by Raa, sensed her unhappiness. She was afraid. He did not try to draw her out. Words could not soothe her. Only a healthy baby would restore her confidence.

He himself was struggling to walk. Uni had produced a crutch that bit the tender flesh under his good arm and raised blisters on his palm that soon turned to thick calluses, but he could at least move haltingly from his room to the garden, dragging his left leg behind him. He spent many hours learning to negotiate the steps of the portico. He was also better able to make himself understood, although his speech remained slurred. Tani told him, giggling, that he sounded drunk all the time, but at least with great effort on his part and concentration on the part of his hearer, he could communicate. Fiercely he disregarded the fatigue, the disappointment, the black depression that crept over him every sunset. He wanted to be ready to ride when the time came.

His naming day had been celebrated on the third day of Phamenoth. He was now thirty-seven years old. He was able to stand in the temple and make the offering of a bull for a thanksgiving and he watched Tani dance proudly in his honour with the other temple women. She was now fifteen. In the following two months the twins would turn twenty-one and in the summer Ahmose would become eighteen. Seqenenra, seeing Tani dip and swirl in her garland of bright flowers, tinkling systra in her hands, felt a stab of apprehension at the swift passing of time. Life was a dream that slid by while he stood in his sleep and followed it with his eyes, unable to reach out and grasp a corner of the pageant, slow it down, force it to stand so that he could consider its implications properly.

A public message came from Het-Uart and was read in the market-place of Weset to the dusty, restless crowd. The King would attain his fortieth year in the month of Mesore, and in recognition of his naming day and the Anniversary of his Appearing, taxes would be lowered. The citizens of Weset, traditionally an independent and haughty breed, did not cheer and clamour. They simply waited until the herald had finished and then walked away, talking among themselves. Of more interest to them was the fact that their Prince had been able to stand throughout his own naming day ceremonies in the temple and had received their mayor with gifts of two days of holiday and an extra hundred acres to be drained and cultivated for them for one year.

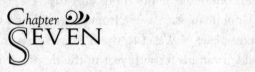
R AMOSE HAD COME, sailing to the water-
steps one morning in the middle of
Phamenoth and fending off Behek and the other dogs as he
walked to the house with his escort. Seqenenra was sitting in
the garden, Uni behind him and Tetisheri reclining on a mat
beside him, her cushions piled around her, when the young
man came to pay his respects. Isis and Mersu stood some way
off. Isis was flinging blooms into the water of the pool to stir the
fish that flickered, a sullen gold, in the murky depths.

Ramose came forward and bowed, his two bodyguards and his
steward following suit. Then he straightened and waited for Seqenenra to speak. Seqenenra felt the man's eyes on his mouth,
his eye travelling his body, but the appraisal was open and kindly. "Greetings, Ramose," he enunciated carefully. Ramose's gaze
flew to his face. There was a moment of deciphering that Seqenenra had become used to. It had taught him patience.

Then Ramose said, "I greet you, Prince, for myself and on
behalf of my father who was most distressed at the news of your
misfortune. I almost expected a scroll from you telling me not
to come. I would have understood." He turned and bowed
slightly to Tetisheri. "Princess, I am honoured to see you again."
Tetisheri smiled, shading her eyes as she looked up at him.

"Ramose, you become more handsome each time I see you," she answered. "You have your mother's even features and your father's big eyes. How is your mother?"

"She is well. She has sent you and her cousin a vial each of a new perfume being mixed on Asi. She hopes you will like it. I will have it unpacked later, as I have brought many gifts for Tani also."

Tetisheri chuckled. "New perfume! And has she sent me a man to appreciate it also? Thank you, Ramose. The gift is a generous one." Seqenenra waved him down. Ramose ordered his escort back to the boat and sank into the sycamore's spreading shade with a sigh.

"Your hurts are grievous, Prince," he said frankly, as Tetisheri sharply commanded Mersu to have a greeting meal brought from the kitchens. "I am appalled. How could a fall of rock cause such damage?" Seqenenra looked at him blankly and then remembered the letter that had gone to Het-Uart from Kamose.

"The chariot was rolling fast under an overhang," he replied, pausing between words to make sure that Ramose understood. "I thought of nothing but the lion to be shot. Something loosened the rocks and I remember nothing more than the sound of them falling."

Ramose nodded. "Father wishes to know if you need anything, another physician, the loan of overseers?" Seqenenra's hand went to the linen cap tied around his head. He fingered it absently.

"Thank him for me," he replied, "but I need nothing. My physician is the best in Egypt."

There was a movement by the house and Tani stepped into the sunlight with Heket trailing her dutifully. As she saw who had come, her wide mouth broke into a smile and she held both hands out to Ramose. He scrambled up and took them.

"How lovely you are, Princess!" he exclaimed, kissing her cheek. She pulled away, gazed at him for a moment, then settled herself beside Tetisheri.

"So!" she said. "Are we to be betrothed this visit, Ramose? I must confess I am tired of waiting. Father is perfectly capable of putting his name and title on the document, and if you tell me you did not bring your father's signature and seal I shall throttle you!" Yes, Seqenenra thought. A betrothal quickly now, and then a marriage. He glanced at Ramose who had resumed his cross-legged position.

"I have brought the betrothal document," he said. "It needs only your father's name. But my father is insisting on a six-month waiting period before the marriage." Tani threw up her hands. The sun glinted on her ringed fingers.

"Oh really!" she snorted. "As if we are all strangers! Why? Teti is such an enthusiast for protocol. I shall dictate a stinging letter to my future father-in-law, and..."

She prattled on. Tetisheri was watching her with amusement. The servants were smiling. But Seqenenra had withdrawn into himself. Teti is waiting to see what I will do, he suddenly knew without a doubt. He does not want to be allied to a family tainted by treason. Does he know I was attacked by an assassin? He has been burned by the flame of revolt in his own family and will be doubly cautious over this marriage. Somehow I must tell Tani that, unless I win through to Het-Uart and become Egypt's King, Teti will no longer be willing to have her in his home.

"Tani, that is enough!" Ramose broke in sternly, and surprisingly Tani closed her mouth, though she managed to shrug eloquently. "My father is willing for the betrothal contract to be signed and sealed now. He will prepare festivities in Khemennu and you and your family will come in six months for the final celebrations. I do not know his reasons for this further wait, but you and I have waited for months already so it will not make much difference. Perhaps it is the dowry?" He glanced politely at Seqenenra, who did not answer.

At that moment servants appeared, bringing wine and shat cakes. Behind them the rest of the family straggled and Ramose rose to bow to Aahotep and embrace the three young men. All settled by the pool and the conversation became general. After a while Ramose and Tani got up and Seqenenra gave them permission to leave.

Ramose put his arm across the girl's slim shoulders and they strolled towards the river. Behek had risen and lumbered panting at their heels. The sound of voices slowly faded, to be replaced by the rustle and piping of birds in the reeds and the hum of insects in the flowering shrubs. The branches of the palms met over their heads, casting a stiff shade on the white, dusty path. Tani dug her toes into the powder as they went. "I am very angry with Teti," she said. "And I imagine that Father is insulted. He is after all a Prince, Ramose. He deserves more deference from your father than he gets."

"He is well aware of the honour Seqenenra is doing him in letting me have you," Ramose replied hesitantly. "It is not second thoughts or pride or a need to try your father's authority." He came to a halt and she with him. Turning her, he smoothed her eyebrows with thoughtful fingers. Behind and before them the sun-dappled path twisted into green gloom. "I must be honest with you, Tani," he admitted. "I love you very much. There are strong rumours that Seqenenra was struck by Apepa's hand because he was planning rebellion. Is it true? My father thinks so."

"I care not one fig what your father thinks!" Tani flashed. "He is a fat old man with more dignity than he deserves! How dare he hesitate over me, a Princess with royal blood in her veins!" Ramose stepped away from her flushed face and furious eyes.

"I am angry also," he said evenly. "I do not care either what your father or mine think or do. But we are obedient children, Tani, and we will remain so until our parents die. You did not answer my question. Do you not trust me?" She considered him, her head on one side.

"My loyalty belongs to my family," she said frostily, "and you are not yet a member of that family or me of yours." He reached out and shook her gently.

"If you tell me the truth, I shall swear by Thoth, totem of Khemennu, not to tell a living soul. Not even my father." She took a deep breath.

"Very well, Ramose. I am angry with Father also for putting himself in the position he did and bringing down on himself the King's wrath. I love him so much and I am so sorry for him. But you must promise to keep it to yourself. I shall utter a curse tonight that will take effect if you ever tell." He nodded.

"I agree."

"Then it is true. Father put up with Apepa's insults and pricks for as long as he could, and then he got a letter telling him he had to kill the hippopotamuses. Can you imagine anything more foolish? Father is clever and he managed to avoid such a cruel thing, but then the King wanted him to build a temple for Set here." She bit her lip and turned troubled eyes to his. "I suppose he might have considered a small shrine, but Weset belongs to Amun. It was impossible. Father gathered a small army and was ready to start north and then someone tried to kill him. We don't know who. We will probably never know." Her voice shook. "We all believe that Apepa's hand was in it." Ramose took her waist and they began to walk again.

"I am sorry to cause you this distress," he said, "but you do see, don't you, that my father must be careful of his reputation? He must wait six months to make sure that Seqenenra has learned his lesson and will stay quiet from now on."

"How tactfully you express it!" Tani blurted, stiff against his hand. "You speak as though my father were an unruly dog to be whipped into submission!"

"You have always had frankness from me," Ramose rebuked her. "There is no point in dancing around the subject, Tani. Our future depends on it."

"I suppose you think of my father as a deceitful traitor and an insane man too?"

They had reached the watersteps. He drew her down onto the white stone. The water lapped with tiny sucking sounds at their feet. A family of ducks broke from the reeds and arrowed smoothly towards one of the small islands between the east and west banks, their wake spreading behind them. The far cliffs wavered, hot beige against a cloudless sky. "I think that his cause is just but his method misguided," Ramose answered, his eyes narrowed against the sun and his gaze fixed on the ducks, now waddling one by one onto the rocky shore. "I do not share my father's comfortable acceptance of our Setiu masters. I would like to see an Egyptian god on the Horus Throne some-day. But it will not be in our lifetime." He forced her to look at him. "Your father is a brave man, but I trust that his moment of rage is over."

Tani did not answer. She smiled at him briefly and looked away. His rage is not over, she thought. It will never be over. As for the army, it has gone home. I can hope fervently that it will not be called back, but I do not like it when Hor-Aha and Kamose cluster around him for hours on end and Kamose and Si-Amun quarrel every time they are together. Something else is brewing and I am afraid. No one tells me anything. They think I am still a child because I am the youngest and must be spared.

All at once she grasped Ramose's fingers. "Am I a woman to you, Ramose," she asked him urgently, "or a pretty girl who has captured your affections and whom you treat kindly and lightly? Is this simply an advantageous marriage for you?"

"Tani," he chided her, "there are a dozen women at home who are pretty and whom I treat kindly and lightly. I have watched you grow from a fey child into a lovely young woman with a quick mind and an equally quick temper. I love you. As for an advantageous marriage, well," he sighed in annoyance at his thought, "you may be a Princess but your family now lives under the cloud of the King's disapproval and my father is worried about it. Why this sudden doubt?" She rubbed her cheek against his warm upper arm.

"I want to be happy," she whispered. "I want to live at Khemennu with you forever. I can hardly bear to look at Father any more, to be cheerful around him, to pretend encouragement. He was so straight and graceful, Ramose, so lordly! Every time I force myself to go to him, it is with a terrible anger against the King and an ache of remembering how things used to be. Please take me away."

He had nothing to say. Gathering her to him, he stroked her silently until he felt her relax and then they spoke of other things. But when they joined the rest of the family for the evening meal, he found that he was watching them, the proud Taos, with detachment and wariness. The night was hot, the first creeping breathlessness of summer.

Seqenenra, dressed only in a thin kilt-linen, ate little. His crutch lay discreetly behind him where Uni stood. The wrap around his head was a patch of white in the ill-lit hall. He pushed food quickly into his deformed mouth as though hoping no one would see, and his eyes roamed the company. Ramose thought of his own father, oiled and bejewelled, gesturing expansively and speaking in his low-pitched, cultured voice to each of his guests in turn as they ate at his flower-strewn ivory tables. Teti was like a huge owl, benign and wise. Seqenenra was a wounded hawk, battered yet alert, with a watchful malevolence behind the darting eyes. Ramose smiled at the drama of his image and Seqenenra, catching the stare, suddenly smiled back. Ramose nodded and looked away.

The Princess Aahotep was at Seqenenra's elbow, a darkly beautiful woman whose every movement held voluptuous grace. There was little of his own mother in her, Ramose reflected, although they were related. His mother was comfortably middle-aged. This woman with her full lips and burnished skin was as sensuous as the King's concubines who gathered languidly on their cushions around the fountains of the harem on a summer afternoon. He saw her lean back to speak to Hetepet, her servant, lean sideways to put her mouth against her husband's ear, supple and easy in her movements.

Ramose sipped his wine and let his mind wander with his eyes. The twins, Kamose and Si-Amun, sat together on mats, sharing a table littered with the remains of the meal but not speaking. The constraint between them was almost palpable. Although it seemed as though there was one man looking into a mirror when they turned to each other, black eyes, long thin faces, sharp noses, a mass of dark curls, there was a gulf between them that set them apart. What is it? Ramose wondered.

He felt Si-Amun's gaze on him, had felt it often through the evening hours while the musicians played and danced and the servants wove to and fro with lotus garlands and perfumed oil. It made him anxious. Kamose turned often to speak to the wild-looking Medjay warrior at his elbow, a man of slow gestures and quick, cold eyes, while Si-Amun seemed to sink lower on his mat, his ringed fingers fidgeting in the food.

Ahmose, scantily clad, had finished his meal long before and was wandering through the diners, sling in hand, delving occasionally into a leather bag at his belt from which he drew small pellets. The clatter of their striking punctuated the conversations. Ahmose sang snatches of some jaunty melody as he whirled and let go. No one paid him any attention. He was obviously too good a shot with the sling to cause anxiety. The great lady Tetisheri sat a little apart, surrounded by her retinue of retainers, a straight-backed, glittering old woman whose sharp gaze encompassed everyone and whose slightest movement resulted in a flurry of obedience around her. Ramose shuddered inwardly. She had always terrified him as a boy, and even now as a man he was in awe of her. Mersu, her steward, answered a command, the words lost in the general hubbub, bending towards her politely. Ramose considered him. He had a relative or a friend in Teti's household, his father's Chief Steward he thought. They were always together when the Taos came to visit. An impressively calm man.

His Tani was sitting on a mat beside her sister, knees drawn up under her filmy red linen, braceleted arms hugging them, waving hair bouncing against her neck as she talked. His heart melted. He did not know what it was about her that called forth such a response. She was so unlike the rest of her family and yet her spasm of anger today, while he had deliberately not reacted to it, had taken him aback. She, too, possessed the overwhelming Tao pride.

Her sister, Aahmes-nefertari, was a younger version of her mother, dark, well-curved, with piercing black eyes and a haughty mouth. She was pregnant, Ramose knew. Another Prince, he thought. Another Tao to spit at the King and dream their long dream of power and ancient Ma'at. By Thoth, I admire them! It would not do to let them know, for I, too, come of a venerable family and have my pride, but I am glad to be sitting here where the air is somehow cleaner and a less complicated Egypt tugs at my mind. But they are dangerous too. As unpredictable as bulls, even my Tani in her way. It is in their blood. Osiris Mentuhotep neb-hapet-Ra . . . I know my history.

His reverie was interrupted by a movement and a rustle beside him. He turned. Prince Si-Amun was settling himself on the floor. Ramose smiled at him warily. He was holding a goblet with great care, and to Ramose, noting his flushed cheeks and brilliant eyes, he seemed already more than a little drunk. "Prince," Ramose nodded. Si-Amun nodded back.

"Well, Ramose," he said. "we used to creep up on the crocodiles in the Khemennu swamps together and hunt for ibis eggs. Do you remember when Kamose and I tied you to a skiff and dragged you through the river? You nearly drowned. And now you are to be my brother-in-law. It seems fitting. Do you have any doubts?" He swilled his cup, drank, and held it out for more. The servant hovering behind them filled it and stepped back.

"Why, no, Prince," Ramose answered. "I love Tani and she will make a fine wife. The marriage is a respectable and suitable one."

"Even considering the trouble Father has been in?" Si-Amun's face came close to his own. "You know people are saying that Apepa had Father attacked. We are not exactly in the King's good graces." Ramose tensed. Beneath Si-Amun's wine-slurred words and glazed eyes he sensed a sober questing.

"Rumours always abound in the estates of the noble and powerful," he said carefully, "and our god is of a suspicious nature. I do not believe either that Seqenenra has been traitorous or the King vengeful. I do not listen to gossip, Prince." A curious expression, half relief and half disappointment, swept over Si-Amun's eyes.

"So you know nothing of it," he urged. Ramose spread his hands.

"Only what is passed from mouth to mouth on idle afternoons. It is all so silly, Si-Amun, but I suppose it troubles the family. The hunting accident—it is a tragedy." He hoped that he sounded convincing. Si-Amun did not know that Tani had told him the truth and he must not betray her confidence.

"And your father?" Si-Amun pressed. "Teti is one of Apepa's favourites. What does he know?" The words were low, the tone almost desperate. Ramose hid his bewilderment, sensing something close to despair in the Prince.

"If you are suggesting that my father knew anything about an attack on your father, an attack that Seqenenra himself admits was a hunting accident, you are overstepping the bounds of our blood ties," he said. "If there was an attack and if my father knew about it beforehand, he would have warned Seqenenra." His indignation was genuine. Si-Amun stared at him for a moment then laughed, a quick, humourless gust of wine-laden breath.

"I am sorry," he said, still choking on his wine. "Of course he would. Forgive me." He began to come unsteadily to his feet. Ramose caught his arm.

"Si-Amun," he said sharply, "are you ill? Or is something troubling you?" Si-Amun looked down on him for a long time.

"I envy you, Ramose," he said finally. "I used to be like you. I would give Amun anything his heart desired if I could be like you again. Tani is a fortunate girl." He graced Ramose with the parody of a smile and walked away. As he went, Ramose noticed the steward Mersu staring after him.

There are nasty undercurrents in this hall, Ramose thought, putting down his wine. What could Father possibly know about Seqenenra's attempted murder? He would tell someone surely, he would warn the husband of his wife's cousin, he has loyalties to the relationship between our families. Doesn't he? Si-Amun's irrational speech had set up a pulse of disquiet in him.

He caught Tani's eye. With a jerk of his head he indicated that they should get Seqenenra's permission to go into the garden. I wish that I could take Tani and go home, he thought, moving towards the Prince's table. I feel like a child in a maze, and the night is coming. I will leave tomorrow as soon as the contract is signed.

In the morning Seqenenra scrawled his name and title on the betrothal scroll. "You may tell Teti," he said to an uncomfortable Ramose who strained to understand the garbled but vehement words, "that I am insulted and displeased at the six-month delay in the nuptials. I have paid a good dowry. Tani has a unique blood line. If there are any more problems, I shall withdraw my consent and demand compensation from Teti." The left side of the Prince's face was a frozen, inert mask but the right side glowed with irritation. Ramose put aside his dread of this formidable man.

"My father did not make his reasons clear to me," he said. "But I must respect his decision, Prince. When I come for Tani in six months' time my conscience will thus be clear. He forced himself to meet Seqenenra's eye. "You forget, lord, that out of love for your daughter I am as disappointed as you." Suddenly, surprisingly, Seqenenra put his right arm around Ramose and embraced him tightly.

"I like you," he said. "I like your courage. I see you have gifts. Go and give them to her. I will not be at the watersteps when you leave, but I wish you a safe journey."

He hobbled away and Ramose watched him go before signalling for the servant to pick up the box at his feet and follow him to the women's quarters. If I did not know better, Ramose thought with worry, I would imagine those words as some kind of permanent farewell.

Tani clapped her hands and exclaimed over the presents, sending for her mother and sister to admire them. There were bolts of linen of the first quality in many different colours, jars of gold dust to sprinkle on her kohl and eyepaint, ebony anointing spoons with gold inlay, dyed ostrich feathers from Kush, earrings of silver and jasper and a small alabaster hippopotamus with black obsidian eyes and ivory teeth. Tani cradled it ecstatically. "How thoughtful of you, Ramose," she said, happy and suddenly shy. "You remembered how I love them." Ramose laughed.

"I could hardly forget, seeing the number of times I have been dragged to the marshes to admire them!" he retorted. "I must be going, Tani. I will send word in six months when the festival preparations are made and then I need not say goodbye to you again." He bowed to Aahotep. "Thank you for your hospitality, Princess. I will make an offering to Thoth so that your husband's health may continue to improve." Aahotep turned her dark-lashed eyes to him and laid a warm palm against his cheek.

"Greet the family for me, Ramose," she asked in her husky voice. Removing her hand, she glanced at Tani, back to Ramose, and he wondered at her sober expression. He kissed Aahmes-nefertari, and he and Tani walked to the watersteps where his barge lay rocking on the slight swell, its pennants stirring limply in the almost motionless air. There he embraced her once more, she near to tears, and he ran up the ramp.

His captain gave the order to cast off. Behek began to bark deliriously as the boat slipped away, seeking the north-flowing current. Ramose leaned on the railing and watched Tani recede, a small, upright figure in flowing white linen, the dog bounding about her knees. A lump came to his throat. She is very brave, he thought. Brave and loyal. The strength of his emotion startled him and he waved once and disappeared inside the cabin.

The next three months passed on the estate like the thick stillness that always precedes a khamsin out on the desert. The crops turned from supple green to a brittle golden ripeness. Seqenenra's overseers tallied the fields, saw to the sweeping of the granaries, and consulted last year's yield lists. But Seqenenra himself could take no interest in the affairs of his domain.

Kamose and Si-Amun celebrated their birthday, Kamose genially but Si-Amun with a quiet embarrassment that bordered on sullenness. Seqenenra had held a reception for his sons and had invited all the dignitaries of Weset and his nomes. He had watched Si-Amun's efforts to be gracious with a puzzled concern. "You had better talk to that one," his mother had advised. "Something is eating him up." Seqenenra had tried, but Si-Amun had been politely evasive. The problem was obviously not the young man's health or that of his wife. Aahmes-nefertari was sunk in the lassitude and contentment of her second pregnancy.

Seqenenra, finally annoyed, his head throbbing and his shoulder and back aching from the crutch, told him sharply that if his trouble had to do with the coming fight he could be released from any obligation to march. Si-Amun had tried to answer, his mouth trembling, but in the end he had sunk once more into silent discomfort and then fled.

Seqenenra had approached Kamose, but Kamose was as mystified as he. "I do not know," he had told his father. "He avoids me. We do not even wrestle any more. Sometimes he goes with Ahmose into the marshes. You know how easy it is to be with Ahmose. He spends most of his time with Aahmes-nefertari in the women's quarters." Tetisheri had lost patience with her grandson a long time ago and spoken roughly to him, so that he avoided her, but his mother continued to fret over him and did her best to draw him out, to no avail.

Seqenenra was forced to dismiss his concern for Si-Amun.

He was involved in his own worries, forcing his body through a series of strenuous exercises that he hoped would make him fit for the chariot and the ride north. He swam every day, floundering in the Nile and grimly ignoring the secret opinion of those watching. He knew he looked ridiculous. He dragged himself around the practice ground in the blazing sun, sweating and cursing, his muscles burning. At the back of his mind had been the belief that if he only had enough time and worked hard enough, life would return to his arm and leg, but through all his exertions the limbs hung on him like a burden of rebuke.

Several times he had himself carried to the valley where Osiris Mentuhotep-neb-hapet-Ra's deserted temple smouldered, but the presence of his ancestor merely angered him and he resolved not to go there again. Fate had not dealt with Mentuhotep as it had with him, Seqenenra. Mentuhotep had not marched north to war maimed and broken. The site conjured self-pity, and Seqenenra did his brooding in the friendly gloom of the old palace. He could no longer climb to the roof, where in spite of much scrubbing the stain of his blood was baked brown into the bricks. He sat on the dais of the throne room, his twisted face turned to the dim friezes on the walls, and tried to maintain an optimism within himself.

In the last week of Payni a letter came from the King, brought by his Chief Herald, who was not on his way to anywhere else but who came ashore at Weset escorted by twenty warriors in royal blue and white, his unsullied linen and gleaming helmet discreetly protected from the sun by the gilt canopy under which he strode to the reception hall. In one hand he carried the white staff of his office and in the other a sealed scroll. Uni, unperturbed, showed him a chair and offered him refreshment, ignoring the bristle of spears around him, the leather belts hung with knives that girded the massive waists of the bodyguard, then leaving to summon his master. "So many soldiers!" he spluttered behind Seqenenra in the passage. "It is an insult!"

"Of course it is," Seqenenra answered wearily. "But we are used to that, are we not?" He limped into the hall. The herald rose, bowed perfunctorily, and watched him come. Seqenenra left him standing. He did not speak, so that the herald was unable to open his own mouth.

Seqenenra held out his hand and the scroll was placed in it. Quickly he broke the seal and read, then passed it to Ipi who had followed him, palette ready. "File this," Seqenenra ordered curtly. He regarded the herald, who was endeavouring to keep his face expressionless, but the man's affront at being forced to remain mute was evident. Seqenenra relented. "I offer you my hospitality," he said. "Will you use my guest quarters tonight?" The herald's face cleared but became cool.

"My thanks, Highness, but I come well-victualled and since I must leave again for Het-Uart with the dawn, I ask your indulgence. I will dine and sleep on the barge."

"In that case," Seqenenra responded equably, "you are dismissed."

He carried the contents of the scroll in his mind like a dark disease all that day while he struggled with his exercise, rested sleeplessly on his couch, and shared the evening meal with his listless family. There were questions from Tani and Ahmose, who had passed the watersteps and inspected the gilded barge from the bank with curiosity, but the rest of them knew Seqenenra would speak when he was ready.

He waited until he returned from the temple. The moorings were empty. The barge had gone. Then he summoned them to the reception hall, sitting waiting, his crutch on the floor beside him, Ipi at his feet, while they straggled into the room. All looked wary, even his mother. They ranged themselves before him, eyes fixed on him apprehensively. The last time he had formally called them was years ago when Apepa had paid them a state visit. He surveyed them quietly.

"Apepa has spoken," he said without preamble. "He is himself planning a temple to Sutekh here in Weset, beside Amun's home. His architects and masons will arrive to survey the site after the harvest in two months' time. They will go on to Swenet to choose stone. We will provide the labourers. This time the scroll was perfectly intelligible."

No one stirred. He could tell from their faces that they had understood his laboured words. He touched a finger to his drooping lip. "We will have no temple to Sutekh here," he enunciated emphatically. "No architects, no masons, no northern foreigners. We are Egyptians. Our god is Egyptian. We go to war immediately. Kamose, if you, Hor-Aha and the officers scatter, you can have troops here in a month. Uni," he turned to his steward, "get out the victual lists and weapons tally. Ipi, bring me the Scribes of Assemblage." He realized that he was speaking too fast and garbling his words. Taking a deep breath he forced himself to be calm. "Ahmose, you will not come. I want you to stay here and prepare to assume my title if I or the others do not come home." He would have gone on, but Ahmose stepped forward looking injured.

"That is unfair," he protested. "I am the best shot in the five nomes. I attained my majority two years ago. I will be eighteen soon. I can handle horses better than either Kamose or Si-Amun." Aahotep made a gesture towards her son, half-protecting, half-rebuke, but Seqenenra cut her off.

"There will be no argument," he said sternly. "Ahmose, I am sorry but you know why the survival of at least one male in the family is vital."

"You speak as if we are all to die!" Si-Amun burst out. "Suicide is wrong, Seqenenra!" He had never before called his father by name and the word put an immediate gulf between them. Kamose pulled him back.

"Be quiet, Si-Amun," he said in a low voice. "It has all been said before. We are going and that is that." Si-Amun glowered at him and flung off Aahmes-nefertari's hesitant arm.

"I am tired of all the talk." The voice was Tetisheri's. "Do it, Seqenenra, and then have done with it." Seqenenra managed a wintry smile at her before turning to Tani. She was regarding him with a steady enquiry.

"I am afraid this means that your marriage will be postponed, probably indefinitely, Tani," he told her. They were the hardest words he had ever forced past his misshapen lips. He searched for something more to say, something comforting, but she saved him from the necessity.

"A year ago I could not have borne such news," she answered huskily. "Now I am able to accept the inevitable. This is why Teti insisted on the six-month wait, isn't it, Father? He suspected us all. I know my duty. Yet if you become King, I shall expect payment for my faithfulness!"

Seqenenra could not even smile at her clumsy attempt at humour. His rancour sat in his breast, a hard, cold weight. Teti will not join me as we pass by, he thought, but Ramose might. I wish I could force Teti to honour the contract and let them marry now and stay away from this tragic chaos. "There is one thing more," he said. "I will command in the field. I cannot fight well but I can lead the men who will be depending on me for their morale." Si-Amun took a breath and would have shouted, but Kamose's hand descended on his arm like a vise.

"Amun will vindicate us," Kamose said with finality. Seqenenra could stand no more. He dismissed them with a flick of the wrist. When they had gone he turned to Uni.

"Give me my crutch and your arm, Uni," he said. "I feel as

though I have already run to Het-Uart and back. Shall I come back, do you think?" It was an uncharacteristic plea for reassurance. Uni grunted.

"Ask Amunmose, not me," he retorted. "I am not a prophet." Nor are you a tactful servant, Seqenenra thought, amused, and at that his sadness fled. This time there would be no assassin's blow in the night. He would have himself guarded constantly until they left. This time they would surely march.

Si-Amun left the reception hall and was almost at the end of the passage leading to his own quarters when Mersu slid out of the early shadows and bowed. Ignoring him, Si-Amun tried to push past but the steward took a step to bar his way. "Well, what is it?" Si-Amun snapped. Mersu bowed again.

"Your pardon, Prince, but I would like to know what your father had to say. It is most unusual to see him summon the whole family at once." Si-Amun could hardly look at the man, his distaste was so strong.

"That is none of your business."

"Perhaps," Mersu answered in a low voice, glancing about the deserted passage. "But it may be the King's business."

"Apepa has ordered the building of a temple to Sutekh here at Weset," Si-Amun croaked. "Now let me past before I strike you." Mersu did not stir.

"And what will Seqenenra do, Prince?" Si-Amun began to flush.

"He has not decided. Get out of my way!" Mersu leaned closer and his voice dropped even farther.

"I must remind you, Si-Amun, that if you do not take me into your confidence I will tell your father how the attack on him came to be. I have nothing to lose, you see."

"How hateful you are!" Si-Amun burst out. "You do not deserve to live, and if Father wins, I will kill you with my own hands. Traitor!"

"So Seqenenra is to march?" Mersu said, unmoved by Si-Amun's venom. "When?" Si-Amun gave in.

"Immediately. The word is going out even now. We will assemble and move at the end of next month."

"Epophi," Mersu said thoughtfully. "My thanks, Prince."

Si-Amun's response was a stinging slap that caught Mersu full on the face. The steward staggered back, a hand going to his cheek, but he recovered himself quickly. He even smiled. Si-Amun strode past him, suddenly desperate for clean, moving air.

Instead of going to his quarters, he ran into the garden and stood by the pool, gasping and shuddering. After a while, he had calmed down enough to go about his business. I do not even have a friend I can confide in, he thought as he went. No one to share this burden of guilt and hatred, to propose an impossible solution, to offer understanding and sympathy. I hope Apepa's warriors kill me on the field. It is all I deserve.

By the end of Epophi all preparations were complete. The soldiers were back in their village on the desert. The donkeys were corralled by the river ready to receive their load of victuals. The horses were trained and groomed. The officers were closeted with Kamose and Hor-Aha, receiving last-minute advice.

On the last night Seqenenra, tired, obstinate and in a mood of fatalism intensified by the baking darkness, sent for Ahmose. The summer was at its height, the land acquiring its other identity of barren ugliness. The gods seemed hostile at this time of the year. Ra the supreme burned his subjects. The wisdom and gentleness of Amun paled in the fierce days and stifling nights. Cow-headed Hathor was too drowsy to answer the prayers of the women who beseeched her for beauty and vigour in the midst of a heat that wrinkled the skin and drained energy from her supplicants.

Because of his ailments, Seqenenra did not like to go naked

as so many did. He was wearing the long gown of a vizier as Ahmose requested admittance and came to him over the tiles. Ahmose's hair glistened with water. His skin, as he embraced Seqenenra, was damp and cool. "You have been swimming," Seqenenra observed unnecessarily. "Would you like beer?" Ahmose nodded and poured from the jug on Seqenenra's night table, sinking onto the floor with the cup in his hands where he settled, one arm along the couch. Seqenenra stood as close to the window as he could, but the night air hung motionless, a palpable thick curtain. "Do not be insulted that you must stay home," Seqenenra said frankly, watching the minute shifting of Ahmose's tight muscles as he drank and adjusted his position. "Someone must stay and order the women and see to a governor's duties." It took Ahmose a moment to decipher the halting words, his eyes concentrated on his father's mouth. Then he shrugged and smiled good-humouredly.

"I have perhaps wasted more time than I should in hunting and fowling," he admitted, "but being the youngest son I never expected to have to consider the responsibilities of an active princely rule. I have had fun, Father. I have loved my life. Eating, sleeping, getting drunk on long winter afternoons under the palms, knowing that nothing was required of me save to exist. Every god has indulged me, not to mention my dear mother and my sisters. But life is strange, is it not?" Seqenenra agreed, a lump in his throat. Ahmose with his carefree cheerfulness had always somehow leavened the family, shrunk without knowing it the cares and troubles that regularly arose. "I gave my tutors a difficult time in my childhood," Ahmose went on. "All I cared about was fishing, knocking ducks out of the sky and stalking hyenas. But I am not stupid. I think you worry about leaving the governorship in my hands." He swallowed the last of his beer and set the cup on the floor beside him, beaming up at Seqenenra. "I daresay I shall make a few mistakes but my instincts are good. They are after all the instincts of a ruling house. Besides, there is Grandmother to cuff me if I falter, and Uni to prod me if I weaken. Do not worry, Father. I shall not let you down."

No, you will not, Seqenenra thought, looking into the handsome face that glowed with vitality and good humour. You are an honest man and the seeds of the kind of greatness that compels men to follow you are already sprouting. I wish that I could live to see them blossom.

They talked a little more, both unwilling to acknowledge the passing of time and neither referring to the coming morning until Ahmose scrambled up. "I am sweating again," he said. "I think I will swim once more before I try to sleep. The Nile is beautiful by starlight, the water dark and the ripples silver." Awkwardly he looked at his feet. "Father, I will not be at the assembling tomorrow to see the army leave," he muttered. "Amunmose will perform the rites in your place while you are gone, but I think I will join him tomorrow."

"I understand." Seqenenra hobbled to him and kissed him warmly. "I love you, Ahmose. You are dismissed."

"May the soles of your feet be firm, Prince." Ahmose smiled tremulously and was gone.

Seqenenra knew that Aahotep would be coming to him soon. He dreaded her brave front, her lingering touch, the fear and bereavement her eyes would not be able to conceal. He loved her deeply but he wanted to lie alone on this, his last night. He could not face giving comfort yet again when he needed to gather in his meagre resources. His body servant entered, washed him and helped him into his sleeping robe. He endured the man's ministrations mechanically and absently, frowning over the details of tomorrow, and had just collapsed onto his couch when Uni came in. "Si-Amun is here," the steward said. "Will you see him?" Seqenenra's heart sank but he nodded.

"Let him come." Uni retired. Si-Amun closed the door behind him and came hesitantly to the side of the couch. There were black patches under his eyes and his skin had a sallow tinge. Seqenenra patted the sheets and Si-Amun sank down beside him. "You are ill?" Seqenenra enquired abruptly, wondering if this was some ploy of Si-Amun's to avoid the march, but Si-Amun denied it.

"No, Father, I am not ill. I just wanted to tell you . . . to tell you . . ." His lips quivered. "There will be much confusion tomorrow and little time for idle talk in the days to come. I may not have a chance to say this again." He glanced into Seqenenra's face. "I love you, my Father. I regret deeply all the pain I have caused you. If I could bear your infirmity I would. Believe that I will fight beside you with all my strength, and willingly. Thank you for the life you have given me." He was so distressed that he could hardly form the words. Seqenenra was shaken.

"The only pain you have caused me has been in seeing your misery and in being unable to help," he replied, mystified. "Even now you suffer and yet keep it to yourself. Share it with me, Si-Amun." Tears began to run down the young man's cheeks.

"I cannot," he said. "Believe what I have told you, Father. I am nothing as a man, nothing, but my arm will be raised in your defence. Forgive me."

"But what for?" Si-Amun turned convulsively, teeth and fists clenched.

"Forgive me!"

"How could I not forgive you anything?" Seqenenra replied, deeply disturbed. "Calm yourself, Si-Amun." For answer the young man smiled through his tears and ran to the door, wrenching it open and disappearing into the darkness beyond.

All at once Seqenenra was blindingly aware of the pain in his head. His eyelid was twitching. "Uni!" he shouted. "Go to the physician and bring me poppy. I cannot sleep with this pain!" He was answered by Aahotep.

"He heard you, Seqenenra." She had slipped into the room, followed by her steward Kares, who was carrying a folding camp cot yhat he proceeded to set up beside the couch. Aahotep then waved him out. "We have not made love in months," she said determinedly. "I understand why, even though I think you are wrong. I have not come to argue with you. I merely wish to spend the night here. Amun only knows when I shall see you again."

He lay not speaking, watching her movements as she shed the thin cloak and reached for her sleeping robe. She was all smooth curves. Her hips quivered. Her breasts swung. Her skin was softly bronze in the light of the night lamp. Expertly she pulled a comb through her straight black hair, holding it in one hand while she worked at the knots, her head on one side, then tossing it back where it lay glossy and tamed beyond her shoulders. She lay down at last, pulling the sheet to her waist. "How hot it is!" she exclaimed. "As I was coming in I passed Si-Amun leaving your room. He almost knocked me down. What did he want?"

Seqenenra found his voice. He felt awkward and foolish, smitten as always by her natural sensuality yet cursing himself for his lack of faith in her love for him. What did she think when she looked at him naked now, with his lumpish, useless leg and the arm that slithered here and there of its own accord, the mouth that could not form a kiss, the eye closed in a permanent half-wink? No matter how she protested her affection, she was a mature woman accustomed to the attentions of the lusty man he had been. Surely somewhere behind those sooty eyes there was a shrinking, a contempt? "I do not know," he answered slowly. "He told me he was pleased to fight beside me, and that he was sorry, and then he left."

There was a discreet tap on the door. Uni entered bearing a tray on which perched a small phial. Seqenenra breathed his relief. He tipped back the phial, tasting the bitter medicine, then closed his eyes. Uni padded out. Aahotep was silent but for her light breathing. Seqenenra felt the slow balm stealing through his body, and with it came drowsiness. The pain ebbed. His thoughts diffused, and he slept.

He half-woke at some time in the night to find Aahotep stretched out beside him, her lips moving leisurely over his chest. He grunted a protest but was too sleepy to do more. "Hush," she whispered. "You can always pretend that I am a dream."

"I am not that much of a coward," he murmured back, "but do not give me your pity, Aahotep." For answer she bit him.

"I know of no one less deserving of pity," she hissed back. "Are you going to leave me with this hunger unsatisfied?" Her mouth was now questing his stomach and he felt himself responding. "Put your pride away," she begged. "You do not need it with me. I love you, Prince." With an inner twisting of despair he did as she had asked, but the passion he felt could not dispel his humiliation.

At dawn he was boated across the river and then carried to the large area of scuffed ground where the army was assembling, Aahotep riding beside him in her litter. They did not speak. There was nothing to say. Seqenenra had been dressed in a blue kilt and sturdy leather sandals. His head was enveloped in the stiff blue helmet of the charioteer. His spear lay beside him and a knife hung at his belt, but he had relinquished his bow and arrows.

As they swayed towards the temporary mustering ground, the distant babble of voices became a roar emerging from the dry dust cloud that powdered the brown trees and hung fine and white in the air. The bearers slowed. Seqenenra saw the women of the family clustered behind a protecting canopy.

Aahmes-nefertari looked sleepy. Tani had dressed with care, wearing many of the jewels Ramose had given her, but her tight, simple sheath was blue, the colour of mourning. Tetisheri sat with Isis and Mersu to either side, her wig dotted with gold flowers and her earrings swinging. She had donned yellow, a triumphant colour full of promise, and Seqenenra smiled to himself in appreciation. His mother, of all the family, had no doubts about the outcome of the conflict.

The litter came to rest. Kamose hurried out of the murk, Si-Amun beside him. "You will have to address the troops in my place," Seqenenra said to them as they helped him to stand. Uni eased the crutch under his arm. "Are the chariots yoked?"

"Yes. Will you wait here until the army has formed marching ranks?" Kamose urged him. "The High Priest has just arrived to give us Amun's protection. When he has done so, I will speak."

Si-Amun said nothing. As Seqenenra's heir it was his place to talk to the soldiers, but he merely set his mouth in a thin line and beckoned impatiently for a chair. Seqenenra sank onto it. Kamose and Si-Amun melted away and presently Seqenenra could hear a barrage of crisp orders barked. "Captains of Fifty! Captains of a Hundred! Form up your men! Commanders to the dais!" He felt a soft hand on his shoulder. The girls had gathered by him.

"Father, as you pass Khemennu please tell Ramose how much I love him and try to persuade Teti to honour the contract," Tani pleaded. She bent and kissed him. "Be careful. Stay away from the fighting. You are the Prince, you can command without danger if you choose." Her voice faltered. Seqenenra nodded dumbly and reached up to stroke her face. Aahmes-nefertari was crying, the swollen eyes so like her mother's huge with tears. He took her hand briefly, wanting to cry himself. Aahotep was at his side, still silent. Her linen stirred against his knee.

The shouts and scuffles around them grew, then slowly faded into a waiting silence. Gradually the dust cleared. Amunmose was mounting the dais in his long tunic and leopard skin, an acolyte beside him bearing a smoking censer. He began the prayers for victory and protection. Taking the censer, he moved it above the stiff ranks. By his side was a large gold cup brimming with bull's blood that would be sprinkled on the soldiers as they marched past the dais.

Seqenenra listened to the clear, echoing voice of his friend, his heart constricting with foreboding, wondering if any but he knew the full fruitlessness of this gesture of his. He was the instrument of destruction for Tani, for Aahmes-nefertari and her unborn child, for his wife. He dared not think of the twins, both standing tall and thoughtful on the dais in their battle gear. He dared not consider the King more than six hundred miles away. Only the thought of his own fate gave him peace. Selfish, he said to himself. I had no choice, yet I wish that he and I could have met in single combat before I became the useless hulk I am now.

Ra had lifted above the eastern desert to spark gold on the tips of the hundreds of spears forested on the plain and slide brightly along the spokes of the chariot wheels that rolled to and fro as the restless horses whickered and fidgeted. Beyond the Nile the walls of Seqenenra's estate rose tall and the temple glowed sturdy and brown. On the shrunken surface of the river the light splintered and sank into the gentle, constant swells lapping the bank. The western cliffs lit suddenly, jagged and beautiful. Ah, Weset, Seqenenra thought. Quiet, hot and sleepy. A place where a man might dream his life away in perfect contentment. The pain of losing you is like a knife under my ribs. Farewell.

Amunmose had fallen silent. Si-Amun left the dais and came to assist his father who went slowly to meet him. Together they mounted the few steps, Si-Amun's arm around Seqenenra. Kamose began his address but Seqenenra, balanced precariously on his crutch, hardly listened to his son's powerful tones. Words of Ma'at, majesty and cause flowed over him. He surveyed the orderly lines, his eyes wandering from the stern faces of the Braves of the King directly below, bows slung over their massive shoulders, past the chariots with their blue-plumed horses and blue-helmeted drivers, to the files of infantry standing attentively and soberly beyond.

The Medjay stood out with their black bodies, a head taller than their Egyptian fellows. Their hair, like Hor-Aha's, lay long and plaited on their naked chests. The Egyptian conscripts had also grown their hair, a soldier's superstition and an attempt at protection, and it hung darkly gleaming to their shoulders. More bowmen than I had hoped, Seqenenra thought. That is good. How fine they look, how predatory! But how few, my Division of Amun that is not a division. Amun, you of the Double Plumes, be with us in the coming days and shield us with your might!

Kamose had finished. Hor-Aha called hoarsely and the men began to stride past the dais as Amunmose took the cup of blood and began to sprinkle them as they came. Their eyes fled from him to the Prince, his distorted face watching each one as they received the blessing and went to form marching ranks along the river road. Si-Amun touched his arm and obediently he left the dais, waiting at the foot while his chariot was brought. A chair had been tied to the chariot's frame, with a high back against which he could lean. Over it arched a canopy. Aahotep and the girls came to embrace him and their hands followed him as he climbed into the chariot and Si-Amun settled him on the chair, tying him into it securely. Seeing him thus, immobile, his spear now in his hand, Aahotep flung herself into the chariot. Her arms went around him. "I love you, Seqenenra," she cried out, her head pressed into his neck. "It is hard to see you go like this!"

For one delirious moment he inhaled her warm odour, then he pushed her away. "Ahmose will need you," he said steadily, "and you must comfort the girls. See that a shrine to Montu is kept open in the house, and the sacrifices made. The god of war will listen." She recovered herself and got out of the chariot. The girls stood with her. Seqenenra heard the order to march. Presently Si-Amun leaped up before him and picked up the reins.

The chariot jerked and began to roll. Si-Amun waved to his mother and brandished his whip. With difficulty Seqenenra looked back. They were still standing where he had left them beside the track in the dust churned afresh by the marching feet behind him. Aahotep had her arms around the girls. Tetisheri, well back and surrounded by her servants, had come to her feet in salute. They seemed so small against the backdrop of the river, their figures framed by the temple pylon beyond the water where the flags rippled in the new breeze. The farther bank was crowded with a sea of quiet citizens who had come out to watch their Prince go off to war. They had not cheered. There was no mood of joyous anticipation. Their faces were anxious and solemn.

After one long look Seqenenra turned away. Before him were the splayed legs and flexing back of his son and the thud of the horses' little hooves in the hard-packed sand. Behind him some of the men were singing. He glanced back once more but a bend in the road led through a straggle of trees and hid his view. Only the tips of the temple flagstaffs could be seen, even now dropping to be lost in the jerking palm leaves. Weset was gone.

Chapter EIGHT

T HEY MADE GOOD TIME that day. Spirits were high in spite of the fiery heat and three hours after Ra had been swallowed by Nut they made camp beside the river at Kift. Seqenenra was exhausted. They had stopped briefly once to eat, but he had nibbled his bread and drunk his water still tied in the chariot. In spite of the shade his canopy afforded he was weak and dizzy by the time Hor-Aha came to help him down. "A good day, Prince," the General remarked as they entered the tent and Seqenenra's body servant came forward. "If we continue to cover twenty miles a day we should arrive at Qes in another ten or eleven days. But, of course, we will not. We must allow for lame horses, sick men and other mishaps. Say twelve days." Seqenenra smiled at Hor-Aha as he sank gratefully onto the camp cot.

"I will need twelve days to become hardened," he admitted ruefully. "See to the men, Hor-Aha, and when you have eaten, bring me my sons. Qes marks the boundary of my governorship according to our ancient agreement with Het-Uart. We must decide how to proceed once it is behind us." The General bowed and went out.

Seqenenra's body servant gently removed his sweat-stained helmet and rumpled kilt and began to wash him. Seqenenra lay with eyes closed against the blinding headache that knifed every time he moved, feeling his bruised, tired muscles relax under the trickles of the blessed cool water. He heard his body-guard take up their station outside with a cough and a low word or two. Beyond them the soldiers were still arriving and break-ing step, scattering to their assigned eating fires with much shouting and laughter. The body servant covered Seqenenra with a sheet, and lighting the one lamp that hung from the central tent pole, he went away to fetch the evening meal. Seqenenra dozed. He was woken by the man setting a tray con-taining smoked fish, bread and dried fruit beside him and he struggled to sit up and eat. He was suddenly ravenous.

He was nursing a cup of wine when Kamose, Si-Amun and Hor-Aha pushed into the tent. Dismissing the servant he told the men to sit and they folded onto the carpeted floor. Si-Amun was enveloped in a white tunic and his feet were bare. His face was red and his nose blistering from the long hours under the sun. Kamose had also changed, but into a fresh kilt and helmet. Hor-Aha wore his customary woollen cloak under which his weapons could be glimpsed. Seqenenra poured them wine and they drank greedily. "Kamose, dictate a message to the family," he said. "Tell them we are well. Has there been any activity on the river?" Hor-Aha shook his head.

"No royal skiffs or barges," he answered. "I have scouts well ahead of us. Things must be quiet in Kush, and of course now that Apepa has decided to build the temple at Weset he need send no more letters until the architects and masons arrive."

"If any heralds are intercepted, they must be killed," Seqe-nenra warned. "We cannot risk detection yet. We are still pass-ing through my nomes, so we are safe for a while."

"What do you intend to do once Qes is past?" Si-Amun asked. "Do we push on to Het-Uart with all speed or conquer as we go?"

"We must conquer as we go," Seqenenra said slowly, his words more unintelligible than usual because of his fatigue. Speaking was an effort. "We cannot become an island in a sea of enemies. I wish to absorb any mayors or governors who can be persuaded to join us and who have warriors at their disposal."

"That is not likely after Qes," Kamose cut in. "From there north, all the men with power are Setiu."

"But their subjects are not, nor their minor officials. The villages are isolated along the river. We will take the men as we go. At the seats of government we will meet with the ministers and try to persuade them, and if that is not possible we will kill them and then sweep up their underlings." Seqenenra paused to summon his strength. His eyelid was pricking. "Did we lose any donkeys?"

"No, Prince," Hor-Aha assured him. "The supplies have now caught up with us. The men are being fed and guards have been set. We may look to a quiet night." The words were balm to Seqenenra's throbbing ears.

"Then you are dismissed. Si-Amun, find my physician. I need something to still my head." Seeing his distress they murmured their good nights and left.

Presently the physician came, examined him, and saying little, poured a draught of poppy. Seqenenra drank eagerly. For a while he thought of Aahotep, of Ahmose and Tetisheri probably still closeted together with mountains of administrative scrolls, of Tani perhaps sleepless and alone, but his thoughts ran together and dissolved into dreams and he slept.

At Iunet and Quena he was received by the towns' administrators, nervous and worried men who had already provided peasants for Kamose's conscription. They had no news for Seqenenra. As far as they knew, all was quiet in the few miles north where their jurisdiction extended. A summer lassitude lay on the countryside.

Seqenenra thanked them and resumed his march. He felt
weaker every day, knowing that this journey taxed even hardened soldiers accustomed to Hor-Aha's strenuous training. His
own small programme of exercise saved him from complete collapse, but he began to suffer fevers that rose in the evening and
kept him alternately shivering and sweating until the dawn.
His physician begged him to turn back, to deliver the army into
the hands of his sons, but Seqenenra knew that, maimed and
useless as he was, the common soldiers still regarded him as
their talisman and the heart would go out of them if he crawled
back to Weset with his tail between his legs. He did not know
how he was to reach Het-Uart, weeks away. He tried not to
think of it. He concentrated on Qes.

At Aabtu the whole army went into the temple where the
head of Osiris was buried and did homage to Egypt's most ven-
erated deity. The Prince of Aabtu, Ankhmahor, had sent many
soldiers to Kamose and he had brought together a further two
hundred men for Seqenenra. "But these are good farmers, Highness," he reminded Seqenenra. "They are needed in this nome
once the Inundation recedes. Please send them home as soon as
you have taken Het-Uart." Seqenenra, overcome with gratitude
and giddy with fever, agreed. They were five days out of Weset.

The following time passed like the sullen, muddy flow of the
river itself. During the day Seqenenra grimly endured the heat
and dust, the ever-present flies, the jolting of the chariot. At
night there were the fires, the tents, a brief conference, then
the blessed release of drugged sleep.

He had sailed by these towns—Thinis where the first Kings
of Egypt had built their palaces, Akhmin where he had personal acres under cultivation, Badari of the doum palms—innu-
merable times, gliding past on his barge, beer in his hand as he
lounged under the shade of canopies with Aahotep on their
way to Khemennu. But to roll through them in a chariot, mile

following weary mile of dead fields, dry canals, barren shrubs and knotted bare trees, was to experience a different Egypt, a merciless country of ugliness and waste. He knew it was only summer, only the discomfort and misery of a land lying parched and waiting for its miraculous rebirth, but more than once he asked himself if this was what he was risking his titles, his estate and his very life for, this sun-beaten strip of aridity beside a stinking, thin dribble of water. Only pride kept his head high behind the sweating back of his son as the hours crawled by.

They reached Qes without incident on the eleventh day. No fort or physical boundary marked the limit of Seqenenra's contro; indeed, there was not even a sizeable town. The cultivated land on the west bank gave way to a large patch of desert that was interrupted by cliffs through which a narrow defile snaked. The desert continued untrammelled on the other side. Beyond the cliffs was a small village.

Here also was a temple to Hathor. With her gold-sheathed cow's horns and her bovine, enigmatic smile she presided over a silence broken only by the few villagers who came to lay bread and flowers at her feet. With the coming of the Setiu her support had waned. Her priests had been forced to look elsewhere for their livelihood, and Hathor dreamed on alone. Seqenenra had promised Aahotep that he would visit the temple and make prayers to the goddess on her behalf. On a windswept, golden evening, while the army spread out on the plain before the cliffs and gathered in groups to polish weapons, wolf down their rations or sleep, he had himself carried through the short cut in the cliffs and into Hathor's forecourt.

Everywhere there was evidence of decay. Weeds, now brittle and dead, had pushed between the paving stones. Desert dogs had left their litter of dried offal and bones strewn over the floor of the inner court. One wall and part of the sanctuary roof were sagging. But Hathor herself was still within, gazing past

Seqenenra as he stood, hands full of wine and food, her comely body painted in a white sheath, her neck decorated with lapis lazuli and gold.

Si-Amun had accompanied him, and together, Seqenenra awkwardly standing and his son prostrate on the cracked and broken floor, they prayed for the health and long life of the women in their family. There were no priests to receive the offerings. They laid the goods at the feet of the statue, backed out of the sanctuary, and Si-Amun with difficulty forced the doors of the tiny room closed. Before long the inner roof would collapse, enabling visitors to scramble into the presence of the goddess, but it was not right that she should be exposed day after day to the curiosity and perhaps even blasphemy of anyone who might wander into the holy precincts.

Seqenenra's heart was heavy as he regained his litter in the outer court and was carried back to the camp in the now-violet splash of late evening. No forcible destruction could equal the sadness of this slow disintegration, he thought, noting Si-Amun's silent preoccupation. The same aura of pathos enveloped them both. The Setiu conquered us without spear or bow, did not burn the temples and kill the priests, yet slowly, slowly, the face of Egypt is changing. Neglect accomplishes in time what swords and arrows cannot.

By the time they got off their litters it was fully dark. Seqenenra had his cot brought outside and lay propped up, eating his sparse meal and listening to the orderly confusion around him. He was just finishing when Hor-Aha came, squatting in the dirt beside him. "I have decided to double the watch tonight," Hor-Aha said. "Word of our progress might have reached the King by now. His scouts might be on the move, though of course it is too soon for them to have reached Qes. The nearest large town is Khemennu and there is a small force of troops stationed there. In any case, it is as well to be prepared." Gloom seized Seqenenra. Tomorrow the work would begin in earnest.

"So many 'mights,' Hor-Aha!" he acknowledged. "At dawn tomorrow gather the officers. We will set the Amun shrine out in the open and make a sacrifice before we leave. How many days do you think before Apepa's forces try to stop us?" Hor-Aha frowned, considering.

"Three days to organize his troops. No more than that, given the fact that the standing army in Het-Uart is very great. Two weeks to march to Khemennu, and we will be moving north to meet his army." He looked up and smiled coldly. "It is very difficult to say, Highness, but we should be ready to give battle in five days and every day from then on."

"What do the scouts say?"

"Up until yesterday all was quiet. But they have not returned today." He shrugged his cloak to cover his hands, his usual gesture of anxiety. "They should have been back before sunset." Seqenenra became alert.

"Have you sent others out after them?" The General nodded.

"We may hear nothing from them until the morning. Prince, I do not advise that we move on until they have returned." Seqenenra disagreed.

"You said yourself that Apepa's army cannot possibly be close yet," he said. "We cannot afford to keep four thousand men sitting about eating." Hor-Aha gave him a startled glance, then both men burst out laughing.

"All the same," Hor-Aha cautioned, his mirth gone as quickly as it appeared, "it is foolish to destroy ourselves needlessly."

When Hor-Aha had gone, Seqenenra dictated his nightly letter to Ahmose and the family and gave his instructions for tomorrow to Kamose, Si-Amun and the officers. They would be on the move early, on full alert, with the chariots and the

Braves of the King in the forefront, ready to take the brunt of whatever hostility they might encounter. There was little to add, no intricate strategy to plan. My campaign, Seqenenra reflected later as his body servant pulled the sheet over him and he drank the remedy the physician had sent, is crudeness itself.

At sometime in the night he was woken by urgent voices outside the tent. Fighting to clear the drug fumes from his head he sat up. His body servant was already struggling from his pallet on the floor and reaching to replenish the oil in the lamp. "I cannot disturb the Prince's rest," Seqenenra heard one of his bodyguard say. "If you wish, I can have you escorted to the General Hor-Aha."

"No!" someone retorted sharply. "I must see Seqenenra now!"

"That is Ramose's voice," Seqenenra said aloud, and to the servant, "Have him admitted."

He licked his lips, dry from the poppy. His tongue felt twice its normal size. Manoeuvring himself carefully, he poured water and drank thirstily, replacing the cup just as Ramose was ushered into the tent. The bodyguard with him stood uncertainly, one hand on the knife at his belt. Seqenenra nodded at him. "Thank you for your vigilance," he said. "I am quite safe with this man. You can go."

Ramose came forward. He looked drawn and dishevelled. Wordlessly he bowed and at Seqenenra's invitation, folded onto the mat beside the couch. Seqenenra was astonished to see him here, in the tent, unpainted and looking ill. "Ramose, where have you come from?" he finally asked. "Where are you going? Are you on your way south and stumbled onto my army?" Ramose shook his head.

"Your pardon, Prince, but I would like some wine. I am somewhat unnerved." He was indeed trembling. "I should not be here. I left my tent nearly two hours ago with orders to my servant to tell any enquirer that I could not be disturbed until morning. The poor man is terrified but loyal. If I am discovered, I shall be executed." Seqenenra's servant did not need to be told. He had slipped out and returned a moment later with a jug of wine and a cup. Ramose thanked him, poured, and drank. He was calmer by the time he had wiped his mouth on the back of his hand.

"What are you doing at Qes?" Seqenenra asked bewildered, but a horrible suspicion began to form in his mind. "Are you hunting out on the desert?" Ramose shook his head. He passed his palms slowly back and forth over his knees.

"Prince, you have been betrayed," he said huskily. "The King's General Pezedkhu is camped just beyond Qes. He has a division and a half with him. Apepa did not know how many soldiers would be marching north with you, you see, so he ordered out a number large enough to overrun any army you might have assembled. If you march over the boundary of your jurisdiction, you will be routed. If you strike camp and go back to Weset immediately, you can avoid a bloody conflict." Seqenenra stared at him, the blood turning sluggish and cold in his veins.

"But that is not possible!" he exclaimed, the force of his emotion rendering him almost inarticulate. He slammed a finger against his sagging mouth. "Not unless..."

"Not unless someone sent word to Apepa long ago, before you even began to gather your forces," Ramose finished for him. "I am sorry, Prince, but that is what happened. Word reached my father at Khemennu more than a month ago as to your intention and he forwarded it to Apepa. I knew nothing of it, I swear, until the day my father unsealed a scroll from the King telling him that an army was on the way to wipe you out as far south as possible." Ramose looked down. "I was appalled. I could not believe that my father would inform on you, his relative by marriage, his friend. But our family has suffered in the past." He looked up pleadingly. "If Teti had not sold you to Apepa, then his motives in keeping quiet would have been suspect. Apepa would have believed that Teti was aiding you, even though my father would, of course, have denied it. Seqenenra, I am ashamed."

"I understand your father's perfidy," Seqenenra responded sadly. "So many divided loyalties, Ramose, so many private agonies! But how did Teti know what was discussed in the privacy of my home? I have a traitor still at Weset?" Ramose nodded miserably.

"The same man who attacked you. The scrolls have been coming from Mersu." Seqenenra cried out in shock.

"Mersu? Impossible! My mother trusts him completely, for years he has served diligently, he is . . . he is . . . Are you sure?"

"Yes." Ramose cleared his throat. "My father told me so. No deceit is impossible in the Egypt of today, Prince." He rose. "Forgive me but I must go. Please do not tell me what you will do. I do not want to know. I must fight beside my father tomorrow, but I swear I will not take arms against you or your sons. You are my friend." He stood there, anguished. "How could I harm Tani's family?" Seqenenra looked up at him.

"I know what it has cost you to come to me tonight," he said. "I thank you, Ramose. I do not yet know what I shall do but I am forever grateful for your loyalty." With his hand on the tent flap, Ramose hesitated.

"One thing more, Highness. Your scouts were captured by Pezedkhu yesterday morning. They were all executed, but not before one of them had told him the strength of your forces and the fact that you and two of your sons will be in the field."

"This Pezedkhu," Seqenenra said. "What is he like?"

"Young, athletic, a fine tactician. He laughs a great deal but his laughter is nothing, an affectation. Under it he is a cold man. Good night, Prince, and may Amun guide your decision." Ramose bowed and was gone.

For a long time Seqenenra was incapable of movement. He sat on the edge of the cot, his healthy arm clutching his lifeless one, rocking slightly, breathing hard. Mersu. Mersu. With a supreme effort he forced himself to see the tall, dignified, quietly smiling man as a traitor, as his enemy, as the one who had crept up behind him in the darkness and raised a Setiu axe, but behind the attempt was Mersu the defender and supporter of his mother, the smoother of her affairs, the tactful adviser, the steward who asked for nothing.

With a sick shudder Seqenenra knew that Mersu's defection had not been the action of a man terrified by the consequences of rebellion. Mersu had cool nerves. Nor did he think it had been a matter of divided loyalties with his allegiance to Apepa winning. No. Mersu the silently efficient was Setiu, from his crisp brown hair to his neatly cut toenails, and probably held the house of Tao in disdain if not in outright hatred. Am I being too harsh? Seqenenra asked himself, inwardly groaning. Can any but the gods see into the heart of a man in these terrible days? I must summon Hor-Aha and my sons. I must decide what to do. The inevitable conflict has simply been moved ahead, that is all. Upon us now instead of a week, two weeks, hence. We would be no better prepared then . . .

Stiffly, with great difficulty, he found his crutch and limped to the tent flap. The guard outside turned at his coming. "Bring the Princes Kamose and Si-Amun and General Hor-Aha to me at once," he commanded. "Find out how many hours there are until Ra is reborn." His body servant, squatting just outside, stood inquiringly, but Seqenenra waved him down and went back into the tent. A fatalism was on him now and he was not afraid.

They slipped into the tent, all three alert and expectant.

Quickly Seqenenra told them of Ramose's clandestine visit and his news, his eyes moving from one to the other in the dim light. Kamose sighed and his shoulders slumped. Hor-Aha absorbed the shock quickly, and Seqenenra could see fresh plots and possibilities forming on his face.

But there was no surprise in Si-Amun's expression. The colour drained from him. He looked around wildly, Seqenenra presumed for wine although he did not touch the remains of Ramose's jug, then with a visible effort he folded his arms and stared at the floor. "If we had barges, we could ferry the men across the river tonight and simply march past Pezedkhu on the opposite bank," Kamose said bleakly, "then straight on for the Delta, leaving him and his men behind. It would take a long time for him to get his hordes across."

"But we have no barges," Hor-Aha pointed out, "and even if we did, the night is too far advanced for such an undertaking." He turned to Seqenenra. "There is a break in the cliffs by Qes. Could we take the army through it and march north in the desert?" Seqenenra considered. "It is two miles to the cleft," he replied, "and there is not another until Dashlut where we could rejoin the river. We might escape notice going out onto the desert but would we be ambushed trying to return to the river?" He regarded their tense faces. "However, your suggestion is the only one that gives us the slightest chance of winning through. There is no time for anything else, for we are trapped. Our only open road lies to the south, and that way I will not go. I have made my decision." He spoke adamantly. "If I run home, retribution might be delayed, but it will surely fall sooner or later. We have not expended this supreme effort to be routed without one arrow being fired. Pass the word to the officers. We strike camp immediately and in silence. No noise, no fires and no lights. We will make for the cleft and pray all are through it by dawn."

They discussed the matter for a while longer but there was little more to be said and in the end they scattered to rouse the bleary, grumbling soldiers and order the supplies packed and loaded onto the donkeys. Seqenenra, after summoning his servant, sat on his cot in mingled worry and a perverted kind of relief. It was some time before he realized that Si-Amun had not uttered a single word.

They filed across the dead fields and into the blinding darkness of the rocky defile between the cliffs, the scouts fanning out ahead, the chariots and the Braves of the King divided and going before and behind. Kamose had ordered the horses' harnesses muffled and the only sounds were the soft thud of hoofs on the hard-baked ground and the creaking of leather. The plain beside the river slowly emptied. Seqenenra, strapped behind Si-Amun, felt every muscle tight with apprehension as they crawled forward. He sensed rather than saw that the sun was about to rise. The air was stale and motionless so that he shivered, not knowing whether he was hot or cold. Occasionally the horses' hoofs struck sparks from the small, sharp stones that littered the way between the soaring cliffs he could not see. He heard Hor-Aha give a soft, curt command and presently Si-Amun reined the horses to the right.

The desert opened out before Seqenenra, a flow of pale, churned sand running to meet a black sky thick with stars. He took a deep breath. The village of Qes, a jumble of lightless huts, lay to his left and was already receding, the grey lines of Hathor's tiny temple with it. Seqenenra swallowed. The chariot jerked as the wheels ploughed into sand. Then the horses found the firmer ground beneath the cliffs and picked up their pace. They were once more facing north, and the boundary of his princedom was behind him.

The darkness began to thin. Soon Seqenenra could make out the silhouette of the rocks rearing jagged and tiered above him on his right. The desert stopped flowing indistinctly and became hollows and dunes, still a lifeless grey but beginning to throw out spidery shadows. With difficulty Seqenenra twisted around. Behind him his army snaked, the men trudging with heads down and eyes on their feet, for the terrain was one moment clinging sand and the next hard-crusted soil. He saw them as dim wraiths, their forms unclear, their obedient silence otherworldly, as though the battle had already been fought, the soldiers murdered, he himself leading an army of ghosts towards eternity. It was only the approach of the light-without-Ra, he knew, but he could not dismiss the premonition that possessed him.

The sky faded to pearl. The stars went out. If he braved the spray of fine sand the horses kicked up and craned to the side, he could see ahead to where the Braves' chariots were wheeling out on the desert. The cleft at Dashlut was nine miles away. Their progress was slow. They should reach it by early afternoon. Seqenenra wondered when the scouts would return. Probably not much before the army itself slowed to negotiate the winding track back towards the Nile. He forced himself to remain calm.

The sun had now risen. The army marched on the western flank of the cliffs in the blessed cool shadow that would shrink as the morning progressed. But now the men were cheerful, the order of silence lifted, and their white teeth flashed in their dark faces as they sang. Occasionally an officer rolled by, saluting Seqenenra as he inspected the ranks, the blue plumes on his horses waving in the morning breeze.

Just before the sheltering shadow shrank to nothing, Seqenenra called a halt. The men broke rank and cast themselves on the ground, waiting for the distribution of water and bread. Seqenenra had his chariot backed against the cliff, and ate and drank in his bonds. He was beginning to worry about the

horses. Without water they tired quickly. They were not creatures of the desert. With luck they could be led to the Nile this
evening.

By the time he had swallowed his allotment of warm, brack-
ish water and dry bread, the shade had disappeared. Orders
rang out and the men stretched, picked up their spears, and
formed rank once more. Seqenenra had his canopy attached.
The sun had appeared over the top of the cliff and immediately
attacked them all. There was no more singing. The men strode
doggedly, sweating and thirsty. Amun, Seqenenra prayed as he
watched Si-Amun's bronze back become slippery and his kilt
transparent and sticky with his body's moisture, let us not have
to fight in this. If we do, then Ra, more than Pezedkhu, will be
the death-dealer.

It was with immeasurable relief four hours later that he saw
the cavalcade slow and at last come to a halt. The horses were
wheezing and trembling, their sides drenched and white with
foam. Si-Amun sank onto his haunches, the reins loose in his
hand, and rested his head against the burnished prow of the
chariot. Presently Kamose came up and stepped from his vehi-
cle. "The corridor to Dashlut is ahead," he told his father. "The
scouts returned about an hour ago and reported a clear passage.
The land between the exit and the river seemed empty but I do
not like it. There were not even any peasants about."

"Pezedkhu's scouts will have discovered our last camp at Qes
at dawn," Seqenenra pondered aloud. "Will he believe that we
turned around and started back to Weset or will he suspect the
truth? If I were the General I would send scouts south to verify
our flight, but I would also take my troops to Dashlut so that
every eventuality would be covered. He can move more swiftly
than we. He has not had to battle the sand." He shaded his eyes
and looked at Kamose. "What do you think?"

"I think that one does not become the King's General unless

186 / LORDS OF THE TWO LANDS

one is wily as well as a good warrior," Kamose replied. "We must presume that he is hard on our heels. Can we continue to march along behind the cliffs?"

"I don't think so," Seqenenra answered. "The horses need water. The next break in the cliffs is at Hor, beyond Khemennu, and to reach it we would have to detour many miles into the desert to get around the cliffs that sprawl in great spurs out into the sand. Teti hunts there often. The rock provides good shelter for lions." He resisted the urge to reach up and rub the old wound on his head which was itching fiercely. "The men must rest. We could camp here and guard the entrance to Dashlut, in which case Pezedkhu would have the time to arrive and cut us off at the other end, or we can march through and camp briefly by the Nile, just long enough to sleep for an hour before pressing on. Either way we do not have enough of a start to outrun Pezedkhu entirely."

"Then let us go through to the river," Kamose said. "We have ample food on the donkeys but water goes at a terrifying rate and if we are cut off from the river we die of thirst in a very short time. Better to give battle than give Apepa the satisfaction of having killed us without a blow!" Seqenenra nodded.

"So be it." He watched Kamose spring into the chariot, shaking sand from his feet as he did so, and suddenly he wanted to run after him, to embrace him tightly, to feel his hot, taut flesh pressed close. Kamose brandished his whip and was gone in a whirl of dust. Si-Amun stirred. "Has the sun made you sick?" Seqenenra asked him anxiously. Si-Amun came to his feet, gathering up the reins. He gave his father a queer, twisted smile. "No," he replied. "It takes more than mighty Ra to make me quail. I am sick with the need to kill." To that, Seqenenra had no answer. Si-Amun whistled at the horses and the chariot started forward. Already the vanguard of the Braves had disappeared into the narrow gap in the cliff.

The strip of land between cliff and river, thick in winter with green crops springing from the marshy ground, but now lying like the parched bed of some long-dried-up lake, was wider at Dashlut than at Qes. Seqenenra, emerging from the sweet coolness of shade between the cliff sides with the hair at the base of his neck standing up, looked anxiously towards the Nile. It was dauntingly far away, and seemed farther than it was because of a heat haze that made the ground shimmer.

The horses, smelling water, tossed their weary heads and picked up speed. The army tumbled after, men's spirits rising now that the threat of the desert was behind them. Seqenenra heard Hor-Aha's voice raised above the babble of excitement. "What are you doing, you fool! Don't take them out of harness! Where are the stable boys with the buckets?" The confusion was orderly. Servants moved among the stationary chariots, some watering the beasts, some checking the harnesses. The charioteers were gathered around Hor-Aha, their blue helmets bent to hear his words. Guards were already taking up their stations on the perimeter. The soldiers were dipping ladles into the skin buckets being carried from one group to another. Seqenenra's servant came bowing, water in his hands, and Seqenenra and Si-Amun drank greedily.

The group around Hor-Aha broke up. Kamose came striding up to his father. "What are your orders?" he asked. Seqenenra gazed to the north, then to the south. He was uneasy but the scene that met his eye was peaceful. The river seemed empty, flowing shallow and turgid below its banks. The tired trees bent under the weight of the sun. The acres across which the army was sprawled was shadowless.

"Pass the word among the officers that the men may sleep for an hour if they wish," he said, his eyes returning to Kamose, "but they must do so in battle formation, weapons to hand. Charioteers in their vehicles, horses yoked. Divide the Braves.

Put half of them on our south flank and half on our north. I do not like this summer afternoon, Kamose. It sends shivers down my spine." After Kamose had gone, Si-Amun eased himself down onto the floor of the chariot.

"Let me untie you, Father, so that you can at least lie down for a while," he begged. "I would like the physician to take a look at you." Seqenenra hesitated. It was true that his back ached, not to mention his head. It would be a relief to stretch out. Again he surveyed the countryside, asleep under the sun's drug. Many soldiers had cast themselves on the ground, kilts drawn up to cover their heads.

"Very well," he answered after a while. "But no physician, Si-Amun. There is nothing he can do." Si-Amun untied him and gently helped him to lower himself onto the floor of the chariot, just out of reach of the sun's rays. He relaxed with a sigh. Presently he said, "Si-Amun, I know that I am putting you in grave danger. You should have a warrior at your back to fight while you manoeuvre the chariot. I have instructed one of the Braves to follow us closely, and if I fail he must take my place. Neither must you try to protect me at the risk of your own safety. Agreed?" Si-Amun turned his head. He was lying beside his father, arm touching arm. Now he smiled, and their dry, hot breath mingled.

"Agreed," he said. "I am where I wish to be, Prince. I am a good driver and a good warrior. Stop fretting." Seqenenra grunted sleepily, but was too tired to say more. He fell into a restless doze.

He was woken by the sound of a horse screaming. In the second before he came fully awake he wished irritably that Ahmose would understand that at certain seasons the stallions should not be stabled next door to each other, then he was fighting to pull himself up in the chariot, Si-Amun grabbing for the reins that had been looped over the front bar. His army, now scrambling to its feet and groping for its spears, was surrounded by a sea of chariots whose horses sported the blue and white plumes of royalty. Beyond the chariots the royal infantry stood, the men fresh and terrible, the late sunlight glinting red on the forest of spear tips, the sturdy shields and the axes hanging from their belts.

Si-Amun reached for his father with one arm, trying to control the frightened horses with the other, but Seqenenra clung to the chariot's side and pushed him away. "I can balance here!" he shouted. "We must take the offensive! Move, Si-Amun!" Even as Si-Amun turned, lashing the horses, and they began to roll over the baked ground, Seqenenra heard a volley of yelled commands echo against the cliff face and his army was galvanized.

He saw Kamose draw a knife and cut the throat of the horse that had been felled by an arrow before leaping back into his chariot behind his driver and vanishing into the whirl of dust the other chariots were making. Behind them the soldiers had begun to run in orderly ranks, spears canted under their arms, shields raised. Seqenenra, teeth clenched, the fingers of his good hand locked tightly around the smooth bronze bar of the chariot, spared a glance behind.

What he saw made him breathe a prayer of thanks to Amun for his decision to divide the Braves, for Pezedkhu had anticipated his move and had held back half his division to the south, sending the rest to the north of the Dashlut rift. We are trapped, Seqenenra thought as his spear rattled against his feet, unless we can somehow escape through the cliffs and re-form on the desert where there is room to move. I was a fool to come through. I should have stayed out there in the sand. One charge to hold them off, and then a retreat. But is there time?

Hor-Aha was in control of the north-facing troops. His voice rose clear and confident above the roar of the first engagement. The chariots flung themselves at the opposing forces. Si-Amun cried a warning a moment before Seqenenra's chariot came to an abrupt halt which nearly tore his arm out of its socket. In the small hiatus, Seqenenra shouted, "Order a retreat through the cliff path! The Braves and the chariots can defend!" Si-Amun nodded, volleying commands to those around him who ran to pass the word. Arrows clattered against the chariot and Seqenenra instinctively ducked, bending with difficulty to retrieve his spear. Now he had to stand with his back against the chariot to maintain his balance. He was gripping the spear with his good hand. Other chariots milled about, the charioteers trying to manoeuvre them into the best position for the warriors to shoot their arrows right into the enemy, and Pezedkhu's men were doing the same. Thrown spears, the first onslaught, littered the ground. Already the foot soldiers were shrieking and hacking at each other with axes and knives.

Seqenenra marked a man who had just jerked a dagger from the belly of one of his Medjay. The soldier was gasping, looking about for another victim to engage. Hafting his spear, Seqe-nenra sent it slicing through the air, but the small movements of the chariot spoiled his aim, unbalanced him, and he toppled onto the floor. With an oath Si-Amun dropped the reins and turned. The soldier was running towards them, axe raised for a throw. Coolly Si-Amun pulled a knife from his belt and it flew in a glittering arc to bury itself deep in the man's chest. With an expression of surprise he fell inches from Seqenenra's sweating face. "Stay down there, please, Father!" Si-Amun yelled at him. "The engagement is too fierce for a retreat."

A Brave had seen the exchange. He jumped into the chariot, bow at the ready, and straddling his Prince he began to fire arrows into the thick press of struggling bodies. Seqenenra watched. His heart gave a bound. It seemed as though his soldiers were holding their own here on the north flank of the battle. The lines had not been pressed back. Some of his chariots had freed themselves from the melee and were wheeling by the river, shooting the enemy on his perimeter.

The enemy, Seqenenra thought bitterly. Look at them! Few of them are Setiu. They are good Egyptian men killing good Egyptian men. How far we have come from the holiness of Ma'at! With the heat and terror of the moment his left eye had closed altogether and the lid was convulsing. His head was pounding. He heard the Brave shout, "They are breaking on the south front, Prince!" and for one delirious moment believed that he was speaking of Pezedkhu, but Si-Amun groaned.

The chariot swung about and began to move, bumping over the bodies of the slain. Seqenenra's line of vision changed. All at once he saw in the distance a chariot whose sides gleamed gold and whose spokes shot fire into the broiling afternoon. He took no notice of the charioteer, for behind him stood a tall young man whose arms sported silver Commander's armbands and whose blue and white helmet was banded in gold. He was pointing and shouting. It was Pezedkhu. Around him clustered his Braves, and beyond them the lines of the southern defence were grimly disciplined and orderly.

Before them, Seqenenra's soldiers were falling back, dying, fighting desperately, blocking any retreat through the mountain cleft. Their courage was a pathetic thing to see, bringing tears of anger to Seqenenra's eyes, but they were outnumbered. Desperately he sought Kamose and found him, his horses felled, fighting hand to hand from the rear of his chariot, his face and arms and the front of his kilt mired in blood.

Suddenly Seqenenra knew what Si-Amun was doing. He was trying to circle the conflict and slip into the rocky break in the cliffs. "I forbid you!" Seqenenra tried to shout up at him. "I do not want to be saved, Si-Amun! I do not want the shame of it!" But he found that he was groaning gibberish. Under such stress his deformed mouth no longer obeyed him.

For a long time Si-Amun tried to negotiate the groups of panting, bloody men who were hacking at each other with dedication, but he finally had to admit defeat. The way was completely cut off. Seqenenra could hear him muttering, could sense him looking to the north, to the south, desperate for a place to hide his father, while Seqenenra lay huddled between the stalwart legs of the Brave defending him.

The chariot came to a halt. Si-Amun crouched to peer into his father's face. "We are slowly being squeezed together," he said. His face was running sweat. "I cannot get you away. We are about to die, Prince." Seqenenra nodded. He did not try to speak. Si-Amun leaned down and kissed him. "This is my fault," he said. "All mine. May I take your axe and knives, Father?" Without waiting for an answer he lifted the heavy bronze weapon from Seqenenra's belt and slipped the short daggers into his hands. Then he stood. Seqenenra tried to pray but found he could not. The din around him was reaching deafening proportions, and in it was an hysterical note of panic. His men were about to be routed. Suddenly the man above him gave a hiccup. Blood spattered Seqenenra, a warm red shower, and the Brave was gone. With his good hand Seqenenra lifted his kilt and wiped his face.

Si-Amun shouted something. The chariot gave a great lurch and began to career. Seqenenra tried to brace himself but he was rolling towards the edge. He cried out, twisting, but Si-Amun could not help him. He was gone. The reins flapped loosely against the curved prow. With every ounce of strength he possessed Seqenenra tried to grab for them, while jamming his good leg against the side of the chariot, but the horses were in full flight. The reins slapped just out of reach of his straining fingers.

All at once the chariot struck an obstacle, began to cant, and Seqenenra tumbled out. The chariot tottered and fell. Dazed, Seqenenra felt pain explode along his healthy leg. He was lying in the shade of the chariot which half-lay above him. He heard Si-Amun calling, "I'm coming, Father, I'm coming!" Where is Kamose? Seqenenra thought. Hor-Aha? Are they dead? Dear Ahmose, try to carry on, try to hold what is left of the family together even if you must run . . .

He had a sudden, vivid vision of his garden in the cool silence of a long winter evening, the pool scarcely rippling, the trees scarcely quivering. Aahotep was sitting on the edge of the pool, one brown foot stirring the smooth depths. "It has been a glorious season, Seqenenra," she was saying. "So bountiful, so beautiful. There will never be another like it." Aahotep! he thought with anguish, teeth clenched against the pain. It has indeed been glorious, and terrible, and wondrously strange, this life of mine, yet I wish that I had been born in another time, a simpler time, when accepting my destiny might not have hurt so much.

His hand, groping spasmodically through the filthy earth, felt the hilt of a knife and he shook it free and clutched it fiercely. A man loomed above him, feet bare, kilt torn, raised axe crusted with blood. Seeing Seqenenra's helplessness he bared his teeth in a weary grin. Taking the axe in both hands he swung it over his head. Seqenenra swiftly jerked the knife towards the man's ankles but the man simply stepped aside. Amun, Seqenenra thought in the split second before he died, grant me a favourable weighing . . .

The last thing he saw was a glint of sombre red from the setting sun as the blade descended.

The axe struck Seqenenra above the right eye, rebounded to smash his right cheek, then glanced off the bridge of his nose. The soldier was tired and had not put as much strength into the blow as he had thought. Swearing, he raised it again and this time it cracked the bone under Seqenenra's left eye. Panting, the man clumsily wrenched it away and peered at the body. The chest was still trembling lightly. Catching up a spear from the disorder around him, he turned Seqenenra's head with one foot and drove the weapon into the skull behind the left ear. The body convulsed once and then was still. The soldier stumbled away.

Si-Amun had seen the man approach his father, consider, and heft his axe. With a scream he plunged forward, but one of Pezedkhu's unhorsed charioteers blundered into his path, knife at the ready, and Si-Amun was forced to engage him. By the time the man lay jerking at his feet it was too late. Horrified, Si-Amun saw the spear haft protruding from his father's neck. Once more he tried to cover the intervening ground and once more his way was blocked. Insane with grief and rage he began to lay about him, tears pouring unnoticed down his filthy cheeks. He was driven farther and farther away from his father's body still pinned under the chariot.

Chapter NINE

BY THE TIME THE sun had sunk red and sullen behind the western cliffs the field belonged to Pezedkhu. Those of Seqenenra's pitiful army who had not been killed or did not lie wounded on the scorching ground had run for the shelter of the tumbled rocks beneath the cliffs and it was there, close to the defile through which they had marched such a short time before, that Si-Amun found Kamose and Hor-Aha together with a few officers. They were hidden in a sandy gap about a quarter of the way up the rocky incline. They could look out upon the chaos of the battlefield without being seen and could if necessary defend their position for a little while. Si-Amun, scrambling mindlessly among the boulders, had almost fallen on them. He greeted them without enthusiasm. Kamose had been wounded in the side and his cheek had been laid open by a knife thrust. Hor-Aha nursed a shattered shoulder with his usual taciturnity. "Where is Father?" Kamose demanded as Si-Amun collapsed into the sand and closed his eyes. "You were supposed to guard him, Si-Amun."

"Don't be a fool, " Si-Amun croaked. "I tried, the Braves tried, but what could we do once the battle began to go against us? I was knocked from the chariot when the horses panicked and ran. Father was pinned under it. He was helpless. Immediately I began to fight my way to him but I was too late."

"He is dead?" Hor-Aha demanded softly. Si-Amun nodded. Kamose stared at him, noting the tracks his tears had made in the dirt of his face, the blood and mire encrusting him.

"Is there any water?" Si-Amun asked faintly. Kamose shook his head, fingering the red slit on his cheek and wincing.

"No water, no food," Hor-Aha answered. "We need both, and the physician, wherever he might be. If Amun has been merciful we will find all when we can go into the defile where the supply donkeys should be waiting. There is such a mess before the path. We must hope that the donkey drivers have been clever enough to withdraw towards the desert and Pezed-khu's men are too tired to explore, particularly at night."

Si-Amun crawled to the tiny vertical split in the rock and looked down towards the river. The sun's afterglow lit the land in a deep scarlet haze. The air was full of dust and still very hot. Pezedkhu's soldiers were moving among the slain, knives drawn. Some were recovering the chariots that lay overturned and horseless among the dead, and others were gathering up the precious bows, but most were going methodically from body to body, kneeling to saw off a hand from each one. Si-Amun withdrew. "They are collecting our bows and taking hands for the tally," he said. "How many died, I wonder? We must recover Father's body as soon as possible. Pray Amun they do not find him to take a hand from him!"

No one replied. Hor-Aha sat propped against a stone, his shoulder a mess of mangled flesh, his eyes drooping closed. Kamose lay with his head pillowed in a cloak, his hand pressing a wad of dirty kilt against his side. The officers sat or lay quietly, some nursing wounds, others trying to tend them. Si-Amun, his throat swollen with thirst, curled up in a hollow in the sand he had dug for himself. There was nothing any of them could do.

They slept fitfully through the night. Occasionally one of them would wake and crawl to the crack to watch the activity below, lit by the fires of the army's camp. Not much moved down there. Pezedkhu's soldiers were also exhausted.

Dawn came. To the men wracked with thirst and pain Ra seemed to leap into the sky with a spiteful speed and their hiding place was soon as hot as a crucible. Below, work began again. Few chariots remained. The bodies were being buried efficiently and quickly. "We must find Father soon," Kamose whispered. "He must be beautified, taken home to the House of the Dead. Otherwise, in this heat . . ." He left his sentence unfinished. Hor-Aha was in the grip of a fever and had begun to murmur nonsense. Si-Amun found a cloak and tried to make some shade for him.

The day dragged on with frightening slowness. Si-Amun went to Kamose and lay beside him. Kamose turned his head and smiled faintly. "We were not able to fight side by side as I had hoped," he whispered. "We have not been as close as we used to be, Si-Amun. I am so angry."

"It is not your fault," Si-Amun assured him. "Try and sleep now, Kamose. It will make the time go faster."

With an impudent lack of haste Ra reached his zenith and sailed towards the west. On the plain the victorious soldiers sang and laughed as they leisurely prepared their evening meal, cleaned their fouled weapons, and tended to their cuts. In their hiding place the men, feeling the approaching blessing of darkness, stirred to life. Hor-Aha was weak but now lucid.

At last the fires below were extinguished, the chariots yoked, the men formed into marching ranks. Si-Amun watched the activity as the sun sank behind him. There was a hush on the plain. In the last pink light a chariot rolled towards the cliffs and stopped. Its sides were of polished gold hammered into the likeness of Sutekh with his tall ears, his long snout and wolfish grin, his Setiu ribbons. Beside the chariot ran a soldier with a trumpet. At a gesture from the man standing in the chariot he raised it and blew. The sound echoed harsh and mournful among the rocks. Pezedkhu lifted an arm and Si-Amun saw his dark, kohled gaze travelling the face of the rocks.

"Proud Princes of Weset!" the General called, his voice strong with a taunting triumph. "The Lord of the Two Lands has answered your act of treason with death. He is mighty! He is invincible! He is the Beloved of Set! Crawl home if you can, and lick your wounds in shame and disgrace. Meditate upon your folly and upon the King's mercy, for he has granted you your lives. Life, health and prosperity be upon him who lives, like Ra, eternally!"

Kamose groaned. Si-Amun watched and listened with a wildly beating heart. Pezedkhu's arm dropped. The chariot wheeled away. Behind it Apepa's army began to move, a ponderous worm, into the evening dusk. Si-Amun saw them go. It took a long time. Darkness had fully fallen before the plain dissolved into its customary silence, broken only by the screech of a hunting owl and the rustle of mice along the bank of the river.

For a long time the men did not dare to stir. Then Si-Amun rose and stretched. His lips were cracked, his tongue swollen. "I will try to find the supply train and the physician," he said. "Two of you," he indicated the officers, "come with me. Another of you, go down to the river and bring back water. Have you a bottle?" One of them produced a leather skin. "Good. But go carefully. It is possible that Pezedkhu has left scouts to take us once we leave this place, although I am sure he does not really know who survived and was simply following the King's orders when he addressed us so magnanimously. Kamose, are you awake? Did you hear me?" His brother's faint assent came out of the darkness. Si-Amun glanced up at the sky. Soon the moon would rise and his going would be easier. Carefully he climbed out of the hollow and began to wind his way to the floor of the plain.

It was not far to the break he was looking for, and as he picked his way through the debris Pezedkhu's soldiers had reckoned not worthy of plunder, the moon rose above the eastern horizon, its blind fingers groping pale towards the river. Si-Amun breathed a prayer of thanks and shortly plunged into the blackness between the cliffs.

He trudged for over an hour, aware of nothing but his thirst and the protesting of his abused muscles, stumbling over sharp stones, slipping on shelves of gravel, until at last he heard the braying of a donkey far ahead. Before long he saw a flicker of yellow light off to his left, deep in a tributary path. Too tired to be cautious he half-ran, half-fell up it, almost into the arms of one of the soldiers left to guard the supplies. The man challenged him and at his answer drew back. "I need food, litters and the physician," Si-Amun managed. "Is he here? Have you water with you?" The man held out a bottle and Si-Amun snatched it and drank. It was the sweetest water he had ever tasted.

"The physician arrived last evening," the soldier told him. "He said the battle was lost. I will find him and bring you supplies." Refreshed, Si-Amun sank onto a rock.

"Keep the donkeys hidden here," he commanded. "We need a light also." The man went away and Si-Amun sat listening to the night silence, aware of the weight of stone around him, the black funnel of sky above. Suddenly, with a shock of horror, he thought of his father lying with the spear thrust through his skull. I am the governor of Weset now, he said to himself. Great Amun! I am the Prince. And I am also the rightful King of

Egypt. As soon as I return to Weset I must send a message to Apepa, an apology, an expression of obedience. This family must not suffer any more.

At the thought of the estate he was reminded of Mersu, of Teti and the courageous Ramose, and he squirmed and closed his eyes. I did not see Teti or Ramose in the battle, he went on in his mind, but I am sure they were there. May the gods have dealt Teti a swift death! How can I go home and have Mersu killed without a trial? For he must die. He opened his eyes. No. It must not begin again, the lies, the deceit, the shame. There on the battlefield I felt clean for the first time in months. I will tell Kamose everything and accept his judgement.

He led the physician and servants carrying litters and food back along the track to the place where the wounded men huddled. The physician immediately set to work, loosing the strings on his pack and unfolding his herbs. One of the servants lit a fire so that he could have hot water. Another set a lamp on the sand. Si-Amun withdrew and watched, feeling normality creep back with the sure, absorbed movements of the physician, the quiet efficiency of the servant's movements, the steady beam of the lamp. Hor-Aha's shoulder was washed and immobilized. Kamose had his side packed with herbs, bound, and his cheek sewn shut. Both men were soon drowsing on a poppy sea. The physician sighed, sat back on his heels, and turned to Si-Amun. "Where is my greatest charge, Prince?" he asked. Si-Amun looked away.

"My father is dead," he replied tonelessly. "He fell in the battle. We will find his body in the morning." The physician fell silent and presently returned his attention to his charges. The lamp was extinguished and the stars became visible, flaming stronger as the moon waned. Si-Amun left his rock and, wrapping himself in a cloak, fell asleep.

As soon as they could see each other, Si-Amun took two

servants and a litter and went down onto the plain. For a long time he paced the churned floor, trying desperately to remember exactly where the chariot had lain. Pezedkhu had removed them all and there was not a wandering horse to be seen. Si-Amun and his men stumbled over broken spears, stained axe heads, ripped and useless pieces of linen that had been kilts, scored leather harnesses. Occasionally they averted their eyes from a dismembered limb, black and grotesque in the grey dust. Dismally Si-Amun thought that they might be compelled to open the mounds that marked the mass graves of the combatants, but find his father they would. It was terrible enough that he had been maimed and then slaughtered while he lay helpless. Was he to be denied a place in the paradise of Osiris because his body could not be beautified?

Then a servant shouted and Si-Amun hurried to where the man stood over a depression in the ground close to where they had left the cliff. The man was flinging clods of earth at a hyena who now slunk away, whimpering. Furious and terrified at the damage the beast might have done to his father's corpse, Si-Amun raced forward. Seqenenra lay as Si-Amun had seen him last. The soldiers that had hauled the chariot upright and dragged it away had ignored him. There had been nothing to distinguish him as the lord of Weset. Somehow the spear that had pierced him had broken off near the tip and the corpse had slid down into the depression and been overlooked by the men taking hands for the tally.

Si-Amun knelt and carefully withdrew the remains of the spear. Seqenenra's eyes were full of sand. His lips were drawn back over his teeth in his final agony. With one loving finger Si-Amun reverently traced the mutilated face, then emotion overcame him. Sitting, he drew his father's body into his arms and wept, rocking to and fro in his grief. His men stood in silence, looking away.

The morning heat began to intensify. Vultures began to congregate on the cliffs behind, their mighty wings sending shafts of shadow over the plain. At last Si-Amun laid the body down and rose awkwardly. "He is putrefying already," he said unevenly. "How are we to return him to Weset for burial?" He gestured, and the litter was lowered. Seqenenra was laid on it and covered with linen. "Take him to the supply train," Si-Amun decided. "Find a box long enough for a temporary coffin. Fill it with dry sand and place him in the middle. We must hurry home." The thought of his mother, his grandmother, was too dreadful to contemplate. With an oath he began to run towards the cliffs.

After a hasty meal Si-Amun had the donkeys brought to the edge of the river and Kamose and Hor-Aha were placed on litters and carried to join them. They set off for home in the long, coloured evening. Seqenenra's makeshift coffin went first, guarded by Si-Amun, who strode beside it. As they moved slowly away from Dashlut, following the river road, other survivors joined them, soldiers who had fled to the cliffs as they did when all was lost. Si-Amun scarcely acknowledged their salutes as they took up positions in the rear, but Hor-Aha's black eyes followed them as they paced dejectedly past his litter. By the time the accursed plain of Dashlut had disappeared from view, he had counted more than two hundred of them.

It took the preoccupied and miserable cavalcade a night and almost all the next day to reach Qes. Many of the soldiers had minor wounds, and those carrying Kamose and Hor-Aha had to go carefully for fear of jolting their charges. Si-Amun, his thoughts on his father's slowly rotting body, was feverish to keep going. While the servants made camp and the physician examined his patients, he scouted the riverbank for boats. The donkeys, laden with all the supplies Seqenenra had painstakingly gathered for the march north, could be returned at leisure to Weset, but Seqenenra himself must be properly embalmed so that both the gods and his ka might recognize the Prince and give him life in the next world. His father's death weighed insupportably on Si-Amun's conscience. He knew he would go mad if Seqenenra arrived at the House of the Dead too late. But Qes had nothing to offer but a few tiny reed fishing boats and Si-Amun had to wait, gnawing his lips impatiently, while the men ate and slept the following night away.

In the morning Hor-Aha refused to lie on his litter. "It is my shoulder that is injured, not my legs," he snapped at the physician. "I am sufficiently rested now. I will walk." He joined Si-Amun at the head of the column as they set off once more, and there was some comfort for the Prince in Hor-Aha's long stride, his black braids moving rhythmically against the grubby folds of his woollen cloak, the occasional dart of his clear, dark eyes when they exchanged a word or two.

Three days later, at the town of Djawati, Si-Amun found what he was looking for. While the dignitaries of the place came out to gather around Kamose, shocked and unbelieving, and many sank to the ground by Seqenenra's coffin and began to grieve, Si-Amun went to the quay and commandeered two flat barges used for the transport of grain to the Delta, ordering helmsmen and rowers at the same time. He had Kamose and his father carried aboard one, and the rest of the soldiers and necessary supplies loaded on the other. The river was nearing its lowest level and scarcely flowed.

Leaving a couple of officers to oversee the donkeys' slow progress on the river road, Si-Amun settled with relief onto the floor of the barge and gave orders for canopies to be erected as it swung out from the shore. Only then did fatigue overtake him. He lay back. Servants had begun to distribute the afternoon's water. Si-Amun watched them draw nearer but before the cup was offered to him he was asleep.

At noon on the tenth day they rounded the familiar bend and Weset slipped into view. Si-Amun and Kamose, reclining side by side, watched silently. Boats of every description still clustered against the town's straggling wharves. The huts and houses still jostled each other haphazardly among the palms where stray dogs lolled in the shade and naked brown children squatted in the dirt. The temple pylon, its smooth sides gleaming under a sun that stood at its zenith, still sported tall flagstaffs upon which the triangular flags rippled, and beyond it the temple rose, its lines sharp against the blue of the sky. On the west bank the tumbled rise and fall of the cliffs, an uneven horizon as well-known and dear to Si-Amun as the angles of his own body, shook in the dust haze.

The barge slowed and at the helmsman's shout began to veer towards the family's watersteps. The old palace still bulked sleepily and mysteriously behind its crumbling walls and beside it, so dear, so achingly, poignantly precious, were the groups of flowering shrubs, now bare, the sycamore trees and trellised grape vines that provided an arboured walk through from the river to the garden and the pond and the unseen portico of Seqenenra's low, rambling haven of peace. Si-Amun, his eyes drinking in every shabby, cheerful detail, felt his throat swell with emotion. "It is as if we have been away for years and have aged beyond imagining," Kamose said beside him. Si-Amun nodded, overcome.

Now he could see a figure on the paving at the top of the steps, someone doing a dance of frantic, panic-stricken welcome. It was Tani, her bronze bracelets sliding up and down her bare arms, her long white sheath pressed to her legs in the wind. Si-Amun wished that he might die immediately and never have to look into his sister's questioning eyes.

The barge bumped the steps. Servants appeared from behind Tani and ran to tether it. The ramp was run out. Si-Amun rose and Tani flung herself into his arms. "I have been watching here every day since the scrolls stopped coming," she cried out. "Grandmother took to the roof where she could see the river better. Mother spent her afternoons praying. Oh, Si-Amun!" She hugged him tightly, still oblivious to all else. After a moment he disengaged himself.

"Tani," he said, "where is Ahmose?" At his tone she sobered. Her glance took in the rest of the barge, halted at Kamose, and she walked to kneel beside him. Her hand went to the bloody bandage under his arm and the swollen stitches on his cheek. She paled.

"We lost, didn't we?" she whispered. "Where is Father?"

"Yes, we lost," Kamose said steadily. "I think we would have lost in any case, dear Tani, but we were betrayed very early. Father is dead. His body is over there." Her gaze flew to the crude wooden box and she would have rushed to it but Kamose gripped her hand. "No," he said. "It is not a sight for you. Go and find Ahmose." Numbly she got to her feet and left the barge, walking as if in a trance. Si-Amun knew that the shock had not yet hit her. He shouted to one of the servants waiting for orders on the bank.

"Run to the House of the Dead and bring sem-priests! The rest of you, help your Prince onto the steps."

By the time Kamose had been laid gently in the shade above the watersteps and Hor-Aha, after a brief word with Si-Amun, had gone to see to the dispersal and settling of the surviving soldiers, Ahmose, Tetisheri and Aahotep had arrived. Si-Amun did not notice them at first. They stood back on the path under the grape arbour, Ahmose watching, Tetisheri standing regally, Aahotep close to her, both hands clutching a robe under her chin.

Si-Amun helped the servants to unload the coffin and place it reverently under a tree, then he gave an order. The barge was untied. The helmsman clambered up to grasp the steering oar and the boat swung ponderously towards the west bank. Only then did Si-Amun turn and meet his family's hesitant gaze. He ran towards them, and their arms opened. For a moment he was enveloped in the familiar touch, the soft flesh and the smell of them that carried him back vividly to the days of his early boyhood, then he stepped away. "You must be brave," he said. Ahmose blinked.

"It was doomed from the start," he said unsteadily. "We all knew that. But I had hoped Father's life might be spared. We have prayed so hard . . ." He swallowed convulsively. "I have done my best to keep all in order for him."

"Open the coffin," Tetisheri said tonelessly. Si-Amun hesitated.

"He was grievously wounded about the head," he warned, but she brushed him aside. Aahotep took her arm and together they walked out under the blinding sun. At a nod from him, the man guarding the coffin took out his knife and prised off the lid. Ahmose joined the women, but Si-Amun went to Kamose, squatting beside the litter, head hanging. When next he looked, his mother was on her knees brushing sand away from the corpse. She did not cry out at what she saw as Si-Amun thought she would. When Seqenenra's face with its terrible gaping wounds was revealed, her hands were stilled. It was Ahmose who uttered a moan.

For many seconds Aahotep knelt, her fingertips light on the swollen, black flesh, Tetisheri's motionless shadow over her, then she rose and bending, pressed her lips to Seqenenra's open, agonized mouth. She straightened. Her shaking hands went to the low neck of her sheath and in a gesture of ancient grief she tore it from neck to waist, then she sank in the dust beside the paving and began to trickle the dry soil over her head.

Tetisheri turned on her heel and stalked towards the two young men, Ahmose behind her. Her face was stony with rage. Beyond her Si-Amun could see two sem-priests hurrying from the direction of the House of the Dead, their heads down and their robes held tight to their bodies for fear they might contaminate anyone unwary enough to brush by them. "Are your wounds serious?" Tetisheri asked Kamose through stiff lips.

"No, Grandmother," he replied. "A spear thrust to the side and a knife in my cheek, that is all. I will be myself in a week or two." She nodded once and turned her terrifying gaze on Si-Amun.

"Aahmes-nefertari is still on her couch," she said. "She gave birth to a son yesterday at sunset. Go to her when you can. She does not yet know that you are home." At that she left them, stalking into the house, her spine straight and her shoulders set. Si-Amun knew that none of them would see her weep. He got up and went to the coffin where the sem-priests were examining the corpse.

"Can he be beautified?" he asked peremptorily. One of the priests answered with his face averted so that he might not breathe on Si-Amun.

"It is not too late, Prince," he said. "The sand has slowed the process of decomposition. But we cannot repair these wounds. The skin is already too dry to take stitches." Relief flooded Si-Amun.

"That is not important," he told them. "Do the best you can. Take him away." He could no longer bear to look down on the black and battered face of his father. Abruptly he went to Aahotep. She was kneeling with her dusty hands in her lap. Soil clung to her hair and stuck to the paint on her face. Si-Amun squatted before her but she turned away.

"Leave me alone, Si-Amun," she whispered. "Go to your wife. There is nothing you can do for me." Obediently he rose.

She was strong, his beautiful mother. She would grieve by herself, she would mourn for the seventy days, but she would live.

Kamose's litter was just disappearing into the shaded garden, Ahmose and Uni following. Kares, his mother's steward, passed him with a bow and took up his station a few steps from Aahotep, folding his arms. Si-Amun wondered anxiously where Tani was licking her wounds, and like cold water flung in his face he remembered Mersu and what must be done. Mentally shaking off the panic that had begun to wrap itself around him, he started towards the women's quarters. I will deal with one thing at a time, he thought. Aahmes-nefertari first, and my son.

Her room was cooler than the burning hands of the sun that beat upon the walls. Puffs of stale air entered from the windcatcher on the roof, stirring the plaited reed window hangings and the wisps of disordered hair that lay on Aahmes-nefertari's cheeks as she drowsed, propped high with pillows. Si-Amun motioned to Raa, on a stool by the couch, and with a welcoming smile the woman crept out. Si-Amun approached and kissed his wife's pale lips. She woke with a start, shrieked in joy, and twining her arms about his neck, drew him down. "Si-Amun! I cannot believe it! We have been so worried since the scrolls stopped coming. Have you seen him yet? He is so strong, so lusty! What has happened? Is Father in Het-Uart already?"

He silenced her chatter, kissing her with a sudden ferocity in order to shrink the weight of his pain and loss, but already it was stopping his breath and squeezing his heart. "Si-Amun!" she exclaimed, pulling free. "You are crying!" He nodded helplessly, laying his head against her breasts, no longer trying to quell the sobs that shook him. She held him loosely and waited until he had spent himself, then she offered him a corner of the sheet on which to wipe his face and pushed him down onto the stool. "Victory was too much to ask," she said.

"I know." He did not feel foolish for breaking down. Not

with her. She was eyeing him warily, fear of the unknown making her face suddenly all questioning eyes, and he knew that he must tell her everything. His guilt had begun to put a wall between them long before he left Weset. It had poisoned their relationship slowly. Now he must put it right.

He began incoherently, not knowing where to start, whether with his discontented life here on the estate, his boredom and disdain for Weset, or with the visit to Teti where in a moment of spiritual greed he had succumbed, but gradually his story grew sane, and cold, and terrible.

Her eyes never left his face. Occasionally they wandered to his mouth, to his curly black hair, but returned always to his gaze. He read disbelief, shock, sympathy and pain there, but towards the end he did not see what he had feared most. There was no scornful condemnation in her face. When he had finished, she lay back and stared at the ceiling. "Father is dead?" she asked, her voice thin. "The sem-priests . . ." He swallowed. "Yes."

"But he would have died anyway, Si-Amun, surely you see that? On the plain of Dashlut or in the canals outside Het-Uart, what does it matter?" She sat up and turned to him urgently. "The rebellion was doomed from the start, with or without the things you have done in secret!" Her fists clenched. "I do not want to lose you! Say nothing, my brother. Have Mersu killed. Persuade the others that no trial is necessary. Ramose did not know about you, did he? Then neither must anyone else. I do not want to lose you!" Her voice had risen.

Si-Amun sat dumb. She was speaking without thought, her first female instinct one of preservation for herself and her baby that overrode conscience or the thought of consequence, and he let her express it.

When she had fallen silent, her head moving agitatedly on the pillow, he leaned forward and imprisoned both her hands in his. "I cannot," he said. "I must confess everything and take what comes. How could our life go on as before? It would lie between us, you as my accomplice, until perhaps you might grow to hate me. And as for me, a man with a dishonest secret gradually loses his pride and his virility. It seeps away, Aahmes-nefertari, until only the secret and the guilt are left. I cannot live that way."

"But if you deliver yourself up to justice, the family will execute you! They will have no choice!" Her knees came up under the white bedding and her tight fists pounded them. "It will not bring Father back nor avert the King's retribution." With a sudden thought she twisted towards him, sitting bundled on the edge of the couch. "You are the eldest son," she pressed, eyes taking fire. "You are now Prince of Weset and governor of the Five Nomes. Oh Si-Amun, justice is in your hands and yours alone! Pardon yourself!"

"Aahmes-nefertari," he said lightly, distinctly, "how could I respect myself? Dispense justice to others? How long would I hold your regard?"

"Well, what of me? What of your son? Raa!" The woman opened the door and bowed. "Bring the baby for Si-Amun to hold!" She turned back to her husband tensely. "If you insist on destroying yourself, what of us? I love you, I need you, your child needs a father, Si-Amun do not leave us!"

She had scarcely finished speaking when Raa appeared cradling a tiny sheet-shrouded form. With a lump in his throat Si-Amun rose, holding out his arms. His son opened his eyes and gazed up at his father sleepily. One small red hand was clutching the corner of the linen that surrounded him. With a shock Si-Amun recognized Seqenenra's strong cheekbones and slightly slanted eyes. The baby smelled sweetly of natron and warm new flesh. Aahmes-nefertari watched them with a painful eagerness. "He is so helpless," she hissed. "So am I, Si-Amun.

Please!" Si-Amun kissed his son's damp forehead and passed him back to Raa.

"Forgive me, my sister," he said. "I cannot." He tried to take her in his arms but she pushed him away savagely and buried her head in the pillows. She was sobbing by the time he had reached the door. Justice is in my hands alone, he thought with despair as he shut out the sound of her weeping and started along the passage. She spoke more truly than she knew. My hands alone.

After leaving his wife, he sought out Tani. He found her on the roof of the old palace, in the place where Seqenenra had been struck down, her linen in shreds where she had torn at her clothes, rocking back and forth silently. Seeing him come, she threw herself into his arms and he comforted her as best he could before persuading her to go to her quarters.

On the way back from the palace he saw his mother still huddled in the dust, but now she was protected from the sun by a canopy and both Kares and Hetepet stood nearby, waiting for her grief to be spent. Si-Amun left her undisturbed. Ahmose had disappeared, probably into the marshes to indulge his sorrow alone. Many of the servants who bowed to Si-Amun as he passed were in tears.

He himself wanted nothing more than to shut himself away, to husband whatever energy was left him, but he forced himself to enquire after Tetisheri. Fortunately his grandmother's steward was nowhere to be seen. Isis answered his knock and told him that Tetisheri was resting and did not wish to be disturbed. Incense drifted into the passage through the open door and Si-Amun thought he heard the low chanting of Tetisheri's priest.

He went away with relief and sought Kamose, who had ordered his litter to be placed by the pond in the garden. Si-Amun sank gratefully into the grass beside him. "There is such peace here," Kamose said as Si-Amun folded his long legs.

"Next to the desert, this place has the power to heal and bring all into a proper perspective." When Si-Amun did not comment, he went on, "Are they all right? How is Tani?"

"I handed her over to Heket. She is taking it very hard."

"She is carrying a double load." Kamose stirred and winced, fingering the bandage under his arm. "She needs Ramose more than she needs any of us. Tell me, Si-Amun, what do you intend to do?"

Si-Amun was startled. "About what?"

Kamose grunted. "You are Father's heir. You must make the decisions now."

"You sound so pompous!" Si-Amun flared and Kamose apologized hastily.

"I am sorry, brother. But something must be done about Mersu. If he suspects that we know what he has done, he will simply disappear, and soon."

Si-Amun nodded unwillingly. "I know. I intend to have him arrested before sunset. But we are in mourning, Kamose. He can be tried but not executed until Father goes to his tomb. It would be simpler to put a knife through his throat in the dark."

Kamose's head rolled towards his brother. "Simpler but against every law of Ma'at," he answered. "Whether we like it or not, Mersu must be properly tried before us, the mayor of Weset, and Uni as the estate's Chief Steward. How Apepa must be laughing at us! "

I knew as much, Si-Amun thought, watching the play of moving shadow across Kamose's naked legs splayed on the litter, but it was worth a small probing. Kamose might have agreed to have Mersu quietly put away if he thought a trial too humiliating and painful for us all.

"What will Apepa do now?" he mused softly.

"Apepa can take his time and then do anything with us that he chooses," Kamose said. "If I were him, I would slay all of us as an example to any other would-be agitators, but that might mean antagonizing the hereditary nobles of Egypt. The Setiu have seldom worked that way. Apepa is no different. I expect us to keep our skins but lose everything else." He twisted to glance up at the servant standing a few paces away and the man came quickly, offering him water which he drank thirstily. He lay back on the litter. "I would give anything to get my hands on Teti!" he growled. "I would administer the five wounds myself before digging my knife into his well-fed paunch!" Si-Amun cringed mentally at his brother's bitter tone. If only you knew, dear Kamose, he thought.

"Yet I can understand his actions," he put in. "True Ma'at is hard for many to discern in these days. I feel pity for Teti." Kamose did not deign to answer, and after a pause he changed the subject.

"What will you call your son?" he asked.

"The astrologers have not completed their deliberations," Si-Amun replied. "I will abide by their decision." As long as it is not Seqenenra, he thought to himself. That has become a name clouded by suffering and death. Oh, my father, so pure, so implacable! He rose. "Apepa will observe the period of mourning," he said, "but we can expect our punishment immediately afterwards. Until then we must relish each day." Kamose's eyes were closed. He was falling into the sudden sleep of the convalescent.

"Yes," he murmured. "Yes . . ."

That evening the family gathered in the hall to eat together, a subdued throng with swollen eyes and little appetite. Si-Amun had sent an invitation to Amunmose and to the mayor of Weset, and when the food had been picked over silently and the serving staff had withdrawn, Si-Amun prepared to address them. He was acutely conscious of Mersu's tall, shrouded form as he rose. The steward was in his usual place behind Tetisheri, alert in his stillness for any need she might express. Uni, Kares, Isis and the other senior servants remained also, ready to listen to Si-Amun seemingly without involvement, but Si-Amun knew that only their training kept their faces bland and their bodies controlled.

Aahmes-nefertari was absent, still recuperating from the birth of their son. Kamose was propped on a camp cot, Hor-Aha beside him. Aahotep had washed and put on clean linen, but she sat behind her low table unadorned by any of her jewels. Ahmose chewed his roast goose thoughtfully, his calm demeanour belied by the ravages of grief on his face. Only Tetisheri had come to the meal in formal attire, fully painted.

She is like the queens of old, Si-Amun thought, catching sight of her as he rose to speak. The arrogance of her station strengthens every bone in her body. She loved her son fiercely and longed to see him on the Holy Throne. Her suffering is great, yet only those of lower station will see her cry. What did you think today, Mersu, when you waited upon a broken and distraught woman? Did you regret what you have done as I bitterly regret it? He saw Tani, sitting on Kamose's other side, her hand in her brother's. He smiled at her and won a weak grimace in return.

The company turned its eyes on him expectantly. A deep quiet fell so that Si-Amun could hear the soft soughing of the dry night wind through the pillars. He caught Hor-Aha's eye and saw the General tense in anticipation. Taking a deep breath, he began to speak.

He told them of Seqenenra's march, of the arrival at Qes, of the coming of Ramose in the middle of the night with his message of betrayal. Out of the corner of his eye he saw Tani jerk upright, but Mersu did not stir. Si-Amun marvelled at the coolness of the man. With an increasingly dry throat he described his father's attempt to outflank Pezedkhu, his failure and his

cruel death. No one moved. Only the lamps showed a sem-
blance of life, their flames rising and sinking in the alabaster
containers while shadows gyrated slowly on the walls.

At last Si-Amun signalled and Hor-Aha came to his feet.
"The man who viciously attacked Seqenenra, who kept Teti
and thus Apepa informed, is here among us tonight," Si-Amun
finished huskily. "Mersu, you are under arrest. Your fate will be
decided when we have buried my father." He wanted to say
more, to speak of the heinous nature of Mersu's crime, to
denounce him in loud tones, but his own involvement stilled
his tongue.

Hor-Aha strode to the steward, and bowing to Tetisheri he
waited. Mersu stepped to his side, still encased in his self-
possession. Without a glance to anyone he left the hall, walking with dignity behind Hor-Aha. The watchers suddenly
loosened.

"He is not truly Egyptian," the mayor said with obvious
relief. "He is Setiu."

"Ramose told you this?" Tani cried out. "He risked his life to
warn you?" Si-Amun nodded, glad to see an emotion other
than deep grief suffuse her face. Ahmose dabbled his fingers in
the water bowl his servant was holding out for him.

"Who else heard Ramose speak?" he asked sharply. "There
must be witnesses, Si-Amun. This is too great an accusation to
consider without corroboration." Si-Amun stared at his brother
in surprise. Ahmose's customary sleepy self-absorption had been
replaced by intelligent eyes bright with his query.

"Only our father heard Ramose's words," he admitted. "But
we, Kamose, Hor-Aha and myself, were summoned to him that
night, moments after Ramose had slipped back to the enemy's
campsite. We can all testify."

"It is still not enough." Ahmose dried his fingers on the proffered cloth and stood up. "Mersu will have to confess."

"Are you calling our father a liar?" Si-Amun, at the end of his tether, was shouting.

Ahmose raised his eyebrows.

"No, of course not. Father was an honest man and besides, what possible reason could he have had for lying? It is simply that we have a man's life in jeopardy here. We must be careful. Am I dismissed, Prince?" Si-Amun let him go. Tani left Kamose and came close to Si-Amun.

"By any chance," she said in a low voice so that only he could hear, "did Ramose leave any message for me?" At a moment like that? Si-Amun wanted to retort scornfully. Don't be ridiculous! But he bit his tongue and forced himself to be kind.

"No, Tani, he did not," he replied. "He was very anxious to speak with Father and then run. If he had been caught crossing into our lines he would have been killed, you know."

"Oh, of course." She put a hand to her cheek. "How stupid of me. It is just . . ." Si-Amun took her shoulders.

"You know that he loves you," he insisted. "He would have warned us in any case because he is an honourable man, but surely you were in his thoughts as he made his way towards Father's tent that night. Be brave, Tani."

"I am tired of being brave," she said. "I want to be other things. I want to be happy." She spun away and ran from the hall. Aahotep, who had not said a word, got up and followed her.

Si-Amun went to his grandmother. I feel like a nursemaid, he thought with a flash of desperation. Like a mother with five crying children. Why do they all look to me for comfort, for decisions? The answer came as he squatted before Tetisheri, immobile and resplendent in her glittering jewels. Because you are now Prince and governor. You are the head of the family. "Grandmother?" he said. She put out a shaking hand. Grasping it, Si-Amun felt it as cold as a snake's skin.

"I trusted him," she rasped. "Gods, I even loved him! His shame covers me. I cannot hold its weight." She turned her mask-like face to Si-Amun. "Must we wait for the mourning to be over?" Her superhuman control was more terrible and more pathetic than Aahotep's outburst in the garden or Tani's free tears. Si-Amun knew then what he had to do. Seventy days of mourning, a funeral and a trial that would inevitably become public would strain the members of the family more than they could bear and corrode their unity and strength, already fragile and desperately maintained. Looming over all this was the certain prospect of the King's judgement. It was too much. Scarred they would be, but not disfigured. Si-Amun made up his mind to see to that.

"Perhaps not," he said softly. "Go to your quarters, Grandmother. Uni!" The steward came quickly. "Escort the Princess to her rooms and for the time being assume the duties of her servant." Tetisheri rose with difficulty, supported on Uni's arm. Suddenly she showed all of her sixty-two years. Si-Amun glanced at the mayor but he and Kamose were talking urgently.

Si-Amun beckoned to the High Priest. Amunmose hurried over. Si-Amun drew him towards the night heavy garden. Outside, beyond the reach of the yellow lamplight, the empty flower beds and shrivelled lawn lay enveloped in a close darkness. A thin, pale moon hung netted in the tired stars, its light too faint to cast any reflection in the murky surface of the pond. The bare shrubs were hardly discernable black smudges against the wall of the old palace.

Si-Amun led the High Priest down the warm stone steps between the pillars and stopped where the night rushed to meet them. "Amunmose," he began quietly, "we do not know each other very well, you and I. We speak at Amun's festivals, at the feasts, but the business of the god belonged to you and my father, not to me." He hesitated, searching for words.

Amunmose, misinterpreting the train of his thought, put in anxiously, "You need have no fear that I will not do my utmost to perform my duties to you as I did to your father, Prince. You are now governor. The welfare of Amun's servants and the privilege of directly communing with the god are now in your hands." Si-Amun forced a smile. Amunmose's face was a pale, worried oval in the dimness.

"I am not doubting your honesty in carrying out your duties," he reassured the man. "The god we serve with the most sincere devotion here in Weset may be almost unknown in the centres of power in Egypt, but no other god has a more loyal priesthood than you and your assistants. No. I have a favour to ask you."

He stopped speaking. A voice within him had woken and was whispering to him, "This is your last chance to turn aside. Ask something innocuous. You are so young, Prince. You have so much to lose. What of your wife, your son?" The night breeze made him shiver suddenly. Amunmose was watching expectantly. Si-Amun took a deep breath.

"I need you to prepare a poison," he said carefully. "I know that the priests of Set are more adept at such things than any other, but I do not want word of my intention to leak north."

"Lord," Amunmose cut in huskily, "before I do this thing I would need to know the purpose. I am Amun's priest. I will not break a law of Ma'at nor endanger my chance of a favourable weighing under Anubis's eye in the Hall of Judgement." The lines of his face had deepened and become strained. He looked cadaverous under the colourless moonlight.

"You know that Mersu will be tried for his betrayal," Si-Amun said. "You also know that he cannot be executed until my father is buried. I wish to carry out my own sentence on him for two reasons." He held up a hand as he saw Amunmose open his mouth to protest. "Hear me before you refuse, High Priest. Father will not be buried for more than two months. In that time Mersu must be guarded on the estate, a constant source of grief and rage to the members of my family, already aching with more than they can bear. My other reason is this. I do not intend to give the King time to command me to release Mersu. I think he will try, if he believes that Mersu has been exposed. Any excuse will do. A post in the north, a summons to consult with his own steward, anything. And I would have to obey. Mersu is not to escape judgement. I will kill him myself."

Amunmose was silent. His head had dropped. Si-Amun could no longer see his face, only the slight gleam of his shaven skull and the bulk of his body. He waited with a fatalistic patience. You will be my judge also, he thought. If you refuse me, I shall seek ways to go on living, but if you agree I shall consider your words as a message from the gods that I, too, must die. He felt perfectly calm. The cold shudder that had gripped him had gone.

Finally Amunmose raised worried eyes to Si-Amun. "This thing stalks the borders of Ma'at," he pointed out, "and its rightness or wrongness depends entirely on the character and virtue of those involved. Yet you are asking for more than a cup of poison, Prince. You require a decision on my wider loyalty." I suppose I do, Si-Amun thought with surprise. I am glad I did not offer him gold for the poison. He nodded.

"I had not considered that before," he admitted. "Your loyalty to this family has never been in question as far as I am concerned. May I have an answer, Amunmose?" The High Priest sighed.

"I trust you, Prince, to do what is right, as your father did. I will make poison for you. Mersu deserves to die."

"Thank you." Amunmose took the words as a dismissal, bowed, and retreated. Si-Amun watched him for a moment, gliding in the direction of the watersteps where his litter bearers drowsed as they waited to carry him back to his quarters in the temple. Then the shadows swallowed him. Si-Amun turned away, finding his legs weak.

Before collapsing in the sanctuary of his rooms he forced himself to go to Mersu's cell. The steward was being held in his own small room and as Si-Amun approached, Hor-Aha rose stiffly from the floor beside the closed door. Two guards saluted. "You do not need to be here," Si-Amun said to Hor-Aha, noting the General's pallor. "Get your shoulder dressed again and then sleep. You are exhausted." Hor-Aha bowed.

"I know," he replied. "I sat down to wait for reinforcements after I had locked the door and somehow could not find the desire to stand again. It has been a sobering day."

"Has Mersu spoken?" Hor-Aha shook his head.

"He is remarkably composed. So much so that I am suspicious, even though I know there is no other way out of his cell." Si-Amun approached.

"I want to see him. You are dismissed, General. Sleep well, and in the morning bring me a report on what has been salvaged from my father's disastrous campaign. But not too early!" Hor-Aha bowed again and left, pulling his cloak tight around his swollen shoulder and walking away under the torchlight. Si-Amun beckoned to a guard. "Open the door."

After a moment it swung wide and Si-Amun walked in, kicking it closed behind him. Mersu rose and bowed profoundly. He had been sitting on his cot, rolling a pair of knucklebones in his fingers. As Si-Amun stepped into the dimly lit room, he placed them on the lid of his chest and Si-Amun, momentarily at a loss under the steward's calm demeanour, noticed how high a gloss the bones had, how much they had been handled. Everyone liked to play the game, but he had not imagined Mersu a devotee of something so frivolous. The thought unmanned him and thus made him angry for a second. He controlled himself with a conscious effort.

"You are remarkably unflustered, Mersu," he said. The man shrugged lightly.

"Why waste energy and suffer the loss of my dignity by railing against fate?" he answered. "I have done my duty to my King. My conscience is clear. I shall sleep the sleep of the just, Prince." Si-Amun searched for impudence in the smooth face but the only insolence lay in Mersu's confident words.

"You believe that the King will have you released before Seqenenra is buried," he said slowly. "That is why your arrest has not troubled you." Mersu smiled.

"Perhaps," he acknowledged. "But Prince, I also have confidence in your clemency."

"What?" Si-Amun started forward furiously but Mersu stood his ground.

"If you do not find me innocent, or at least dismiss my case for lack of direct evidence, I shall tell your brothers and anyone else who cares to listen the part you yourself played in Seqenenra's downfall. Are you brave enough to stand beside me before the judges, O Prince of Weset?" Now his tone was mocking, the smile still fixed on his mouth. "In two months' time I expect to be on my way to Het-Uart. I do not mind being imprisoned in the meantime. I have worked long and hard for your grandmother. I need a rest."

Si-Amun was speechless. His blood cried out against not only the steward's callousness but also his rudeness, the complete disregard for Si-Amun's rank and station inherent in the coarse words. We are provincial upstart lordlings to him, Si-Amun thought in angry dismay. He is ashamed to have served us. He thinks himself worthy only to serve a King, and our claim to that Kingship is a source of embarrassment to him. Well, we shall see who is the power in this part of Egypt, you Setiu worm!

Stepping forward he struck Mersu briskly on the mouth.

"How dare you speak to me in that fashion!" he snapped. "Peasant! While you await your trial you can busy yourself with the weaving of reed mats for the cells of your fellow servants to remind you of your correct position. Tetisheri spoiled you. You have a less noble spirit than the commonest peasant farmer sweating over the shaduf."

"And what of you?" Mersu whispered. He made no move to rub his cheek where the marks of Si-Amun's hand showed white. "What of you, proud Tao?" Si-Amun held his gaze, at the same time painfully aware of the odorous stream of thin black smoke from the untrimmed lamp, the uneven, cool dirt floor under his feet, the rumpled coarse linen sheet on the cot behind Mersu's rigid figure.

"So be it," he forced through stiff lips and, turning on his heel, he left.

Chapter TEN

THAT NIGHT HE LAY alone and sleepless on his couch, listening to the grief of the people of Weset. The women were keening in the streets for Seqenenra, their high-pitched, ululating wails carrying far over the river and echoing against the walls of the old palace. The seventy days of mourning for the Prince had begun. In the House of the Dead his body lay disembowelled and packed in natron, guarded by sem-priests who recited the obligatory prayers over him at intervals before returning to their strange meditations.

Two days later Amunmose returned. Si-Amun, leaning against one of the pillars that gave out from his father's office to the portico steps and listening to Hor-Aha's dry voice accounting the disposition of the remaining soldiers, watched the High Priest make his way through the garden. He was dressed in an ankle-length white kilt, stiffly starched, its pleats rustling. His sandals were red leather, the pectoral lying against his brown chest was gold and jasper, and his eyes were ringed in black kohl. The leopard skin lay over one shoulder, the beast's snout almost brushing the ground. Two acolytes flanked him, one carrying his white staff with the gold plumes of Amun and one bearing a small wooden box.

Si-Amun held a hand up and Hor-Aha stopped speaking. "We will resume later," he said to the General. "Amunmose is here in an official capacity, I think with the name of my son. Send to Aahmes-nefertari. Tell her to prepare for a visit from the High Priest." He scarcely heard Hor-Aha take his leave. His eyes were fixed on the innocent-seeming box in the hands of the small boy as Amunmose came to a halt below him and bowed, and it was all he could do to greet the priest and invite him in under the relative coolness of the portico roof.

Amunmose mounted the steps, sweat beading on his forehead. "Courage, my friend!" Si-Amun smiled, waving him within. "Only a few more days to the Inundation. Have you brought a name for my son?" But as he spoke, his glance kept straying to the acolyte standing obediently outside in the sun. Amunmose bowed again, seeing his abstraction.

"Indeed I have, Prince. I have also brought the thing you requested. Be careful how you handle it. A drop on the skin will burn." Si-Amun wrenched his attention back to the priest.

"Let us first discuss life," he requested quietly, although a thrill of horror shot down his spine. "What do the astrologers say?" He waited anxiously, thinking of his first child, the little boy he had been unable to get to know and who now lay in an unfinished tomb. Amunmose smiled.

"I think you will be satisfied," he said. "They have chosen the name Ahmose-onkh." Ahmose-onkh. Si-Amun felt his heart lighten. It was a good, solid name, conservative and reassuring, familiar and comfortable as the passing of dreaming time in Weset. It was right that the child should bear the name of Ahmose, who alone among the male members of the family had remained sunny and untouched directly by war and destruction, and the suffix "onkh," a derivative of the ankh, the sign of life itself, reinforced the name's vitality. Si-Amun returned the High Priest's smile.

"It is entirely acceptable," he said. "Go to Aahmes-nefertari now and tell her." But first Amunmose clicked his fingers and the little acolyte came running up the steps. Bowing to Si-Amun he presented the box.

"A gift for your son, from me," Amunmose said for the benefit of the acolyte and with a warning glance at Si-Amun. "It has great value, Prince. Guard it well."

Si-Amun took it, placed a hand on the acolyte's black head, managed to dismiss the priest, and turned into the empty office. The wood was warm in his fingers and a scent of cedar drifted to his nostrils. Trembling, he lifted the lid. An alabaster pot lay within, its stopper sealed tight with wax. Si-Amun stared at it, then resolutely closed the lid. Tucking it under his arm, he made his way to his rooms and thrust the box under his couch. Then he went in search of Aahmes-nefertari.

He found his wife on the roof sitting under a canopy on her cushions, the baby asleep in a basket beside her. Raa was dripping lotus essence into a bowl of water in which a cloth was soaking. On seeing the Prince come walking across the roof, she bowed and withdrew. Aahmes-nefertari smiled and held out her arms. She was naked, her sheath crumpled on the mat. "Are you pleased?" she smiled. "I think it is a lovely name. Amunmose has just gone and I decided to come up here and have Raa bathe me. How hot it is this afternoon!" Si-Amun knelt to be enfolded. Her skin was hot and dry, smelling faintly of persimmons. The hair that drifted against his face was also warm, as soft and light as river mist. He pulled back a little and kissed her unpainted lips.

"I think it is a lovely name too," he smiled. "Ahmose will be delighted." He turned his attention to the child. Ahmose-onkh slept in the abandon of utter bliss. Surfeited with milk, he lay with his tiny brown limbs splayed on the sheet, his black eyelashes fluttering against his chubby cheeks, his mouth, like an early lotus bud, slightly open. Si-Amun stroked his satiny skin with one wondering finger. "How perfect he is!" he exclaimed, and with the emotion came a heightened awareness of all around him.

The baby's skin was dewy, the sheet under him dazzling white. Si-Amun, bemused, could count every intricate warp and woof. One of Aahmes-nefertari's hands lay relaxed on a blue cushion. Enthralled, Si-Amun noted with a kind of passion the faintly paler patches on her fingers where she usually wore her rings, the ridges of her tendons, the tiny almost invisible hairs between her knuckles. His eyes travelled the brown, glowing journey of her naked leg, the ankle turned, the toes sturdy and calloused, and then lifted to the view beyond. He felt breathless, as though he had run a long way.

The tassels lining the edge of the canopy stirred red against the profound, strong aquamarine of the summer sky. Past them the outlines of desert and temple, the complex rise and fall of Weset's buildings, the complicated arrangement of bare shrubs beside the river's silver curves smote Si-Amun forcefully as something foreign and exotic, something already apart from him, to which he did not belong. A channel had opened between his eyes and his heart, carrying exquisite though unintelligible messages that bypassed his consciousness. The summer colours, all beige, silver, tan, imposed against a vivid blue, burned him like a hot sword.

"Aahmes-nefertari," he said, hardly recognizing his own voice, "let's stay up here for the rest of the day. Send Raa away. I will bathe you. We can talk. We can have food sent up at sunset instead of going to the hall." She turned to him astonished, ready to tease, but something in his expression gave her pause.

"Very well," she agreed. "Raa can take the baby with her." But he prevented her.

"No. We can take care of him." She settled back on the cushions and grinned at him.

"The sun has turned your head, Si-Amun! So we shall be lazy? Good! Bathe me!"

They ordered Raa inside the house and as the sun slowly arced towards the west they talked. Si-Amun adjusted the canopy accordingly. Twice they dozed, slumped against each other on the disordered cushions. Si-Amun trickled the scented water over Aahmes-nefertari's dark supple body. He watched her suckle their son. They spoke together of their father, of their childhood, but by unspoken agreement they did not mention the future. Si-Amun would have liked to make love to her there on the roof under the softening sunlight, but she was still healing from Ahmose-onkh's birth.

Towards evening servants appeared with barley beer and red wine, raisins and figs, pomegranates, bread and honey cakes. As Ra was slowly swallowed and the red tide of his struggle flooded the land, they at last fell silent, lying side by side in a companionable embrace and watching him disappear.

When the light had faded and the stars began to flutter in a sky that still held a hint of the palest of blues, Si-Amun took his son in his arms and walked Aahmes-nefertari to her quarters. Once there she turned to face him. Behind them Raa was lighting the lamps, setting out fresh water for the night, and turning down the sheets on the couch. "It has been a glorious afternoon," she sighed, reaching to kiss him. "If we were not mourning for Father, if there was no sadness, it would have been perfect. But you are not yourself, Si-Amun." He returned her kiss, feeling the small weight of his son leave his arms as Raa took the boy away towards the nursery.

"None of us are ourselves," he said. "Perhaps we will never again be as we were. How can we be? The future is very dark,

Aahmes-nefertari. I love you, and nothing else is worthwhile but that." For a moment his gaze travelled her face, the tight skin tanned almost black, the brown eyes clear and soft without paint, the well-formed, mobile mouth only slightly paler than the rest of her. "Sleep well," he finished. She smiled, nodded, and closed her door behind him.

The passages were empty of all save the guards as Si-Amun made his way to his quarters, and the house was quiet, the inhabitants exhausted by a day of heat. He wondered, as he listened to the slap slap of his sandals on the tiling, what the members of the family were doing. The impulse to turn aside to investigate was strong but he resisted it, seeing it as an attempt of his ka to divert him from his purpose. Nothing would be served by it. He knew where they were. They were his flesh and blood, their characters, their habits, grooved beside his own in this shabby old house. Tetisheri would be praying or listening to stories in her room. His mother would be talking with Isis, recalling all her memories with Seqenenra. Aahmes-nefertari . . . Better not to think of her holding up her arms so that Raa could pull the diaphanous sleeping gown over her head and then walking through into the nursery to bend one last time over the loose form of the sleeping baby. Kamose, now on his feet but still stiff, would be sitting alone and without light in the garden, thinking the thoughts that no one in the family shared, reluctant to go to his couch, and Ahmose was probably wandering by the river with a guard. Tani would be asleep.

Si-Amun answered the grave salute of the guard on his door and stepped inside. The room was empty, but his servant had left a light on the table by the couch, opened his small Amun shrine, and placed grains of fresh incense in the holder beside it. Si-Amun went to the shrine, ignited the charcoal, tossed some grains onto it, and passing the holder over the shrine, began his evening prayers. Before his father's death he had seldom bothered to perform this ritual, but lately, feeling the responsibilities Seqenenra had laid upon him, he had begun to approach the god each night as part of his duty to the family and the governorship he now held. He prayed carefully, then closed the shrine. He did not know whether what he was about to do was within the laws of the gods who had ruled Egypt or if the terrible monster Sebek, always waiting by the scales, would annihilate him. But this is the only way I can make myself clean, he thought grimly as he pulled the box out from under his couch and placed it on the table. I must spare them all the misery of my trial.

Going to the door he sent a servant for a palette. When the man returned, Si-Amun took it, and sinking cross-legged in the correct pose, placed it across his knees. He murmured the prayer to Thoth, picked up a reed brush and began.

It did not take him long to explain to his family, in neat black hieratic script, his guilt and his shame. He resisted the urge to justify himself, for here at the last he knew that any justification was false. He had done wrong and he must pay. He signed himself Si-Amun, Prince and Governor of Weset. The papyrus quickly absorbed the black paint. Si-Amun rolled up the scroll, and going to his chest he selected his favourite knife, a bronze dagger with an ivory hilt his father had given him years ago. He drew it slowly across the back of his hand and saw blood spring up like a boat's wake in its path. It was sharp enough. He opened the box, removed the stone vial, and let himself out into the passage. He handed the scroll to the soldier. "Give this to Prince Kamose when you have finished your watch," he said, and without waiting for a reply he set off along the passage.

Mersu's cell was close to the women's quarters. Si-Amun went steadily, eyes fixed unseeing on his feet, allowing his mind to fill with a succession of images from his short life that he deliberately did not imbue with any emotion save the futility of it all.

He was almost outside Mersu's door when someone touched his arm. He started, coming to a halt, and Tani materialized before him. She was barefoot and holding a cloak against her. Si-Amun fumbled and almost dropped the alabaster container. His heart gave a bound. "Tani!" he exclaimed. "What are you doing wandering about alone?"

"I cannot sleep," she confessed. "Heket is already snoring on her mat and my other servants are in their quarters. I talked to the guard on my door for a while but I made the poor man uncomfortable so I decided to walk a little." She bit her lip. "I am lonely, Si-Amun. I have no one to share with. Grandmother relishes her isolation. Mother withdraws into her own grief and I do not want to trouble her with mine. Kamose is still wounded and you know what he's like. Even though he talks to you, you get the feeling that he's in some other world. I need Ramose."

All at once she noticed what he was carrying. Her eyes darted from the knife and vial to his face and back again. "What on earth are you doing with those?" Si-Amun could find no ready answer. Her appearance had shocked him and he felt disoriented. As he cast about for a light reply, she stepped closer, a frown on her face. "Where are you going, Si-Amun?" she asked sharply, a hint of fear in her voice. "Why do you need a dagger inside the house!'" Suddenly he felt himself gripped. She had both hands around his wrist. "You're going to kill Mersu, aren't you?" she hissed. "Aren't you?" He was about to tell her to mind her own business and send her back to her rooms, but there was nothing childish about her expression, intense and fiercely questioning. She is not a child, he thought with shock. She is fifteen. Only two years younger than Aahmes-nefertari. How self-absorbed I have been!

"Yes," he said, still feeling her little nails biting into his wrist. "I am going to kill Mersu. It is cleaner and less agonizing than a trial, Tani, and Amun knows he deserves to die." He expected her to gasp, recoil, let loose a spate of argument and indignation, but she stared at him calmly. Gradually an odd light dawned in her eyes, something cool and accepting. She let him go.

"You are right," she said. "Let him pay for Father's death, not us. Strike well, Si-Amun." With a dignity he had never seen in her before, she turned and retraced her steps, disappearing around the corner in a flurry of floating linen. She had not glanced back.

The encounter left Si-Amun with a feeling of vague anxiety. Kill Mersu but choose to live yourself, his inner self demanded. Tani is changing and who but you has noticed? The family needs you. Weset needs you! He groaned, an admission of the temptation, and a moment later found himself outside Mersu's cell.

The guard saluted. Si-Amun smiled at him. "A quiet night, soldier?" he enquired. The man's spear butt hit the floor with a tiny thud.

"Indeed, it is, Prince," he replied.

"And the prisoner?"

"He ate soup and bread two hours ago. General Hor-Aha came at sunset to make sure all was well and Uni sent a bundle of reeds so that the prisoner need not be idle." In spite of his state of mind Si-Amun chuckled at the mental picture of the proud steward sitting on his floor, waist deep in reeds.

"Good. I am going in. You are to stay at your post and not respond to anything you hear within. Do you understand?" The man nodded.

"I am my lord's servant." Si-Amun laid a hand lightly on his shoulder and went inside.

The guard closed the door behind him and at the sound an aura of unreality folded itself around Si-Amun. Bending, he set the alabaster jar on the gritty floor beside him, feeling as though each muscle was responding solemnly to the dictates of an obscure religious rite fraught with mystery. As he straightened, he would not have been surprised to find himself garbed in priestly linens and hooded with the ceremonial mask of Set. He resisted an impulse to touch his face.

Mersu was lying on the couch, legs crossed, arms behind his head. In one corner of the ill-lighted room lay a disordered pile of reeds. The remains of the steward's simple meal lay on a tray on the floor. At the sound of the door he had looked up, and seeing who it was had begun to rise. Now he stood, hands loose at his sides, and Si-Amun, watching him closely, saw uncertainty for the first time blossom on the inscrutable face as Mersu saw the knife. This time Si-Amun did pass his fingers in front of his eyes, sure that he would feel Set's grey, furred snout and sharp fangs, for at Mersu's expression a thrill of exultation shook him, the cold excitement of the executioner. "Yes," he said, his voice coming flat and controlled. "I have decided not to put you or myself through the tension of a trial, Mersu. You did not think I had the courage, did you? This is your judgement," he indicated the knife, "and that," he pointed to the jar, "is mine. If by some chance you should pass the Weighing of the Heart, you need not expect to be welcomed into the presence of Osiris, for I have written a scroll for my family, and when it is read your body will not be embalmed. Neither, perhaps, will mine." Mersu had blanched. Si-Amun saw him back up until the couch was behind his knees, its edge supporting him. "Will your name survive anywhere?" he went on. "Will the Setiu god Sutekh perhaps rescue you and reward you for your loyalty to his minion Apepa?" He was becoming vindictive, the bitter gall in his soul rising in a fume of hatred to his

tongue, but he was royal, he was a Prince, and with superhuman effort he reminded himself that Mersu was not to blame
for his own lack of virtue. "Do you wish to speak before I kill
you?" Mersu swallowed, licked his lips, then seemed to gather
strength. His face remained as grey as a corpse's but he was
standing straighter.

"There is nothing to say," he croaked. "Perhaps it is better
this way, Prince. I am saved the humiliation of a public execution and you the shame and censure of your family. As for the
fate of my ka, well, the gods of Egypt are no longer as powerful
as the Setiu deities. I shall survive." He managed a shrug, a gesture that was meant to be one of bravado but that struck Si-
Amun with its pathos. "I would not be good at weaving reed
mats in any case." He closed his mouth and fixed his eyes on
Si-Amun.

For a moment they stared at each other and it seemed to Si-
Amun that in the silence the steward was gaining confidence,
returning to his insolent self and weakening him, Si-Amun, in
the process. The exultation was draining away, leaving him
shivering with confused resolve and softening will. He knew
that if he did not strike soon, he would slink away, forever dis-
honoured. The ivory hilt was warm against his palm.

Changing his grip he strode forward. Mersu watched him
come. Only the rigid cords of his neck and the spasm of a muscle by his mouth betrayed his mounting terror. Si-Amun took a
quick, deep breath, and plunged the dagger into Mersu's stomach. With a grunt the steward's hands went to the weapon,
folding in agony around the blade. Blood drenched his kilt and
began to run down his legs. Si-Amun felt it, warm and wet, on
his own fingers. "That is for me," he whispered. Mersu's eyes
were round with shock. Bracing himself against the steward's
chest Si-Amun hauled the knife free, grasped Mersu by the
back of the neck, and pushed the stained bronze under his ear

and into his skull. Mersu twitched and fell to the floor. "And that is for my father," Si-Amun gasped.

He collapsed onto the couch and sat breathing heavily, looking at his hands. Blood encrusted them, and had splashed him to the elbow. His chest was smeared with it and his kilt mired. Mersu lay curled before him, staring sightlessly at his feet. Si-Amun waited for his heart to stop pounding, forcing himself to be aware only of the happening of each second. As it gradually settled he found himself pitying it, and smiled at the idiocy.

The alabaster jar stood where he had placed it an eternity ago. Getting up, he went to it and carried it back to the couch. Kamose will be a better governor than I ever could, he thought as he wrestled with the seal. He cares little for appearances and much for the welfare of the nomes, while I could only ever think of the glories of Het-Uart and a place beside the King. Curse him! Kamose will marry Aahmes-nefertari, that is the way of Ma'at for us, and he will adopt my son. He squeezed his eyes shut against the vision of his wife with the baby beside her, both naked and drowsy in the heat of the afternoon. Then he looked curiously into the jar. A small amount of dark liquid quivered under his gaze. He sniffed it cautiously. It had no odour. Carefully, so that none spilled on his hand, he lifted it and drank, grimacing as he did so, for it tasted rank and bitter.

Immediately his throat began to burn. Sweat broke out all over his body. With teeth clenched against the fire spreading through his stomach, he replaced the stopper and put the jar on Mersu's table, then found he could not straighten. He wrapped his arms around himself, rocking and groaning, soon unable to stifle his shrieks as the pain engulfed him. He could not think, but his last emotion was one of an overwhelming loneliness.

Kamose was dreaming. The dream had recurred so many times that even in his sleep he was conscious of a sense of well-being and anticipation. In its opening scene he could be anywhere on the estate—in his quarters, in the garden, by the river, even in the reception hall, but wherever he was, the same sense of pleasurable expectation would steal over him. On this night he dreamed that he was sitting in the garden. It was dusk. Ra had just disappeared into the mouth of Nut and the pool reflected a calm, heavy red sky. Evening was beginning to render the lawn, the flower beds, the shrubs and clustering trees indistinct, and in the house a few lights had begun to shine out. With the irrationality of dreams Kamose found that he could still see quite well. He was on a mat on the verge of the pool, one hand trailing in the warm water. Lotus pads nudged his fingers and their blooms sent out a heady fragrance.

For a while, in the dream, he was content to savour the evening, but then his senses grew alert and the familiar excitement prickled over his scalp and stilled his fingers. He was facing the path that ran through the grape arbour to the water-steps. He knew it was winter, for the lushness of the growth all around him spoke of an Inundation not long over, yet grapes hung heavy and black from the vines, their clusters dusty and ripe. She is coming, he thought in the dream, his stomach tightening. She is coming. Sometimes she would be walking slowly away from him and he would run to try and catch her. Sometimes she would appear suddenly, always facing away from him, and he would scramble to confront her before the dream faded, but he was always too late. For many months the dream had been wrapping him in its delicious languor but he had never seen more than her back.

Now he looked towards the arbour where the path veered in under the darkness of the vine-hung trellis and yes she was there, standing with one hand raised, about to pluck a grape. Under the transparent white sheath that hung about her ankles her brown body flowed inward to a tight waist and then curved in the gentle slope of two rounded hips. She was tall. Between her shoulder blades the golden counterpoise of a pectoral hung suspended on a silver chain against her satin skin. She held her head erect. Her hair was thick, black and straight, with the sheen of a crow's feathers in sunlight, and Kamose could see the gold band hung with tiny ankhs that encircled her forehead. Rising above it, just visible, was the back of a cobra. Armbands of electrum set with lapis lazuli gripped her soft upper arms, and the long fingers she held out towards the grapes were heavy with rings.

Kamose felt faint with desire and something more, for this dream did not have the quality of the tiring and lustful dreams of youth. This unknown woman was the sum of all his longing. She took a grape between thumb and forefinger, turning slightly as she did so, and Kamose held his breath. Slowly, quietly, he came to his feet and began to creep towards her. The vine swayed as she pulled the grape free and bore it to her mouth. Kamose caught a tantalizing glimpse of her cheek as she did so. He moved carefully, not daring to make a sound. In dreams past he had called to her, stumbled after her, shouting, but at any sound from him she had melted away. So now he resorted to stealth. Her hand had fallen to her side. Kamose saw the silver-shot linen stirring at her touch. With lips parted in concentration, fists clenched, he eased closer. He was almost there. She stood very still as if listening. Now he could smell her perfume. The aura of myrrh around her made him dizzy with delight. He had never been able to get so near to her before. His heart was racing madly as he stopped. His hand went out reaching for her shoulder and for one delirious second his fingers touched her. She was cool and his touch slid over skin like soft oils.

But he felt his wrist gripped and he was no longer in the garden. He was on his back, on his couch in the dimness of a stifling summer night, and someone was bending over him. Aching with loss and full of confusion, he struggled to sit up.

"Kamose!" a voice hissed in his ear. "Oh please wake up! I am worried." He came to a sitting position, trembling. His neck rest had tumbled to the floor and he had been sleeping with his head on the naked mattress. He rubbed his shoulders.

"Tani!" he said in surprise, still struggling to retain the dream, still liquid with his loss. "Whatever is the matter?" She sank down by his knees.

"It's Si-Amun," she blurted. "I couldn't sleep tonight and I was wandering about the house. I met him in the passage close to Mersu's cell. He had a knife and a jar in his hands. He admitted that he was going to kill Mersu and I agreed that his reasons were good ones. But the jar . . ." She clutched at him again in her distress. "I'm frightened, Kamose. He seemed so detached, so cool, but his eyes were strange. It didn't strike me until a little later. What was in the jar?" Kamose put a soothing hand on her head and swung his legs over the edge of the couch.

"Don't worry," he said, though unease was filling him too. "He should not have taken the law into his own hands, even though Mersu deserved to die. It is not easy to kill a man, Tani, not even in the heat of battle. No wonder if Si-Amun looked strange. Wait outside. I will wrap on a kilt and we will find him."

"Thank you, Kamose. You are a very comforting person." She left the couch and hurried to the door. Kamose stood up and pulled a kilt from the chest by the wall. Comforting, am I? he thought. Oh Tani, you should see me in my dreams! Si-Amun, I wish you had not lost your head over this business with Mersu. A proper trial and execution would have been more in keeping with Ma'at. Grandmother will have sharp words for you. He joined Tani in the passage.

Night still hung thick in the house and the torches fixed on the walls were guttering. The two of them set off for Si-Amun's quarters, not far from Kamose's own. Tani's hand slipped into his. On the way they passed Ahmose's door. Ahmose's guard acknowledged them and they were about to walk on when the door opened and Ahmose's bleary face appeared. "What is going on?" he said. "I heard the guard salute someone a while ago, and now you two."

"It must have been Si-Amun," Tani exclaimed. "Did he come back?" she asked the soldier.

"No, Princess," he answered. "He spoke to me briefly and went on. I have not seen him since."

"Well, we will look in his rooms anyway," Kamose decided. "Come with us, Ahmose." He did not understand the formless anxiety tugging at him. Ahmose was clutching a sheet. He wound it around his waist.

"Si-Amun has killed Mersu?" he said as they rushed on. "How very odd! He is such a stickler for the right way of doing things. I can hardly believe it!" So he is, Kamose thought with a jolt. Si-Amun, lover of protocol and defender of the rules by which Princes live.

Presently they came to Si-Amun's door. It was closed. Kamose greeted the guard. "Is my brother within?" he enquired. The man shook his head.

"No, Prince, he is not. He went out about an hour ago. He told me to give you this when my watch was over." Kamose took the scroll. The anxiety that had been growing in him was now a silent shriek of haste. He wanted to run to Si-Amun wherever he was, but did not know why. The message was not sealed. Kamose unrolled it, and holding it under the light of a torch he quickly read. With a cry he read it again. Then he thrust Tani at the soldier.

"Stay here!" he ordered. "You are not to move, do you understand? Wait for me. Look after her," he flung back over his shoulder at the guard as he ran down the passage. "Ahmose! Come!"

"What is in the scroll?" Ahmose panted behind him. "This is insane!"

"Yes, it is," Kamose spat back at him grimly. "Our spy was Mersu but Si-Amun had been passing information to him all the time. He intends to kill Mersu and then himself. Hurry!"

"Gods!" Ahmose managed. They spun towards the women's quarters. Before long they were tumbling to a halt outside Mersu's cell. The guard, pale and visibly relieved to see them, saluted shakily.

"Oh, Prince Kamose, I am so glad to see you! Prince Si-Amun is inside. He ordered me not to enter the room no matter what and I cannot disobey him, but something terrible has happened in there and he has not come out."

"You fool!" Kamose snapped. "A good soldier must sometimes use his own judgement! Unlock the door and go in."

The man fumbled with the door and pushed it open. Laying down his spear, he drew his knife and went cautiously inside, Kamose and Ahmose after him. The light was very dim. The lamp by the cot was already sputtering, exhausted of oil, and cast gyrating shadows around the small room. Kamose almost tripped over the body of Mersu. Swiftly he knelt, his practised eye seeing past the welter of blood, now almost dry and darkening to a murky brown, to the death wound under the ear. He pulled the corpse onto its back. Mersu's abdomen was a torn mess.

Ahmose had sprung past him to the body sprawled across the cot. He stopped as if struck by a spell. "Kamose!" he whispered in a strangled voice. His brother came to his feet slowly, feeling the weight of grim certainty make his movements clumsy. He forced himself to step past Mersu and raise his eyes to the burden on the cot. Si-Amun's face was contorted with his last agony. His lips were rimmed in a black froth. Such pain and resignation were expressed in the rigid features that Kamose

knew the sight was imprinted so vividly on his consciousness
that the details would never fade.

"Si-Amun!" he cried out. "Si-Amun!" He fell across the cot,
and drawing Si-Amun's still-warm body into his arms, began to
sway with his cheek resting on Si-Amun's hair. Ahmose stood
watching as if stunned. Kamose was vaguely aware of his stiff
figure. Though he wanted to shout to his brother to go away so
that he could give full rein to his bitter regret, he forced himself
to consider what must be done. "Ahmose, wake the women and
bring them. Do not let them in, though. Guard, fetch help and
have Mersu's body carried to the stables for the time being.
Alert the servants. I want this room washed and the linen on
the cot changed immediately." Both men left.

For a precious few minutes Kamose was alone with his twin.
He was not given to easy tears, even now. He continued to cra-
dle Si-Amun, stroking his head, his thoughts coherent and loud
to him in the new silence. In better times your weakness would
not have mattered, Si-Amun, he said to himself, consumed by
a cold anger. If Father had been King from the beginning, if you
had not cared so much about what is correct over what is right,
if you could have learned to be reckless . . . He kissed the lifeless
forehead, and as he did so he felt the germ of true hatred begin
to uncurl in his soul. Rapidly it sprouted, a dark and evil sprig.
You, Apepa, Kamose thought with ferocity. You are to blame.
Father and now Si-Amun. The family is decimated and it is
your fault. Setiu pig. Foreign disease. The epithets he flung at
the King eased his grief but they were more than a comfort.
They clung to the roots of this new hatred and fed it so that its
grip on him became firm.

Servants came running, and in a frightened silence interspersed with Uni's murmured commands, they mopped up the
blood and spread fresh sand on the floor. Mersu's body was
taken away. Uni and Kamose lifted Si-Amun so that the sheet

on the cot could be removed and a fresh one laid, then they placed him gently on the sweet-smelling linen. A bowl of hot water appeared and Kamose, glancing up, saw Tani in the act of wringing out a cloth. Tears were pouring down her cheeks. "Ahmose!" he shouted angrily. "I told you to keep the women away!" Ahmose's face peered around the door.

"She insisted," he said. "Grandmother is here, and Mother. Aahmes-nefertari is coming. I will wait for the word to let them in."

"This is no sight for you," Kamose said brusquely to Tani, but she smiled wanly at him, the dripping cloth in her hands.

"It is my fault," she said brokenly. "I was too stupid to see what was happening when I met him in the passage. If I had argued with him. If I had run to you immediately... Let me do this, Kamose."

"It is not your fault," he said harshly. "Si-Amun chose this moment a long time ago." She did not answer. He stood back and watched her wash Si-Amun's tortured face, the crust of blood from his limp hands and motionless chest, her movements sure. He knew that he would never take Tani for granted again.

By the time Kamose allowed the other women into the room, Si-Amun lay composed, arms at his side, white linen draped across his loins. Nothing could be done, however, to disguise the pain and terror in which he died and which was reflected so graphically on his face. Aahmes-nefertari flew to him, and falling beside him, laid her head on his chest. "I did not know that he was suffering so much!" she sobbed. "He told me everything and I did nothing!" She lifted a distorted face to Kamose. "I wanted him to kill Mersu and then keep silent!" She went on crying. Aahotep simply sat on the cot and her hand found her son's thigh. She seemed dazed. Tetisheri stalked to the cot and stood with folded arms over her sleeping robe, her grey hair dishevelled, her complexion drained. Tani, her task completed, squatted in a corner with her head on her knees.

"I have read the scroll," Tetisheri said at last. "He did the right thing. He was weak but the blood of his ancestors won out in the end." Kamose glanced at her. She seemed calm, but she was unconsciously pinching her arms so fiercely that they were already bruising. He was about to go to her when Aahotep jerked to her feet. Her eyes were blazing.

"Is that all you can say?" she shouted. "This is my son, your grandson! No words of love, Tetisheri, no tears for your own flesh? How can you be so cold? I would have spared him this, I would have taken his place if I thought I could put it right, and yet it was his own father he betrayed! To Set with your arrogance, your cruel adherence to an unfeeling code of conduct!" She made an effort to control her agitation. "He is not only guilty of treason," she went on in a choked voice, "he is a suicide. How can he possibly be properly beautified and buried? What god will receive him?" Tetisheri had listened impassively. Now she went around the cot and pulled Aahotep to her feet.

"I did not say that I did not love him," she responded harshly. "It was not necessary. This family is my life. My life! I said that he had done the right thing. I paid him the supreme compliment, my poor grandson. Weset is the only place left in Egypt where men still know what is right." All at once her iron control wavered. Blindly her hands went out, and Aahotep embraced her.

"Kamose, you are our authority now," Ahmose said. "Mersu deserves complete annihilation, of course, and you will order that his body be thrown into the Nile, but what of Si-Amun? Was his last act not one of brave expiation? His suicide was not a matter of a man turning away from his responsibilities or the trials of his life."

"I know." Kamose bent and pulled Aahmes-nefertari from

Si-Amun's corpse. "That is enough!" he said to her roughly. "You will make yourself ill. Think of your son, Aahmes-nefertari. Si-Amun would be ashamed of this outburst." She stopped her loud sobbing and nodded against his chest. "He cannot be properly beautified," Kamose answered Ahmose. "To allow it would be to condone all he has done. But I will not see him forfeit his soul. Let the sem-priests preserve his body whole, without the organs being removed, without the separate prayers, without ceremony. Then he will be wrapped in sheepskins and buried quickly."

"Sheepskins?" Aahmes-nefertari croaked. "Not that, Kamose! That is disgrace! That is shame!"

"It is what he deserves and nothing more," Kamose said, and the tone of his voice brooked no argument. "He would approve if he could, Aahmes-nefertari." Aahotep broke in.

"You are right," she said sadly. "It is just, Kamose." Kamose signalled to Uni, hovering by the door

"Bring the sem-priests and give them those instructions," he said. Uni bowed and disappeared. "Ahmose, please tell Raa and Isis to come. Mother, Grandmother, you need rest. Aahmes-nefertari, I will send the physician to you." Gradually he saw to their needs, shepherding them out, sending a servant for the physician, until at last the sem-priests came to take Si-Amun away. He felt sick, and so tired that his limbs were uncoordinated. There had been no time for memories, not for any of them. That would come later in the long hours of peace, when together they could learn to speak of Si-Amun without grief and exorcise the shame he had brought to the house.

He was about to leave the room that seemed to have been his prison forever when he remembered Tani. Turning, he called her, holding out a hand. She came and grasped it gratefully. "Thank you for not forgetting me," she said. He summoned a smile.

"Come," he ordered, leading her out into the passage. "I will take you to your quarters, Tani." He did not like the look of her. Her eyes were all black pupils and her skin sallow but for the purple smudges under her eyes. Her fingers in his were very cold.

"Kamose," she said hesitantly, glancing back at Mersu's still-open door with a shudder. "Could I please sleep in your room tonight? I do not want to be alone."

"Wouldn't you prefer to be with Mother?" Tani shook her head.

"No," she said emphatically. "You make me feel safe. I want to be with you."

He had his steward set up a cot beside his couch, and while Heket was dressing it he forced a cup of wine between Tani's chattering teeth. "I am so cold," she complained.

"It is the shock," he told her. "Here. Get into bed. Heket has brought extra blankets and she will sleep by the door. There is nothing to fear."

"Yes there is," she whispered as he bent over and kissed her. "There is the future to fear, Kamose. See what life has done to Si-Amun."

He wanted to reassure her, to tell her that Si-Amun's choices had brought their inevitable consequences, but he did not have the heart. Already her eyelids were drooping. He extinguished the lamp and fell onto his couch, knowing that he had lived a lifetime in the few hours since Tani had shaken him awake and he was now a very old man. Apepa will pay, he thought as he plunged into sleep. Justice will eventually be done for you, Seqenenra, and for you, my brother. I shall see to it.

Chapter ELEVEN

H E WOKE JUST BEFORE dawn, fully
conscious, and lay with his hands be-
hind his head listening to Tani's even breathing and watching
the first colourless light diffuse through the room. He knew
that the kitchen and household servants must be about, for
they usually began their chores well before the family rose, but
there were no sounds of cheerful industry, no snatches of song
sung in the passage or slap-slap of busy sandalled feet. I must
gather my energies and get up, he thought. The tragedy must
be faced. Mother, Tetisheri, all of them will want to talk today,
and cry, and they will turn to me because I am now the head of
the family. They will expect me to be strong, to make decisions
when there are none to make in order to reassure them. When
will word of Si-Amun's suicide reach Het-Uart? How will
Apepa react?

With a sinking heart he hauled himself off the couch and
padded to the door. Outside, his steward was waiting patiently
on his stool. "Akhtoy," Kamose said, "send someone to the temple. Tell Amunmose to perform the rites on my behalf this
morning, and have Ipi ready in Father's office after I have
bathed and dressed." When he went back into the room he saw

that Tani was awake. He smiled at her. "Are you feeling better this morning?"

"Yes," she replied without answering his smile. "But my dreams were bad, Kamose. What is to become of us?" A discreet knock was heard. Kamose dropped a kiss on the tip of her nose.

"My body servant is ready to wash me," he replied. "You are not to worry about the future, Tani. It is hidden in the will of the gods and it is also in my hands. Don't you have confidence in your big brother?"

"Of course I do," she retorted, sitting up and yawning. "It is just . . ." He held up a warning finger.

"No more. I will send Heket to you, and I want you to go and comfort Mother today. You are stronger than you think, little Tani. Remember how you used to chatter away to Father when he was recovering from his wound? No one could make him smile the way you could!"

"I am not little Tani any more!" she flashed at him, annoyed. "I shall soon be sixteen. Is twenty-one so old, Kamose? Anyway it was different when Father was only wounded and getting better. I shan't know what to say to Mother." Her voice faltered. He sat on the edge of her cot and took both hands in his own.

"No tears," he rebuked her sternly. "Be strong for me, please, Tani. I need your help today. Try to see Aahmes-nefertari also. Her loss yesterday was the greatest." She rallied under his words.

"That is true," she said with a trace of defiance. "But you will marry Aahmes-nefertari because you are now Prince and she the elder sister. She will have you to protect her and comfort her." Kamose heard what she said with a sense of surprise. He had not considered this duty.

"I will do my best to protect and comfort all of you," he replied. "Come on, Tani. Get up. Neither Father nor Si-Amun would forgive us if we allowed our grief to make us weak." As he went out to find a servant to fetch Heket, he heard her leave the cot.

Once bathed and clad in a kilt, he made his way to the office. He was not hungry, though the aroma of freshly baked bread wafted through the house. The thought of food knotted his stomach and made him feel sick. He needed to get away, to take a chariot out onto the desert where in the heat and silence he could accomplish his own healing as he always did when he needed to be alone, but such self-indulgence would have to wait.

As he entered the office, Ipi rose to bow to him. Beyond the bobbing man early sunlight slipped between the pillars and slanted across the tiled floor and the voices of servants could be heard in the garden. Kamose hesitated on the threshold, his courage momentarily deserting him as he saw his father's plain cedar chair drawn up behind the desk and a pile of scrolls left on the lid of the storage chest by Si-Amun such a short while ago. Then he crossed to the desk and turned to lean against it. Ipi had settled to the floor, his palette across his knees, his face uptilted expectantly.

How to begin? Kamose thought dismally. What do I say? He sighed. "Let us try," he said. The scribe's head bent and Kamose heard him murmur the prayer to Thoth as he picked up his brush. "'To Ramose, my brother, greetings. You know the misfortunes that have befallen us here in Weset and if this letter is answered by your silence I shall understand, but I beg you before you turn away from us to remember the years of closeness and reciprocation there has been between your family and mine. I also beg you to remember the bond that links you and my sister Tani. If you truly love her, do not desert her now. Whether or not you still intend to take her for your wife, come and visit her. She has lost her father, and lately a brother.'"

He paused. Should he tell Ramose everything? No. Undoubtedly Teti would read the scroll. Word of Si-Amun's death was inevitably already spreading north and there was no point in giving that rat the satisfaction of reading about it directly so that he could smack his lips over their troubles. "'She needs you now,'" he went on. "'Set what conditions upon such a visit that you like. I will not object to anything you demand. Only come.'" He considered, then nodded. "That is all. Put the date and I will sign it myself when you have a fair copy."

"Who will carry it, Highness?" Ipi enquired.

"Give it to Uni. I will instruct him. We can do without him for a week or two." He dismissed the man and was tempted to go into the garden, but he resisted. Today grief reigned in Weset and he must enter into it, share it, however much he wanted to go away and howl by himself. Reluctantly he took the passage to the women's quarters.

The weeks of mourning seemed to ooze by slowly, one undifferentiated day sliding into another, so that Kamose began to believe that they had always been grieving, that Seqenenra and Si-Amun had died hentis ago and at their passing time itself had ceased to flow. He went to Amun's modest temple each morning to make his obeisances before the god, to pray and listen to Amunmose chant the Admonitions. He dealt with matters of administration brought to him. He gathered with the other members of the family before the shrine to Anubis, god of beautification and burial, to pray for a correct embalming for Seqenenra and a favourable weighing, and secretly included Si-Amun in his petitions, as he knew the others were doing. Day after day they spoke of their dead with tears, and gradually the tears ceased and the memories became lighter. The Inundation was late. The scorching summer blazed on and in their distress Seqenenra's family could not believe that the Nile would ever rise to fertilize the

land again. It was as though Egypt had died with her most
loyal son.

But Ra rose and set in spite of the introversion into which
the family had sunk, and one day a herald arrived from the
Delta. He did not deign to set foot on the watersteps. Thrusting
his scroll at Uni, who had returned from Khemennu and was
passing on his way into Weset, he called a haughty greeting and
walked back on board his barge. Uni ran to find Kamose. He
and Ahmose had been inspecting the stables together with
Hor-Aha. Several mares were due to foal shortly and Kamose
was anxious about them. The three men had crossed the practice ground and had let themselves through the gate into the
garden when Uni rushed up and bowed. "A message from the
north," he said, holding it out. The men glanced at one
another and Kamose for a moment could not take the proffered
papyrus. All at once the spell of mourning was over. The sor-
rowing oasis of the house had been invaded. The world was
flowing into the gap.

"Thank you, Uni," he managed at last, grasping the scroll.
"You can go." The steward bowed and left.

"There was no tax demand this year," Ahmose said tightly,
his homely face solemn. "I had forgotten about it. Do you
think . . ." Kamose glanced thoughtfully at his brother. Ahmose
had dust clinging to his brown hair and his mouth was parted,
giving Kamose a glimpse of his white, slightly protruding teeth.

"I had not forgotten," Kamose replied. "I just did not think
about it. It did not seem in the least important."

"Dismiss me, Highness," Hor-Aha said, but Kamose restrain-
ed him.

"No," he said. "Stay, General. We have no secrets from you."
He fingered the raised red weal on his cheek where his wound
had healed. "I pray that it may be our assessment but I doubt
that it is." Swiftly he broke the seal and unrolled the papyrus,

scanning it carefully. "No," he said at last, looking up, eyes narrowed against the sun. "It is not. Apepa is coming to Weset. He is bringing the Horus Throne so that he may sit in judgement on this family. He says 'Out of respect for the grief of the great lady Tetisheri, we will postpone our journey until her son has been entombed, but we expect to be received with all pomp and obedience shortly thereafter. If Isis has begun to cry, we will travel the desert roads.'" Ahmose grimaced.

"So we will not even have the Inundation to buy us time," he breathed. "Well, at least Father did not live to see the day of our humiliation!" Hor-Aha was watching Kamose carefully. Kamose felt his black, steady eyes on him in speculation.

"What greeting will you prepare for the King, O Prince?" he asked softly. But Kamose shook his head.

"I would like nothing better than to greet our god with a special Weset welcome," he said, his jaw tight, "but how could we? Our army has scattered, the conscripts are back on their farms, the Medjay are squatting round their fires many nights away. Besides," he gave Ahmose a humourless smile, "there is no heart for fighting left in the family. Not now. It is too soon." Ahmose nodded in agreement.

"We must take our punishment," he said. "Surely even Apepa will see the foolishness of executing blood Princes of Egypt! I wonder what he has in store for us?"

"I will not think about it," Kamose retorted. "What is the point? Hor-Aha, I want you to take all our officers and go into Wawat. Do not return until I send for you. Apepa will not take our lives, but he will want to see you dead."

"Is he clever enough for that?" Hor-Aha snorted.

"I do not know," Kamose answered thoughtfully. "He has always been an invisible presence to us here, sometimes threatening, always disliked, something of a mystery. Father knew him. He came once when I was young. You would not remember,

Ahmose. Neither do I, very well. I want to believe that he is lazy and stupid."

"Even that is not important," Hor-Aha said pointedly. "It is the character of his generals and advisers that matters."

"We must persuade him that we have learned our lesson," Ahmose put in anxiously. "Have we, Kamose?"

Have we? Kamose looked from one to the other. Have we? I am not sure. All I know is that Apepa had better crush us so low that we cannot rise again.

The news of the King's impending arrival caused a stir of resentment and apprehension in the house. It blunted the sadness of their loss, and the prospect of Apepa here at Weset in the flesh further served to propel them all out of their wanderings in the past. Tetisheri, in spite of her hatred for the King, had no intention of receiving him with anything less than the full pomp of which Weset was capable. Her pride would not allow it, and she and Aahotep took charge of the necessary arrangements.

Tani spent a great deal of time with Kamose and Kamose grew used to her pert, pretty face at his shoulder. He had not really expected a reply from Ramose, and as time went on he ceased to look for one. He was angry at the man's fickleness even while he understood that Teti's word was law in his own house, and his heart ached for Tani who seldom lapsed into self-pity and who was gamely trying to remain his helper.

He himself became more tense and withdrawn as the day of Seqenenra's funeral drew closer, for that day would be the last one of peace. Apepa would come, and as Weset's chief administrator, Kamose knew that the brunt of the King's attention would fall on him. All final decisions would be his. Every word would be weighed, every gesture noted. He felt alone, increasingly apart from the life of the house that was slowly returning to normal.

On the day that he heard Aahmes-nefertari laughing with Tani as they played with the baby, he knew that the pain they had all endured was over. Only the poignancy remained. Nothing Apepa could do to them would be as harrowing as the anguish they had lived through. Only he felt permanently changed, set apart from them all. So this is authority, he often thought. This is the potential for power. How did Father handle it with such grace?

By the time of Seqenenra's funeral the flood was in full spate and there was relief under the solemnity of those who gathered to escort the coffin to its final resting place. Kamose, waiting with his brother on the watersteps while Uni strode up and down assigning seats on the barges that would take them all to the western shore, stared moodily into the river's muddy depths. Though he knew that the day was Seqenenra's and he ought to be keeping his mind on the years of care and wisdom his father had given him, his thoughts kept straying north. Had the King set out yet? How many days were left before the herald announcing Apepa's arrival disembarked on these same steps, now gleaming pristine and innocent in the hot sun?

Ahmose shifted beside him. "The sleds are ready," he said, pointing, and Kamose's gaze followed his finger. Across the swollen river four red oxen stood, massively patient beside their handlers, and behind them two red sleds could just be made out. At that moment Tetisheri approached.

"There are two sleds," she said without preamble. "What are you doing, Kamose?" He smiled wryly into the alert, kohl-lined eyes.

"The sem-priests told me that Si-Amun's body is also ready to be buried," he replied. "It seemed wasteful to free servants tomorrow to carry him over and seal him in his tomb when today the sleds, servants and barges are available. He might as well journey with Father." She began to blink rapidly.

"I am trying not to cry," she said vehemently. "Tears will ruin my face paint. You are a wily man, Prince, and a compassionate one. See that you do not endanger the fate of your own soul by acknowledging aloud what is happening today." She stood on tiptoe and kissed him before moving away, Isis behind her.

"Here come the barges," Ahmose observed, his voice unsteady. "And see! One has just left the watersteps by the House of the Dead. It is Father."

Kamose watched the flat vessel move slowly towards the western watersteps, poled by one of the servants of the dead. On it rested two coffins, one large and brightly decorated. Kamose could make out the black Eye of Horus on the side and the lines of hieroglyphs interspersed with gilt ankhs and the symbol for eternity. The other was smaller, a plain wooden box lying in the shadow cast by the bigger one. He had no time to consider his decision to allow Si-Amun to share Seqenenra's rites for Uni was bowing at his elbow. "Please embark, Prince," the steward was saying. "I do not wish to keep the Princesses standing in this heat."

With a curt nod Kamose tore his attention back to the moment and had already begun to descend the watersteps when there was a stir behind him. Ahmose continued onto the barge, but Kamose felt a light touch on his arm even as he was turning back. He found himself face to face with Ramose. He stared at the young man stupidly, bereft of speech. Ramose bowed.

"I came as soon as I could," he said. "My father forbade it and we have had several bitter quarrels, but I do not care much any more for my father's authority." He glanced around him apologetically. "Forgive me for arriving on this day," he begged. "I did not know." Kamose felt relief loosen his muscles.

"Nevertheless, you are welcome," he said. "Go into the house and refresh yourself until we return. Do you know about Si-Amun?" Ramose's face clouded.

"Yes," he replied. "Word spread through the markets in the villages along the river. I cannot tell you how sorry I am." Kamose wanted to ask him how Teti had reacted to the news, but now was not the time.

"We will talk later," he promised. Ramose nodded, and shouldering his way through the crowd waiting to embark, was gone. He made no attempt to speak to Tani, only smiling at her as he passed, but Kamose saw the unbelief on her face blossom into joy before she lowered her head and drew the blue mourning garments around her. That is the one ray of hope in the darkness of our situation, Kamose thought, as he ran down the steps and onto the rocking barge. The seed of rebirth buried in the ashes of death all around us. He lowered himself beside a silent and withdrawn Aahmes-nefertari and waited for the others to come on board.

The trip to the west bank was not long. As the last of the house servants was clambering onto the last barge, the family was already walking to where the sleds, now loaded, lay. Kamose, hearing wailing begin, looked back. The east bank was lined with townspeople from Weset who had begun to keen for Seqenenra. Uni was once more fussing over the formation of the procession behind the two coffins. Aahmes-nefertari, ushered to the front to stand beside Aahotep, suddenly saw why and began to weep. Kamose and Ahmose escorted Tetisheri, with Tani immediately behind. Priests and servants brought up the rear, the women among them already tearing their blue linen and stooping to trickle sand over their heads.

At a signal from Kamose the procession began to move. With a jerk the sleds ground through the sand followed by men from Amun's temple carrying Seqenenra's viscera in four alabaster jars. Kamose put his arm around his grandmother and gave himself up to his grief.

They reached the foot of the cliffs where Seqenenra had

prepared his tomb many years before and gathered round the entrance, Amunmose stepping forward to begin the funerary rite, his acolytes with smoking censers beside him. The crowd fell silent, only the little dancers whispering briefly as they took their places for the dance. Many sidelong glances were cast at Si-Amun's plain coffin lying close by, but no one dared to draw attention to it. Amunmose behaved as though it was not there, stepping around it as Seqenenra's was propped upright against the rock and swung open for the ceremony of the Opening of the Mouth. Kamose watched the sacred knife touch the bandaged body's mouth, eyes, nose and ears, freeing Seqenenra's senses to be used once again.

When the High Priest had finished he wavered, turning an enquiring face to Kamose and indicating the other box with the merest gesture. Kamose considered swiftly. How could the dead smell again, or taste the sweetness of cool water, or see the green glory of the mighty sycamore tree that guarded the entrance to the paradise of Osiris, unless the ceremony was performed? Then he shook his head. It was necessary to maintain the fiction that Si-Amun just happened to be on his way to his own resting place and his conveyance was a matter of convenience, although everyone present understood what Kamose truly intended.

Amunmose signalled for the next rite. One by one the family knelt to kiss the feet of the corpse, so stiff and unyielding in its swathe of bandages, so unrecognizable as the man whose presence had pervaded the house for so many years, and then the dancers began to weave the magic of motion around him, keeping him safe from the dangers of his journey. How fine these people are, Kamose thought as he watched a small hand brush Si-Amun's coffin with seeming carelessness, another lean sideways so that her perfumed hair trailed over the lid. Their loyalty is greater than their fear of breaking the laws regarding suicide, and their warm understanding would put many a fine noble to shame.

The morning became early afternoon. Canopies were erected and cushions strewn over the sand, but many preferred to stand close to the tomb as the rites drew to a close. At last servants took Seqenenra down the steps and into the cool darkness of the vault, lowering him into his stone sarcophagus and arranging his belongings around him. Kamose, watching the women of the house laying flowers on the lid and crying quietly, saw also the furniture, the jars of food, wine and oils, his father's jewels and his cosmetic box. Carved wooden servants stood about to see to Seqenenra's needs and his dismantled chariot had been laid reverently against a wall together with his bow and a quiver of arrows. What use is it all without us? Kamose thought angrily. All these things will only serve to remind him of his family, now divided from him by the ravine that neither he nor we can leap over. Will he finger them with pleasure any more?

Taking Tani's hand he led her back up the steps and out into the blinding white light. For a moment he stood blinking, glorying in the sudden sweep of overpowering sky and shimmering land, then they walked towards the meal that was being laid under the shade of the canopies. Aahotep and Tetisheri were already settled, sitting knee to knee without speaking. Aahmes-nefertari sat on a reed mat as close to Si-Amun's coffin as she dared, already eating, and Kamose did not have the heart to admonish her. She was sharing with her husband, not her father. He, Ahmose and Tani joined the two women, and Tetisheri nodded to Uni. The servants began to serve more food.

Nothing could ever take the place of this, Kamose thought as he broke a loaf of bread apart and a slice of glistening pink melon was placed before him. Nothing in the presence of Osiris could ever compensate me for the loss of this sky, this light, this hot air smelling of desert dryness, those tired palms jerking over the shallow river. The voices of the company sounded like the rhythm of life itself, a gentle confusion that was nevertheless strongly comforting. He thought of Si-Amun, and slipped the melon into his mouth.

By early evening it was over. The temple servants had sealed the door of Seqenenra's tomb, knotting the cords and plastering them with mud into which the imprint of the House of the Dead, the jackal and nine captives, was pressed. Amunmose intoned protective prayers. The barges heaved in the small swell a slight breeze had conjured, and family and mourners made their way finally aboard in the glow of the setting sun while servants buried the remainder of the feast as was the custom.

Si-Amun's coffin, still on its sled, was quietly dragged away towards the small tomb that would now remain forever unfinished. Aahmes-nefertari had run after it, her control finally breaking as she saw it bumping unceremoniously over the rock-pitted ground, and had flung a sheaf of bulrushes over it before Kamose caught her, and picking her up, carried her quickly towards the river. "You must not," he said sharply above her cries, but could not reprimand her further.

He, too, was thinking of their brother lying blind, deaf and dumb, his coffin tossed on the floor amongst the stone chips left by the masons when they obeyed the order to cease their work. So he and his infant son would lie there together with no record of their life on the walls, and Si-Amun's deeds would never come to the attention of the gods. It was terrible, but not as terrible as a body left to rot away, plunging the soul into nothingness. "He has little Si-Amun with him," Kamose sought to calm her as he lowered her onto the barge and into her mother's arms. "At least he is not alone. I will have his name carved on rocks out in the desert, Aahmes-nefertari. Do not worry. The gods will find him."

It was a cold comfort, he knew, and he took his place beside Tani and watched the water ripple in red waves as they were thrust towards the eastern bank. Beyond the welter of garden growth and trees, the house rose like a bulwark of security and sanity and farther along the bank Weset lay in an untidy jumble washed pink as Ra dipped west.

Someone was standing on the paving, arms folded, his stance patient. Tani leaned her head against Kamose. "It is over," she whispered. "Now we can begin to live again, even if it means more pain. That is better than the peace of death, isn't it, Kamose?"

"Even so," Kamose agreed, hugging her, his eyes on Ramose's waiting form. "Even so."

Kamose had to wait for a conversation with Ramose. Tani begged him for permission to see the young noble alone and Kamose did not have the heart to refuse her. "It is not right," Tetisheri had protested irritably when she herself sent for Ramose and was told that he and Tani had disappeared together into the reed marshes in a skiff. Tetisheri had sought out Kamose and found him in the reception hall sitting chin in hand at the top of the steps leading into the garden. "We are not peasants," she had gone on as he helped her down beside him. "We have strict rules governing the conduct of our young women."

"Tani needs him," Kamose had responded firmly. "She will not do anything foolish and you know that very well. She has been through a great deal. Besides, Grandmother, I am now the head of this household and my word is law." She had grunted scornfully but had retreated.

"Then as the head of the household and Prince of Weset you might consider your other duties," she had continued with asperity. "The period of mourning is over. Life resumes its normal course. It is now your responsibility to take Aahmes-nefertari as your wife and her son as your own. This blood line must be preserved without taint for the future."

"For what future?" Kamose had retorted in exasperation, turning on the step so that the lamplight could fall on Teti-sheri's gnarled fingers glittering with rings, her thin shoulders and one side of her delicately boned face. She was resolutely not looking at him, her eyes on the darkness that swept to their feet. "In a few days I doubt if we will have a future. What is the use of pretending any more that we may one day regain the Double Crown? The dream becomes more nebulous, more ridiculous, as one generation succeeds another. I have already decided that I will not marry my sister." He spoke to test her or perhaps himself, he did not know. He remembered the woman who haunted his sleep, who caused him to close his eyes each night in secret anticipation mingled with anxiety and who had for the past several years kept him uninterested in any other.

She had come to him only last night, standing on a rock in the desert, clad in brilliant red, gold-shot linen. Her upraised arms were heavy with gold and the sullen red glow of jaspers, and gold-ringed jasper flowers were entwined in her windswept black hair. There had been something savagely beautiful about her sinuous back under the sheath that flowed like smoke around her and he had been almost afraid in the midst of his fascination.

But Kamose was not so thralled by a phantom, though he ached for her, as to be blinded to the daily obligations of reality. No. His refusal to marry Aahmes-nefertari came from somewhere deep inside, a violent distaste against appropriating the person his brother had loved, stealing her away, enjoying what Si-Amun could never again take pleasure from. The thought made him feel like the basest of thieves and his belief in his heritage was not strong enough to impel him to claim Si-Amun's prize. "Kamose, you must!" Tetisheri had urged, facing him at last. "And before Apepa comes. Then it will not matter what he does to you. If exile is the sentence, Aahmes-nefertari can go with you. If you are sent to be assistant governor of some provincial backwater, she cannot be separated from you! Then no matter what, the blood of your ancestors will be still pure!" Kamose, meeting her intense, intelligent old eyes, had laughed aloud.

"Weset *is* a provincial backwater, dear Grandmother," he pointed out. "The courtiers in Het-Uart shudder at the thought of our nomes and call them Egypt's southern brazier. Your own son married a commoner, don't forget." She sat straighter.

"That is because he had no sister. Besides, Aahotep is not a commoner. She comes of a noble and ancient family."

"A family that produced a dishonourable man like Teti," Kamose cut in quickly. "Let us wait and see, Grandmother. Aahmes-nefertari is entitled to whatever protection I can give her, of course. Why not ask Ahmose if he wants her?" Tetisheri leaned close, eyes narrowed in their cobweb of wrinkles.

"Because you may change your mind. You are a deep one, Kamose. It would not surprise me."

"I have said that I would never marry."

"And I have never believed you!"

They glared at one another until Tetisheri put a hand on his shoulder, heaved herself to her feet, and calling sharply for Isis, melted into the darkness. Kamose sat on, thinking. It has taken Grandmother's forthright tongue to bring my own thoughts clear, he said to himself. I am no longer interested in the quality of my blood. I care only for revenge, but how that is to be accomplished, I do not know.

Ramose stayed for a week, spending most of his time with Tani, but also fitting in remarkably well with the family routine.

Kamose, much to his surprise, began to enjoy his company. They saw little of each other in the mornings, for Kamose, his duties accomplished in the temple, would retire to the office with Ahmose and Ipi, but sometimes in the afternoons he and Ramose would take chariots out onto the desert to race or hunt. The heat of summer was slowly giving way to a winter pleasance as the river filled the parched fields. The two men would sit together in the sand under the shelter of a canopy, drinking beer while their horses cooled down.

Ramose would say little about the rift that had developed between his father and himself, and his distress over Si-Amun's suicide and Seqenenra's untimely death was genuine. Kamose, seeing Tani's new peace, asked him about the uncertain prospects for a wedding. Ramose squinted out past the canopy's shade to the churned pale gold desert shaking in the sun, and did not reply for a while. Then he sighed. "I have done much in defying my father to come here," he said. "I am ashamed of him, Prince, but he is still my father and the head of our household. The matter of a marriage is postponed until the King has decided what is to become of you." He turned a troubled gaze on Kamose. "I love Tani," he said with feeling, "but I cannot risk losing my inheritance or my future. If I marry her now, Father will disown me out of fear of Apepa's displeasure. She is a Princess and whether or not she ever thinks about it, she is used to and entitled to a certain way of life. I must offer her more than simply myself. Those are the facts of my life."

"I do understand," Kamose admitted, surprised that he felt no resentment towards Ramose. "If I were in your place, I would feel the same. But it is a hard thing for Tani to accept. Have you discussed it with her?"

"Of course!" Ramose replied promptly. "She is no longer the starry-eyed child of Hathor I courted. She will wait for the King's judgement, but she knows that it may not be enough for

Father. To put it bluntly, you are all in disgrace. Father is already sniffing out the daughters of several courtiers in Het-Uart. I have told him not to waste his time." He looked back at the desert. "I can wait another five or six years if necessary before being obliged to take a wife in order to perpetuate our line. A great deal can happen in that time."

The words made Kamose shiver involuntarily with foreboding and a despair that bordered on panic. He wanted to jump up and rush to destroy Apepa, take Egypt by storm, brutally force the future into a shape that he could control for Tani's sake, and for Ramose, and for the members of the family who turned their eyes increasingly to him for security and for the assurances he could not possibly give. "You are a good man, Ramose," he said huskily. "I trust you. Tell me, if the wind of chance should by some miracle begin to blow at my back, would you stand beside me?" Ramose was silent for a long time, then he said, "I respect you also, Prince, but forgive me. Bringing a warning to Seqenenra is a far cry from fighting at his side. I cannot answer your question."

When Ramose at last took his leave on the watersteps and then stood on the deck of his barge, waving to Tani until the bend in the river hid him from view, Kamose was sorry. He would miss the young man's quiet amiability. There was a steadiness about Ramose that had served to calm fears and tempers in the house. His presence had lifted the family from its preoccupations and isolation and had helped to place their worries in a different perspective. Tani did not cry as she turned from the watersteps towards her own quarters. Kamose saw her face sink into lines of resignation, and he knew that she was ready to accept whatever fate was to bring.

Chapter TWELVE

T WO DAYS AFTER RAMOSE had sailed away a Royal Herald stepped from his chariot at the rear entrance to the house's enclosure, handed the reins to the barracks servant who had rushed up, and walked through the gate towards the house. Ahmose saw him come and went to greet him, offering a mat in the shade of the garden and a cooling drink, but the man declined. "I bring a message for the Prince Kamose and his family," he said. "The King will grace this home with his divine person tomorrow at noon. He intends to be carried through Weset with the curtains of his litter open so that the people may worship him. He then expects to be greeted by this family on the river road, seeing that it is not under water here. He and his immediate staff will sleep in your house, but his retinue will have tents erected above the flood line outside Weset. That is all."

"That is all what?" Ahmose demanded sharply. The man was gracious enough to flush. He bowed shortly.

"That is all, Highness."

"Thank you," Ahmose said crisply. "You can go."

One for us, Ahmose thought, as he went in search of Kamose. Petty of me, I suppose, but no matter how much in disfavour we are, the King's servants must still show us due respect. I wonder if Ramose encountered the royal entourage? No, I imagine not. The flood that is carrying him swiftly home has forced our King to march either in the desert or well above the waterline where the paths are not much used and are soft or rocky, depending on where you are. It will not have improved his humour and perhaps he will make us suffer for it, but I cannot help taking pleasure in the thought of his frustration and discomfort.

His musings had taken him past the airy entrance to both the office and the reception hall and he met Kamose coming round the corner of the house. Quickly he gave him the news. "There is nothing I can do to help you," he added, "nor will the women want me around. Mother and Grandmother will be in a flurry of cleaning and preparing and will be resenting it all, so that they will be in a foul temper. With your permission I should like to take my skiff and have a look at the hippopotamuses. Will you come, Kamose?"

Kamose considered his brother with mild annoyance. Ahmose was waiting for an answer, smiling with his head on one side, the breeze ruffling his brown curls. Sometimes you exasperate me, Kamose thought. You behave as though you were still twelve or thirteen, naïve and unreflective, and I must make an effort to remember the times when you show far more maturity than your nineteen years. Perhaps I simply envy you your ability to worry about nothing until the time for worry comes. Why should I stay in the house? You are right. I have no obligations today. All I will do is brood. "Yes, I think I will come," he said aloud. "Let me send a message to the others and I will join you by the river."

A few minutes later he and Ahmose pushed off. Ahmose was poling, standing above his brother with wiry legs apart and chattering as he did so. Kamose, with a deliberate effort, gave himself up to the bright promise of the afternoon. The hippopotamuses were asleep, basking in the sun above the flood line, their mighty bodies immobile. For a while the brothers watched them and Kamose envied them their air of sheer abandon. "Let's swim," Ahmose suggested. "They are not going to put on a show for us, so we might as well entertain ourselves." Entertainment, Kamose thought anxiously. What do we have for the King apart from our musicians? Then he mentally shook himself and followed Ahmose, sliding into the cool, reed-choked water with a gasp of delight, his toes sinking into the mud.

They swam for perhaps an hour, gliding back and forth, then Ahmose dived and came up with a handful of black mud which he hurled at Kamose, grinning impishly. Kamose was about to protest when suddenly he was seized with a reckless joy. He did not consciously think of this moment as the last of his freedom or as an overwhelming desire to retreat into the vanished years of his boyhood. He only knew that the sun was hot, the water like satin under his chin, and he had been sober for too long. Sinking, he grabbed up two handfuls of riverbed and surfaced, aiming at Ahmose and then lurching towards him to rub the mud into his face. Soon both of them were yelling and shrieking like demented children, helpless with laughter and covered in black mud. It was Kamose's defiance flung at the King, the future and his fate and he gloried in it, deliriously aware of nothing but this hour. His madness was gone as quickly as it had come and he and Ahmose washed themselves off as best they could and propelled the skiff back to the watersteps, but Kamose felt scoured and content like a newly made pot and courage sprang freshly to life in him.

He rose before dawn the next day as was his custom and calmly made his way to the temple, washing and clothing the god and placing food and wine before him with hands that did not falter, while Amunmose stumbled over the words of the ritual and the sound of the systra held by the singers was ragged and slightly out of rhythm. Only at the Admonitions did the High Priest's voice become more sure as he reminded Amun of the faithfulness of the Princes of Weset and called for the god to vindicate the years of trust. Afterwards in the outer court, both of them shod once more, Kamose invited Amunmose to feast at the house every evening until the King left. "We are proud of our God-of-Double-Plumes," he said, "and we wish the King to know that we honour his servants also. You have been our supporter, Amunmose, and if you do not fear the King's wrath, please represent Weset's Protector." Amunmose was nervous but no coward and he agreed.

Satisfied, Kamose sent a servant into the town to watch for Apepa's approach and then returned to the family who were already gathered in the garden, sitting glumly in their finery as they waited for Apepa. Kamose knew better than to try and cheer them. With a murmured word of greeting he squatted in the new grass and fell silent.

For a long time there was nothing but the constant, scarcely noted babble of birdsong and the rustle of the breeze in the shrubbery. Lizards darted from shade to shade. A frog bounced to the edge of the pond, considered the water, and launched himself towards a lotus pad. "I feel sick," Tani said. Kamose was about to offer a word when the slow sound of many voices began to overpower the music of the birds and grew to a thunderous ovation. At the same moment, the servant ran up out of breath, and bowed.

"He comes, he comes!" he panted. With one accord the family rose.

"My mirror!" Tetisheri snapped and Isis passed her the copper disk. Tani put her hands to her cheeks. Ahmose went to

Aahmes-nefertari's side and her hand slid into the crook of his elbow. Aahotep exchanged glances with Kamose.

"Weset is cheering him," she said. Kamose shrugged.

"Our people are realists," he replied. "They know that a few shouts mean nothing and may please the man they helped us to march against. Are we ready?" He regarded each of them in turn. The finest linen flowed against their limbs. They were wigged and painted, glittering with jewels. We could not pass for courtiers, Kamose thought with a lump in his throat. We have been too far from the fashions of the Delta for too long. But we have something timeless and unmistakable that we share, that I see today in Grandmother's rigid back, in Aahmes-nefertari's unconscious dignity and Tani's regal yet unstudied gestures. The Setiu cannot imitate it. It is unique. "I am so proud of all of you," he managed. "Let us not disgrace our father today, whatever happens. We will have courage. Shall we go?"

They paced in under the dappled shade of the grape trellis, Uni and Akhtoy, today in the long, pleated ankle-length gowns of their station, leading the way. Behind the family came servants bearing the formal greeting meal of bread, wine and dried fruit, on a gold platter to offer the King, but Kamose, after long deliberation, had decided not to present Apepa with any gifts. It would look too much like a craven desire to curry favour, and if Apepa interpreted it as stubborn pride, well, so much the worse. Besides, what could the Princes of Weset offer to the god who had everything? And I will tell him so, Kamose vowed as the pleasant coolness of the trellis gave way to the sun-drenched paved path and the area before the water-steps, if he asks why we do not give him anything. We have nothing to lose.

Yet under his bravado he was full of an uncertainty that grew as they halted facing the river road and a large canopy was unfolded over them. The cheering was subsiding. A small puff of dust drifted into view. Kamose spared a moment to glance across the river to the homes of the dead where Seqenenra lay in the dark cold of his tomb beyond the rugged face of the sun-drenched cliffs. Is your ba fluttering somewhere near, Father? he wondered, and is it distressed to see us clustered here like wary, defiant gazelles run to ground? Ahmose dug him in the ribs and Kamose with an inner stiffening turned to face the King's vanguard.

Two chariots rolled into sight, the horses sporting blue and white plumes, the charioteers wearing blue-and-white helmets. Kamose, squinting into the dust cloud stirred up by the beasts' hoofs, saw that the two men standing easily behind the charioteers sported silver armbands as well as the full regalia of war-spears in hand, bows slung behind them, axes and knives thudding against their linen-covered thighs. He wondered if one of them was the General Pezedkhu who had so soundly defeated Seqenenra. Behind the chariots were two columns of foot soldiers, Braves of the King, perhaps twenty of them, their faces solemn, their spears a phalanx of warning. Still far back, Kamose caught a glimpse of a litter whose closed curtains gleamed with the lustre of gold-wrapped thread. His heart gave a lurch.

The chariots came to a halt. The soldiers smartly divided to line the road. A gaggle of administrative servants was disgorged from two large litters. They stood for a moment, chattering to each other and shaking the grey dirt from their sandals, then one of them detached himself from the group and came forward. He was a tall man with a mild expression and a pair of alert grey eyes. He put his hands on his knees and bowed low, his obeisance somehow managing to include the whole family. "Prince Kamose?" he asked, after running his gaze swiftly over them all. Kamose nodded. The man bowed again, this time directly to him. "I am Nehmen, His Majesty's Chief Steward."

His voice was soft and deferential without being obsequious and Kamose admired the training and control that must have gone into it. "I am responsible for seeing that the needs of the One are properly met while he is here. If you will be so good as to indicate your Chief Steward, I would like to confer with him."

"Very well." Kamose waved Uni and Akhtoy forward. "Akhtoy, my steward, and Uni, my grandmother's administrator of household affairs. They are at your disposal." Nehmen smiled at the two, then returned his mild gaze to Kamose.

"Thank you, Prince," he said. Turning, he barked a crisp command, snapped his fingers, and the little crowd still hovering by the litters broke into individuals who hurried past the family sketching bows as they went and disappeared in the direction of the house. Nehmen, Akhtoy and Uni paced after them.

The way was now open along the road. The King's litter was approaching, carried high on the shoulders of six brawny soldiers and preceded by acolytes sprinkling holy water from the sacred lake beside Sutekh's temple and waving censers over the hard-packed soil, the fragrant smoke scarcely visible in the bright sunlight. Ahead of them a High Priest glided, his shaven brown skull bound with one red ribbon, his leopard pelt held to him by one gold-gripped arm. In the other hand he held a staff topped by the head of Sutekh in silver, its wolf snout snarling a warning to those who watched. He was flanked by we'eb priests who chanted praises to the god and to the King. These took no notice of the family at all.

The water sprinklers reached the broad paved area and began to splatter every stone. Amunmose, himself decked in the garb of his office and attended by acolytes, moved to greet his fellow High Priest. The litter was almost upon them. Kamose felt the expectation and tension around him. The bearers came to a halt and lowered it carefully, then stepped away. Servants rushed to draw back the damask curtains, and as they did so everyone around the litter sank to the ground but for a man who came forward and halted beside the family. He was all in white. His kilt, helmet and sandals and the long staff he now raised were also white, ringed in gold. The Chief Herald, Kamose thought, a whiff of the man's jasmine perfume reaching his nostrils. What was his name? He heard the man draw in a deep breath at the same moment that a brown foot contained in a heavily jewelled sandal appeared from the litter and sought the ground.

"The Mighty Bull of Ma'at, Beloved of Set, Beloved of Ptah, He Who Causes Hearts to Live, The Glorious One of the Double Diadem, Lord of the Two Lands, Awoserra Aqenenra Apepa, Living for Ever!" The herald's strong, vibrant voice echoed against the angles of the house and was thrown back to the river. The King had emerged from the litter and was walking towards them. The Fanbearers on the Right and Left Hands had sprung to pace beside him, the white ostrich fans, symbols of divine protection, held high over his head and quivering against the blue sky.

In the second before Kamose reluctantly bent his knee, he studied the King. Apepa was taller than most of the men who waited on him. His legs were long and shapely, his shoulders, under the white, short-sleeved, loose-fitting shirt and fan pectoral of gold and lapis lazuli, seemed broad. His neck was perhaps a trifle long for the thinness of his face, giving him a pinched and precarious look as though he might lose his balance at any moment.

Kamose did not have the time to study his face. As he went to his knees and then prostrated himself, he had one thought and the rush of one indignant feeling. The King's foreign roots were written all over his body and he had no right, no right at all, to wear lapis lazuli. The hair of the gods was made from the precious dark blue stone with its sprinkling of glinting gold, and only the divine ones, the god Kings and their families, had the right to display it on their persons.

Sheep herder, Kamose thought viciously. It was the greatest insult an Egyptian could conjure. The stone, still damp from the holy water, was warm under his nose and gritty beneath his stomach. He heard Tani's quick, ragged breaths beside him and he hoped that Tetisheri, doubtless enraged at having to prostrate herself to anyone, would keep her mouth firmly closed.

A silence had fallen. Presently a shadow fell across Kamose but he did not dare to move. He could just make out the royal foot, a smudge of henna shadowing the arch that rose slightly from the gilded leather sandal, and a row of turquoise and gold beads across the toes. It was a slim foot. At last Apepa spoke. "Rise," he said. The family scrambled up, not daring to brush the grit from their bodies. Kamose's eyes sought the King's face. He had not been able to remember its delineaments from the brief visit of years ago, apart from the fact that the young Apepa had worn a beard, but now he found he was gazing at someone familiar. He would have done better to keep the beard, Kamose thought, inspecting the high cheekbones and hollow cheeks that promised a firm chin but did not deliver it.

Apepa's chin was a little too pointed, his eyes a little too close together, his eyebrows strong and black. The upper half of his face was indeed kingly, with the eyes, now meeting Kamose's own with calm speculation, large and dark brown under a high forehead slashed by the gold band of the white-and-yellow-striped linen helmet he wore. His mouth curved like a bow, the corners downturned, making him look sullen, but the lines around it did not indicate a discontented nature. They had been carved by laughter. "Lower your gaze, Kamose Tao," Apepa said evenly. Kamose did as he was told.

"Tetisheri!" the King exclaimed, and she came forward and bowed. "I have fond memories of my last visit to your house, in the year of my Appearing when I journeyed throughout my domain. I was comfortable here. It seemed to me then that you and your children lived a life of perfect contentment and ease. But we were all much younger and perhaps less foolish then." Tetisheri smiled frostily.

"Your Majesty is kind," she responded. "But seeing that you are still a man of only forty-one, we may pray that you have many years left in which to grow even more wise."

He did not react to the mild rebuke. He turned to Aahotep, commiserating with her on the loss of her husband as though he had died in some local accident instead of at the hands of first his assassin and then his soldiers. He spoke briefly with Ahmose, asked Aahmes-nefertari how many children she had, and took Tani by the chin, lifting her face towards his own with his deft, graceful fingers. The colour drained from Tani's cheeks but she did not flinch. She stared resolutely straight ahead. "Lovely, quite lovely," Apepa murmured. "I remember you as a chubby urchin of five, dear Tani, but now I can see your father's handsomeness and your mother's beauty in you. You are betrothed to Ramose of Khemennu, are you not?"

"Yes, Majesty," Tani whispered. Apepa released her and there was a slight hiatus.

Kamose beckoned and a servant came bearing the platter of the greeting meal. Kamose took it and knelt, holding it aloft. Apepa inspected it curiously, stirred it with one finger, then politely selected one dried grape and put it in his mouth. "Pezedkhu!" he called. Immediately one of the chariot riders strode forward and bowed.

"Majesty?"

Kamose stared at him. He was swarthy, large-nosed, with coarse features. He was also very young, perhaps still in his late twenties. He must be a military genius, Kamose thought dismally.

"Pezedkhu, clear out every local soldier in the house and grounds and confine them to their barracks while I am here. Set sentries out on the desert as well as along the riverbanks. Assign bodyguards to every member of this family." He turned and smiled very sweetly at an indignant Kamose. "I would never forgive myself if something happened to any of you during my stay," he explained. "My guards are well trained, do not fear. They will watch upon your doors at night and protect you during the day. Yku-didi!" The Chief Herald approached. "Clear my way into the house. I wish to eat and then retire for the afternoon sleep. Where is Itju?" The scribe at his heels bowed.

"Here, Majesty."

"Take instructions for Nehmen. The Throne is to be placed in the reception hall and guarded at all times. Have my travelling couch erected immediately in whatever quarters are the best here. I want the Keeper of the Royal Regalia to sleep beside the throne, with the box in his arms. Have the Treasurer send his assistants into the town and distribute gold to the populace. Open my travelling shrine. I will pray to Sutekh before I retire." He glanced across at his High Priest, deep in conversation with Amunmose. "Have Nehmen check the women's quarters to see whether or not there is room for my wives. If not, pitch tents for these ladies," he waved one languid hand at Aahotep and the others, "in the garden. All but Tetisheri. She is not to be disturbed. That is all for now." The scribe, who had been scribbling furiously, picked up his palette and went away.

Apepa turned to Kamose. "You are right," he said. "I do not trust you, and you need not be affronted because of it. You have an excess of pride, you Taos." Kamose repressed a shudder. He had indeed been thinking with rage of the King's restrictions. "I hope that I will be fed and entertained well tonight," Apepa went on. "We will not speak of the matter that has dragged me here from the pleasant gardens of my palace until tomorrow.

Then you will hear your fate." He did not wait for a reply. Yku-didi was calling and sweeping his staff before him. Servants were already on their faces as Apepa began to move off towards the house. After him went a great procession of litters, runners and courtiers.

"Those must be his wives," Aahmes-nefertari said in a low voice to Tani as the litters swayed past. "Or some of them, at any rate." Kamose barely glanced at the richly hung conveyances, for in the rear, guarded by another phalanx of soldiers, came a litter on which was a shrouded form that could only be the great Horus Throne. Kamose swallowed, thinking of his father as it jerked by. The Horus Throne, upon which none could sit but the gods of Egypt. Beside it paced a little man with a huge casket in his arms. The Double Crown, Crook and Flail. Kamose bowed to it reverently and joined the rest of the family.

"What a crowd!" Aahotep marvelled. "The house will never hold them all!"

"And we cannot feed them all, the parasites," Tetisheri snapped. "I am almost eager to hear my sentence so that they will waft back to Het-Uart before the land becomes denuded of everything. What locusts!"

"He seems to be rather fond of you, Grandmother," Ahmose put in mildly. "He certainly treats you with respect."

"I should hope so!" Tetisheri retorted. "For some reason we found some common ground when he was here eleven years ago. I think strong women fascinate him. Either that, or he has a proper respect for the aged."

"It is hard to tell what he respects," Kamose mused. "I think his haughty pride covers an insecurity, perhaps even an envy of us, that makes him doubly dangerous. Our punishment will be harsh if that is so."

"Yet he removed his beard," Aahotep reminded them. "He knows the Egyptian aversion to body hair. He is not as immune to the opinion of the people as a King should be."

"That is because he is not really a King," Ahmose said loftily. "Let's go into the house and see what is going on. Did you hear the way they talk, those courtiers? Their words so clipped as though their tongues got tired in a hurry? We must mingle with them, Kamose, and keep our ears open. We may hear something useful."

"I don't want to be with them at all," Tani said. "I hope we do get tents in the garden."

"We must behave as though nothing is wrong," Kamose said decidedly. "Don't let them slight or intimidate us. The noblest families in Egypt are represented here, as well as the King's Setiu advisers. We have no animosity towards them."

Yet no one moved to leave the shade of the canopy. The last stragglers in the King's entourage were wandering by. Most of them ignored the little group. Some bowed, whether mockingly or in earnest Kamose did not know. He stood on, one arm around Tani's shoulders, and longed suddenly for the sound of his father's voice.

Nehmen had appropriated Kamose's suite of rooms for the King. It had been Seqenenra's and his father's before him. The rooms were simply decorated with bright wall paintings of day-to-day life but large and airy. The viziers were quartered in Si-Amun's rooms, and Ahmose found himself ousted for Nehmen and Yku-didi. He and Kamose decided to sleep in the barracks with the sequestered soldiers but an order forbidding it came from the King through Nehmen, so they found themselves squeezed into a servant's cell. Fortunately it was not Mersu's.

To Tani's delight, billowing tents of coarse linen were erected by the pool in the garden for herself and her mother.

Aahmes-nefertari had accepted her grandmother's invitation to have a cot put up in her bedchamber and she went to ground there, little Ahmose-onkh beside her in his basket.

All at once the large house with its many passages became uncomfortably crowded. Kamose and his brother, venturing out in the late afternoon with their huge and silent guards padding behind them, found every corner occupied by officials and courtiers who were passing the time before the King left his bedchamber in desultory talk, board games and gambling. Their servants jostled each other as they came and went from the kitchens or the forest of tents that had mushroomed on the ground behind the house where the majority of the courtiers had been assigned space. Kamose's nostrils were tickled by wafts of exotic perfume, hot pastries and precious oils from Rethennu. Jewels winked at him on the prettily gesturing, hennaed hands, the smooth, pampered skin of arms and necks, swung from the ears of painted men and women who glanced curiously at him as he went. Even the servants had gold rings in their ears and seemed to stare at him with a haughty disdain as they stepped aside so that he and Ahmose could pass. "Try the office," Ahmose whispered, but even here there was no oasis of calm. As the two young men pushed open the door they were met by a sudden silence and the regard of several pairs of eyes. Yku-didi and three heralds were there, conferring with the Treasurer, their scribes cross-legged on the floor in a welter of paint pots and scrolls. There was a scramble to rise and bow to the Princes. Kamose nodded curtly and retreated, closing the door. "The garden," he suggested, and he and Ahmose picked their way back along the passage. On the way, scraps of tantalizing conversation followed them.

"... the tax on my date groves. My steward swears by Baal-Yam it is not true."

"... but she caught them by the tamarisks, you know, the

place that's so nice and shady and private behind the temple wall. He says it isn't what it seems but I know . . ."

". . . the negotiations have taken so long. Who do the Keftiu think they are? The whole thing is producing mountains of documents and no results. The King . . ."

"It's a spell to make you remember where you put it, but the cost is high, ten uten, and you might prefer to commission an identical circlet and hope it's ready before she asks where it's gone . . ."

"Oh, I have landed on the House of Spitting! Good luck and bad together! I need a throw of five, five!"

"Hush, it's them! How handsome they are, even if their skin is so dark! If the King wants to banish them he can send them straight to my bedchamber . . ."

It took Kamose a moment to realize that the last speaker, a woman with alluring almond eyes and golden leaves tied into her sleek black wig, was referring to Ahmose and himself. With a wry smile he turned into the reception hall, Ahmose at his heels.

Here there was a reverential peace. A few courtiers stood about in quiet groups, sipping wine and talking in low voices. To Kamose's right, under a tall canopy of cloth of gold, stood the Horus Throne. With one accord the two of them approached it. It was of gold, its arms ending in the snarling muzzles of lions, its sides a beautiful sweep of turquoise and lapis wings where Isis and Neith, the sisters of Osiris, spread their arms to protect and enfold the god who sat upon it. The back was intricately tooled, the gold inlaid with jasper and carnelian showing many ankhs, symbols of life, hanging from the staff of eternity and the stool of wealth. The sides, tiny tiles of ivory alternated with ebony, depicted a King striding forth, Crook and Flail held out before him, Hapi, the god of the Nile, behind him and Ra before. On the rear a great Eye of Horus glimmered. Kamose approached the Throne, pride and a spurt of possessiveness making him blind to all else around him. "Do not touch it, Prince," a voice warned. Kamose looked down. The Keeper of the Royal Regalia was sitting below the three steps of the dais, his charge beside him. Kamose conjured a smile.

"I have no intention of touching it," he answered.

"Look, Kamose," Ahmose whispered. "Here, on the seat. It is Horus in his aspect of the Falcon God of the Horizon. How splendid he is!"

"And look at the footstool," Kamose whispered back. "The King places his feet on Egypt's enemies, the Nine Bowmen, but the Setiu are conspicuously absent!" He and Ahmose grinned at each other, a moment of wicked humour eclipsing all else.

"One could hardly grind one's own ancestors into the dirt," Ahmose hissed, shaking with suppressed laughter. "Oh, Kamose! I feel almost sorry for our upstart King!"

"Hush!" Kamose indicated the Keeper of the Royal Regalia. "We should not linger here, Ahmose. Our guards are becoming uneasy." The two burly soldiers were indeed shuffling and look- ing about awkwardly. Kamose and Ahmose continued on their way through the lofty room.

As they went, a man detached himself from one of the groups and came towards them, bowing several times. "Princes," he said as they halted, "I am Prince Sebek-nakht of Mennofer, erpa-ha and hereditary lord. I am honoured to meet you both." His smile was open and friendly. They returned his bow.

"The Princes of Memphis possess an illustrious lineage," Kamose observed. "My house is not my own at the moment, Sebek-nakht, but I welcome you to Weset. We are at your service."

"Thank you," the man said. "I am a priest of Sekhmet, Lion Goddess of Mennofer. I am also one of the King's architects and my father is vizier of the North. If I can serve you in any capacity, your Highness has only to ask."

"I am grateful," Kamose answered, taken aback and yet touched by the man's courtly words. "I am in no position to request any favours at present but I appreciate your offer."

"The Mennofer Princes have always been very powerful men," Ahmose commented as he and Kamose left the hall and stepped out into the warm afternoon sunlight. "Do you think we have a friend there, Kamose?" Kamose shrugged.

"We have no friends," he replied shortly. "We have no need of a priest or an architect, and the support of a vizier's son means nothing now. It is too late. Where was the mighty erpa-ha Prince when Seqenenra needed him?"

But under the bitter words was a flicker of gladness. Egypt's native sons recognized each other. The nobles of this country could do little more, but Kamose no longer felt alone amid a hostile throng. A sympathy more secret and less courageous than the Mennofer Prince's might exist behind any of these northern faces that displayed the cosmetician's skills. Kamose wondered if the Setiu King might be sitting atop a house of fragile reeds after all.

The feast that took place that night was the most sumptuous ever seen in Weset. The King occupied the dais, sitting in cushions before his gilded table surrounded by pink and green spring flowers. Electrum sparkled as he bent to speak to his Queen on his right, lifted food to his mouth, or paused to survey the company. On his wigged head the Fiery Uraeus, the golden cobra and vulture with their beaded eyes and watchful gaze, reared in protective warning. Below him the Chief Herald stood with his staff. His Fanbearers, holding the ostrich plumes, flanked the dais together with his generals and bodyguard. The Queen was a dark and delicate young woman in a silver-shot sheath, her arms tinkling with silver, her fingers heavy with gold. Behind her, three of his other wives chattered and giggled, garbed in fine linen and buried in flowers.

The crush of diners around the many tiny tables scattered about the floor was intense and spilled out over the portico, down the steps, and into the garden. Dozens of perspiring servants moved to and fro bearing trays of steaming dishes and flagons of wine. Others presented the courtiers with garlands of early blue and pink lotus, strings of blue beads and perfume cones to be tied on their heads. The blending of hundreds of voices was deafening, the mingled aromas of food, flowers and the melting cones overpowering. Occasionally a puff of night wind blew in from the garden but it only served to stir the laden air. The playing of the King's musicians was drowned in the cacophony.

Kamose and the family sat far back against a wall, facing a tumultuous sea of laughing, drinking courtiers and largely ignored. They took their meal quietly. Although they had put on all their finery they felt awkwardly out of place, old-fashioned and slow. They were soon finished and sat with cups before them, the sweet smell of their lotus wreaths mingling with the released scent of the oil that slipped lazily down their necks. "What is that strange instrument?" Tani enquired, pointing to where the musicians were vainly playing. "I recognize the harps and drums and, of course, the finger cymbals."

"It is called a lute," Tetisheri answered. "The Setiu brought it with them. When the dancing begins you will be able to hear it. The sound is stronger than the harp but not as gentle."

"This wine is Charu," Ahmose broke in, licking his lips speculatively, his voice full of awe. "The best wine in the world."

"And the perfume locked in the cones is myrrh," Aahotep cut in. "Are we children, to be impressed by these things? Gold buys everything and means nothing."

"Yet it is hard to look beyond the gold to those through whose hands it passes," Aahmes-nefertari said, her eyes on the Queen, who was listening to her husband, her chin sunk in one hennaed palm.

"We must try," Kamose urged her. "We are not unimportant, Aahmes-nefertari. All this," he gestured at the riotous crowd, "all this is because of us. The King is here, six hundred miles from Het-Uart, because we are more important than any noble in this room. Remember that."

"I would have preferred a visit from a herald with a scroll," Tetisheri complained. "They eat more in a day than we set on our tables in a month. Uni is crazy with anxiety over our stocks of flour and honey. The harvest is a long way off." No one had the heart to remind her that for them the harvest would probably be meaningless. They fell silent, a little pool of worry and sobriety amid an increasingly raucous congregation.

At last the King signalled. The noise dropped to an anticipatory murmur. Servants removed the tables and the diners pressed back towards the walls. The musicians took a moment to gulp their beer and mop their faces. Then the entertainment began. Afterwards Kamose, falling onto his cot in his cramped quarters, remembered that part of the night as a blur of glaring colours, naked bodies and exotic music. Imprisoned in the crush, his head throbbing, he suppressed a wild desire to leap up and run out onto the desert where there was a fresh wind and starlight. Tetisheri was lying back on her cushions, eyes closed, drowsing. Aahotep had her arm around Aahmes-nefetari. Tani was sitting with knees drawn up, mutely watching the activity. Ahmose had disappeared, but Kamose saw him a little later talking to the Mennofer Prince and the men around him. They were all smiling.

With a rumble of drums and the high click of finger cymbals the dancing started. Kamose, no stranger to the delights and intricacies of such expression, took little notice. Everyone loved dancing. The King's troupes were very accomplished. Their skin gleamed with oil, their hair, weighted with silver balls, swung pleasingly. Their supple bodies bent and swayed. But the last dancers were black, their hair stuck with the plumage of strange birds, their loincloths of animal skins. As they danced they uttered hoarse cries. Their eyes roved fiercely over the gathering and they shook strange instruments. Kushites, Kamose thought. A gift, I suppose, to our King from Teti-en, Prince of Kush, that ingratiating governor who preens himself on enjoying Setiu approval and who is so closely bound to Het-Uart by treaties that the King calls him "brother."

The dancers were replaced by magicians who turned wooden sticks into snakes that slithered black and menacing over the floor and made the women shriek, then were grasped by the tail and became sticks again. The magicians were able to clothe themselves in fire, pull singing birds from their mouths, and other marvellous things. But Kamose watched coldly. Outside the moon was shrinking, paling towards the dawn. The swollen river ran swiftly silver and the lush new growth along its banks was shrouded in darkness.

He felt eyes on him and lifted his head. Apepa was staring at him expressionlessly from the dais over the clapping, shouting throng, his face unreadable. Kamose stared back, wondering what thoughts were flitting through the King's mind under the stiff helmet whose wings brushed the royal shoulders. No contest existed between the two men. Apepa was the law and Kamose the criminal. Yet, as he considered the King's blank gaze, Kamose sensed fear behind it, and a challenge. It is between you and me, he thought, as the Queen touched Apepa's hand and he turned to give her his attention. You know it, irrational as it seems. You and me.

On the following morning Kamose rose early, washed and

dressed, and walked to the temple, trailed by the soldiers detailed to guard him. He performed his duty to Amun, spoke briefly to Amunmose, then walked back to the house in the sparkling, fresh air. The flood was at its height. Water lapped at his feet and spread beyond him to the very edge of the cliffs, reflecting a pale sky. Two hawks hung motionless above him as though dazed by the strength of the sunlight and the smooth mirror of the vast pools below. Their presence lightened his heart and he saluted them silently as he approached the house. Already the noise and bustle of the King's retinue could be heard and a strong smell of new bread assailed him as he turned away from the river and headed for the garden.

On the way, Yku-didi came up to him. "The King has commanded that you attend him in the reception hall in one hour, Prince," he said with a bow. "You may not wear jewellery or sandals. A simple kilt will be sufficient clothing." Kamose fought down his apprehension. Criminals appearing for sentencing had to be barefoot and unadorned but he had somehow believed that his rank would protect him from this humiliation. For answer he nodded, dismissed the herald, and returned to the servant's cell. Akhtoy rose from his stool before the door.

"Go to the other members of the family and tell them that we will meet together in the garden in one hour," he told his steward. "Has the King risen?"

"Yes, Prince. He and his train have finished the morning prayers to Sutekh and are taking nourishment."

"Thank you. You can go."

For the first time, Kamose wished that time would stand still, that some mighty cataclysm would come and sweep them all away before he had to stand before Apepa with his loved ones under the eyes of the northerners. He could imagine what their thoughts would be. Relief that the judgement was not falling on them, an avid titillation as the sentence was pronounced, food for gossip for many weeks to come.

He entered his room and stood with eyes closed, breathing deeply, conjuring the faces of his father and Si-Amun in an effort to boost his courage, but their picture only discomfited him further. I am angry with them, he thought in surprise. They left me to face this alone, and I am angry. He turned his thoughts to Amun, whose golden image sat smiling in the temple surmounted by his beautiful plumes. Amunmose would be present in the hall today in his full regalia, praying quietly for those to whom the god owed loyalty. The Princes of Weset have served you faithfully for generations, he said to the god in his mind. Now is the moment of reciprocation. Take up our cause, your cause, and smite the Setiu...

His thoughts trailed away, the words lacking conviction. It had all been said to Amun a thousand times and Kamose did not want to pray any more. He sat on the disordered cot where the hard-pressed servants had not yet had time to change the linen, folded his arms, and set himself grimly to wait.

Shortly before the hour was up Kamose left the cell and went into the garden where the rest of the family was already gathered, a tight, sombre little group staring haughtily back at the courtiers who strolled about waiting for a herald to announce that they might enter the hall. Swiftly Kamose kissed the women. His mother and sisters wore ankle-length, unpleated sheaths. They were without jewels or wigs. Aahotep's healthy, gleaming tresses fell to her shoulders, one streak of grey at her temple catching the sun. None of them were painted but Tetisheri. She stood resplendent in wig, silver necklet, earrings and bracelets. Her sandals were of soft white leather. Blue eye paint smudged her lids and kohl-rimmed eyes. Tani had been crying. Her eyes were swollen red. "Where is Ahmose?" Kamose enquired anxiously, ignoring the flutter of hushed conversation that had broken out at his appearance.

"We do not know," Tetisheri replied. Kamose surveyed her and as he did so he felt his mood change from fearful anticipation to a lightness he had not experienced for a very long time. His grandmother regarded him with her customary cool hauteur. The others had their eyes fixed on him too, their gaze full of expectation. They were relying on him to conjure some magic that would save them, but Tetisheri would always stand on nothing but her blood and her station in life, unrecognized though that might be. She was the wife of a King, the mother of a King, and that was enough for her. "He will doubtless appear at the last moment," Tetisheri went on. "Fetch me a shat cake, Uni. This waiting has given me an appetite."

All at once Ahmose came striding briskly from the house, his legs wet, his tight curls glistening with moisture. "I decided to go fowling this morning with Prince Sebek-nakht and his friends," he said by way of explanation. "The reed marshes are teeming with ducks. Sebek-nakht is a very good shot with the throwing stick and we thoroughly enjoyed ourselves. I came home very muddy though." Aahotep began a furious reply but it was cut short by the sound of Yku-didi's staff of office striking the step outside the hall.

"Enter who will!" he called. There was a rush past him. Ahmose smiled encouragingly at everyone. Kamose squeezed Tani's hand. They followed the crowd into the dimness of the hall.

The courtiers had been shepherded to either side so that Kamose, walking between the pillars, could see straight to the Throne. It was empty. A guard barred his way and another took up his position behind the family. For a few minutes the atmosphere in the hall became charged with excitement and expectation, then Yku-didi reappeared, this time beside the doors at the far side that had been flung open, and began to shout the King's titles.

The royal party filed in. The wives settled themselves on the steps of the dais. Behind them Apepa followed and mounted, turning to seat himself. Kamose, with bated breath, saw that he was wearing the Double Crown, the smooth white dome of Upper Egypt nestling inside the red support of the symbol of Lower Egypt. Fastened above his forehead was the Uraeus. Today the cobra and the vulture had a predatory look to them, their ebony eyes hungry. Kamose repressed a shiver. Strapped to Apepa's chin was the royal beard of plaited leather thongs. Impassively the King surveyed the company. Yku-didi finished his recital and took up his position below the Fanbearer on the Right Hand. Itju opened his paint pot and checked his brushes. A deep hush stole over the courtiers so that the song of a solitary bird could be heard pouring its delirious winter music between the sun-splashed pillars.

Apepa pointed down the hall. Immediately the guards ushered Kamose and the others forward. With heads high they walked the length of the hall. Halting before the Throne, they went down on their knees and then on their faces, prostrating themselves. "Read the charge," Apepa said quietly, his voice falling flat in the packed room. Yku-didi cleared his throat. Kamose heard the rustle of a scroll being unrolled.

"Kamose Tao, hereditary Prince of Egypt, erpa-ha and smer, governor of Weset and her nomes, you and your family by blood are charged with conspiring to commit treason together with the Osiris One Seqenenra Tao, of taking up arms against the Divine One and Ruler of the Two Lands Awoserra Aqenenra Apepa, and of breaking the treaties of mutual trust and aid sealed between your grandfather Senakhtenra and the King. You are charged with attempting to disturb the balance of

Ma'at in Egypt and with blasphemy against Egypt's supreme protector Sutekh. Copies of these charges have been given to Sutekh, Ra and Thoth for judgement. Your guilt has been determined. Life, Health and Prosperity to the One who reigns, like Ra, eternally!"

There was a pause. Kamose closed his eyes, his cheek pressed to the warm floor.

"You may rise," Apepa's voice floated over them, still flat and emotionless. They came to their feet. Ahmose stared frankly at the King. Kamose, beside him, watched as at a peremptory wave of the royal hand the Keeper of the Royal Regalia mounted the steps between the wives, the open box in his arms. Apepa leaned forward and took the Crook and the Flail. The Keeper backed away. "Do any of you have anything to say before I pronounce sentence?" the King enquired. Kamose met his black-ringed, impenetrable gaze.

"I do," he said, his voice loud in the late-morning stillness. "It is beneath a son of Amun to try to justify the rebellion that my father planned and that my brother and I took part in, therefore I will not try. But, Majesty, I beg clemency for the women of my family. They neither instigated it nor actively supported us. They are innocent."

"Are they indeed?" Apepa said politely, his eyes swivelling to Tetisheri standing stiffly in all her splendour. "But who can tell what words of encouragement were whispered in secret, Prince, what seditious desires were fanned in the heat of a summer afternoon? There is nothing temperate here in the south. Not the power of Ra, not the aridity of the desert, not the reckless hot blood of the inhabitants, some of whom, it is said, have more than a tincture of Wawat blood in their veins." Ahmose stifled an indignant exclamation. "Wawat blood foments wars, or so it is said," Apepa went on. "Your plea has been noted." He leaned forward, the Crook and the

Flail held firmly against his chest. "Where are your father's officers, Kamose Tao?"

"There were not many, as your Majesty doubtless knows," Kamose answered smoothly. "They were all killed in the battle." Apepa glanced at Pezedkhu who was standing with the other generals against the wall. Pezedkhu imperceptibly shook his head. Apepa looked back at Kamose.

"Justification may be beneath a son of Amun," he remarked dryly, "but lying is not. However I do not intend to expend my soldiers' energy in tracking down the miscreants. They did not perform well in any case. I will proceed." He came to his feet. All but the family sank to the floor. Kamose felt Tani's hand grip his own as the Crook and the Flail were extended over them. "Hear the judgement of the King all-wise," Apepa said, raising his voice so that it flowed, strong and vibrant, over the people. "Kamose Tao, for the crime of treason you are commanded to report in four months' time to the commander of our eastern stronghold, Sile, where you will serve as one of Egypt's defenders indefinitely. Your nomes are removed from your control. Your property and all your goods are declared khato. They revert to the Crown. Ahmose Tao, you are to report to the Prince and governor of Kush, Teti-en, who will assign you an active post against the tribesmen who refuse to accept Egypt's jurisdiction. Tetisheri, I have prepared an apartment for you in my harem at Ta-she. There you may retire and do such small works as the Keeper of the Door finds for you. Aahmes-nefertari, you are banished likewise from the sight of your family. You and your son will proceed to the Delta where I myself will arrange a suitable marriage for you outside the bounds of Egypt's nobility. Tani, you will travel north with me as my honoured guest. You will live at Het-Uart in every blessing. I do not wish you to be unhappy." Tani's nails suddenly dug into Kamose's palm and Kamose winced in spite of his immediate attempt at control.

Apepa sat down. The company stirred. "Such is the sentence," Apepa went on more mildly. "I have been lenient. You deserve death, but for the sake of your ancient lineage I give you your life. However, on pain of death, you will not see or communicate with each other. I will receive regular reports on your behaviour."

"Majesty," Kamose broke in, feeling Tani's hand trembling violently in his, "perhaps you are not aware that my sister is promised to Ramose of Khemennu. She is already betrothed. Even a King may not break this tie." Apepa seemed unmoved by Kamose's temerity. He smiled faintly.

"The possibility of this marriage died a long time ago and you know it," he rebuked Kamose. "Ramose is a loyal son of Egypt who does not wish to be allied to a traitorous family such as yours. Teti has found him another wife. For his loyalty to me I have given Teti the governorship of Weset and her nomes, this house, and your acres. In four months he and his household will leave Khemennu for Weset. Aahotep, you will remain here to serve your relative in any capacity he chooses. " Kamose dropped Tani's hand.

"No!" he shouted, stepping forward. "It is not just, it is not right! Kill us if you must, but do not give our birthright to such a one as Teti! It is an insult to every noble of Egypt. This house is ours, it has been ours since my ancestors left the old palace and built it!" He wanted to say more, to scream abuse at the lofty, arrogant face regarding him with eyebrows raised under the weight of the Double Crown, but caution won. Panting, teeth bared, he fell silent.

"You have forfeited all your rights," Apepa pointed out. "So has your totem. I know that the High Priest of Amun gave you his support and Amun his blessing. The god will be moved into a small shrine in the centre of Weset. We do not wish to deprive the people of their comfort. Amun's temple will be rededicated to Sutekh, whose likeness will reside therein. This audience is at an end."

Immediately the crowd came to its feet and a buzz of excited talk broke out. The King had already left the Throne and was pacing through the door, his officials before and behind him. The wives were yawning and wriggling on the steps, eager to be gone to the noon meal and more congenial pursuits. Kamose looked about. The courtiers were streaming out into the garden, all but Sebek-nakht, who came towards them sympathetically. "I am sorry, Prince," he said to Kamose. "Be assured that I shall work every day to have your sentences mitigated. It is an outrage to treat Princes thus, no matter what they have done!" There was little for Kamose to say. Graciously he thanked the young man who hurried away and followed the others. Soon no one was left in the hall but the family and their guards.

Tani flung herself on Kamose. "You will not let him take me away, will you, Kamose?" she pleaded hysterically. "You can do something, can't you? Can't you?" Kamose roughly pulled the frantic arms from around his neck. Aahotep, exchanging glances with him, cradled the girl against her shoulder.

"Tani, you must try and understand that there is nothing I can do," Kamose said. "He is the King. His authority is absolute. Mother, for Amun's sake take her away! Aahmes-nefertari, you go too." The young woman was hesitating, white to the lips. Ahmose went to her swiftly and kissed her.

"Do as he says," he urged. "I will come to you later. There is much to be said, Aahmes-nefertari, but not now. Do not despair!" With a dazed nod, she turned awkwardly and followed her mother and sister.

"Apepa hopes that we will kill ourselves," Tetisheri commented coolly, her eyes on the little group now retreating with heads lowered, the guards behind. "He has given us four months for the sentence to sink in and for us to feel the full humiliation of it. Death by our own hand would save him a great deal of trouble." She shifted her steady gaze to Kamose. "What are you going to do?" she enquired. "It is unthinkable that Teti should be allowed to live in my house and rule your nomes, Kamose. Something must be done." Kamose rounded on her savagely.

"What do you expect me to do?" he exploded. "Call down fire from Ra to destroy the King? Wake up, Grandmother! I am not a magician, to pull spells of salvation out of my mouth! There is nothing to be done. Nothing!" She regarded his heaving chest and angry eyes unperturbed.

"Nevertheless, you will try," she responded. "I know you, Kamose Tao. I see into your heart as no other can." Jerking her head towards Uni waiting out of earshot by the doors, she glided regally away.

"Tani is to be more than one of Apepa's guests," Kamose mused, unaware that he had spoken aloud. "She is to be a hostage against our compliance. Of course. That is why he takes her north when he goes and does not send for her later."

"The same thought had occurred to me," Ahmose agreed. Kamose swung to him, startled. He had not realized that he had voiced his thoughts. "How wily he is!" Ahmose went on. "By that one move he has tied our hands more tightly than anything else could have done. Now we cannot even run away."

"Run away?" Kamose frowned. "To where, Ahmose?"

"Anywhere," Ahmose replied promptly, "as long as we are together." Kamose began walking away absently. "Where are you going?" Ahmose called after him. Kamose raised his shoulders as though the physical gesture could relieve him of the weight of despair that had settled on him.

"I need to think," he said. "Go and keep the women calm, Ahmose. You are good at that. I will see you later."

The noon sun struck him as he left the hall and descended

into the garden. Air eddied around him. The grass felt soft under his bare feet. The shrubs and flower beds were alive with the chirp and rustle of birds and insects. The shouts and splashes of jockeying helmsmen came from the river. The reality of the day stunned Kamose. Quickly, with eyes narrowed almost shut, he made for the rear wall and the gate that would let him out onto the practice ground, the barracks and the strip of uncultivated land at the foot of the cliffs. He had his hand on the gate when his guard stopped him. "You are not permitted to visit the barracks, Prince." Kamose looked beyond to where the soldiers were sitting about idly on the scuffed dirt of the parade area. His eyes sought for Hor-Aha until a moment later he remembered that the General was somewhere deep in the wild lands of Wawat.

"I do not wish to visit the barracks," he assured the man. "I want to walk a little under the cliffs." He pushed on the gate but the man stepped apologetically and firmly in front of him.

"I am sorry."

"Very well." Kamose turned back and headed for the break in the southern wall that would lead into the old palace compound. The wary guard padded after him.

The palace was empty, quiet and cool. Kamose took deep breaths as he passed through the dilapidated rooms on his way to the stairs by the women's quarters. Mounting, he came out on the roof and with deliberation sank onto the same dusty spot where his father had often rested and where he had been so cruelly attacked. There was as yet no shade but the winter sun was bearable. Over the wall he saw the garden alive with the multi-coloured floating linens of the restless courtiers. Their conversation reached him as a not-unpleasant susurration of sound. The path from the garden through the grape trellis to the watersteps was alive with heralds and other officials going to and from the river.

Directly below, in a corner of the baking compound where wall met wall and provided a small shadow, a young boy in loincloth and dusty sandals sprawled with his midday meal, oblivious of the man who gazed down on him. The sight made Kamose smile, and his despondency lightened. I need your wisdom now, Father, he spoke in his mind to the ghost of the man who had himself sat here so often that his presence seemed to linger. Show me what alternatives I have. Are we to live scattered and anguished? Are we to die? What choices do we have? Kamose's chin sank into his palms and he closed his eyes. The royal guard lowered himself resignedly into the debris and set his back against the crumbling side of the windcatcher. He did not relish his duty at all.

Chapter THIRTEEN

IN THE LATE AFTERNOON the King sent for Kamose. Kamose had spent several hours in deep thought on the old palace roof, pondering while the garden emptied and the couches and cots in the house and tents were filled with sleeping people, and had been on his way to the cell he shared with Ahmose to wash and change his linen when Yku-didi accosted him in the passage and bade him follow. Kamose did so obediently. He was tired. He had hoped that Apepa would return to Het-Uart without demanding a personal meeting.

Kamose was ushered into his own quarters, where Apepa was sitting in a chair beside the rumpled couch. He had obviously just risen from his afternoon sleep. A square of white linen hid his shaven skull as the law decreed. He was clad in a short, crushed white kilt and nothing else. A servant had the royal foot in his lap and was carefully painting the sole with orange henna. Apepa was sipping water. On the table beside him lay his rings and the Royal Seal. "Prince Kamose, Majesty," the herald announced, then bowed and withdrew. Apepa signalled. Kamose went forward with bowed back and hands on his knees, then he prostrated himself. Apepa allowed him to rise.

"I wish to return to the Delta tomorrow," the King said.

"Unfortunately the river is still too high to navigate safely and I will have to endure my litter and the desert but I cannot wait. I summoned you to make sure that you fully understand your situation before I leave." His cosmetician laid down the henna-stained brush and began to fan the royal foot to dry the liquid. Apepa regarded Kamose quizzically from beneath the loose cap of fine linen, his face creasing as he smiled. "Do you have any questions for me, Prince?"

"Majesty, I beg you to reconsider taking Tani away with you," Kamose said. "She is still very young and has never been separated from her family. She . . ." Apepa silenced him with a wave of one freshly hennaed palm.

"She is sixteen, a woman, and capable of understanding her duty to her King," he replied. His smile widened. He knows perfectly well that I have concluded her true status, Kamose thought. "My advisers recommended execution for all of you," the King went on. "You do not seem grateful for my clemency."

"I would guess that only your Setiu advisers recommended execution, Divine One," Kamose said softly. "I would also guess that your native Egyptian administrators thought the idea horrifying and warned you against such a move for the sake of your security. They were wise." The smile disappeared from Apepa's face.

"My advisers are invited to give me their opinions because I value their wisdom," he snapped, "but I alone in Egypt am all-wise. The final decision was mine." He snatched his foot from the cosmetician's grasp and leaned forward. "You have the arrogance to believe that I fear you, Kamose Tao, that one hint of a threat from you will send me scurrying to Sutekh in prayer for my survival. Not so. You and your family live in a world of old dreams and dead glories where the Setiu are still enemies and you are still Kings."

He held out a hand and a servant approached with an unguent jar. Pouring a drop of oil on the royal palm, he withdrew. Apepa rubbed his hands together and passed them over his face and neck and the heady aroma of lotus flowers filled the room. "I was born here," Apepa said slowly. "My father, my grandfather and his before him, all gods of Egypt. I could have killed Aahmes-nefertari's son, that child of your so-called royal brother, but I do not need to kill. All Egypt worships me, Kamose, for I am the god. I am almost moved to pity you for your delusions and your poverty." He closed his eyes and inhaled deeply as Kamose wanted to do. The flower odour was bewitchingly sensuous. "My forefathers acknowledged your privileged place in the Egypt of old and concluded treaties with your family instead of wiping them out. Now I, too, reverence the past by rapping your knuckles instead of piercing your heart." The royal eyes suddenly opened wide and fixed Kamose with a cold stare. "You will never see Weset again, I promise you. But I will also promise you that Tani will be surrounded with all respect and the luxury she deserves because of her station as a Princess and though your other sister cannot be allowed a noble husband, yet I will choose for her wisely so that she knows no want. Herald!" The door opened and Yku-didi bowed. "Show in the General." A bareheaded, powerfully built man came in, bowing. "This is General Dudu," Apepa told Kamose. "He is to stay here with fifty of his soldiers when I and my retinue leave tomorrow. He will assess all your holdings for appropriation and will send me weekly reports on you until the four months are up, at which time his Second will escort Ahmose into Kush and he will bring you and the others north. You are dismissed. We shall not meet again."

With gritted teeth Kamose went to the floor, rose, and backed out of the room. I should have known that there would be a watchdog, he said to himself furiously as the door was closed firmly in his face. Apepa is right. I am a poor fool wandering in dreams, but they are not yet nightmares. Not yet.

As he strode angrily down the passage he almost collided with Uni. The steward had his arms full of starched linen and a servant trotted behind him. He bowed and Kamose grasped his arm, looking round. The guard was a discreet few paces behind. "Send a runner into Wawat," he whispered into Uni's ear. "Bring Hor-Aha and the other officers back. The King leaves tomorrow." Uni nodded and stepped aside. Kamose went on down the passage.

In the garden the courtiers were gathering, freshly bathed, waiting for the evening feast to begin. Kamose glanced over their heads to the sky. Ra was rimming the horizon, his red sphere flattened and elongated as Nut slowly bit into him. His blood drenched the grass and splashed in long streamers against the walls of the house. The chattering, drifting people glowed in the warm bronze light. Kamose made his way towards the spot where two tents trembled in the evening breeze, scarcely aware of the way the crowd swayed and parted to let him through. He called softly outside Tani's tent and was answered. The guard standing by the opening nodded curtly. He went in.

Tani was sitting hunched on cushions, the playing pieces of a board game scattered on the mat beside her. Several sheaths had been spread across the cot on which she slept. A flagon and cup sat on top of her tiring chest, together with two lamps waiting to be lit. She looked up when he entered. Kamose lowered himself beside her. As he did so, a great gust of laughter rose from the courtiers outside.

"Listen to them!" Tani said disdainfully. "The only worry they have is whether the goose will be roasted correctly tonight and the melons stuffed with enough sweetmeats. How Egypt ever gets governed by that crowd is beyond me!"

"Why are you alone, Tani?" Kamose asked gently. "You should not have been left by yourself."

"They were all here," she answered woodenly. "Grandmother talking of revenge, Mother with her arms around me, Ahmose clucking over Aahmes-nefertari who was swearing to hide her panic and vowing she would rather die than marry some filthy commoner. I sent them away." Kamose looked at her in surprise. She was still deathly pale, but there was no sign of the hysteria that had threatened to erupt in the reception hall.

"Sent them away?"

"Yes. There is no point in wailing and cursing, is there, Kamose? Better to accept our fate, my fate." She smiled at him, the curve of her lips carrying a cynicism he had never seen in her before. The sight shocked him. "I have always loved the old oath we use so freely," she went on. "'As I love life and hate death.' Everyone says it. It has almost lost any meaning. We are indeed a people who love life and hate death, more passionately than the Setiu could ever understand. I have been pondering the words, Kamose. I love life. Love life. As long as I am alive, I may hope that the gods will send me a kinder fate. Is it not so?" He nodded gravely, overwhelmed by her calmness.

"It is so."

"But what he said about Ramose . . ." She bent forward over the hands folded in her lap. "Ramose told me that he would refuse to consider any women his father put forward, that he would wait and see what the future brought. He need not wait any longer, need he?" Kamose felt her agony but admired her ruthless clear sightedness.

"No, Tani, he need not wait. Word of the King's judgement will reach Khemennu very soon. But I think he will wait." She give him a tight smile.

"So do I."

There was a small silence, then Kamose reached over and,

taking both her hands in his, he began to chafe them gently. When he spoke, he lowered his voice. The shadow of the patient guard lay against the sloping side of the tent. The happy noise in the garden was growing but Kamose did not want to take a foolish risk. "Tani, I want you to understand something," he said quietly. "You are not going north simply because the King has taken a fancy to you. You are going as a hostage to ensure that the rest of us make no more trouble." She did not look surprised. She merely raised her eyebrows wearily.

"I suspected it," she replied. "If I were Apepa I would do the same thing." Her gaze became alert and she withdrew her fingers from her brother's grasp. "Is he being unduly cautious, Kamose?" Kamose sat back, pulling his feet further under him. He looked at her directly.

"No, he is not," he answered frankly. "I cannot allow us to be broken and vanish into oblivion without one more attempt."

"What are you going to do?"

"I don't know yet. I'm waiting for Hor-Aha to come back. We have four months' grace, Tani, a gift from Amun, and I cannot waste them in learning to accept my fate." He cupped her face, feeling her olive skin so cool, so smooth. Her eyelashes fluttered against his thumbs. "But you will be the one to suffer," he went on. "As a hostage, the King's anger will fall on you if Ahmose and I stir up another small rebellion. And it will be small." His hands fell to her delicate shoulders. "I am under no illusions about that. If you tell me so, Tani, I will wait here quietly for my escort to Sile and do nothing. It is your life I would be placing in jeopardy, and I will not do so without your permission." Her fingers curled around his wrists but she was not looking at him. She was frowning into the gathering dimness of the tent.

"Do you think that Apepa is capable of executing me in reprisal?" she asked at length. Kamose sighed.

"I do not know. Under his arrogance he is insecure and insecure men are unpredictable, but he is also unnaturally sensitive to the opinions of his subjects."

"So there is a chance that he would hesitate, that he might fear the disapproval of the nobles?"

"I think so." Her hands slid along his arms in an almost voluptuous gesture and she kissed him tremulously before pushing him away.

"Then hazard the throw, dear brother. I would rather think of you as dead when I sit in the palace of Het-Uart than living the life of a common soldier, being hungry and thirsty, sleeping wherever you can, surrounded by strangers, trying to hold onto the memory of our faces as the years go by . . ." Her voice failed her.

"I think of you, all of you, in the same way," Kamose replied harshly. "Ahmose beaten and burned by the Kush sun, Grandmother weakening as she is forced to make bread or weave, Aahmes-nefertari and her little son reduced to the life of a merchant's family and Mother humbled to the station of a mere servant or at best an unwanted companion to her relatives, barely tolerated in her own home. We could do it, Tani, all of us. But the thought of the memories fading, the daily adjustments becoming easier until we begin to take on the colour of our surroundings, the forgetting, the accepting . . . No. Such an end is not for us. Death is preferable." She had recovered a little.

"When is the King leaving?"

"Tomorrow morning. You must be brave, Tani. Are you sure?"

"Yes," she said with a touching grimness. "I am sure. Make another war, Kamose. Perhaps the King will grow genuinely fond of me and be reluctant to see me dead. Perhaps you will win." Kamose thought that in spite of her protestations of desire to go on living, she found the prospect bleak and hardly bearable without Ramose, and his plans meant little to her. She has already suffered as much as any of us, perhaps more, he mused with resignation. Her fate now is not just. "It is my last night with you all," she was saying. "I want us to eat together here in my tent. Let the northerners have the reception hall. A tent is more suitable for the children of the desert anyway." He got up awkwardly.

"I will arrange it," he promised. "And, Tani, do not mention my plans to the others. You are the only one so far who knows." She nodded and fell to playing with the scattered pieces from the Dogs and Jackals game. He pushed out of the tent into the gathering twilight.

Kamose did not seek permission to eat separately. He merely told Nehmen what the family would do and the steward, after a moment's hesitation, agreed. Uni was requested to supply food and servants, and an hour after sunset a small parade crossed from the kitchens to Tani's tent bearing food and wine. The garden was now empty. Sounds of revelry from the hall came in gusts through the open tent flap as Uni and Isis, Hetepet, Heket and other family retainers filled the tent with spicy aromas, trimmed lamps, and bent to serve their masters. Outside, their harpist sat on the grass and played softly.

Tani had asked that Behek be allowed to join them. He lay beside her panting noisily and accepting the scraps she passed to him. Occasionally she threw her arms around him, hugging his grey, massive body. She took no part in the sporadic conversation going on around her, merely listening and smiling, but Kamose knew that she was storing up every detail to be examined later on the long trek north. A burst of strident music reached him from the hall, momentarily eclipsing the gentler tones of the harp. Tetisheri gave an order and the remains of the meal were removed. Kamose bade the servants go to their own quarters and the family settled back on the cushions.

For a long while nothing was said. Tani gazed into a lamp's mesmerizing glow, one arm slung across Behek's sleeping back. Ahmose drank without relish, his legs splayed out before him. Aahmes-nefertari sat close to her mother, toying with the ornaments on her belt. Suddenly she looked around at them all. "This is goodbye to Tani," she said loudly. "The rest of us must linger on here a little longer. It is unbearable. Unbearable! Father began it all. It is his fault. He is dead, he is at peace, while we must suffer the consequences of his foolishness. I am so angry!" No one reprimanded her. She finished speaking, but her bitter voice still coiled about them.

"You forget what Father faced," Tani said mildly. "You forget how Apepa trapped him, baited him until he had no other choice. Be angry, Aahmes-nefertari, but not with him." Behek stirred at the sound of her voice but did not waken. His ears twitched.

"What is to become of my son?" Aahmes-nefertari said urgently. "What man already smarting from the King's order to marry me will want a dead and disgraced noble's son for his own? Ahmose-onkh is an innocent child. He does not deserve this."

"It depends how you look at it," Ahmose said reasonably. "From one point of view we are all traitors and we have been let off lightly. I can see that."

"So can I," Kamose agreed. "Recriminations are vain. Perhaps we are not within the true Ma'at after all and have been deluding ourselves." With one accord they looked at him suspiciously. He spoke brightly, with a smile. "We must not waste the night digging over such old and acrid soil," he went on. "We will be joyful. We will drink and laugh, we will share our memories, hold one another. Aahmes-nefertari, the gods expect that Princes as well as peasants will do good and behave with an honest courage. Let us not fail them." Tetisheri grunted.

"You sound like your father," she said caustically. "Too much pride, too much by half."

Such a comment coming from the proudest Tao of them all cut the tension. They burst out laughing. Tetisheri, after an affronted stare, managed a small chuckle.

The evening became night. The wine passed from hand to hand, the reminiscences and ancient family jokes from mouth to mouth. Our cohesiveness cannot really be assailed by separation, Kamose reflected, watching Tani giggle at something Ahmose had said. It is a matter of the soul. We are all mourning under these gales of mirth, all frightened and lonely, all longing for what used to be, but we know that we are simply pieces of a larger body that will endure and that cannot be dissolved by exile or death.

Much later as they clung half-drunk to each other with nothing left to say, Kamose knew he was right. Seqenenra and Si-Amun were with them also, perhaps hovering unseen in the tent but certainly pouring warm through their veins and being renewed in the red darkness of their hearts where Osiris Mentuhotep-neb-hapet-Ra and the other ancestors also lingered. It was a slim comfort but it was all they had.

After much hugging and tearful kisses they slipped away. Ahmose headed for the river for his customary walk along the bank. Aahmes-nefertari wanted to hold her son. Aahotep would spend the night with Tani. Tetisheri and Kamose walked through the scented darkness towards her quarters, the ever-present guards, sleepy and bored, pacing behind them. "I cannot believe that you are letting her go without a fight, without remonstrance, without a public objection," Tetisheri accused Kamose. "It is almost as though you want to see her taken away! And what of Aahmes-nefertari? Marry her quickly, Kamose, so that at least her fate may be kinder. What is the matter with you?" Kamose fought down his rage.

"I did make a public objection, Grandmother, remember?"

"Yes, but hardly a forceful one!" she hissed back. "Stall him, speak to him of a dowry, anything..."

Kamose rounded on her, and thrusting his face close he hissed back, "Are you entirely mad? I will tell you once, Tetisheri, and then not again. I need time. Tani must go north, the reparation must be paid, we must be docile and accepting. Apepa must be lulled into thinking that we at last will lie quiet. I need time!"

"She is sacrificed?"

"If you care to put it like that—yes. She knows." His grandmother paused. He could sense her thinking furiously in the darkness though he could barely see her face.

"When we take Het-Uart, we can get her back," she whispered. "What of General Dudu?"

Kamose suppressed a burst of wild laughter. Take Het-Uart? Get Tani back? It was fruitless to be angry with Tetisheri, to reproach her, to scorn her grand schemes. She was who she was.

"Dudu is my first order of business once the King has left," he replied, resuming his walk. "You realize it is all hopeless anyway?"

"What I think is not important," she answered more loudly. "What any of us thinks does not matter. It is what we do and what we say. We must always behave as though certain things were going to happen. Good night, Kamose."

"Good night, Grandmother." She is a little mad, he thought as he plunged into the torchlit silence of the sleeping house. I envy her.

Ahmose came to bed an hour later. "There is much activity beyond the walls," he told a drowsy Kamose. "Tents are already being struck and the donkeys loaded. The King wants an early start."

"Good," Kamose murmured before turning over. "I can have

my rooms back if they are not too full of the stink of Setiu incense."

Two hours after dawn the family gathered at the rear of the house to watch Tani leave. Heket had volunteered to go with her and now busied herself in pulling the warm cloak higher on her mistress's shoulders and making sure there were enough cushions in the litter already waiting on the sand, the bearers standing silently beside it. General Pezedkhu himself had been detailed to guard Tani's progress and he watched the family embrace her once more, his soldiers shuffling into rank around him. The plain beyond them was a churned mess where the majority of the courtiers' tents had been pitched. Dead flowers, cracked jars, a broken tent pole, a few scraps of coloured linen that flapped forlornly in the faint breeze of morning, flowed right up to the edge of the training ground. The barracks were devoid of life.

The caravan stretched out towards the north. Donkeys stood patiently with heads lowered. Dogs ran between their hoofs and sniffed at the already shrouded litters. Soldiers and servants checked their gear and exchanged short comments. There was no sign of the King or his immediate entourage. No one had taken leave of the family or thanked them formally for their hospitality. Now that the sentence had been passed they were already forgotten.

Pezedkhu motioned and Tani's bearers straightened and prepared to lift the litter. One by one, her relatives held her, kissing the cold lips and smiling with a feigned encouragement into the dull eyes, giving her the age-old farewell, "May the soles of your feet be firm." Her goods had been hurriedly packed onto the donkeys but each person thrust gifts into her hands before she finally turned and clambered among the cushions of the litter. Heket made as if to join her, but Pezedkhu barred her way. "Not you," he said roughly. "You walk." Tani leaned out.

"She rides in here with me," she said emphatically, "or I shall scream and make such a fuss that you will have to chain me to the litter." Tight-lipped, the General stood back, and Heket scrambled up beside Tani. The bearers stooped, the conveyance was raised, and the soldiers ran to push a place for it in the already moving cavalcade. Tani's hand appeared, twitching the curtains closed, and the last they saw of her was a pale, grim little face and the early sun winking on her rings.

"Pray, Tani!" Ahmose shouted after her. "Pray to Amun every day for our deliverance!" The rest of them were silent. Dust already billowed from the hoofs of the animals and the feet of the walkers, causing Aahotep to lift her cloak over her nose. Tani had disappeared into the murk.

Tetisheri made a soft noise, half-moan, half-exclamation, and turned towards the rear gate. The other followed. Kamose saw Dudu approaching across the practice ground and quickly turned away. Not today, he vowed, seeing Ahmose's arm go around his sister's shoulders. Today we grieve. "Uni," he said as the steward came to meet him. "Keep the General away from me until tomorrow." He strode into the empty, echoing house.

All that day the members of the family kept to their rooms while the servants swept and scoured the house of the remnants of the King's occupation. Kamose lay on his couch, hands behind his head, listening to the industry going on around him and thinking of the coming four months with dread. Capitulation was out of the question, yet where was he to find more men, horses, chariots, weapons, food?

At noon Akhtoy brought a light meal but Kamose was unable to force it down. He wondered how Tani was, where the caravan had stopped for the noon meal, what Apepa was thinking. I am going to have to kill General Dudu, he said to himself, and forge my own dispatches to go north. I don't want to kill him. He is only doing his duty. But he cannot be allowed to live, with the chance that he might find a way to let the King know what I am planning. I will let one dispatch through. I will watch how he seals it, how he addresses Apepa.

But Kamose's thoughts did not stay long on General Dudu. Wearily they once more began to circle the problem of fresh troops and gold with which to equip them, yet under his pondering was the relief that comes after long tension. Apepa had gone. The noises and voices in the house were familiar. Much could be accomplished in four months. Kamose slept.

He had not dreamed of the woman who so often had begun to haunt his waking hours for a long time, but in the hot, slow-moving hours of afternoon, his mind still unconsciously engaged in possible troop tallies, his emotions dark with the loss of Tani and his grandmother's accusations, he found himself walking behind her along the path that ran from Weset, past Amun's temple, and towards the watersteps of his house. It was summer. The river beside him ran with a slow deliberation and the sun was beating on his bare head but he barely noticed his surroundings for she was there, perhaps ten paces ahead and almost abreast of the temple pylon, her long legs moving with supple sureness over the dusty, pitted ground. Light and shadow dappled her from the branches overhead.

She was dressed in nothing but a short, coarse linen kilt that swirled about her thighs. Her feet were bare, her heels grey with dust. Beads of sweat glittered on her spine and her straight shoulders were hidden under a shower of swinging black hair. Such a spasm of desire and longing shook Kamose that he cried out in his dream, but he knew better now than to try and catch up with her. If he ran, she would simply glide faster and the dream would end all the sooner. He wished to prolong this glorious pain. He padded after her. The shadow of the pylon began to engulf her.

All at once she slowed and glanced towards the temple and

Kamose, unprepared, missed a glance at her profile. Cursing himself he tried to keep walking but found he could not. She also had come to a halt, waiting easily, one brown, oil-bedewed leg flexed.

Then Kamose's breath caught in his throat, for between the solid, soaring stones of the pylon a tall figure was emerging. Kamose's attention was riveted on two things. The figure had a garland of fresh winter flowers around its neck, lotus, persea, tamarisk blooms, all damp and quivering although it was high summer. It also wore a coronet of purple gold, that most precious and rare amalgam, surmounted by two white, gently trembling plumes.

Kamose was suddenly afraid. With bated breath, terrified and yet hoping that the figure might turn and pierce him with his mild, searching eyes, he stood still, captivated by the easy ripple of every perfect muscle in that regal body as it moved towards the woman. Will she turn and bow? Kamose wondered. Will I see her face? The god halted. The woman inclined her head, a reverent yet proud gesture, and held out her hands to the side. Only then did Kamose notice that the god held a bow and a dagger in his hennaed fingers, Kamose's own bow, the one he had drawn in Seqenenra's defence, and his gold-hilted dagger that had already drawn Setiu blood.

The woman took them, slinging the bow across her back, and began to move on. Kamose, released, stumbled after her, but by the time he too came abreast of the temple pylon, the god had gone. Glancing enthralled into the outer court, Kamose thought he glimpsed a flutter of gold-tissued kilt and one gold-shod heel disappearing between the pillars leading to the inner court, but he had no time to follow. The woman held his dagger in her right hand. Sun glinted on it as she strode purposefully on. They were almost at the watersteps. The end of the grape trellis appeared on Kamose's right, still with a few shrivelled leaves clinging to the vines.

The woman stopped. Her left arm rose in the direction of the river and Kamose noticed with a thrill that silver commander's armbands shone on her upper arms. He followed her gesture. The river was crowded with craft of every kind—heralds' skiffs, hunting skiffs, fishermen's tiny boats, barges, all empty and gliding gently past on the current. The woman began to turn and Kamose's knees became water. He felt himself buckling, falling towards her, unable to breathe. Then he was sitting up on his couch drenched in sweat, his legs tangled in the damp sheet. He was panting. Someone was rapping on his door and Akhtoy's voice called politely, "Prince, General Dudu wishes to see you as soon as possible. He has been waiting all afternoon." Kamose wanted to pound the door into slivers. If Akhtoy had not knocked and woken him he might have seen her. Seen her!

"Tell the General I will be in my office in one hour," he managed thickly. "Send me drinking water, Akhtoy, and a bath servant."

"Yes, Highness."

Kamose pulled the sheets away from his legs and left the couch, standing unsteadily in the middle of the floor. He felt dazed, his body sticky and odorous, his mind drugged. Another knock came on the door and he said, "Enter," his tongue obeying him reluctantly. His body servant bowed his way in holding an earthen jug and a cup. The water in the jug was cool. It had just been drawn from the huge jar always standing in the passage to catch the draughts passing through the house. Kamose could tell by the way the jug was sweating. He stared at it blankly.

"Water, Highness," the servant said. "Shall I pour it for you?"

He went to the low table and set it down. Kamose watched the transparent liquid slosh to and fro and at once it became more important than anything else in the world. He tensed, praying that for one moment the servant would not move, a bird would not cry, no sound would disturb the revelation he knew was about to burst into his consciousness. Water. Water. His bow, his dagger. The river. Boats, many boats, and a gesture as graceful and provocative as a dancer's. The river and boats. Boats boats . . .

He began to shake. Of course! Boats! "Amun!" he said aloud, his voice a croak. "You have opened the door. Who is she then that scarcely bows to you? Hathor? Your wife Mut? An aspect of Sekhmet? She who takes my bow, my dagger . . . Boats!"

"Highness?" the servant enquired. Kamose turned to him, smiling.

"I will pour for myself," he said. "You can go." The man cast him a doubtful, worried glance and left. Kamose went to the table and lifted the jug, trying to pour himself a drink, but his hands were trembling so violently that he slopped the water onto the floor.

An hour later, bathed and clad in freshly starched linen, a circlet of gold on his head, he sat in the office and received the General's curt bow. He still felt that an aura of dislocation surrounded him. His eyes were swollen, his hands puffy from the effects of the sleep that had been more than sleep, but he was happy and he greeted Dudu with a swift smile. "Why did you wish to see me?" he asked. Dudu looked nonplussed, then embarrassed.

"Highness, it is my unfortunate duty to insist that you confer with me on every decision you take regarding your family and the nomes for the next four months. Everything must be reported to the One."

"An unfortunate duty, indeed," Kamose replied dryly. "I

make no decision today, Dudu." The man bowed shortly. "That may be so, Prince, but I also have a duty to accompany you everywhere. I am afraid I am to be your shadow." Kamose felt a pang of sympathy for him.

"Do you wish a cot set up beside my couch?" he asked, a wicked innocence on his face. Dudu sighed, offended.

"No, Highness, that will not be necessary," he responded stiffly. "One of my soldiers will guard your nights and your afternoon sleeps. With regard to your soldiers, I have released them from the barracks and paired them with my own fifty retainers. One of yours, one of mine. To keep them all locked away for four months would not have been practical." Kamose for a moment admired such a strategy.

"No indeed," he agreed. "Not practical at all. Dudu, I am going to walk to the temple now. You may accompany me if you wish."

"Now?" Dudu blurted. Kamose could see the thoughts written on the bluff face before Dudu managed to control his expression. He was not allowed into the Holiest of Holiest, the sanctuary. Messages could be passed there through the High Priest and Dudu could do nothing about it except post guards at every exit and question all who passed. What foolishness! And who went to pray at this time of day anyway?

"Now," Kamose affirmed, rising. "We are a devout people here in the south," he went on. "Amun receives our regular homage, as does Osiris, Hapi, Ptah. I hope you have strong legs, General, for you will be standing regularly in the outer court for long periods." Dudu bowed without replying and Kamose strode past him, calling for his guard.

He could have taken a litter but he wanted to walk, not to spite his shadow but because he had covered the same ground such a short time ago. The dream was vivid in his mind as he passed under the thick green shade of new leaves alive with nesting birds. The river rushed by, swollen and murky. The sun was hot but not unpleasant. Kamose wanted to sing. His escort, one of his own bodyguards accompanied by a Setiu warrior, tramped ahead stolidly. Dudu followed him three paces behind, his own guard bringing up the rear. A Weset woman holding a small boy by one hand and a donkey's leading rope in the other drew to one side as Kamose passed. She bowed, smiling, and Kamose greeted her.

At the pylon he had a moment of awe and hesitation, remembering Amun's stately appearance here. He ordered the soldiers to relax in the shade of the massive stone structure. He and Dudu went on into the outer court. Kamose stopped a young priest who was hurrying by in the direction of the god's storerooms that ranged along one side of the temple. "Where is the High Priest? Find him for me and send him to the sanctuary. I wish to pray." The boy bowed, nodded, and ran on. With a peremptory gesture Kamose ordered the General to wait. Dudu did not dare to follow him as he passed the gate to the inner court.

Kamose stood while a temple servant approached carrying a bowl filled with water from the sacred lake and a cloth. By the time he had removed his sandals and washed his feet, hands and face, murmuring the cleansing prayers as he did so, Amunmose was waiting by the closed doors of the sanctuary. Kamose answered his bow with a hand on the High Priest's shoulder and together they entered the holy place.

It was dark there and refreshingly cool. Amun sat glowing dully, his smile fixed on his benign features, a smile, Kamose thought, of triumphant complicity. You are a great god, Kamose told him in his mind. You deserve to have the whole of Egypt placed in your open palms and it will be. I promise. He approached the god and knelt, kissing the smooth golden feet and clasping the solid ankles. Laying his cheek against Amun's arched foot he closed his eyes and began to pray, thanking him for the message of the dream, so obvious and yet overlooked by them all, even Seqenenra, who had marched his men in the desert, marched and been defeated. The chance was slim but it was better than no chance at all and the god himself had provided it, therefore the task was not hopeless. Love for this deity, the protector of Weset, the one whose eyes lit the desert and who had turned his august gaze on his son, filled Kamose, and with it came a corresponding scorn for the wild undisciplined Sutekh and his royal sycophant. We will win, he told the god. You and I.

At last he rose. Amunmose stood quietly watching. Kamose walked to him. "I know how I am to defeat Apepa," he said without preamble, "but it will take much planning, much gold. Amun showed me how in a dream, Amunmose, but I need your help. Send priests to every Amun shrine in the nomes and any farther north that you know of. Bring to Weset all the offerings, gold, silver, jewellery, anything that can be used to pay grain merchants and vegetable sellers. Do it secretly and store it here, in the temple." Amunmose nodded in agreement. "I am being followed everywhere by the King's representative," Kamose went on. "This is the only place he cannot enter, therefore, with your permission, I should like to use the sanctuary to pass and receive messages with you as intermediary. It will not be for long," he explained, seeing Amunmose's hesitant expression, "and it will involve no sacrilege, that I promise. I will be able to deal with General Dudu in a week or so. In the meantime news will come to you, not to me, and I will come to the temple twice a day for it." He paused, thinking. "I have already sent for Hor-Aha. Have a priest set up a tent out in the desert to intercept him in the unlikely event that he arrives before I have had time to get rid of Dudu. You can lodge him here. I will send Uni to you

tomorrow. Tell him I want a list of every boat in the area—
fishing vessels, skiffs, barges, all of them, and a list of boat
makers in Weset."

Amunmose smiled. "Is that all, Prince?"

Kamose grinned back at the bite of sarcasm in his friend's
voice. "That is all for now. Make sure Uni brings his information here and does not attempt to give it to me directly. I thank
you, Amunmose."

The High Priest inclined his head. "I am glad Amun
afforded you this vision. I think he has great plans for his town.
Who knows? One day Weset might be the chief and holiest city
in Egypt!"

Kamose laughed, the glad sound echoing against the high
stone ceiling. "Who knows indeed?" he said, thinking of the
town's huddle of mud houses, the noisy market and sleepy
wharf. "I must rejoin my jailor." Prostrating himself before
the god and embracing Amunmose he strode out into the dazzling sunshine, forcing himself to swallow the song that rose to
his lips.

General Dudu's report to Apepa was dictated a week later to
the scribe he had brought with him. Kamose was with his
mother as she inspected the newly planted flower beds against
the house when Ipi came with the news. "He dictated in private, in the rooms assigned to him," the scribe said in answer to
Kamose's sharp question, "but I knew it was to happen because
his scribe and I were talking together in the office when he was
sent for. I followed but could not hear the message, for the
General keeps his door guarded. I had to walk straight past."

"Where is the scroll now?"

"His scribe is in his cell, making a fair copy to send north."
Kamose considered quickly. It was vital that he see the dispatch, not so much for what it said but for the manner of
Dudu's style in dictation, his opening address and the closing
salutation he used.

"Can you lure the man away from his work for a few moments?" he asked Ipi. "Is a herald waiting to take it north immediately?"

"No, Highness," Ipi told him. "There is a box filled with dispatches the King left to be carried into Kush and some for the northern administrators. The herald is due back from Kush tonight and will not start for the north until tomorrow."

"Good. Dudu will be here at any moment, having done his duty. Run to Uni. Tell him I want him to inspect the scroll carefully and he doesn't have much time in which to do so. Take the scribe to the river, give him wine from my own stock, anything, Ipi." Ipi bowed and went away. Kamose saw him bow as he veered past the General who was just emerging from the house.

"What are you doing, Kamose?" Aahotep said in a low voice. Kamose pressed her arm.

"I cannot tell you yet, it is too dangerous," he whispered back. "In a few days, Mother." She nodded, lips compressed, and returned to her consideration of the new plants. A short distance away a gardener was squatting in the wet black earth, his naked brown spine bent as he distributed his nest of seedlings.

"Of course we must continue to plant and see to the crop sowing as well," Aahotep said more loudly as Dudu swung towards them. "There is time for that before we must leave here forever." She turned to the General with a haughty smile. "Even though the King has appropriated our next harvest, we cannot see our peasants denuded also. Come, Kamose." She linked arms with him and began to talk of something else, strolling in the direction of the grape arbour and leaving Dudu to bring up the rear.

By the time Kamose went to the temple the next morning to perform the rites, Uni had visited the High Priest. While Dudu sat in the shade of a pillar in the outer court and glumly watched the colourful comings and goings of the dancers and petitioners, Amunmose gave Kamose Uni's message. "The opening and closing salutations are the common ones," he said. "The King's titles after the greeting and before the General's signature."

"A signature?"

"Yes," Amunmose said. "The General likes to scrawl his name himself and he does not put 'by the hand of my scribe so-and-so.'"

"That is bad news," Kamose said, frowning. "A seal?"

"The General prefers uncoloured wax and he uses a cylinder seal. He must carry it on his person. Uni says that the signature is not difficult to forge, Prince, and he had a chance to try it twice. The General's Setiu name is not a long one, the two syllables being repeated." For a second Kamose reflected on the many skills that were needed to produce a good steward.

"Anything else?" This is the only chance we will get to try that signature, he thought. If I wait until the next dispatch, time will be running too short. I must trust Uni's draughting ability.

"Yes," Amunmose said. "The General's dispatches are always wound three times with plain flaxen string and knotted once. The wax is placed on the knot." If we get through this, I will make Uni a vizier, Kamose said to himself.

"Thank you, Amunmose," he said aloud. "I have been in here long enough. Please get a message to Uni. Tell him that I shall arrange to bring Ahmose to my quarters tomorrow night, very late. The servants' quarters have only two guards in the passage. Perhaps I can be ill. Tell him to try and persuade one guard, preferably the Setiu one, to stay on Ahmose's door while he is escorted to me by the other one. I shall be waiting. If tomorrow night is not suitable, then the next. Can you do that for me?"

"Certainly, Highness."

Kamose rode back to the house, Dudu walking behind the litter, in a mood of tense concentration and a mounting apprehension. He had killed before, but in the heat of battle. He did not know if he could conjure the reckless callousness necessary to murder a man in cold blood. But I must, he told himself, deliberately bringing to mind the King's supercilious face in order to stiffen his resolve. I must. It is the first, the most important move. Dudu must die. But in his mind he was whispering, "Apepa must die," and that thought stiffened his muscles and brought a steadiness to his determination.

Two hours before dawn, when sleep is at its heaviest and vigilance grows weary, Kamose left his couch, went to the door, and opening it, spoke to the guards outside. He was bent over, his face twisted in pain. "I need my steward," he gasped. "I am ill. Please tell him to bring my brother with him." The guards looked at each other. Kamose's personal bodyguard touched him gently.

"Shall I alert the physician also, Prince?" he asked solicitously. The other guard was watching Kamose carefully. Kamose cursed himself. The possibility of that request had not occurred to him. "Very well," he agreed, "but I do not want to alert the whole household if it is just something I ate or drank."

"I will go," the local man said. The other one resumed his stance. Kamose retreated, closing the door, and listened to the footfalls fade along the passage. He was sure that his Setiu guard had been about to suggest that Dudu be roused, but now the man would not dare to leave his post unattended.

Some minutes later he heard low voices beyond. The door opened and Uni appeared, bleary-eyed and clutching his sleeping kilt. Ahmose followed him into the room. Kamose could see three faces in the shadows behind Ahmose, and fortunately two of them were local bodyguards. Kamose, panting now, beckoned his own in after his brother and bade him close the door. "Are you my loyal servant?" he asked the man, straightening and walking to his chest. "Will you obey me whatever the consequences?" The soldier nodded.

"You know I will, Prince. Have I not stood at your door and at your side for many years?" He sounded offended.

"Good," Kamose shot at him crisply. "In a moment I want you to kill the Setiu outside, then go with my steward. Uni, you are to take both the local guards and go immediately to the quarters where Dudu's staff sleeps. If you are unfortunate enough to meet more Setiu men, kill them at once. Set up soldiers around Dudu's servants so that not one of them can walk out of his cell without being seen. They are not to leave, not even to walk along the passage, for any reason at all." He was fingering the contents of the chest impatiently as he spoke, then he stood, a dagger in his hand. Fleetingly he thought how the last time he had seen it, it had been held in the delicate grasp of the woman in his dreams. The soldier was nodding his assent. "Ahmose," Kamose went on, "we are going to kill Dudu now, we hope in his sleep. I do not ask you to strike, only to hold him if he struggles. It must be done quietly. I cannot announce my intentions until I have the soldiers under my command. Uni, the herald left yesterday morning?"

"You know he did, Highness." Kamose was feverish with haste and a fear that he did not betray.

"Then let us make our move." He jerked his head at the soldier who drew his own knife and slipped out the door. Anxiously Kamose, Uni and Ahmose waited. There were a few noncommittal words spoken, an exclamation of surprise, then a brief scuffle. Kamose tensed. The door swung wide to reveal his guard, the other with a look of puzzlement and shock on his face, and a limp body huddled across the threshold. "Bring him in here and then go. Hurry!" Kamose urged. "Come, Ahmose." He knew he could trust Uni to follow his instructions. His heart was beating lightly and rapidly as he and his brother ran back along the passage and plunged into the corridor leading to the guest quarters. Here they slowed to a walk, for Dudu had placed several guards outside his door, none of them local men.

"This is madness, Kamose!" Ahmose whispered across at him. "We cannot take on three of them!"

"Not at the moment," Kamose managed, trying to will his heart and his breath to slow. "They will not refuse to let us in, and afterwards we must take a small gamble." Suddenly he remembered the knife in his hand. He thrust it into his sleeping kilt as they rounded a corner and the three guards came to a surprised attention, saluting with spears thrust forward.

"Greetings," Kamose said. "We must speak with the General. Let us pass." They stared at him then one of them stepped out.

"Where are your guards, Prince?" He enquired politely but with an edge of suspicion in his voice.

"At the end of the passage," Kamose said. "Go and look if you want to. But hurry. It will soon be dawn and our business cannot wait." He saw the mistrust on their faces. They were not stupid men. Yet they hesitated, afraid to offend a Prince of Egypt no matter what the circumstances surrounding him. There had been a natural imperiousness in his tone that no commoner dared to defy, but had not the General given strict orders that neither of these young men should be allowed to walk anywhere unescorted? What business could a disgraced Prince under house arrest possibly have an hour before the dawn?

I have underestimated them, Kamose thought angrily. I am a fool. He glanced at Ahmose, seeing his brother's muscles tighten, and in a lightning moment their eyes met. Ahmose nodded. Both brothers lunged. Kamose grabbed a spear and pulled it violently towards him. The guard, caught unawares, went with it, toppling forward. Kamose's knee struck his groin. In a reflex movement he doubled over, only to have Kamose's fist connect with his chin. He collapsed without a sound. Kamose whirled to see Ahmose's foot fly into one man's stomach, then his arm hook around the straining neck. The third guard was pulling his knife, preparing to leap upon Ahmose. Kamose leaped first, clinging to his back, digging thumbs into his eyes. The man howled and dropped the knife. His fingers closed like a vise around Kamose's wrists but then loosened. He slipped to the floor and Ahmose jumped aside, letting go the hilt of the knife he had slid into the taut chest. Ahmose was sweating profusely. "Not a bad performance for two men who have neglected their wrestling practice lately," he said huskily. "One dead, perhaps two. I think I broke this one's neck, Kamose."

"I am sorry," Kamose said. "If they had not been so obdurate . . ." The door opened and Dudu's tousled head appeared.

"What is happening here?" he asked, then Kamose saw his eyes clear and widen with surprising speed. Before he could react, Kamose flung himself against the door, knocking him off balance. Dudu toppled to the floor but rolled and regained his feet with agility. Not fast enough for Ahmose, however, who ran to step behind him as he rose and pinned his arms behind his back. Kamose pushed the door closed and drew his dagger, feeling suddenly cold and drained.

Dudu had grasped the situation immediately. Kamose saw it in his eyes. But he showed no fear and Kamose found a respect for the man growing. He would have liked to offer Dudu his life in exchange for the General's co-operation but knew that at the first opportunity Dudu would betray him. Dudu was Setiu.

"This will only bring you a short respite," Dudu said huskily. "It is a tiny battle. You cannot win the war, Highness." I am tired of the word cannot, Kamose thought mutinously. A short respite, a tiny battle, as though I were a child fighting by the riverbank with reeds for knives and a bulrush for an axe.

"Not Highness, Dudu," he said, clenching the dagger and

coming closer, his eyes roving Dudu's broad chest for the best place to strike. "Not Highness. Majesty." He saw Dudu take a deep breath before the blade was forced home between the third and fourth ribs. All at once Kamose's hand and wrist were drenched in warm blood. He wrenched out the dagger as Ahmose lowered Dudu and quickly stood away.

"These necessities are terrible," Ahmose said, racing to the cot and pulling off the sheet. "Wipe yourself, Kamose." Kamose took the linen and began to scrub at his hands, first rubbing the dagger's blade clean. Ahmose bent and carefully closed Dudu's glazing eyes. "We have committed ourselves now," he went on, "and even if we wanted it, there can be no turning back. If we lose, it will mean death for us all this time."

"I know," Kamose replied. "But I cannot believe, I refuse to believe, that we will vanish from the flow of history without leaving a trace! We had better go, Ahmose. Ra is about to rise and we must have the soldiers in our control before the rest of the house wakes. I wish Hor-Aha were here."

In the grey light of dawn the soldiers sleeping side by side in the barracks were woken by a sharp command. Coming groggily to their feet they found themselves confronted by the Princes and two bodyguards, all standing with feet apart and bows drawn. "Soldiers of the house to the right," Kamose ordered, "and those of the General Dudu to the left. Quickly!" Still half-asleep the men stumbled to obey, grouping themselves against the bare mud walls as he had commanded.

Kamose, outwardly stonyfaced, watched them anxiously. His control hung by a thread. If one Setiu officer gave the order to charge, the four of them they would be helpless in a moment. Ahmose and his escort moved imperceptibly, training their weapons to the left. Kamose's gaze travelled his own fifty soldiers and he did not speak again until he had satisfied himself that he recognized all of them. "Sit down," he shouted at them, and at once they sank to the floor. "Do not move," he went on. Then he turned his attention to the rest. "Give me your name, place of birth, station and family history," he said. "You first." Dudu's men stared at him as though he had gone mad, but his own guard sensed what was to come. A murmur passed through their ranks like a breath of winter breeze.

The soldier Kamose had pointed at stepped forward and saluted. "Ptahmose of Mennofer, Highness, foot soldier in the Division of Set. My father and his fathers before him were scribes in the village school just outside the city." Kamose nodded curtly.

"Sit down. Next."

One by one the fifty gave their details. Those with Setiu names, whose families inhabited the eastern Delta, he commanded to remain on their feet. In the end there were twenty left standing. Ahmose slipped close and muttered in Kamose's ear, "If you are going to do what I think you are, can you at least give them some kind of a choice? This is barbaric!"

"We cannot take the risk, not with soldiers," Kamose hissed back. "I like it no more than you, Ahmose. If they were peasants or simple townsmen it would not matter so much, but I cannot allow trained military men to wander loose here whether they have sworn loyalty to me or not. They all believe us to be defeated before we begin."

Swiftly he singled out twenty of his own men and told them to distribute their weapons. "Take these twenty out onto the desert and shoot them," he said. "Bury them in the sand. Do not throw them in the river. I do not want their bodies floating downstream to tell a tale." His soldiers obeyed, stumbling in their alacrity. The victims stared at him in dumb amazement, unable to believe the sudden fate that had fallen upon them. Some stooped to gather kilts and other personal belongings, clutching them to their chests as though they were to be transferred to some other barracks. Ahmose told them to drop everything they held. Kamose nodded to his personal body-guard and the man sprang to take charge, ushering out the Setiu men and their executioners.

There was a short silence inside the building. The command to form ranks and then to march came clearly in the strength-ening light, then the sound of bare feet pounding the packed dirt that faded away. Ahmose does not realize it yet, Kamose thought as he surveyed the remaining white faces, but this is only the beginning, and sometimes we will be unable to separate friend from foe. May Amun forgive me. He felt deathly cold. "You that are left," he said to the thirty now stiffly at attention, only their darting eyes betraying their uncertainty, "I have spared you because you are native Egyptians even though you serve in the army of Apepa. You must now swear loyalty to me. If you do so, you will be welcome in Weset. If you break the vow you are about to make, you will be subject to the five wounds and immediate execution as traitors. Come forward." His fifty retainers sat watching in obvious relief as the thirty came one by one to kiss Kamose's feet and hands in token of their new fealty.

When the last had crawled forward, Kamose spoke directly to the Captain of the fifty. "These thirty are to be paired with those whose honesty is not in question," he ordered. "They are not to leave the confines of the estate, nor may they be given guard duty in the house. Work them hard at weapons practice and in the stables and watch them. I shall expect regular reports on their words and attitudes." The man bowed and even before he straightened Kamose had left the vast room and was walking towards the house, filling his lungs with good, cool morning air. Ahmose ran to join him.

"You look ill," Ahmose said. "What now?" Kamose passed a weary hand over his face. His skin felt loose and rough.

"Now we pass the same rod of testing over Dudu's servants

and impose the same restrictions on them," he said. "I would like to kill them all. Body servants and house servants usually grow the greatest loyalty. But word must not be spread that I am so ruthless as to murder innocent native Egyptians. I must be seen as a liberator, Ahmose, an Egyptian fighting on the side of other Egyptians to free this country from foreign oppressors. Half my work will be done for me if the right gossip goes before me in the towns and villages. But not yet."

"Is that how you see yourself?" Ahmose asked curiously. They had reached the garden. Kamose paused and turned black-ringed eyes on his brother.

"No," he said with a twisted smile. "I am Seqenenra's avenger and Egypt's god."

Before the noon meal, nine of Dudu's staff had been taken out and killed and the rest had been placed with the kitchen staff under Uni's omnipotent eye. Kamose's bodyguard came back with a report of the deaths of the twenty soldiers. Ahmose had gone to the rest of the family to tell them that the house was once more their own, but Kamose refused to see Tetisheri who had come hurrying to the office as soon as Ahmose had left her.

"Keep them away from me," he had ordered Akhtoy. "I am not ready to discuss any affair with them. I need sleep." Akhtoy had politely but firmly sent Tetisheri back to her quarters.

Kamose had sent for Uni and sharply demanded a report on his request for information regarding boats and boat builders. When Uni had mildly reminded the Prince that there had so far been neither the time nor the opportunity to do more than brief his understeward and send servants into Weset, Kamose flew into a rage. Uni was unimpressed. "You need sleep, Prince, and you also need to wash. You still have blood on your kilt." Kamose looked down on his crusted linen and the streaks of dry brown blood still clinging to his arms.

"You are right," he admitted. But have I covered everything? he thought anxiously. Is the house really secure? Shall I wake to a knife in my throat?

He allowed his bath servant to wash him, then he went to his quarters and fell across his couch. Vivid pictures of his dagger piercing the General, of the bewildered soldiers' ashen faces flashed through his mind. Blood on my hands, he thought dimly. Too much to forget. Too much to turn back. He placed his palm beneath his cheek and slept.

Uni's report on the boat builders was in Kamose's hands within the next week. Most of the vessels in and around Weset were too small to convey more than a few fishermen. But Kamose appropriated several barges from merchants who traded up and down the Nile. He gave Uni the authority to commission a hundred reed ships to hold fifty men each, the construction of which was to begin immediately. Uni was aghast. "Highness, such expense! How are we to pay the builders?"

"They will be given an acre of my land each when they have completed the work."

"But, Highness," Uni expostulated. "You need your Weset holdings to keep the household supplied and your servants fed!"

Kamose stared between the pillars of the portico and out to where Aahotep and Tetisheri sat on mats in the garden. They were not speaking. Aahotep's hands had fallen still over the beads she was threading. She was staring into her lap. Tetisheri was reclining on one elbow, her eyes on the blue dragonflies over the placid surface of the pool, her expression pensive and unguardedly sad. Kamose could feel their fear. "Uni," he said wearily, his face still turned away, "the King has appropriated all my holdings in any case. If I do not give the land away, Teti will put his loathsome feet on it or else the King's overseers will see it farmed for the court. In either case it is only mine for another four months." He smiled grimly. "A little less than four months now. Dudu, of course, was supposed to prevent me from doing anything foolish, but as he is no longer living, I shall have proper deeds drawn up and signed so that the builders' claim to the acres cannot be contested by either Teti or Apepa. If I win, the whole of Egypt will pour tribute into my lap. If I lose, we all die. It does not matter any more." Uni cleared his throat.

"Very well. You are my master and I will do as you wish. But where will you get the men to fill a hundred ships? There will be room for a division!" Kamose breathed deeply and closed his eyes, opening them again to turn back into the room. He cast himself into the chair by the desk.

"I will begin with men from Weset and the nomes. I will not ask for those who can be spared. I intend to conscript every male fourteen and over. I will not march as my father did but sail swiftly from village to village, making them mine by oath or force, I do not care which, and taking away the men. If the soldiers ride in boats they will not become tired with marching. They will be fresh at every stop along the way. If necessary, I will slaughter the headman of the villages and the mayors of the towns, but I do not think it will be necessary. They will swear allegiance to me and give me aid." He glanced up at an indignant Uni. "It is what my father should have done."

"Highness," Uni countered with a patience he obviously did not feel, for he was tapping a scroll rhythmically and unconsciously against his palm. "The boats can be ready in two months but the men and boys you intend to conscript will be needed on the land. The sowing is less than two months away. And how will you pay them?" Kamose drew in his legs and folded his arms.

"They will not be paid until my campaign is over. I will promise them booty in the Delta and we will commandeer grain and supplies as we go. I shall take my women's jewels and trinkets, everything of value from the house, and have it traded for initial supplies. I will not leave anything for either Teti or the King. As for the sowing, let the women and children do it."

"Highness!" Uni was speechless.

"Is that all?" Kamose asked, amused in spite of himself at the steward's affront. Uni bowed. "Good. Ipi?" The scribe left his corner and came to sit at Kamose's feet, his brush ready. "Send to the south, to Nekheb. I need navigators, and Nekheb breeds good sailors. Word the message in any way you wish, but make it a command. Do you have Dudu's seal, Uni?" The steward nodded. "Then it is time to dictate a scroll to Apepa from the General, telling him how very well behaved the Weset wild-men have become, and how resigned their women."

Ipi dipped his brush in the black paint and held it poised expectantly over the papyrus but Kamose was suddenly sunk in thought. "Uni," he said after a while, "is it difficult to obtain lapis lazuli?" Uni blinked at him.

"Why yes," he replied. "It must be mined in the desert and is quite rare. Even the King pays much gold for it, but it is said that he and his Queen own a great deal and have had it inlaid in their chairs and tiring boxes and suchlike." Kamose looked up.

"Send someone to the temple and ask Amunmose if there is any in Amun's storehouses. Tell him to deliver it to my jeweller. I have a fancy for a lapis pectoral."

"But High—" Kamose cut him short with a slapped palm on the desk.

"I am a King," he said peremptorily. "I am the son of Amun, his Incarnation, am I not? The people will see me arrayed in lapis as I sail and they will remember. Do I have to explain my every command to you, Uni?" Uni bowed stiffly.

"No, Prince. I am sorry."

"Get about my business then. And do not forget to find a runner who can wear the insignia of a herald. Someone entirely trustworthy to carry the scroll north. He can say that he was accompanying the regular herald who fell ill at Aabtu, in case Dudu's real herald is well known in Het-Uart. Choose someone reasonably cultured, Uni. Apepa will doubtless question him. Send him to me before he leaves. Now, Ipi. I will dictate."

The message to the King was brief, but Kamose could not resist a comment on Tani as though from Dudu's mouth, a hope that she was being treated well. He did not dare to ask for news of her. That night, lying sleepless on his couch, the ivory head-rest cool under his neck and the night light flickering spasmod-ically on the walls of his room, he thought of her with pain. I did not spend enough time with her, he told himself. None of us did. She was always little Tani, underfoot, sometimes a pleas-ure to indulge but more often dismissed absently. Her strengths were submerged under our other preoccupations. Amun care for her and give her courage. He was barely dozing when there was a light knock on the door and Uni peered around it.

"I am awake," Kamose said, sitting up.

"Your Highness, the General Hor-Aha is here and wishes to speak with you." All drowsiness fled.

"Let him come in," Kamose bade, rising, his heart lightening as the familiar tall, cloaked figure strode into the dimness. Uni closed the door behind him. Hor-Aha came to a halt and began to bow but Kamose with an uncharacteristic impulse embraced him. The Medjay warrior smelled of sand and stones. His long plaited hair and white cloak were dusty. Kamose felt the thin whipcord muscles flex as the embrace was answered, then Hor-Aha completed his bow. "Welcome back," Kamose said. "I am more relieved to see you than I can say. Have you heard the news?"

"Yes, Prince." Hor-Aha shed his cloak and it fell to the floor in a cloud of fine grit. He had a dirty loincloth twisted about his hips. Against his naked waist lay his leather belt hung still with his knife and an axe. Kamose felt as though he had never left.

"The priest waiting for me out on the desert told me everything. The execution of the Setiu soldiers was unfortunate."

"Was there an alternative?"

Hor-Aha's white teeth gleamed briefly. "No. But I hate to see good men wasted."

"Are you hungry? Thirsty?"

Hor-Aha shook his head. "I am very tired, Highness, that is all. I shared food with the priest before his servant packed up his things and they returned to the temple. So we go to war again?"

Kamose indicated a stool. He sat on the edge of the couch and watched the lean figure fold forward. Hor-Aha sighed in relief.

"We do. Let me tell you how." Quickly he outlined his strategy, scanning Hor-Aha's dark face for approval or doubt. When he had finished, the General sat very still, considering. Then he nodded.

"You have no choice," he said. "The decisive moment is approaching. Many Medjay were killed in Seqenenra's battle, but if I send one of my tribesmen together with an Egyptian officer, it should be possible to recruit more. Wawat craves the protection of Egypt from the ever-present threat of a Kushite invasion and Apepa ignored the Medjay, preferring to treaty with Teti-en in Kush. A successful conclusion to your war will mean security for Wawat. Have you begun the conscription?"

"Not yet. I was waiting for you." For a minute they fell silent, Kamose becoming aware that for the first time in many days he was completely relaxed.

Then Hor-Aha said, "I regret the exile of Princess Tani. I would have done the same thing in Apepa's place but it was cruel all the same." Kamose rose and immediately Hor-Aha was on his feet.

"Go and rest," Kamose advised. "There is much to do tomorrow." Hor-Aha retrieved his cloak and shook it vigorously before swinging it around his shoulders.

"I will check the barracks first," he said. "The soldiers' village your father had built still lies unmolested on the west bank, Highness?"

"Yes."

"Good. Tomorrow, then." Kamose lay down again once the door had closed behind the General. Tomorrow, he thought with a pang, whether of excitement or apprehension, he did not know. Tomorrow.

In two months the hundred reed ships lay rocking at anchor along the east bank of the river, vast golden hulks so light that they drew little draught and so would be able to navigate the shrinking Nile until well into the summer. Kamose had deeded his land to the builders without a qualm, although his mother had cried with despair when he had told her what he intended to do. She, Tetisheri and Aahmes-nefertari had gathered together their jewels and handed them to him in mute resignation to a fate they all accepted as the sodden earth began to emerge from the slowly sinking water. Kamose had the precious things traded for last year's grain and onions, beer and linen.

Armed with the conscription edict his officers travelled dozens of villages, herding the peasants away from the fields and commanding that their women should see to the sowing. There were few protests. Men began once more to stream across the Nile, fill the barracks and soldiers' village on the west bank, and finally overflow into tents that mushroomed over the desert. Kamose did not bother with chariots and horses. His plan of campaign relied almost exclusively on the ships, still swarming with the builders who perched on the high prows tying the last of the reed bundles and overseeing the attaching of steering oars and cabins.

The Medjay returned in stronger numbers than his father had drawn, and Kamose suspected that Hor-Aha had concluded treaties with other Wawat tribes about which he had not told his Prince. Kamose was grateful. The wild sons of the desert had no love of water and would doubtless embark with hesitant wariness, but when the fighting began their confidence and skill would return.

Kamose continued to send regular scrolls north, dreading possible replies brought by the hand of some Setiu herald or officer who would have to be detained or killed, but Het-Uart was silent. Nor did any word come from Ramose. Kamose had not expected any. He wondered if Teti and his son were receiving news from the capital that also included indirect references to Tani's welfare. He also wondered, in the small hours of the morning when the night grew stale and he paced, sleepless with the thousand eventualities on which success depended, what he would do once he won through to Khemennu and what Ramose would do. Teti must die, that was certain, but he did not want to fight Ramose to do it. The worry was fruitless. It belonged to the future and as such should have been dismissed.

But Kamose found that he could not set his problems in a sensible order. Tomorrow's need for sustained target practice, with the bows the craftsmen were frantically turning out to replace the ones the Setiu had retrieved, battled for attention with the nebulous directives associated with a siege of Het-Uart many weeks away, and in his feverish state of mind Kamose could not separate the two. To run from burdens that threatened his reason was not in his nature, but on several nights he went to bed drunk on palm wine and more than once he invited a servant girl to his couch before turning from her in something like disgust because her skin did not have the dull sheen of the woman of his dreams, or her hips did not curve to flow into the long, graceful legs whose movement he knew now as well as his own.

She has ruined me, he thought without emotion on the occasions when he lay watching the servant's naked back disappear out his door. She has forced an obsession on me, this beloved stranger who does not bow to the gods and who handles my dagger, my bow, as though they belong to her. My flesh cries out only for her, for her.

Amunmose sent him a quantity of lapis lazuli from the temple storerooms without comment. Kamose stood for a long time holding the dark blue, gold-shot stones under the shaft of white sunlight that fell between the pillars into the office before sending them to his jeweller. He knew he held the value of a ship and all its men in his admiring fingers but he did not regret his vanity. The lapis was a symbol of his right to revenge and divine justification.

In the third month Kamose invited the Egyptian nobles of the cities in his nomes to join him in Weset and captain themselves the men he had conscripted from them. He did not want to do so. It was customary for a King to assemble a war council made up of his generals and the two viziers, but Seqenenra had had no senior officers and Kamose would have preferred to go on relying on Hor-Aha and Ahmose alone. He hated delegating authority or power, but he knew that the household had become dangerously self-reliant, turning in on itself with every onslaught against it. If the campaign grew, it would become unwieldy without men in charge who could act independently when necessary.

Kamose intended to keep the officers he knew for the command of his personal bodyguard, the Followers of His Majesty, and for the shock troops, the Braves of the King. He would offer the Princes good commands under Hor-Aha as General-in-Chief. Military training was part of every young noble's education. They would perform well and in return he would promise them court positions. Eyes and Ears of the King, Fanbearer on the Right Hand and Fanbearer on the Left Hand, Vizier of the South, of the North . . . of the North . . .

They came respectfully and warily, Mesehti of Djawati with his light eyes and weatherbeaten face, Intef of Qebt, the great ancient trading centre of the south in the days of the old Kings, Iasen of Badari, Makhu of Akhmin and the haughty Ankhmahor of Aabtu, whose blood ran almost as blue as Kamose's own. At the same time Paheri, mayor of Nekheb, arrived, and with him the sailors Kamose had requested that Uni send for, including the same Abana who had served under Seqenenra as Guardian of Vessels and his son Kay. Kamose immediately sent them across the river.

Tetisheri greeted the Princes with the pomp only she could summon and Aahotep saw to their quarters. Kamose feted them as grandly as he could, aware that their pride was as touchy as his own. They had polite words for him, looked askance at Hor-Aha, and inspected the ships and the burgeoning army without comment.

On the fourth day Kamose summoned them to the office, seating them around Seqenenra's huge desk, with Hor-Aha on his right hand, and laid his plans before them, his eyes going deliberately from one to another. When he had finished speaking, there was a long silence, full of busy conjecture. Mesehti's pale gaze was fixed on the foliage tossing in a high wind beyond the pillars, his face blank. Intef tapped the table with one ringed finger. Prince Ankhmahor openly studied Kamose over the rim of his wine cup, eyebrows raised. Ahmose, also present, was sitting back in his chair, one arm hooked over the back, seemingly indifferent, but Kamose felt his tension.

Finally Ankhmahor put down his cup and passed a slow tongue over his lips. "We are all nobles here," he said. "I myself, as everyone knows, am an hereditary Prince and erpa-ha of Egypt. None of us deny your superiority, Kamose, as governor of the Weset nomes, or your claim to godhead through Osiris Mentuhotep-neb-hapet-Ra Glorified. Yet next month your control over the nomes ceases and you go into internal exile." He folded his carefully manicured hands around the cup before him and leaned forward. "For a few more weeks you are within your rights to conscript our peasants and commandeer what supplies you wish from us and for this we are blameless before Apepa. You are the governor. But you ask much more of us. Much more." His glance went coolly round the table and was answered by nods from the others. "You request active co-operation in your revolt. You want us to form new divisions as men are collected on your way north. In other words, you want us to choose between you and the King and not passively either. Is this not too much to ask of us, Prince?"

Kamose smiled into the smooth, exquisitely painted face. You are completely in control of yourself, he thought. In all probability you know exactly where you stand and it will be on the side of blood and history, yet with a courtier's graciousness of speech you challenge not my revolt but the worthiness of my character to grasp the Crook and the Flail after so many years of my family's eclipse. Ankhmahor has not forgotten my ances-tor's weakness in passing the emblems of godhead to a foreign power, no matter what the reasons. How good it is to be in understanding with one of my own kind! "I think that my father insulted you all by not acknowledging your right to be included in his designs," he replied equally steadily. "I apologize for his thoughtlessness. I do indeed ask too much of you. I ask it as your god. I ask it as your friend. But most of all, I think, I ask it as one Egyptian to another."

"You are right," Mesehti broke in emphatically. "Seqenenra behaved as though he was the only Egyptian Prince in the south. The insult was in his lack of trust, Kamose. He did not confide in us, pay us the compliment of placing his safety in our hands." He spread his own before Kamose dramatically. "Hands that have always worked for our country and our gods."

"I can only repeat that I am sorry," Kamose reiterated calmly. "My father's revolt was the first hint of unease in a long time. I do not excuse his silence. It was impossible for him to trust anyone, as the savage attack on him here proved."

"He might have asked himself why we chose to linger in the south, away from any court opportunities, although as nobles we could have been exercising our influence and increasing our wealth in Het-Uart!" Intef snapped. "My grandfather was Sandal Bearer to the King, in attendance on him at all times. Now I rot in the provinces no matter how much I love the south."

"I do not deny that your talents are being wasted, and if my father did not recognize why, I do," Kamose interposed equally forcefully. "I need them, Princes! Cast your fate with mine, I beseech you."

"I repeat," Ankhmahor said softly. "You ask too much. As well as our property here we have grazing land in the Delta, even as you did. If we are defeated, Apepa will confiscate it all. It is not proper for Princes of Egypt to lose their birthright, for their sons will curse them and they will dwindle into obscurity." Kamose had not missed Ankhmahor's subtle "we." He reinforced it.

"But we are all dwindling into obscurity," he pointed out. "Slowly but surely the foreign ministers and the members of Egyptian aristocracy who breathe the breath of the Setiu gather the power that was once ours to themselves. You have nothing to lose by fighting with me, and if I win you will not be forgotten."

"Our noble brothers have pulled out their tongues that they might all speak together in swearing fealty to Apepa," Iasen agreed. "We signed tribute agreements but we did not take any vow to the King. I suppose that if we lent you our support our honour would not be impugned." *Your honour lies in returning Egypt to Ma'at,* Kamose thought. Aloud he pressed them.

"If I know my countrymen, their oaths to a foreigner lie only skin deep. As long as the Setiu make them rich they tell themselves that they are content, but I believe that beneath this contentment lies a deep unrest. I speak to you plainly, Princes. If I can confront them with you beside me, lending my claim not only credibility, which of course it does not need, but also the obedience and loyalty of Egypt's most ancient lineages, I can revive their devotion to a proper Ma'at and gain their support."

He had not meant to pay them a hollow compliment and they knew it. Their guarded faces relaxed as they sensed the genuine respect in which he held them. Prince Makhu sniffed delicately. Intef cast a sidelong glance at Mesehti, then waved at Hor-Aha. "This man may be a Medjay but he is not Egyptian. It is not customary for blood Princes to defer to someone of lesser station, let alone of lesser nationality, in battle or anywhere else." Ahmose laughed.

"In our position we cannot be too concerned with protocol and precedence," he said. "Ability reigns supreme, Intef. Yet if anyone deserves elevation to the nobility for his service, loyalty and sheer craftiness, Hor-Aha does. Well, Kamose?" Kamose grunted. I should have done it a long time ago, he thought. Ahmose is right. Hor-Aha has not been greedy enough and I have been too selfish. He turned to his General, meeting the black eyes with a hint of amusement in them, the tiny smile.

"Are you willing to carry a title, Hor-Aha?" he asked softly. "It means a final commitment to me and to this country, something stronger than your tribal oaths." Hor-Aha nodded.

"I do not need a title in order to serve you, Prince," he answered equally softly as though he and Kamose were engaged in a private conversation. "But your brother is right. I deserve it. Later I will take the estates, servants and preferments that go with it."

"Very well. Please rise." Hor-Aha did so, standing easily as Kamose drew close. Kamose touched him with slow solemnity on the forehead, shoulders and heart. "Hor-Aha, General," he said as he did so. "I make you erpa-ha, Hereditary Prince of Weset and all Egypt, you and your sons after you, forever. I, Kamose, King of Egypt, beloved of Amun, Son of the Sun, make it so." Hor-Aha knelt and kissed Kamose's feet.

"I will try to be worthy of this honour, Majesty," he said.

"Rise," Kamose ordered. "You are already worthy. Sit." They both resumed their seats. The other Princes had watched impassively. "Well?" Kamose pressed them. "To what avail is my strength when one usurper is in Het-Uart and another in Kush, so that I sit here between a Setiu and a Kushite, each in possession of his slice of Egypt, and I cannot even pass to Mennofer without permission? My new erpa-ha is a fitting match for Pezedkhu. Are you with me?" Ankhmahor sighed ostentatiously.

"Alas for my cattle!" he said. "Yes, we are with you. But, Majesty, we will exact a heavy gift from you when we win." Kamose did not thank them. To do so would have been unbecoming. He immediately passed to the matter of their responsibilities.

"Before we move north there is the matter of Pi-Hathor to be dealt with," he said. "As you all know, even though the town lies twenty-three miles south of us here at Weset, it is considered part of Apepa's holdings. The Setiu have always needed its limestone and, more importantly, its ships. It is their halfway point for trade with Kush and it represents the southern boundary of their control. It pricks our tender underbelly like a thorn." He leaned forward. "The population of Pi-Hathor is predominantly native Egyptian, and I do not wish to expend troops, energy and time overrunning it, two reasons why I intend to attempt negotiation with its mayor. I will not request active aid from him. That would be dangerous. All I need is his oath that he will not move against Weset or impede any of my river traffic, that he will preserve a state of neutrality with me. I think he can be convinced. Therefore I ask that you all accompany me south so that Pi-Hathor may see that I have the weight of serious purpose behind me. We will leave tomorrow at dawn. Are you agreed?" They nodded without comment and Kamose sat back, gradually relinquishing the conversation to Hor-Aha, who was not in the least in awe of them. He and Ahmose sat quietly sipping wine and listening until the light in the room changed to red and Uni knocked to admit the servants with lamps.

"Does it feel strange to be called Majesty?" Ahmose asked him later as they walked together, tired but satisfied, by the river. The sun had long since set but the new-risen moon was full, its reflection lying broken into silver shards on the surface of the quiet river water. Before and behind them their watchful guards paced the shadows.

The dark, empty ships towered beyond the river growth, moving ponderously against their anchors, the men set to guard them invisible on their decks. Kamose inhaled the dry, sweetish odour of their reeds. He answered Ahmose's question with a sense of shock.

"No, not strange," he said. "Indeed it seemed quite natural and I did not notice the use of the title until afterwards."

"I did," Ahmose answered softly. "For a moment it set you apart from me, Kamose, but only for a moment. We love each other, do we not? And it reminded me that if anything should happen to you, I will be Majesty." Something in his tone made Kamose stop on the path and turn to him, urgently seeking his face under the sickly moonlight.

"Nothing is going to happen to me," he said reassuringly, taking Ahmose's arm. "Amun himself has decreed that I should win through to Het-Uart. Are you afraid for me, Ahmose?"

Ahmose's eyes were hollow in the weak light, his expression sombre.

"No, not for you," he answered quickly. "You are the most self-sufficient person I know, Kamose. You need no one. God-head set you apart long ago in a different way from Father, a cold and unapproachable way to those who do not know you well. You will not mind dying alone if that is your destiny and I will not mind for you. It is for myself that I am afraid. I do not want to be King, ever. Princedom suits me far better." He tried to smile at Kamose. Is this a premonition? Kamose wondered. "You should have a son!" Ahmose went on vehemently. "A Horus-in-the-Nest, so that if necessary I might be Regent but never King!"

"Ahmose, I have been meaning to speak to you of this matter," Kamose said, squeezing his brother's arm before releasing it. "I want you to marry Aahmes-nefertari. You know the reasons why. You spend much time with her and she seems to confide in you. Would it be onerous for you?" Ahmose began to walk again and Kamose swung in beside him.

"Not at all," Ahmose said. "I want her, but by rights she should go to you. I did not want to speak until you had decided whether or not you would do your dynastic duty. Seeing you will not, then I will do it for you."

He understands everything, Kamose thought with relief. I need say no more. They fell silent, each wrapped in the beauty of the night, and strolled on, elbow to elbow, until the dull orange lights of Weset came into view.

Chapter FOURTEEN

IN THE COOL SILENCE OF dawn Kamose and Ahmose set out on the barge, accompanied by Ipi and a contingent of bodyguards. The river was running strongly and at first the rowers had to strain against the rapid current that slapped and gurgled beneath the craft, but as the day brightened a wind out of the north began to blow and their progress became smoother. Mesehti, Intef and the others sat together on cushions under the billowing awning beside the cabin, Ahmose cross-legged beside them, but none of them spoke. Kamose, leaning on the deck rail, his eyes on the riverbank gliding by but his attention fixed on the men behind him, did not think that their mute immobility was a result of the wine they had drunk at Aahotep's modest feast of the night before. They were afraid, each one deep in his own assessment of a desperate situation, perhaps thinking more of all they might lose than of the as yet nebulous rewards their new allegiance could bring. He was afraid himself, but his fear was an old companion and he was able to greet it and then turn from its grey face.

Hor-Aha stood beside him and there was comfort in the Medjay's quiet support. "Have you sent ahead to warn the mayor of Pi-Hathor of your coming, Majesty?" the man asked at last. Kamose shook his head, feeling the warm weight of the lapis pectoral his jeweller had delivered to him move slightly against his naked chest. His fingers came up, caressing its smooth curves. At its base the god of eternity, Heh, knelt on the heb sign. In his outstretched hands he held the long, notched palm ribs that made up the sides of the ornament and that represented many years. Around his neck went the ankh, symbol of life. Above Heh's head, the royal cartouche enclosing Kamose's name was encircled by the wings of the goddess Nekhbet, the Lady of Dread, vulture protectress of the King of the south, and she was entwined in the embrace of Wadjet, the Lady of Flame, serpent goddess of the north, she who would spit venom at any who dared to threaten the sanctity of the King's person. The whole was of lapis lazuli set in gold. Between Kamose's shoulder blades, in the one place where demons could strike at the body, the pectoral's counterpoise contained no lapis but was all of gold, an oblong in which Amun and Montu stood side by side, invincible guardians against any attack by the coarse gods of the Setiu. Curling above it was the delicate feather of Ma'at.

"No," he replied, his hand closing around the symbols of his hope. "I do not want to give him any presentiment of my purpose. It is better if we descend upon him unawares and dazzle him with our combined authority. We must not fail at Pi-Hathor. If we do, my Princes will begin their service to me in an even greater hesitancy than they now feel, and worse, I will be marching north with a potentially worrisome enemy at my back. Small perhaps, but even a tiny thorn can inflict a nasty scratch."

"Yet Pi-Hathor worries me," Hor-Aha rejoined. "It is too close to Weset. What if the mayor chooses to attack your town while you are engaged farther north? You are leaving no one but the Princesses to see to the safety of your domain."

"I know." Kamose faced him directly, squinting in the bright light. "It is a calculated risk, my friend. Pi-Hathor has no garrison of soldiers. The men there are quarry workers and shipwrights. If the mayor wishes to march against Weset, he will have to train his peasants to fight and that, as we are aware, takes time. I will place a spy in the town who can report to my mother while I am gone. That will have to be enough." Hor-Aha pursed his lips, then nodded.

"It is all in the lap of the gods, Majesty. If they desire your success, nothing will stand against you." He bowed and strode away, folding himself onto the deck in the thin shade cast by the arc of the prow, but Kamose stayed where he was, watching Egypt slide past.

The two hills that formed a backdrop for Pi-Hathor drifted into sight just after sunset when the last shreds of Ra's fiery garment were still being dragged below the horizon and the sky faded from dark blue above to a flush of pink against which the hills stood out black and rugged. Between them and the river the town huddled, a motley confusion of mud-brick buildings interspersed with narrow streets. In the centre, the temple of Hathor reared, its stone pylons and pillared façade casting long shadows towards the Nile's bank, where watersteps ran the whole length of the town's frontage. Kamose, now sitting with the others amid the flotsam of the evening meal and craning forward, could clearly see the island with its deep bay that lay offshore from the town.

Here there was a different kind of confusion. Quays ran out into the water like the spokes of chariot wheels, all of them lined with craft of every description, some of cedar, some of reeds, some with their bones waiting to be fleshed, some drawn up onto the sand of the bay and listing like beached monsters to expose their damaged flanks. Smoke from cooking fires cast a faint haze over the peaceful scene and blended with the subdued din of cheerful activity. Coming to his feet, Kamose hailed his captain. "Find us a mooring to the north, away from the skiffs unloading the workers from the island," he called. "Hor-Aha, select four soldiers to accompany us and deploy the others to guard the boat. Neither they nor the sailors are to speak to any curious townsmen who might wander by. It is one thing to be visiting the administrator of Pi-Hathor," he added to Ahmose who had come up to him, "and quite another to start a premature rumour that could undo us. If the Princes have finished dining, we can prepare to disembark." The craft nudged the watersteps, and at the captain's curt command a sailor jumped out, rope in hand, to tether it to one of the poles sunk into the river. Others lifted the ramp. With a long, slow breath, Kamose glanced around the gathered company, but there was nothing to say. The ramp settled against the water-steps, and one by one they silently followed him off the boat.

With two guards before and two behind, they paced the street that led straight from the Nile to the precincts of the temple. The crowds they met were moving away from the cen-tre of the community, intent on reaching their own doors after a day of labour, and the conversation around the group was merry. Few spared Kamose and his companions more than a friendly glance. Pi-Hathor was used to travellers from Kush or the Delta who came on business for the King's overseers.

Kamose knew that the offices of the mayor and his assistants lay behind Hathor's domain, on the edge of the square of public meetings and town celebrations. He hoped that the man had not already gone to his house, for as he and the Princes approached the temple, there were already torches being lit, and lamps flickered in the open doorways they passed. Dusk was deepening. Under the now black shadow of the looming pylon they veered left, followed Hathor's outer wall, and came at last to the dusty square. They crossed it, and Kamose saw to his relief that light still poured from the mayor's office and a servant still sat on a low stool beside the door. He rose as they approached, bowing clumsily, and the little cavalcade came to a halt. "Is your master within?" Kamose enquired. The man cleared his throat.

"Yes, lord," he replied uncertainly, "but he has finished his business for the day." Kamose jerked his head at one of his soldiers.

"Take this man to the nearest tavern," he ordered. "Buy him beer and a meal. Keep him under your eye until you are sent for."

"But, lord, I may not leave my stool," the servant protested. "Who are you? Let me announce you."

"It is not necessary," Kamose smiled, and at a further gesture one of his guards came forward, grasped the man's arm politely but firmly, and led him away, still objecting. "That is one pair of ears dealt with," he murmured. "Let us go in."

The mayor of Pi-Hathor was rising from his chair behind an imposing desk that almost filled the small room, a short, stooped figure with mottled hands, wrinkled face and a pale skull. His scribe was also unfolding from his place at his master's feet, palette in one hand and a roll of papyrus in the other. They had obviously just completed a dictation. Both looked rumpled and weary and Kamose, in the fleeting second before they turned to him in surprise, thought how heavy this man's task was with the dual nature of the town's industry. He would not be ignorant and easy to placate. "Het-uy, mayor of Pi-Hathor?" he said gently. Het-uy nodded, his dark eyes moving perplexed over the stern men ranked before him and coming to rest on the three remaining guards, one of whom stood in the doorway looking out warily into the gathering night.

"I am," he acknowledged slowly. "But who are you and what is your business with me? Where is the servant who should have announced you?" His gaze narrowed. "I think I am addressing the Prince of Weset, am I not?" The bewilderment on his face had given way to suspicion.

"You are," Kamose said swiftly. "I am Kamose Tao. My brother Ahmose and the Princes Mesehti, Intef, Iasen, Makhu and Ankhmahor are with me. This is my scribe, Ipi. Dismiss yours, Het-uy. We have an urgent and private matter to discuss. You may sit." The mayor lowered himself behind the desk. His palms found its surface and rested there. Kamose noticed that the fingers did not tremble, nor did the voice when Het-uy answered him.

"My scribe is discreet, as all good scribes are," he objected. "You will forgive me, Prince, if I ask that he might stay. You are under an interdict of disenfranchisement and banishment and I would be wise to retain a witness to any business you might wish to conduct with me. Your sudden appearance without a formal message from a herald, in fact with no warning at all, does not indicate either a social visit or a frivolous affair."

"You will be wiser to do as I command," Kamose snapped, with a testiness he did not feel. Het-uy was going to be difficult. "The King's judgement with regard to my fate does not become effective for another two weeks. Until that time I am still a Prince of Egypt and you, Het-uy, are merely a mayor. Send him away. Guard!" His man on the door turned. "Go to the other offices and fetch chairs. We will all sit." Kamose returned his gaze to the mayor, eyebrows raised, and with obvious reluctance Het-uy nodded at his scribe. With a bow to his master and one to the company he backed out, palette clutched to his chest. Immediately Ipi went to the floor, set his own palette across his knees, and prepared to write. Other than the small sounds he made as he opened his pen case, uncapped his ink and unrolled his papyrus, the room fell silent. The mayor's hands remained motionless on the desk. He scanned each solemn face before

346 / LORDS OF THE TWO LANDS

him, his own expression impossible to read. I wish I could gain this man's loyalty, Kamose thought. He has great inner strength, but it is all for Apepa. Such is the pity and the sadness of these days that men like this, intelligent, honest and incorruptible, are become the enemies of the very country they believe they defend. They are outside the bounds of Ma'at without ever knowing it.

The guard returned with the chairs Kamose had requested, and there was a general loosening as the company relaxed onto them. The man regained his station, blocking the door. Kamose touched Ipi's shoulder, and taking up one of the lamps from the desk, he handed it to his scribe. "Say the prayer to Thoth," he advised. "Begin the recording." He crossed his legs and looked straight at the mayor. "I have come to ask you to sign an agreement of non-intervention with me," he said without preamble. "My House is indeed under a decree of banishment from Apepa, but I have decided not to allow the members of my family to be scattered and my land go to khato. The blood of the Taos is ancient and honourable and cannot suffer such a final outrage. I intend to return to Weset this night and in two days begin a campaign against the invaders. Before the next Inundation I intend to besiege Het-Uart." At last he had punctured the mayor's composure. The man's eyes widened and his hands slid to the edge of the desk and gripped it in a spasm of shock.

"Prince, you are mad," he said huskily. "Will you compound your father's grave error? Seqenenra fomented revolt and died. The One has been more lenient with you than any in Egypt believed safe for the stability of the Double Crown or the country. All that can happen is your defeat and the execution of every member of your household! What can you mean by non-intervention?" Yet he glanced rapidly from one of Kamose's silent party to the other and his fingers slid into his invisible lap.

"I ask nothing more from you than this," Kamose went on

deliberately. "That you will swear to remain here in Pi-Hathor and go about the business of the city, neither conjuring war on Weset while I am away nor impeding any of my messengers that might pass by on their way farther south."

"Ridiculous!" Het-uy almost shouted. "My duty is to send at once to my King and then sit back and watch you die! Highness, we all grieve at the eclipse of your House," he went on more soberly. "For years beyond years your lineage has been rooted in the soil of Egypt. Yet your father committed treason, and now you threaten to do the same. For the sake of your ancestors, of your unborn descendants, do not allow such illustrious blood to dribble away forever into the sands of ignominy!"

"My ancestors were gods in Egypt," Kamose broke in softly. "They were Kings. Why am I not King, Het-uy? Answer me that." He uncrossed his legs and, placing his elbows on his knees, leaned forward so that his face was level with the mayor's. "You cannot, because the only words you could form would be words of that very treason of which you accuse my father. You would have to say that I am not King because base foreigners have overrun this land and their chiefs have made themselves Kings. Deny it if you are able!" But Het-uy only stared at him mutely and Kamose sighed and sat back. "I have one hundred ships already launched on the Nile at Weset," he said flatly. "I have a division of soldiers waiting to board them. If you refuse me this agreement, I will be forced to bring my army here and raze Pi-Hathor to the ground before I go north. I have not wasted the time Apepa so kindly and naïvely gave me, Het-uy, and I do not intend to squander much more of it here. Yes or no?" The mayor whitened, his eyes going to Mesehti on Kamose's left, and Kamose pressed him. "These Princes have already sworn their loyalty to me and put their own hosts at my disposal," he said brutally. "Ask them, if you doubt me. Ask them!" But the mayor shook his head.

"Prince, you are brave but stupid," he managed. "And these

great men with you, they will pay a terrible price for their so-called loyalty. Apepa will crush you all. You do not seem to understand that, if I comply with any agreement you thrust on me, I am inviting my own portion of the One's righteous anger." I have him, Kamose thought in a wave of exultation. But he was careful not to let the relief show on his face.

"Not so," he said. "I am not asking you or your town for any active support. All I want is your assurance that you will not move against Weset. That would be difficult for you in any case, for there are no soldiers here, only quarrymen and ship-wrights. If Apepa defeats me, why you are absolved from any liability because of it. But if I win through to Het-Uart and snatch up the Double Crown, I will show my gratitude to the man and the city that did not impede my victory. Either way, Pi-Hathor is guiltless."

Another silence fell. Het-uy blinked, sighed, looked to the ceiling, then down at his lap. Ipi's pen was stilled. The shadows ceased gyrating on the walls of the room. Then the mayor let out a gust of breath. "Very well, Prince," he said crossly. "You can have your agreement. Two copies, one for you and one for me to hide away. But I do not do this willingly!"

"Of course not," Kamose smiled. "Thank you, Het-uy. In anticipation of your co-operation I have already dictated the document and Ipi has made a copy." He gestured at his scribe who reached into the leather bag beside him and passed two thin scrolls to Kamose. One was placed in the mayor's out-stretched hand. "As you can see," Kamose reiterated smoothly, "it contains nothing we have not discussed. The wording is very simple." Het-uy unrolled his scroll and scanned it briefly, then he looked up.

"You have no guarantee that I will not immediately break this arrangement and send it to the King with a warning," he remarked. "You have, after all, threatened and coerced me into conniving at treason and my conscience would not awaken should I choose to betray you." Kamose met his gaze.

"But you will not break it," he said quietly. "Unwillingly or not you have given your word, and you are an honourable man. You will keep it so long as you may do so without repercussions, and that is all I have asked of you, Het-uy. However, all messengers and heralds coming up from the south will be stopped and questioned at Weset. In these dark days I think I may be forgiven for not putting my trust in spoken or written assurances alone. Ipi, give the mayor a pen." Het-uy's mouth set in a thin line. Without further comment he took the brush Ipi held up to him, and now his hand did shake, so that a drop of black ink sprinkled the desk. Kamose took the scroll he signed, passed it to Ipi, and gave him the other, watching while he inscribed his name again. "That one you must keep," he ordered, coming to his feet. "We will not insult you now by accepting your hospitality. Long life, Het-uy." The others had also risen. Het-uy bowed stiffly but did not return the greeting, and with a few steps Kamose was outside.

Sending one of the guards to search the taverns for his fellows, Kamose set off down the street. Full night had fallen. Lamplight from the open doorways he passed pooled yellow into the dust, seeming to carry with it the gusts of laughter and quick conversation that swelled out, only to be sucked up by the darkness. Faint chanting came from the holy precinct of Hathor's temple, but the sweet, high female voices only reminded Kamose that he must warn his mother to keep a careful watch on the river traffic and pay close attention to the reports of the spy he would send here to Hathor's city. "Will he make trouble, do you think?" Iasen was voicing Kamose's own thoughts, but it was Ahmose who answered.

"No," he said. "Het-uy will regard his dilemma as a moral one, not a matter of expediency, and as such he will be torn between his obligation to Apepa and the commitment he made when he set brush to papyrus. He will lose sleep over it but will do nothing. Such is the way of a man who can decide swiftly when the issue is between what is right and what is forbidden, but who becomes impotent when the scales are balanced."

"He is a good man," Intef remarked as they came to the torchlit expanse of the watersteps and swung left. Kamose looked past the torches to the indistinct hump of the island and the dim line of the east bank beyond it. A good man, he thought. So many of them, good men. How many good men will I have to kill before a greater good can be established? A wave of depression swept over him, a feeling of futility he was too tired to fight. Answering his captain's challenge, he walked up the ramp. "Take us home," he ordered. "There is no profit in spending the night here unless it is too dark for the helmsman to steer." The captain glanced up at the sky.

"The moon is three-quarters to the full," he said, "and we will be moving with the current, not against it. I think we may cast off, Prince." Kamose nodded. The others had already settled on their cushions under the lamp that hung in the stern and were quaffing the wine being offered to them with obvious relief, while a polite distance from them the cook crouched over his brazier. The tempting aroma of grilling fish wafted to Kamose's nostrils. One of the sailors had begun to sing, his voice coming and going under the sharp commands to cast off and man the helm and the thud of the ramp being drawn up. The barge trembled under Kamose's feet.

Making his way to the cabin, he entered, letting the curtain fall behind him and standing for a moment in the close darkness. He did not like what he had been forced to do to the mayor of Pi-Hathor but that, he thought grimly, is the least of what I will be called upon to do in the name of freedom over the coming months. Amun, give me the resolve to be ruthless without courting the destruction of my ka, the wisdom to discern friend from foe when both speak to me in the accents of my beloved country! Sinking to the floor, he drew up his knees, laid his head against the wall, and closed his eyes. The lively voices of his friends, his allies, came to him, weaving with the clink of wine jugs against cups, the slow, rhythmic slap of the oars as they bit the water, the intermittent snatches of song the sailor was still crooning, all part of the sweet reality of an Egyptian night that pierced his ka with a longing for all that had gone. He had never felt so alone.

Just after midnight the captain ordered their craft into a small bay so that the sailors could rest. They did not move on again until dawn and the barge nudged the watersteps at Weset late in the afternoon of the same day, its low, sleek lines dwarfed by the vast reed ships that rocked on either side. At once Kamose ordered Hor-Aha, Ahmose and the Princes across the river. "I want your assessment of the troops," he told them. "Hor-Aha is my second-in-command and he and Ahmose have been training the men, but I would like an opinion on their readiness from the rest of you. Hor-Aha, find Baba Abana. He is an accomplished sailor and will give us his views on how the men should be distributed on the ships. He must take charge of everything to do with our efficiency on the river. Time is now our enemy. Come what may, we must begin our offensive the day after tomorrow." He left them then, walking towards the house in the company of his guards, and before he reached the entrance his steward met him, bowing. "Send to my mother and Tetisheri," he said. "I will come to their quarters before dining. I want to see the Scribe of Assemblage at once in my office. And bring beer, Akhtoy. I am very thirsty."

The office was cool and silent. Kamose sank into the chair that had so often held his father's form and for a moment inhaled the atmosphere of calm and good order that had been so much a part of Seqenenra's character, but he refused the temptation to close his eyes and succumb to its peace. Do I send the Princes on ahead to their nomes to have their conscripts waiting for me or do I keep them beside me? he wondered wearily. Can I trust them absolutely or only until my campaign encounters a difficulty? Will they take orders humbly from Hor-Aha or will their pride result in arguments and hostility towards a mere Medjay? The five thousand Medjay tribesmen Hor-Aha brought with him are fierce warriors but unruly, unused to military discipline. Hor-Aha knows how to speak to them, but will he be able to rule Egyptian soldiers? I must remind him not to appoint any Medjay to officer positions over native Egyptians no matter how capable they prove themselves to be. Or am I wrong? Is it more important to promote men who can forge the conscripts into an efficient fighting force than to worry about resentments within the ranks?

His head was beginning to ache, and when Akhtoy appeared with a jug of beer, he drank gratefully. The Scribe of Assemblage had arrived on the steward's heels. Kamose acknowledged his bow, bade him sit, and pushed the cup and jug towards him. "I presume that by now you have been able to obtain an accurate assessment of what provisions we can load onto the boats and how long they will last," he said. "Give me your estimates." The man finished pouring his beer and took a judicious sip.

"In obedience to your command, Highness, I have had the granaries emptied and the stores of dried fruits and preserved vegetables packed. I have calculated their attrition on a figure of five thousand Medjay and twenty-five senior officers who will, of course, be entitled to better fare than the ranks. The desert men can exist on less food than Egyptians, but I did not think it wise to presume that you would indeed expect them to do so." Here he smiled, and Kamose smiled back.

"You are right," he agreed. "Nor do I want myself or my

officers feasting while the men squat over their meagre bread and onions."

"But surely, Highness, a little wine, a simple platter of shat cakes..." Kamose held up a hand.

"A little wine perhaps. But we are on no punitive march into Kush, remember. Old rules do not apply." The Scribe sighed.

"It is a detail, Highness. By my reckoning we may feed the army bread, goat cheese and a few dried figs each morning and in the evening, bread, radishes, garlic, an onion, a handful of chick peas and a little honey. The rowers can fish at sunset and whatever they catch can augment this diet. There is plenty of oil and enough beer, I think. Nothing but the fish needs to be cooked, so the army will not be slowed down." Kamose nodded his approval.

"How long will the supplies last?"

The Scribe shrugged eloquently. "I have taken the most pessimistic view," he replied, "and assumed the worst. With no replenishment from the nomes of your Princes, the supplies garnered will last you two weeks. I told my men to take only the reserves of grain and fruits from your peasants, so that the women and children can survive for the next two months until the harvest."

"Two weeks." Kamose repeated. "And two days out of Weset we will be tying up at Qebt and then Kift, both in the Herui nome and both governed by Intef. Make sure that you bring enough of your underlings with you to swiftly organize and load supplies from these towns. This is good. Very good. Find Paheri, the mayor of Nekheb. He is with the army on the west bank. Tell him in your capacity as Scribe of Assemblage to send to Nekheb for as much natron as the town can spare. It is produced there, so he should be able to provide us with plenty. It can follow us. We will need it for washing." He met the other's eye and he knew that the Scribe was echoing his own unspoken thought. We will need it for burying also. "That is all," he said at last. "You may begin to load the boats. You have one more day in which to complete the task. Thank you." The man rose at once, bowed, and left the office, and Kamose also stood, stretching until his spine cracked.

The light in the room had acquired a reddish tinge. Ra was falling slowly into the waiting mouth of Nut and it was time to confront the women and send across the river for the Princes. Kamose would have liked to bathe and change his linen but such amenities would have to wait. He drained the last of the Scribe's cup of beer before closing the door of the room behind him.

Three heads turned to him expectantly as he was admitted to his grandmother's suite. She was sitting stiffly on the chair beside her couch, her knees together, her be-ringed hands folded. Aahotep occupied the stool before Tetisheri's cosmetic table. She was clad in a loose white wrap. Isis stood behind her, with a mouth full of pins, as she smoothly wound her mistress's thick hair into a coil. Aahmes-nefertari had pulled cushions onto the floor and was reclining on them. As her brother approached she scrambled up and took a step towards him, her clear glance full of worry. Kamose surveyed them gravely. "I love you very much," he said. "And I know that you love me. No, Isis." He turned to the servant who was about to bow herself out. "You may stay." His attention returned to his women. "You know what I have planned," he went on. "The day after tomorrow I leave Weset with my army. We must not look back, any of us. This is Apepa's birth month and also the Anniversary of his Appearing. Celebrations will be going on all over Egypt, but especially in the Delta. There is no better time to begin a war of recovery. I do not know how long I will be gone." He spread his hands. "It is all in the wisdom of Amun and we must trust him. Weset and this nome are in your hands.

I am asking you to undertake a crushing responsibility. First, you must organize the peasant women to harvest the fields and the vineyards. Second, you must set a constant watch on the traffic coming up from the south. Every craft must be intercepted, every scroll opened and read, without exception. Remember that Pi-Hathor supports the Setiu, and in spite of our treaty the mayor may try to get messages through to Het-Uart. He may even try to overrun you here. I have spared a hundred soldiers to remain with you. I am sorry it is so few, but if they are deployed sensibly you should be able to hold off a rabble of shipwrights and quarrymen." He saw panic flare in his sister's eyes, but his mother was frowning in speculation and Tetisheri continued to regard him with cool immobility.

"The High Priest and his inferiors will fight if they have to," she said, "and gardeners have strong muscles. It is not such a large step, from hoes to swords. Do not fret over us, Kamose. We are entirely capable of running this nome in your absence and repelling a few malcontents if necessary."

"You must send me regular reports," Kamose told them. "Include everything from the progress of the harvest to how the wind smells. Sacrifice before Amun every day on my behalf." Aahmes-nefertari stirred.

"And what of Tani?" she whispered. "Have you forgotten her so soon, Kamose?" He strode to her and grasped her shoulders.

"No!" he said harshly. "But Tani knew what I would do and she accepted any consequence my actions might bring down on her. She is a Tao, even as you are, Aahmes-nefertari." He let her go and ran gentle fingers down her glossy head. "If it will comfort you, I do not think that Apepa will revenge himself on her. Such an action would prejudice many Egyptians against him who might otherwise fight on his side. It is one thing to punish a Prince. It is quite another to execute a young Princess."

Tetisheri grunted her agreement. "He is a mongrel, with a

mongrel's vulgar sense of morality," she declared, "but in the matter of self-preservation he is a greyhound. He will not harm our Tani."

Aahotep had not spoken, but, as Isis was settling the braided wig over her hair, she said, "You wear lapis now, Kamose. You go north as a King. The succession must be assured against your possible death." It had cost her a great deal to force out the words and the full mouth trembled as she raised her gaze to his. "Will you sign a marriage contract with your sister and consummate it before you go?" He shook his head.

"I have already arranged this with Ahmose," he answered. "You love him, Aahmes-nefertari, and he will be a good father to Ahmose-onkh, if he comes home. There is no time for the proper feasting that should accompany a royal wedding and I am sorry for that, but tomorrow you and he will stand in the temple and receive the blessing of the god, and tomorrow night you must bed together. Do you accept this?" The girl inclined her head.

"But you, Kamose," she interjected. "What of you? Will you never marry then?"

"I do not think so," he said, wondering what they would say if they knew that he was in love with a phantom who haunted his dreams. "My disposition has always been a solitary one, and I am grateful that Ahmose can so willingly fulfil my duty on my behalf." She smiled at that and he walked to the door.

"Tonight we fete the Princes for the last time," he said as he opened the door. "Let us drown ourselves in fine wine and have music in our ears and cones of precious oil on our heads. We will celebrate life."

As he paced the darkening passage to his own quarters, a thousand concerns fought for his attention, but he denied them all. Not now, he told the inner clamour. Now is the time for hot water and royal linen, for eye paint and hennaed palms, for a final embrace that will encompass past and present before the future unfolds its murky wings.

Standing on the bathing slab under his body servant's ministrations, he forced his mind to sink beneath the messages of his senses: the gurgle of the scented water as it coursed down his limbs and disappeared into the drain in the floor, the friction of a towel wielded vigorously between his shoulder blades, the sudden heavy odour of lotus as the man unstoppered a jar of oil.

At a murmured request, Kamose lowered himself onto a bench and deliberately luxuriated in the tingling of his skin before relaxing under the soothing coolness of his servant's oiled hands. But a thought came to him unbidden, sharp and painful as the cut of a knife. *That is where the demons strike, there between the shoulder blades. Assassins also, unless a man is completely unaware of his danger, sleeping perhaps, or pondering deeply. Oh my father, surely even now sitting in peace under the sacred sycamore tree where Osiris rules, pray for me! And you, Si-Amun my brother, dead by your own hand, where are you? Would a plea to the gods from your ka bring me a blessing or a curse?* He groaned and the man's fingers were stilled. "Did I hurt you, Prince?" he asked solicitously. Kamose moved his head against the narrow pillow, a denial. *It is my heart that hurts me,* he replied soundlessly, and *try as I might I cannot banish that distress. May the wine tonight be rich and strong!*

The dining hall was almost full that night, for Kamose had invited not only the five Princes but his officers, the mayor of Weset and his administrators and their wives, and the priests of Amun. Flowers littered the tiny dining tables scattered over the tiled floor, trembling in the drafts from floating linen and sending their perfume gusting into the room. Every lamp Aahotep could muster had turned the dim expanse into a golden day. There were no shadows. The stewards bent with brimming wine

jugs over guests who held up their cups eagerly. Servants threaded their way through the chattering throng, holding high the
trays laden with the last of the family's delicacies. Duck, fish
and gazelle meat smoked under fresh leaves of pungent cilantro.
Stalks of celery, sprigs of parsley and round brown chick peas
nestled on beds of crisp lettuce. Sycamore figs soaked in honey
from the persea trees and little crumbling sweet cakes were offered, and the beer was flavoured with pomegranates and mint.
Kamose's musicians plucked and tapped valiantly, the melodies
almost lost under the clamour around them.

The family sat on the dais above the throng. The women
and the two brothers also had donned their most colourful
linens and adorned themselves in such jewellery as remained to
them. Eyes black-kohled, lips and palms hennaed orange, their
braided wigs glistening with the melting saffron oil, they
seemed detached from the revellers. In spite of their smiles,
their warm glances, their gestures as they ate or raised the
blooms to their faces, there was an invisible rift between them
and the noisy crowd at their sandalled feet. They were marked
for death or for glory, not the anonymous death of a common
soldier or the glory of mere temporal success, but a formal execution or the confirmation of divinity. All knew it, and the
knowledge wove a thread of gravity through the increasing din.

Ahmose had his arm around his sister as they ate, and when
they had finished, they talked quietly together. Tetisheri had
both hands around her cup, but she was not drinking. Her calm
gaze remained fixed above the heads of the people. Aahotep
was bent over the table, one cheek resting in her palm, still
frowning. But Kamose drank steadily, no longer tasting the fine
vintage regularly replenished in his goblet. The seductive
aroma of the wax cone on his head filled his nostrils. The air in
the hall was warm and redolent with life. The wine slipped
down his throat, cool and comforting, but he was not consoled.

In the flushed faces below him he fancied that he caught his father's glance, the swift tossing of his dead brother's head, but when he looked again there were no ghosts, only Intef smiling up at him briefly and Ankhmahor turning to answer his neighbour's question.

Before the feasting had begun, he had instructed the Princes to return to their nomes at dawn so as to prepare their stores and conscripts for his arrival. One day will not be enough, he thought hazily. I should not have taken them to Pi-Hathor. Now the army will have to linger at Kift and perhaps also at Aabtu while the ranks are swelled and the food replenished. I only have four months before the next Inundation. Four months to take Egypt back and bottle up Apepa in the Delta. Oh, for Set's sake, Kamose! he berated himself inwardly. You will go insane before you set foot in your boat if you do not control this pointless gnawing at what cannot now be changed. Get drunk and sleep. He drained his cup and held it out unsteadily to be refilled.

He woke at noon the following day to a pounding headache and the news that the Princes had gone north in obedience to his instructions. Pushing aside the food Uni had placed beside him on the couch, he gulped down several cups of water before making his way to the bath house to have the poisons of his last excess massaged from his pores. The air was stale with the atmosphere of silent exhaustion that often followed a night of carousal. Servants moved with quiet purpose, clearing away the debris of a feast that had spilled from the hall into the passages of the public area and out to the garden. The smell of baking bread gave Kamose a wave of nausea before he entered the humid dampness of the bath house and acknowledged his body servant's bow, but by the time he emerged, washed, kneaded and ready to be dressed, his appetite was returning and he ate a few mouthfuls of bread and goat cheese while his kilt was wrapped about his waist and his face was painted. For once, his mind, as drained as his body felt, was still.

Ipi was waiting for him in the office. "The family expects your summons, Highness," he said in answer to Kamose's question. "The Prince and Princess are ready. The contract is before you."

"Bring them then," Kamose ordered, "and have the litters ready outside." He went to sit behind the desk, the scroll under his fingers, but he did not unroll it. It was a simple, standard marriage agreement with Ahmose and Aahmes-nefertari's names inserted. He felt a twinge of doubt as he looked down at it. Is this the right thing to do? he wondered. Give her to Ahmose instead of taking her myself? What if Ahmose is killed in the coming battles but I survive to rule? Would I serve as regent for whatever child results from this union? Or would I then marry her in my turn? Where is she, the beloved of my dreams? I have not seen her now for a long time. Has she deserted me because I am set on the right path or because I have wandered unknowingly into error? No, he decided. She is near, but no other sign is needed. I am in the will of Ma'at.

They entered mutely and came to stand before him, their mother on their left, Tetisheri on their right. All looked pale and tired, even Ahmose, who was usually alert and cheerful no matter how he had spent his nights. Ipi placed his palette before them and uncapped the ink. "Are you still willing to do this thing?" Kamose asked them. The question was a formality, couched in his own terse words. They nodded. "Then sign your name and titles. Mother, Grandmother, you will witness the signatures together with me." Solemnly, in a silence broken only by the almost imperceptible abrasion of brush against papyrus, they bent and complied. Kamose wrote last, and it was over. He passed the scroll to Ipi. "Lock it away in the archives," he said, rising. "Now come. The litters are waiting to take us to the temple."

The early afternoon was a dazzle of bright sunlight with a hint of the greater heat Shemu would bring in a few weeks, and Kamose found his mood lightening as his bearers paced the path that ran from the estate to Amun's home. The Nile, glimpsed between the lushness of growth along its bank, sparkled. An intermittent breeze lifted the edge of the litter's curtain and fluttered it against his naked calf. To right and left the family's bodyguards, the Followers of His Majesty, strode easily, their sturdy leather sandals kicking up little puffs of dust.

All at once Kamose heard his sister exclaim. Leaning out he saw her peering up at the sky. "Oh look, Ahmose!" she called out. "Look up! Horus gives us his benediction! It is a favourable omen!" Kamose scanned the blue vastness above him and drew in his breath. A great hawk was hovering over the cavalcade, its red-tipped wings outspread. It was so close that Kamose could see the sun reflected in its shiny black eyes and the tiny slits of its nostrils. Its beak was open, and even as he gazed, it gave a raucous shriek and dropped further towards them. Kamose flinched involuntarily, but with an audible rustle of feathers and another harsh cry it swooped over him, paused above Ahmose's conveyance, then rose straight up to be lost in the brilliance of the day. Kamose found himself trembling as a babble of exhilarated chatter broke out among the bearers. A mighty omen indeed, he thought as they moved on. The God of the Horizon has spoken. But his holy sanction was not for me. Not for me.

Leaving the litter bearers to squat in the shade of the trees that lined Amun's canal, the family crossed the outer court, removed their sandals, and entered the inner court. Amunmose was waiting for them before the open doors of the sanctuary, his acolytes holding lighted censers whose smoke curled almost invisibly into the limpid air. Bowing, he preceded them to where the god sat in the cool gloom of the Holiest of Holiest, golden hands on golden knees, his feet surrounded by the flowers and food presented to him that morning by his servants. Ahmose had brought him the gift of an amulet and Aahmes-nefertari a necklet of electrum, as well as the offerings of wine, food and oil prescribed by custom. Poor trinkets indeed, Kamose thought as he watched his brother and sister pass their burdens to Amunmose and kneel to prostrate themselves. But Amun knows that there is little left to bring to him until such time as I may fill this sanctuary with the riches of the whole of Egypt. He listened attentively to the prayers and responses of thanksgiving, the requests for happiness and the added blessing of children, his spirit calmed under the steady golden regard of his god.

When the appointed rites were over, they returned to the house where a meal had been set out for them in the garden. Relief had replaced the mood of heavy soberness in which they had signed the marriage contract, and Ahmose and his new wife were toasted with laughter and many gentle jokes. They sat close together under the sheltering canopy, holding hands and smiling into each other's eyes over the rims of their cups while Ahmose-onkh, released from his nurse's care, crawled over them, prattling delightedly in his own unintelligible language. Their happiness soothed Kamose. I have done the right thing, he told himself, whether or not the future will bring them divinity. They were born for one another.

As the afternoon slipped away, Tetisheri and Aahotep sought their couches and Ahmose-onkh, protesting volubly, was retrieved and carried into the house. Kamose rose also. "If I eat at all this evening, it will be in the office," he said, looking down on their flushed faces. "Do not worry about tomorrow,

Ahmose. I will take care of the last details before we set sail. I will see you at the watersteps at dawn." He hesitated, wanting to say more, to tell them to treasure the moments remaining to them, to assure his sister that he would do everything in his power to return her husband to her safely, for he sensed that the sad shadow of Si-Amun's fate lay over her, but he could not. His words would have held only a hollow promise. Smiling briefly, he left them.

Inside his own quarters he summoned Akhtoy. "I want to see the Scribe of Recruits, the Scribe of Assemblage and General Hor-Aha in the office as soon as possible," he ordered his steward. "Have my body servant bring hot water and fresh linen. I will wash and change my clothes." By the time he had finished his ablutions and had walked through the house, the men he had summoned were already in attendance. All three were weary. Kamose noted their dusty kilts and drawn features without comment, and bade them sit. "This will not take long," he said. "General, I want the Medjay on board the boats and settled by dawn. Is that possible?" Hor-Aha nodded.

"They are ready," he answered. "All I have left to do is to assign a boat to each five hundred under the appropriate officers."

"Have the mayor of Nekheb and his townsmen been of any use to you?"

"Yes, indeed." Hor-Aha leaned forward. "Paheri and Baba Abana have organized the men into shifts of rowers and appointed the junior officers as those who call the strokes. It was something I had not considered fully. The desert men are not pleased to be travelling on water. Both men of Nekheb have been invaluable in making them more familiar with the boats and explaining to them how best to cope with the experience."

"Good." Kamose turned his attention to the others. "Scribe of Recruits, are my conscripts ready?" The man inclined his head.

"Yes, Highness. There has been some unruliness among the younger boys and many of the conscripts are grumbling because they must march while the Medjay sit in the boats, but the General has done his utmost to explain to them why this is necessary." A difficult task indeed, Kamose mused. A Medjay general trying to inform Egyptian farmers and artisans why foreigners may travel in comfort while they sweat under the sun. I should have seen to that myself. The doubts regarding Hor-Aha's supreme authority he had so lately endeavoured to put to rest returned to him and he glanced across to find the General's black eyes fixed on him. Was it a challenge he saw there? Hor-Aha smiled without humour.

"I did not do the explaining myself," he said, and Kamose was convinced that the man had read his thought. "I seconded a native Egyptian officer to the task. He made it clear to the nome troops that it was merely a matter of good tactics, not a slur against their blood. The Medjay are primarily archers and they have keen eyesight. They need the long view they will have from the boats. I made sure that the officer pointed out the superiority of Egyptians in the business of hand-to-hand combat." His smile widened. "Of course, for the majority of the nome troops, well-trained as they are, it is not true. Only those of them who fought with your illustrious father, Majesty, have seen any action at all. But the officer's tact seemed to mollify them."

"It was a wise thing to do," Kamose replied. "Once battle is joined and the army works as one, these foolish divisions will fade." To that, Hor-Aha had no response. Uneasily Kamose returned his gaze to the Scribe of Recruits. "Then get them across the river," he ordered. "They can sleep on their mats by the road. The boats will move faster than they can march in any case, so they will have a chance to become real soldiers in the wake of the first onslaughts, before any pitched battle is likely. Scribe of Assemblage, are the stores divided and stowed?"

"Everything, Highness. The custodians and cooks are ready. Tonight the donkeys accompanying the foot soldiers will be loaded."

"Good," Kamose repeated. "Very good. Then that is all. I will not be available for the rest of the night, but I will be down by the river at dawn. If there are any problems, take them to the General. You are dismissed." They rose as one, bowed, and left him.

For a moment Kamose sat on, drumming his fingers on the desk. I should go to Mother and Grandmother, he thought. I should spend a portion of this night reassuring them, reiterating their instructions, telling them what I intend. I should use up the rest of the hours remaining in the temple, in prayer. But when he left the office and greeted Akhtoy who had risen from his stool and was waiting for instructions, Kamose found words other than those he had planned to say leaving his mouth. "Tell the women that I cannot be with them tonight," he said. "Send to the temple and bid the High Priest come to the river to bless the troops at dawn. But first bring me a warm cloak and a lamp full of oil, Akhtoy. I want to go to the old palace. Tell no one where I am unless it be a matter of extreme emergency." He did not know where such a quixotic impulse had come from, but as he crossed the lawns towards the crumbling cleft in the ancient wall that separated his estate from that of his ancestors, the cloak over his arm and the lamp he carried casting a tiny circle of wavering light in the increasing dimness, he knew it was right.

Although a vestige of the day lingered in the wide courtyard across whose rubble-strewn stone flags he cautiously picked his way, it was already night inside the palace. Cold, musty air greeted him as he stood for a moment just within the lofty entrance to what had once been the mighty reception hall, a breath out of the past from the lungs of the dead. He shook off the fancy, allowing himself to gradually become aware of the rows of pillars marching away into the gloom, the patch of paler air far to his left where part of the roof and a wall had fallen in hentis ago and scattered bricks and deep dust over the chipped tiling of the floor.

He had intended to go straight to the stairs leading to the roof above the women's quarters, but his feet seemed to have a mind of their own and he began to wander the huge, dilapidated rooms where his lamp cast no more than a feeble glow against a weight of silence and lofty space. Here and there a remnant of life sprang out at him; the baleful glare of a Wadjet Eye that regarded him with hostility before sinking into obscurity as he moved quietly on, a splash of dull yellow, all that was left from some painted scene of a happier age, a seated likeness of some god or King that seemed to emerge from its corner as though it were about to rise, its serene features gazing steadily into the motionless decay around it. Kamose had the uneasy notion that if he spoke to it, it would reply, that to address it would unleash some force that had lain dormant in this, the sacred home of his forebears. He shook his head at his foolishness, but he was careful to make no sound until he had left its vicinity.

He had not been allowed to play here in the old palace. Seqenenra had forbidden it as being too dangerous, and as he grew, Kamose had not often been tempted to explore its secrets. It was stark and cold, a place of tumbled masonry, a home for bats and rodents. Yet now as he paced like a ghost himself through rooms that opened out into other rooms, along corridors whose uneven floors led to doorless black pits or cracked terraces or yet another series of empty, half-ruined apartments, it came to him that its greatest danger did not lie in loose bricks or sagging walls. With his senses heightened, he seemed to catch errant whispers, soft laughter, the flicker of jewelled linen just beyond the periphery of his vision. The true danger was more subtle, more seductive, a siren call of past glories that had conspired with Apepa's constant jibes to lure Seqenenra into the rebellion that had cast him, maimed and broken, into his tomb. Kamose felt the intoxication himself, stealing through his veins like a gentle elixir, the promise of purification, restoration, restitution. It was not a trap. The cause was just, it was right. The palace did not hold an evil magic. Its spell was redolent with Ma'at, the Ma'at of an Egypt gone, an Egypt that the ancestors who invisibly crowded this place waited for him to revive.

At last Kamose found himself in the throne room, standing before the dais on which the Horus Throne had once rested, that holy seat against whose gold and electrum back the spine of a usurper curved. He turned and faced the dusky vastness of the pillared chamber. "Hear all of you," he said in a low voice. "I swear that, if Amun wills it, I will return victorious and I will set the Holy Throne once more upon this dais and I will rebuild this place so that once more the glory of Egypt will reside here. I swear it!" The echoes woke and murmured the words back at him, but with them came a long sigh and the flame of his lamp guttered suddenly as though a draught had found it. Controlling an urge to flee, he walked slowly towards the women's quarters.

He emerged onto the roof and lowered himself beside the remains of the old windcatcher, blowing out the lamp and wrapping himself tightly in the cloak. It was here that Father used to come when he wanted to be alone, he thought, and it was here that Mersu attacked him. It is fitting that my last night of certitude and peace should be spent in this spot. Below him the halls of the palace dreamed on in stillness, but up here the stars and a moon almost at the full showed Kamose the vague outlines of the garden and part of the sleeping house.

His glance moved from there to the vine trellises and the dark palms clustered before the watersteps. Torches lit the night with their orange flares, some on the river, their reflections wavering on the water, some on either bank, both clustered and strung out along the river path. Shouts and the murmur of many voices came to him. His army was massing in obedience to his command, in faith that he would lead the soldiers well. Watching it all from his high vantage point, he had a moment of despair coupled with deep inadequacy. I have done all this, he thought. I, Kamose, Prince of Weset. And who am I to accomplish what my father could not? They trust me, my mother and grandmother, my brother and sister, the officers below, the Princes even now gathering themselves for the gamble. They believe that I can perform that which I have promised. Oh, Amun, I need you now! And you, Osiris Seqenenra, my dear father, be here with me tonight!

He drew up his knees and closed his eyes against the ordered chaos. Through the hours while Ra was passing through the body of Nut, he alternately dozed and prayed until the sky in the east began to pale and the time for prayer was over. Then, rising and massaging his cramped limbs, he picked up the lamp and made his way down the stairs, through the now mute precincts of the palace, and out to where his fate awaited him.

END OF BOOK ONE

Select BIBLIOGRAPHY

BOOKS

Aldred, Cyril. *Jewels of the Pharaohs: Egyptian Jewelry of the Dynastic Period*. rev. ed. London: Thames and Hudson Ltd. 1978.

Aldred, Cyril. *The Egyptians*. rev. ed. London: Thames and Hudson, 1987.

Baikie, James. *A History of Egypt: From the Earliest Times to the End of the XVIII Dynasty*. Vol 1 and 2. Freeport, New York: Books for Libraries Press, 1971.

Baines, John, and Jaromir Malek. *Atlas of Ancient Egypt*. New York: Facts on File, 1987.

Bietak, Manfred. *Avaris the Capital of the Hyksos: Recent Excavations at Tell el-Daba*. London: British Museum Press, 1996.

Breasted, James H. *A History of Egypt: From the Earliest Times to the Persian Conquest*. New York: Charles Scribner's Sons, 1905.

Breasted, James H. *Ancient Records of Egypt*. Vol. 2 and 4. London: Histories & Mysteries of Man Ltd., 1988.

Bryan, Cyril P. *Ancient Egyptian Medicine: The Papyrus Ebers*. Chicago: Ares Publishers Inc., 1930.

Budge, Wallace E.A. *A History of Egypt: from the End of the Neolithic Period to the Death of Cleopatra VII. B.C. 30*. Vol. 3, *Egypt under the Amenemhats and Hyksos*. Oosterhout: Anthropological Publications, 1968.

Budge, Wallace E.A. *An Egyptian Hieroglyphic Dictionary*. Vol 1 and 2. rev. ed. New York: Dover Publications, Inc., 1978.

Budge, Wallace E.A. *Egyptian Magic*. London: Routledge & Kegan Paul, 1986.

Budge, Wallace E.A. *Legends of the Egyptian Gods: Hieroglyphic Texts and Translations*. New York: Dover Publications, Inc., 1994.

Budge, Wallace E.A. *The Mummy: A Handbook of Egyptian Funerary Archaeology*. New York: Dover Publications, Inc., 1989.

Cottrell, Leonard. *The Warrior Pharaohs*. New York: G.P. Putnam's Sons, 1969.

David, Rosalie. *Mysteries of the Mummies: The Story of the Manchester University Investigation*. London: Book Club Associates, 1979.

Davidovits, Joseph, and Margie Morris. *The Pyramids: an Enigma Solved*. New York: Dorset Press, 1988.

Gardiner, Sir Alan. *Egypt of the Pharaohs*. Oxford: Oxford University Press, 1964.

James, T.G.H. *Excavating in Egypt: The Egypt Exploration Society 1882-1982*. London: British Museum Publications Limited, 1982.

Mertz, Barbara. *Temples Tombs & Hieroglyphs: A Popular History of Ancient Egypt*. rev. ed. New York: Peter Bedrick Books, 1990.

Murnane, William J. *Guide to Ancient Egypt*. New York: Penguin Books, 1983.

Murray, Margaret A. *Egyptian Religious Poetry*. Westport: Greenwood Press Publishers, 1980.

Murray, Margaret A. *The Splendour that was Egypt*. rev. ed. London: Sidgwick & Jackson, 1972.

Nagel's Encyclopedia-Guide. *Egypt*. Geneva: Nagel Publishers, 1985.

Newberry, Percy Edward. *Ancient Egyptian Scarabs: An Introduction to Egyptian Seals and Signet Rings*. Chicago: Ares, 1979.

Newby, Percy Howard. *Warrior Pharaohs: The Rise and Fall of the Egyptian Empire*. London, Boston: Faber and Faber, 1980.

Porter, Bertha, and Rosalind L.B. Moss. *Topographical Bibliography of Ancient Egyptian Hieroglyphic Texts, Reliefs, and Paintings*. Vol. VII, *Nubia, The Deserts and Outside Egypt*. Oxford: Griffith Institute Ashmolean Museum, 1995.

Richardson, Dan. *Egypt: The Rough Guide*. London: Penguin Books, 1996.

Shaw, Ian, and Paul Nicholson. *The Dictionary of Ancient Egypt*. London: Harry N. Abrams, Inc., 1995.

Spalinger, Anthony J. *Aspects of the Military Documents of the Ancient Egyptians*. London: Yale University Press, 1982.

Watson, Philip J. *Costumes of Ancient Egypt*. New York: Chelsea House Publishers, 1987.

Wilson, Ian. *The Exodus Enigma*. London: Guild Publishing, 1986.

University Museum Handbooks. *The Egyptian Mummy Secrets and Science*. Pennsylvania: University of Pennsylvania, 1980.

ATLASES

Oxford Bible Atlas. 2nd. ed. London; New York: Oxford University Press, 1974.

The Harper Atlas of the Bible. Edited by James A. Pritchard. Toronto: Fitzhenry and Whiteside, 1987.

The Cambridge Atlas of the Middle East and North Africa. Cambridge, U.K.: Cambridge University Press, 1987.

JOURNALS

K.M.T. a Modern Journal of Ancient Egypt. San Francisco.
Volume 5, number 1, *Hyksos Symposium at the Metropolitan Museum*.
Volume 5, number 2, *Amunhotep I, Last King of the 17th Dynasty?*
Volume 5, number 3, *Decline of the Royal Pyramid*.
Volume 6, number 2, *Buhen: Blueprint of an Egyptian Fortress*.